THE CLOUD BORN

A Tale of the Nepheleid

By Marisol Charbonneau

ARCANA ELEMENTS

The book is dedicated to all my friends, family, and strangers who supported us since the genesis of the Nepheleid series, and especially to Heather Lee Mills, who kindly edited this tome even after moving half a world away …

Finally, I would also like to dedicate this book to Georges Brossard, who taught me that all things, great and especially small, have their place in the web of life.

Repose en paix, oncle Georges.

Chapter One

There was once a garden long ago, by the storied shore of the apple-bearing Hesperian Coast, at the very edge of the known world. There, a maiden Goddess-Queen planted the tree of the golden apples, a gift bestowed to her by Gaia, the Earth-Mother, upon her marriage to the newly crowned King of the gods. Tended by the Hesperides nymphs, and fed by streams of ambrosia that flowed from the deepest recesses of the Earth, the garden was forever bathed in the golden light of sunset to celebrate the bridal of the ruling Queen and King of Heaven.

The goddess' cherished garden flourished for aeons untold, until a mortal hero whose very name evoked the Lady's glory overcame the loyal serpent-dragon that guarded the tree of the golden apples. Emboldened by the slaughter of the garden's protector, the Pleiades, daughters of the Titan Atlas and sisters to the Hesperides, stole the precious fruit. That is, all save for one, which would one day become the prize in a beauty contest that would decide the fate of the world.

Robbed of her treasure, and absent a worthy sentinel, the goddess sequestered her pillaged garden far beyond the westernmost horizon, where for millennia Okeanos' vast reach denied sailors the sight of distant shores. Hidden from the sight of gods and men, the ravished garden fell to ruin, forgotten save for a few tales told of the goddess' loss, and the dreams of its bereft mistress. But for all her sorrows, the Lady knew that her garden held at its very roots a far greater treasure than the ghosts of her past glories. It held the seeds of hope and life, which she will spread across the stars when her children take to the Heavens beyond the utmost reaches of starry Olympus, her former abode. For she is Hera, the golden-throned Queen of the gods, Crucible of heroes and Mistress of all Life, known by countless names since the dawning of human consciousness in the many nations bordering the inland sea at the navel of the ancient world.

In her wildest and most blissful dreams, the venerable Hera remembered herself as she once was: an ancient being, far older than she knew herself to be, for much of her former life was forsaken from memory in the few centuries before she reluctantly bound her fate to that of loud-thundering Zeus, King of Olympus. She did not know then, nor could she possibly have remembered when winged Eros drove her bridal chariot to her bridegroom on her wedding day, that Zeus had once cast her into the ghastly Lethe River in the Underworld, hoping that she would forget another King she had loved before.

No one living today knew the full extent of who her lost love, a most noble son of Gaia, had once been. Even Hera could scarce recall her first husband, the fabled Eurymedon, save that he had been the King of the Giants and the father of her long-estranged firstborn son who, until merely a decade ago, she had not known still lived. Her memories were mostly of those days long past when she was a Maiden Queen and ruled alone, though she had been bride to many Consorts, of whom the faithless Zeus was but the most recent. Hera commemorated her most eminent nuptials by planting sacred gardens across the broad-pathed Earth, from fair Eden to the East, bathed in the gentle light of dawn, to her beautiful, doomed sunset garden of the Hesperides at the westernmost edge of the world.

In these cloistered sanctuaries she had kept other precious tress, all guarded by powerful serpent-dragons whose ancestors' bones long dwelt in the bosom of the Earth-Mother. There, her mortal children had once lived. They were precious treasures risen from lowlier creatures and subsequently crafted in the image of the gods, innocent and protected from all harm that could befall their fragile kind. Few learned mortals today tell the tale of how her brazen Consort in the fair land of Eden, having grown jealous of the love her children bestowed upon her, greedily cast the goddess out of her garden. With deceitful intent he told her children that he alone had made them out of clay, just as he alone had made the entire world in six days.

As her children grew to believe the lies their father told them about their nature, the serpent in the garden of Eden, taking pity upon the goddess' progeny, told them the truth about their exiled mother, and of her despair at having become alienated from her own creation. Spurred by the serpent's wise counsel, the children rebelled against their father's tyranny, and in his wrath the petty god of Eden cast his children from their home. Many wandered the world for years without end, scraping what they could from the bounty of whatever wilderness upon which they trod, while a blessed few made their homes within their mother's other gardens across the broad-pathed Earth.

Still, Hera wondered what happened to her mortal children who had not found a welcoming hearth in the safety of her many gardens West of Eden. How had they prospered, cast out from their home by their father, deprived of the loving embrace of their mother? Had these mortals fared better than her newfound firstborn son Prometheus, benefactor of humanity, long punished for his effort to ease the wretchedness of mortals with his gift of fire from Olympus? For in many ways loud-thundering Zeus, the goddess' ultimate Consort, had not proved himself possessing a more meritorious character than his predecessor, the Lord of Eden.

Not only had Zeus taken a dim view of Prometheus' kindly deed, he did all that he could to keep mortals in a state of abject ignorance, fearing that they would grow arrogant in their knowledge and eventual mastery over the world. And grow arrogant they did, a mirror-image of their ornery Sky-fathers, whose greed for power knew no bounds, likewise their contempt for the generous Earth-Mother that sustains all that lives.

In her dreams, Hera often remembered how mortals came in great throngs to worship at her temples, anticipating with bated breath the moment when her wood-plank effigy was bathed at the confluence of rivers, then tied to the Sacred Tree, binding the goddess' fertility to the bounty of the land itself. In those halcyon days, her bridegrooms had been the River-gods and streams, sons of Okeanos and Tethys, the Father and Mother of Rivers and the source of all life. How many of her loves had since become her foes, spurned from memory by her unwitting bridal bath in the Lethe, whose waters make gods and men forget that which came before?

How many mortals in how many lands had called her Mother, long before the son of Kronos, her own brother, finally claimed her as his bride, ending her reign as the Great Goddess of the inland sea? How many names had her mortal children called her through the centuries? How many gardens had she sown, how many trees had she planted, how many Consorts, mortal and divine, had known bliss in her loving arms, and met their reward in the glory of a short season?

And now the goddess' garden lies in ruins, and the living world cries out to her.

But in her dreams, the Lady knows that she will soon plant anew the seeds of many gardens yet to come, when the worthy among her children set sail with her across the stars.

Nepheleid

Such are the dreams of the Goddess of a thousand names, Asherah, Hathor, Uni, Juno.

Such are the dreams of the Lion Lady, perennial Queen of Heaven, whose hands hold the reins.

Such are the dreams of Hera, the exalted and maligned.

Such are the dreams of Hera, the Mother of Mortals...

Chapter Two

Only one more hour until the lesson is over, Apollo thought as he led the children across the vast underground laboratories at the CARINA campus at Borealis. CARINA, or the Centre for Aerospace Research and Innovation of North America, was located deep in the heart of the Canadian wilderness. As was the custom among the offspring of the learned mortals and other immortals who worked within these hallowed halls of science, the pupils followed their teacher in a single file into the central wing of the cavernous ALSESTIS facilities. Named after an ancient mortal Queen whose love for her husband empowered her to overcome death, the Alternative Life Support for the Exploration of Space and Terra-forming Implementation Systems division of the CARINA venture lay mostly empty, its primary components long since relocated to the city-ship Nephele high above the Earth.

As Spring was well under way, the installations were awash in the eerie green glow emanating from the inverted translucent domed ceiling that contained the artificial lake atop the laboratories, like a giant offering bowl to the blooming forest beyond. Since all the children present had been told for years that they were soon to follow their parents to the Nephele, Apollo saw it fit to focus today's lesson on the basics of terra-forming. Indeed, should the crew of the heavenly citadel ever come upon a wandering world rife with all the conditions needed to seed Earthly life, it would fall upon these youngsters and their eventual progeny to see the great work of their forebears to completion, and make new homes out of the vast expanses of rock and ice beyond the Heliosphere.

"Now children, the first thing you must know about natural terra-forming, is that this process usually takes millions of years," Apollo pontificated, his words well-rehearsed. "That is, if we are to use our own world as a baseline. However, with the right technology, there are ways to accelerate it down to a few centuries…"

"And by that time, these sprouts will be long dead!" said a wag near the edge of the gathering crowd of pupils still filing into the hall.

Nepheleid

"Oh hush, Eris!" a small girl chided her chaperone good-naturedly. "For all anyone knows, we will sleep the whole way through!"

"That is correct, Junia," Apollo replied, smiling benevolently at his gallant defender, yet resisting the urge to flush at the indignity of having his honour safeguarded by a wee child, even if she happened to be the daughter of Hera, and the very reason for his presence among this lot. "That is why in the meantime, you will all be made to learn the importance of maintaining viable long-term habitats in the vacuum of space while exoplanets terra-form," he continued.

"Teacher's pet!" a barely shaving mortal lad of thirteen called out mockingly.

"Why don't you just marry him already!" jeered another, while his friends attempted to lead the other children into a familiar chorus, "Junia and Doctor Archer, sitting in a tree! K-I-S-S-I-N-G! First comes love, then comes... Ow! What the hell, Eris?"

The children laughed as one of the instigating brats rubbed the spot on his arm where Junia's minder had pinched him. They all fell silent when the boy turned around to face Eris and raised his fist, his countenance rife with fury, while a tall, imposing figure emerged from the shadows.

"Ares, no!" Junia shrieked, while Eris leapt upon her twin, averting the god of war in a nick of time from smiting the irate lad.

"Oh, dear," Apollo said, heaving a weary, theatrical sigh. Far be it for the Lord of the golden bow to balk at assuming the role of humble school-teacher, even among his clever colleagues' offspring – mortal or otherwise. This was simply a kindness he had agreed to perform for Mnemosyne, Mother of the Muses, while the Titanide was away as part of their Queen's retinue on her journey at the heart of the continent to bid farewell to the gods and Manitous who dwelt in this most ancient land. And yet here he was, questioning once again Hera's wisdom for naming Eris as Junia's minder while she and Klymene, her loyal friend and co-parent, were away, all the while tasking Ares with keeping his firebrand twin in check. As it turned out, Eris spent most of her time censoring her brother against those whose hearts he believed harboured ill will towards Junia for being the daughter of ALSESTIS' Director of Operations, as Hera was known among the learned mortals of CARINA. At times, Apollo questioned whether Eris was due for a change of career, abandoning her former vocation as the goddess of chaos, confusion, and strife, to become instead her youngest sister's unlikely nanny.

As he rolled his eyes for effect, the Lord of the golden bow spied Prometheus watching him from within the observation deck high above the installations. Beside him stood his lively and equally astute wife Asia, daughter of the primordial Titans Okeanos and Tethys, the Father and Mother of Rivers. The benefactor of humanity and his bride, Apollo knew, had taken a brief leave of absence from the Nephele in order to look after the young Junia while Hera and her cortege journeyed to the heart of Turtle Island. Prior to Hera's departure, the task of shadowing Junia fell upon Hermes, who had sworn to safeguard the estranged Queen of Olympus and her young daughter from being taken back to Zeus' Court against their will. However, as Hermes had also gone with Hera, Klymene, Mnemosyne and their entourage, perhaps Prometheus and Asia felt it a wiser course of action to keep a watchful eye over the child, lest Eris and Ares make a mess of things despite their best intentions.

The Seasons had turned from Winter to Spring since Apollo joined Hera in this wondrous place in the convalescing woodlands of Turtle Island. In fact, almost four months had come and gone since Hera, Apollo, along with a bevy of learned mortals, local immortals, and a growing number of exiled gods and goddesses who once made their homes on starry Olympus, had presided over the lighting of the Nephele. This event, witnessed by all the living beings of the broad-pathed Earth, signalled the moment when this city-ship, the newest and most sophisticated spacecraft in the CARINA fleet, attained full autonomy from its base of operations at Polaris, a decommissioned and refurbished aircraft carrier anchored at the heart of the Arctic Ocean. Since that most glorious moment, a great number of the learned mortals and other immortals stationed at CARINA Polaris relocated to Borealis, while a small crew stayed behind to repurpose the ship's tiered decks into facilities dedicated exclusively for the launch and accommodation of space-bound equipment and personnel in the decades to come.

Though the Nephele remained in the final stages of construction in low Earth orbit, hundreds among its future crew were soon to make their way once more to the base of the Hub, CARINA's massive space elevator at Polaris, by Summer's end. There, the learned mortals and a few immortals, would make the final ascent towards the city-ship and dwell at the edge of where the sky meets the void of space, until the Nephele was ready to leave Earth's orbit to join its sister-ship, the mining vessel Corona, at the boundaries of the asteroid belt, high above the orbit of Mars. All the while, their children had attended the school at CARINA Borealis, where Mnemosyne, Mother of the Muses, had served as headmistress since shortly before Hera, and the newly conceived Junia, fell from the sky and landed, rather improbably, on the thawing waters of Lake New-Agassiz above these very laboratories in which Apollo now stood.

Shortly before she made her memorable entry at Borealis and assumed the role of ALSESTIS' Director of Operations, Hera had discovered in the most bizarre way imaginable that Prometheus was, in fact, her son by her first husband Eurymedon, King of the Giants, whom Zeus smote with his thunderbolt under the pretext that he had raped his dear sister. When she finally learned the truth, Hera emphatically repudiated Zeus, and exited the heavenly throne room through a portal of swirling stars, with her firstborn son by her side – and her unborn daughter in her womb. For almost nine years thence, the Father of gods and men ordered his Court to find his errant wife and their progeny, but in her absence the Queen, through her most singular skill, had somehow found a number of accomplices willing to keep her whereabouts secret. For many years Hermes, Athena, and Apollo, along with swift Iris of the rainbow wings, and other immortals who dwell at the boundaries of the Earth, humoured their King mercilessly, pretending to search for one whom they knew had no desire to be found. This farce ended on the ninth Summer of the Queen's absence, when Apollo reluctantly confessed to Zeus that he had divined that Hera and her young daughter were hiding somewhere that was nowhere in the world.

With hope renewed, the Thunderer sent Apollo and wise Athena to search for his quarry aboard the Nephele, high above the broad-pathed Earth, while Hermes and Herakles were dispatched to search for them in the Underworld. For several weeks Apollo and Athena dwelt with Prometheus and Asia and the rest of the learned crew of the Nephele, until Hermes and Herakles, newly returned from Hades' Kingdom, emerged with Hera and the young Junia atop the utmost deck of the Polaris. When Zeus appeared with the entire Olympian Court to reclaim his wife and child, Hera flatly refused to reconcile with the King, and Junia blithely displayed her contempt for the one who had caused so much hurt to her mother and eldest brother for so many centuries.

"Now, children," Apollo chided softly. "You really need to pay attention. This is valuable information that will be of great importance..."

We need to speak with you, Apollo heard Prometheus say wordlessly within the confines of his mind. *Let someone else continue the lesson... There will be no harm done, the young ones are already quite distracted by the antics of the red-haired twins ...*

Looking up at the observation deck, Apollo saw Prometheus and Asia staring at him once more, their expressions rapt and anxious in equal measure.

"Good afternoon, Doctor Archer," a mellifluous female voice called out from behind. "Good afternoon, children."

Apollo turned around and saw kind Demeter, who brings forth gifts, smiling at him. Since Zeus had decreed that Hermes could not return to Olympus without Hera and their young daughter, Athena and Apollo, along with Hephaestus and Eris, volunteered to remain on the Polaris in solidarity with their brother, as well as their Queen. In the days and weeks that followed, they were joined by a growing number of blessed gods who had left Olympus, each in turn taking on roles they found palatable among the learned mortals at CARINA. Apollo eventually took a place of high importance among the chief scientists of the space-faring venture, though today he sorely regretted assuring Mnemosyne that he did not mind replacing her as Headmistress at the school for their colleagues' gifted offspring.

"Good afternoon Doctor Summers," the youngest children, Junia included, answered in unison.

"Doctor Summers," Apollo answered his aunt courteously, whom he noticed was appropriately clad in a white laboratory coat. He suppressed a grin, unaccustomed as he was at some of his fellow deities' aliases among these learned mortals. "Will you join us for the lecture? I was about to explain the applications of fungi in terra-forming, and how it binds soil and sustains life even in the most inhospitable environments here on Earth…"

"A lesson in botany!" Demeter exclaimed cheerfully. "Would you like me to assist?"

"Truth be told," Apollo said, "I would be most grateful if you took the lead, as you are, without a doubt, our utmost expert on the matter. Wouldn't you agree, children?"

The youngest pupils acquiesced mirthfully, while the older ones grumbled their assent with varying levels of apathy.

"But of course," Demeter replied with a knowing grin, conveying to Apollo that she had also heard Prometheus' call. Turning to address the pupils, the goddess of the grain took a deep breath, and began. "Who among you have heard of Frazer Island, off the coast of the Australian archipelago?"

Turning to face the observation deck, Apollo sighed wistfully at the memory of the transcendently beautiful Frazer Island, as well as many other landmasses that had slipped beneath the waves in the last two centuries. But such matters were long settled and now he, like Hera and Prometheus and the learned mortals and immortals at CARINA, had set his mind on helping Earthly life recover from humanity's past hubris.

Apollo quickly climbed the steps to the observation deck, where Asia had kept the door open for him.

"Thank you," he said softly as he shut the door behind him.

"It's a sad day when the Lord Apollo must suffer the heckling of young boys," Asia jested.

"It's not like Derek to act out like that," Prometheus said.

"Derek did not act out," Apollo replied. "He was just teasing Junia. It was his friend Paul who tried to make a ruckus... I cannot believe I would ever say this, but I am glad Eris was there, before Ares made short work of the two of them!" That would have been a pity, Apollo thought, for in truth he knew the boy Derek to be quite fond of Junia, despite her being four years his junior. Though not as clever as Hera's youngest daughter, this lad happened to be quite the wunderkind in his own right, with a sharpness of wit that could put many of the blessed gods of starry Olympus to shame – including Ares.

"I thought Derek and the older boys were mostly fond of Hera," Asia bantered. "Aren't all of the adolescent boys in these parts enamoured with the legendarily beautiful lady who literally fell out of the sky, and whose miracle progeny not only survived the 'shuttle crash' against all odds, but also made it to full term in an incubator?"

"The very same technology Zeus does not know might have made his child mortal," Apollo added.

"Hence Hera's goodwill 'farewell' tour of Turtle Island to thank all the local gods for ensuring her daughter's safety on the continent of her birth," Asia added. "She would have been far better served by leaving the child with her sister Demeter in her absence, if you ask me. But she didn't, and here we are."

"Yes, and you would think that the children ought to have gotten used to Junia being flanked by unstable bodyguards of late," Prometheus said wearily. "At least the red-haired twins are getting a top-notch scientific education in the meantime!"

"Yes, all three of them!" Asia chortled, referring to Junia's equally fiery bronze-coloured mane.

"Until that time Eris tried to goad the children into creating new hybrid lifeforms using the old CRISPR protocols last week, under the guise of learning about restorative genetic engineering from scratch," Prometheus quipped.

"I believe she wanted Junia to craft a giraffe-saurus-rex," Asia said mirthfully.

"That is why we no longer allow children in the ALSESTIS labs without competent adult supervision," Prometheus replied, his tone deadpan.

"And by children," Apollo enquired for effect, "You mean Ares and Eris? The small ones can be trusted far more than these two?"

Prometheus nodded. "That is why Demeter is here, and not with Hera and the others."

Asia turned to face her husband. "Where are they at, right now?" she asked.

"Pine Ridge. With the Lakota Calf Maiden, presiding over the Sun Dance," Prometheus answered calmly, though Apollo saw him flinch.

The benefactor of humanity obviously loathed the thought of others having their flesh pierced, albeit willingly, in fulfillment of a sacred obligation to the Creator, even if this was nothing like the torment he endured for centuries, in punishment for the crime of giving fire to humanity against the Thunderer's orders.

Prometheus took a moment to regain his composure, then turned his gaze toward Apollo. "We've had no recent sightings of Zeus in the clouds above Borealis," he said. "Not since Hera left on her journey."

"You don't think he followed them to the heart of Turtle Island?" Apollo asked, with a hint of alarm.

Nepheleid

"Even he would not dare to attempt such a thing," Asia answered. "We think he retreated back to Olympus."

"And this worries us," Prometheus added. "Almost as much as Hera's recent state of mind."

Apollo raised an eyebrow.

"Our Queen has had troubled dreams of late... You have seen this as well, Phoebus," Prometheus continued. "Surely you know that Hera's prophetic gift never errs, even if she is unaware of this while she slumbers."

Apollo nodded. On the eve of her final exit from Olympus, Hera had shared dreams and memories with Apollo inside the confines of his mind. These experiences had left an indelible mark upon his psyche, cementing his allegiance to one whose thoughts and deeds never failed to reveal their rectitude in the end.

"Hera would never compromise us, nor would she ever abandon her mission until it is brought to completion!" Asia interjected animatedly. "That is not in her nature!"

"She would, if it meant saving us all from the wrath of her King," Prometheus replied truthfully.

"Zeus cannot stop us from launching the Nephele!" Asia cried out. "Otherwise he would have done so last Summer, when he found Hera and Junia on the deck of the Polaris! Besides, we already have Junia, and he does not, nor will he ever dare to retrieve her without having Hermes suffer the penalty of breaking the Oath of the Holy River Styx! Zeus is the Keeper of Oaths. He cannot act against his nature, any more than Hera ever could!"

Prometheus shook his head. "We have a contingency plan of Hera's own devising," he said dolefully. "In case the day would come when Zeus decided to deal the coup de grâce to our venture. At best, this would buy us some time."

"What did you see inside Hera's mind?" Apollo asked Prometheus. "If the thought of disclosing such things does not trouble you..."

Prometheus took a deep breath. "When our Queen began to bid farewell to what remains of the living Earth," he answered, "she did not realize the magnitude of her grief at leaving all that she has ever loved and protected, from the time she lived as a maiden in the House of Okeanos and Tethys at the boundaries if the Earth, to her long reign as Queen of Olympus. In her melancholy she has grown rather heedless, and there is a chance that her slumbering mind might have called out to Zeus in a fit of nostalgia." Prometheus took another deep breath.

"There is much that Zeus does not know," Asia answered in his stead. "He has no inkling that the power the Sky-Kings have wielded on Earth for millennia will be rendered meaningless beyond the boundary of Earth's orbit. He knows almost nothing of the means through which we intend to conceive and sustain the generations to come. He does not even know about the circumstances surrounding how Junia came into this world."

"Even if he has heard the tale mortals at Borealis have told of Hera's crash landing," Prometheus added. "He does not know that we placed Junia in the incubator to save her life. If he ever found out, he might see it fit to declare Hera an unfit mother. Then coerce her into agreeing to return to Olympus in such a way that Hermes remains safe from the penalty of the Oath of the Holy River Styx."

"What do you mean to do?' Apollo asked, the gravity of the situation finally dawning upon him.

"We must initiate the Hesperides Protocol," Prometheus said at last, his tone sombre yet determined.

Asia closed her eyes. "Hera will not be pleased," she said without humour. "So be it."

Nepheleid

Chapter Three

A gentle Spring breeze swept through the vast hilly meadow at Pine Ridge, at the heart of the Oglala Lakota Nation, where many generations ago a great battle for the soul of Turtle Island was fought and won by all the tribes of mortals who dwell upon this land. There, the defenders of the sacred Earth gained victory not by the might of searing weapons, but by the righteousness of their calling to bring low the wicked, greedy men who for centuries devoured the Earth for their own gain. Today their descendants gathered for the Sun Dance, welcoming their brethren from all corners of the continent, as well as the posterity of the many nations of settlers from around the broad-pathed Earth who have made their homes on Turtle Island.

Golden-throned Hera, venerable Goddess-Queen from the distant shores of Hellas and its surrounding inland Sea, looked upon the mortals on the meadow from the unseen bower of Ptesanwin, known to the People of the Plains as the White Buffalo Calf Woman. The Queen and her retinue were guests of this most esteemed herald of Wakan Tanka, the mightiest among the spirit-people who have dwelt upon Turtle Island for as long as mortals could remember. And remember they did, for the Sun Dancers gathered each year at the first stirrings of Spring to recall the time when Ptesanwin bestowed the Sacred Peace Pipe upon the people and taught them her holy ways when hunger threatened to eradicate the Lakota from the face of the Earth. It was she who taught the people to treat the land and all that lives with reverence, and that all life and all things were interconnected and equally sacred in the eyes of the Great Spirit. When her work was done, Ptesanwin took the form of a black buffalo calf, then before the mortals' eyes she changed the colour of her coat from black to red, then to yellow, then white, and told them to look for her in this ever-changing guise as a sign of her eventual return among their kind.

Concealed from the sight of mortals, Hera stood beside her illustrious hostess, the daughter of Turtle Island with whom the Cow-Eyed goddess of the ancient Aegean and Mediterranean Seas was most often confused. Even Klymene, Hera's loyal handmaiden and, as far as the mortal men of Borealis knew, domestic life partner, grew fond of remarking what a striking resemblance her Queen bore to the Lakota Calf Maiden, one that went beyond their shared fondness for ungulates. Flanking Hermes, loud-thundering Zeus' unwittingly exiled herald and messenger, Hera and Ptesanwin surveyed the scene before them. All beheld the scores of mortals dancing in step around the tree pole at the centre of the gathering, where according to custom, a select few had fastened themselves to the pole with ropes, the ends of which were hooked into their very flesh. These few mortals, Hera and her entourage had been told, would chant and pray as they circled the pole in wide arcs until they broke themselves free from their bonds.

As a show of respect for Ptesanwin, Hera did not allow her lovely features to betray her disquiet at the sight of these Sun Dancers' asceticism, as Hermes and her other acolytes had done despite their best efforts to remain stoic. Though Hera understood such mortifications as a show of bravery and piety, these displays reminded her all too well of times long ago when mortals closed the Tonaia ceremony by binding her own likeness to her sacred tree at the confluence of rivers. Like the Sun Dance, this long-forgotten rite heralded the turning of the Seasons from Winter to Spring, when Hera concluded her journey to the boundaries of the Earth and returned among the people on the shores of Hellas. At its climax the goddess' image was bathed in the river, then tied to a tree to bind her power to the Earth and to all the living world for another year.

Not once had the mortals who attended the Tonaia ever bound themselves to the sacred tree with piercing hooks fastening their flesh, Hera thought queasily, trying to not hear Rhea's voice in her mind, chiding her for having grown soft in recent centuries. Indeed, the staunchest displays of pious devotion she had ever witnessed were those of her mother's Galli priests who, prior to Roman times emasculated themselves upon their sacred pine tree shortly after the Spring Equinox on a day known as the Day of Blood. Hera had always found such proceedings excessive and needlessly gory, even though her own chariot races, which mortals celebrated every year in her honour, seldom concluded without the untimely demise of a hapless charioteer at the precarious radius turn.

Still, Hera considered after a moment, it is far more dignified to meet your doom on the field of battle, or even in the throes of an athletic contest dedicated to the glory of the gods, than to be maimed or killed by trees, as trees are meant to uphold and preserve Life by binding Earth and Sky. The sacred groves mortals had sown around Hera's ancient temples, as well as all the hallowed trees she had planted in all her nuptial gardens throughout the course of her long life, stood for the alliance of the chthonic forces below with the powers of Sun and Sky that became known in later centuries to the mortals who had made their homes in the lands of the Aegean and beyond. In prior centuries, before her many successive marriages to Sky-Kings from far and wide, Hera had favoured river-gods as her preferred species of bridegrooms, and for many an aeon she had gifted to the Earth, through the holy rite of Tonaia, the fecundity of her holy womb to bolster the bounty of the land, after her yearly nuptials with the many sons of Okeanos and Tethys.

Though few mortals whose ancestors had come to this land from the ancient shores of Europe remembered such deeds by the venerable Goddess-Queen, the gods of Turtle Island quickly came to learn of Hera's wondrous ability to bestow her vitality to the land to foster healing where waterways lingered in distress, poisoned as they were by the deeds of foolhardy, long-dead men. Within weeks of her defection from starry Olympus, Hera, newly awakened from her long slumber, and her womb empty of her still-growing unborn daughter, caught the attention of local gods when she took pity on an ailing stream, and promptly set out to purify it by bathing in its waters. A wandering Manitou spied the goddess as she sank beneath the waters, absorbing within her holy form all manners of miasma, then expelled the offending substance into receptacles provided to her by her immortal Oceanid handmaidens at CARINA Borealis. Before Summer had come to full bloom that year, Hera had thoroughly cleansed in this manner a major watershed, and soon her renown had grown far and wide among the gods of Turtle Island.

In gratitude for her generous and invaluable indulgence, the gods and Manitous of this land agreed to protect Hera's daughter Junia against those who would abduct her from the only home she had ever known to take her back to her father, whom they knew to be a mighty Sky-King in far Olympus. However, a year ago, before the Seasons turned from Summer to Autumn, Hera's husband found Hera and their child hiding among the mortals of CARINA in their floating citadel at Polaris. Bringing his heavenly Court with him over the Arctic skies, he tried to intimidate the Queen into returning with their daughter to starry Olympus. Unfortunately for him, a few among his other deathless children who dwell on holy Olympus ended up joining Hera at CARINA to aid their Queen in her quest to send mortals to the stars to seed the Cosmos with Earthly life. As her purpose among the gods and mortals of Turtle Island had neared completion, Hera prepared for her imminent departure by teaching the clever mortals at CARINA how to perfect their devices to heal the land and waters from their old wounds, with the ample means provided by lofty-minded Prometheus' philanthropic venture.

A few short weeks ago, when Winter surrendered to Spring, Hera undertook a final journey at the time appointed by the Seasons. This time to pay a final visit to the gods of Turtle Island who had befriended her during her sojourn upon their land. She meant to thank them for welcoming her in their midst for so many years, and also for allowing Prometheus and his ilk to do their work within their quiescent woodlands for the last few decades. The hallowed meadow at Pine Ridge, where worthy mortals reclaimed the very heart and soul of Turtle Island from the clutches of avarice, was Hera's final stop on her journey before she and her young daughter, along with hundreds of CARINA's cleverest and bravest, made their way to the Nephele at Summer's end.

"Honoured friend," Ptesanwin addressed Hera, gently tugging at the sleeve of her white beaded buckskin coat to pull her aside, away from the others. "If watching the Sun Dancers upsets you, we can move on to my tipi beyond the hill. The People will not see us, unless I let them. Except for the children, who see all the spirits of the Earth, as they are the closest to the Creator. They will see us, but they will show respect and leave us be."

"This ceremony does not upset me, Calf Maiden," Hera replied truthfully, taking her cue and following her hostess away from her retinue. "It's just the sight of all the People gathered has me longing for days long past when mortals use to gather in my honour."

"Some of them think we are one and the same," Ptesanwin said with a smile in her voice.

"This amuses you," Hera remarked, a smile curling on her lips as well.

"There are those who think that all the Wakan are one and the same. That is no more true or false as it is with the People. We are all reflections of one another."

"That is a rather kind way of looking at mortals," Hera replied. ' I prefer to let the virtuous ones find me, as I am, instead of letting them think I am another. Although, to be perfectly honest, there are far worse things than to be confounded with the one who brought the People such a gift as the Peace Pipe."

"And I don't mind being thought of as the one who purifies the waters, and who for her deeds has earned the name Sky River Woman among the Wakan," Ptesanwin answered. "But are you sure you don't want to move your women and your son to my tipi? Your boy keeps getting paler each time I look at him…"

It took Hera a moment to realize that Ptesanwin was speaking of Hermes, who even in his banishment from Olympus continued to obey Zeus' command to follow his Queen wherever she may roam.

"He is not my son," Hera said a little more curtly than she would have liked, as the gentle Spring breeze became a strong gust bearing down upon the meadow.

"I thought… because he follows you everywhere you go, like a shadow."

"He follows me because his father told him to," Hera replied as the gale intensified. "And he has the gall to act as though he has nowhere else to go. Oh, I know full well that my ex-husband ordered him to spy on me, and so he does, the ungrateful little shit."

Ptesanwin looked at Hera, her eyes growing wide. "He is an ingrate?" she inquired, surprised at having caused her guest a sudden outburst of anger, which even the Wakan knew had once constituted the stuff of legend.

"He absolutely is," Hera answered, her tone softening. She waited a moment to continue, banishing with her mind the dense, green-hued thunderheads on the vast horizon. "I raised him because my ex-husband saw it fit that he should live on Olympus," she said with forced calm, "while his whore mother and her sisters pilfered my beautiful sunset garden. And how did he show his appreciation? By constantly lying to me and undermining me, slaying my heroes and overall making a fool of me. He is the reason why I can no longer have nice things, not on Earth for that matter..." Hera took a breath. "I apologize, Calf Maiden. Hermes' continued presence by my side is not of my choosing. It vexes me, and yet I do not have the heart to exile him any further, not the way his father did. That was simply cruel and uncalled for. Zeus will have to let him return to Olympus eventually, as I doubt Hermes will choose to accompany us all to the Nephele."

"So, it's decided then," Ptesanwin said gravely. "You and your smallest daughter will be leaving with the People who have helped heal the Earth, never to return..."

"There will be ways to return to Earth from the Nephele once it joins the Corona," Hera replied evasively. "Those who long for home will be given the opportunity to return at appointed times, and as for those who will choose to leave the sister-ships permanently and remain here on Earth, well, we shall find others eager to replace them. The children of those who will be boarding with us this September will be given that choice once their schooling is concluded, in the cities beyond the skies. But that window will close in a few decades. By then we anticipate that our fleet will have grown exponentially, and then we shall set out from the Heliosphere to interstellar space."

"But you, you will leave us forever, and without making peace with your husband, the Sky-Father to the East."

Hera looked at Ptesanwin quizzically. "Now, where did that come from, if I may ask? Has Hermes delivered any threatening tidings to your people, unbeknownst to me, on his father's behalf? If he did, I assure you that these threats have no teeth. Zeus has no power on Turtle Island, and he is not so foolhardy as to pick a fight with you lot."

"No... no one threatened us, not yet anyway," Ptesanwin answered, shielding her eyes from a sudden, intense gust of wind.

Hera softened her gaze as the gale died down.

"Your husband will not let you go without a fight," Ptesanwin continued. "And I know that you promised Sedna, the Sea-Maiden of the far North, that you would never let any harm befall the People and Animals and Land of Turtle Island because of your unresolved quarrel with your husband… The Wakan of the North told us that he only wants you to return to him so that you can both raise your child in the land where you're from. They heard him say as much when he met you on your big ship at the top of the Earth. Would it be so bad if you made your peace with him, and maybe stayed longer on Earth among us, at least until your daughter comes of age and chooses for herself whether to join the others in the cities in the stars?"

"Believe it or not," Hera replied uneasily, "I have given this quite some thought. But keeping Junia as far away from Olympus as possible is the only way I can do right by her. So long as I remain on the same world where her father dwells, War and Strife will follow me wherever I go. It was his unholy lust for me that brought them into this world, and in a roundabout way is the ultimate reason why the gods of Olympus have become estranged from the Earth-Mother. If I stay, all the blessings I have bestowed upon this land, all my good work will come undone. There is no other way."

"That is a hard judgement you cast upon him," Ptesanwin said. "All beings can learn to live in harmony according to the ways of the Wakan. Even one such as your husband."

"I am afraid it is not so, Calf Maiden," Hera answered determinedly. "You have not heard the tale told of how I came to bear my twins, Ares and Eris, the truest children I could ever have borne one such as loud-thundering Zeus. It was the price I paid for choosing his side in the War against the Giants, which unbeknownst to me began the moment when Zeus struck down their King, a favoured son of Gaia, the Earth-Mother. His name was Eurymedon, and he was my first husband, my first love. Zeus wanted me all to himself, so he put it into his mind that Eurymedon had abducted me against my will. That is the pretext he gave everyone after he smote him, until there was nothing left of Eurymedon but a pile of ashes and a smouldering crater. Once the deed was done, Zeus stole the son I had borne my husband, then he erased my memories and forbade everyone who saw what he had done to me from ever speaking a word of it ever again. Afterwards my mother sent me away to the boundaries of the Earth, and there I was raised by Okeanos and Tethys, the eldest children of Earth and Sky. For years I wondered why my mother sent me so far away, but now I know that she only wanted to take me as far from Zeus as she thought possible, for my own good. It did not matter, though, for Zeus found me at the boundaries, and he greeted me like a long-lost lover. At the time I thought that perhaps after he had had his way with me, he would move on to another conquest and let me be, but I was sorely mistaken.

"Many years later, I set out on my own and became a Queen at many a Court. For some time I dwelt beyond the shores of Anatolia, far to the East, and after that… I made my way back West, back home, to the many isles of Southern Hellas, then to the mainland, and afterwards around the far shores of the Inland Sea. All the while, Zeus ceaselessly petitioned for my favour, claiming that he loved me above all others, but I knew he only wanted me to marry him so that I would choose him as King among the gods, as I had once chosen the King to succeed Baal when I was Queen at the Court of El. I refused Zeus at every turn, because by then I knew his reputation well. Besides, he was my brother!

"My mother warned me long ago against falling for the charms of my one-time Saviour, as she had hers. Having dwelt among the Oceanides, I knew what fate had befallen their sister Metis, Zeus' first wife, and the mother of Athena, his firstborn. My sister Demeter, who brings forth gifts, provided her own cautionary tale as to why I ought to never wed Zeus, as he had gone so far as to rape Persephone, their daughter, to sire a longed-for son. It was Demeter who beckoned me for my help in disposing of the bastard child, and I felt so awful for Demeter and Persephone that I could not in good conscience refuse her request. Zeus knew all along of my complicity in the deed, and yet he never once desisted in his pursuit to make me his wife! Never in all my years had I seen anyone let his lust get the better of his own judgement as he had. You must understand, for all his amorous persistence, this above all else made him all the more off-putting.

"The Earth-Mother herself tried to warn me several times against marrying Zeus, but by that time he had recruited the help of that wench Aphrodite, my long-time rival whom I'd known by different names when I dwelt in the lands far to the East, between the rivers of the Levant. With her help he tricked me into agreeing to become his bride and crown him King. To seal my fate, he invited all the gods of Earth, Sea and Sky to bear witness to our nuptials, and beckoned Eros to drive my bridal Chariot and the three Fates to seal our bond, so that all would know that I now belonged to him, in a way he never truly belonged to me.

"Gaia told me once what Zeus had done to her son, my first husband, and in my outrage I helped her bring forth the monster Typhon to end him. But some dark trick, perhaps love, blinded my judgement, and I returned to Zeus in a nick of time, which ensured his victory against his foe. In her anger at her failure Gaia brought forth the Giants from her womb, brothers to my lost Eurymedon, and set them loose upon the broad-pathed Earth to make themselves as much a nuisance to the gods of Olympus as any being could. I am certain you have heard that tale told, Calf Maiden."

Ptesanwin nodded. "I have," she said. "Even here on Turtle Island, we have our own tales of the Wakinyan and their battles against the Unktehila."

"You must understand," Hera continued. "All the while, all I ever wanted was for our blessed kind to be at peace with Gaia and her progeny. I never wanted to battle the Giants. As far as I knew, the Earth was vast enough for us all to live in peace. I wanted no quarrel, but they brought the quarrel to us, so we met them on the battlefield for almost ten years, each side equally matched. One night I snuck away from Olympus and tried to beg Gaia to call off her sons and let us all live in peace, but instead I heard my father's voice from gloomy Tartarus telling me to listen for Gaia's words to the Giants. With my gift of prophecy, I heard the Earth speak of the herb of invulnerability, which would end our stalemate and ensure victory to the side that found it first. The message was meant for her sons, but I heard it nonetheless with the power of my gift. And with my second sight I also foretold that we would never truly win the War without the aid of a lion-skinned mortal.

"Zeus listened to my ramblings in my deep trance and found the herb where I said it would be. And as surely as you gave the Peace Pipe to the People once they embraced your Wakan ways, my alliance with Zeus brought forth War and Strife in the end. We won the fight, but he seeded my twins, Ares and Eris, into my womb on the night my prophecy turned the tide in our favour. All I wanted was peace, but since that night, War and Strife have never left me. When I told Zeus that Ares and Eris would be the last children I ever bore him, he went ahead and sired countless children with innumerable goddesses and mortal women, and even boasted that so long as goddesses bore him children such as Artemis and Apollo, he would never care less about me or my jealousy. Can you imagine? Of course, he said that when I was away from Olympus, otherwise I would have abandoned him right then and there, never to return. Perhaps I should have, come to think of it. And even then, he wasn't done! He even went ahead and sired a race of heroes by my Priestess, Io, just to spite me. The last among her lineage turned out to be Herakles, the lion-skinned mortal who bore my name, the one I had to bring back with us to the field of battle to finish the War against the Giants. Herakles, who was my enemy before he became my son, the hero whose deeds brought my most beautiful garden to ruin, and whose reward after his mortal death was Hebe, my firstborn daughter, as his wife among the gods who dwell on starry Olympus."

"But all these children are now with you, as your allies," Ptesanwin interjected.

"I suppose so," Hera said, a hint of exasperation in her voice. "Apollo was an early convert, in the parlance of mortals, but I suspect he was always more interested in Junia than the righteousness of our cause. As for Artemis, well, she only came here to be with her twin, and believe me, I made it abundantly clear that as long as she dwells on Turtle Island, she is not to hunt or even chase another living creature so long as I dwell among you here on Earth. I told her in no uncertain terms that if I ever caught her looking at so much as a squirrel with murderous intent, I would immediately banish her back to Olympus, even if that meant losing Apollo's support. It's just as well if we did, as most of my own children, all except Eileithya, have joined me at CARINA since last year. There is absolutely nothing surprising in all this, since Zeus never cared a whit for any of the legitimate children I bore him. He never concerned himself much with Hebe or Eileithya, and Hephaestus he threw from Olympus on the day he was born! Ares, most of all he loathes, though he never could deny him as anything but his own son. Eris, he dismisses as the Bringer of Chaos, yet she above all others grants me her own brand of justice whenever Zeus' judgment strays towards folly. It took me quite some time to come to that realization, but Eris always takes my side, for good or ill. It took me centuries, literally, to understand the whole ugly business with the Trojan War was her way to avenge me for all the wrong Zeus had done to me in prior years.

"That is why you should never believe Zeus when he claims to only wish for me to return to Olympus so that we can raise our daughter there. He cares nothing for her, of that I am more than certain. I would rather have Eris raise her here on Turtle Island than have her suffer exposure to even the most agreeable of Zeus' whores, of which he has in baffling abundance. Eris is a genial counterpoint to Zeus' hubris, as she seeds chaos where he seeks to impose his own despotic species of order. That is why I chose her as Junia's protector. She will always keep her safe, even after I return from my final journey upon the broad-pathed Earth."

Hera took a deep breath, allowing her hostess to grasp the full magnitude of her words. After a few tense, tacit moments, the White Buffalo Calf Woman turned to the Cow-Eyed goddess of ancient Hellas and the Inland Sea, and said, "I heard your tale, Sky River Woman. There is much bad blood between you and your husband, but you left out the part where you broke the spell by bearing him another child. Your bellicose twins are no longer the last children you ever bore him. There is hope for Peace yet."

"I was afraid you'd say that," Hera answered coyly. "And Peace there will be, once Junia and I, as well as any among my kin who wish to follow me, have left this place to dwell in our citadels among the stars. This was the promise I gave Sedna, many years ago. I intend to keep my word, for what kind of Queen would I be if my word were not my bond?"

Ptesanwin nodded gravely. "Let us hope you are right, Sky River Woman," she whispered almost inaudibly, her serene gaze fixed upon the last Sun Dancer breaking free from his bonds.

Nepheleid

Chapter Four

On the highest rampart of Olympus' heavenly citadel, loud-thundering Zeus stared wistfully into the firmament, basking in the vanishing golden glow of sunset as day surrendered to dusk. He knew better than to look due North, for there the Nephele, locked in geostatic orbit at the top of the Earth, shone brighter than the Moon at the very edge of the Heavens over which he rules. The gilded jewel of the night, as some among the few blessed gods who remained on starry Olympus had grown to call the prized CARINA city-ship, provided a constant yet eerily beautiful reminder of all that he had lost since he last saw his Queen the previous Summer, under the Arctic skies at the boundaries of the world. As the bright day slipped away, Zeus fought the familiar, oppressive melancholy bearing down upon him, brought about by the absence of so many among his children who had joined Hera in her quest to seed the Cosmos with Earthly life. The banquet, he knew, would bring him little joy, nor would retiring to his bedchamber for the night bring him any solace, for his bride would not be waiting for him in their bed.

The turning of the Seasons from Winter to Spring a few fortnights past marked the tenth year since golden-throned Hera last set foot on high Olympus, where she had ruled by Zeus' side since the hallowed day when the Fates sealed their union before all the gods of Earth, Sea, and Sky. Until that wretched morning when she decamped from the throne room in a swirl of stars with that ingrate Prometheus, Hera had been the most faithful of wives, even if at the worst of times she had proven herself a rather mutinous Queen. Still, Zeus dared not blame his beloved for her last exit from Olympus. That egregious blow to the peace and serenity of the abode of the gods was all Prometheus' doing, for he above all others had the most cause to defeat and humiliate the Father of gods and men for slights inflicted upon him long before the denizens of Olympus fought and won the War against the Giants.

And so it was that on this night, like every night since he last saw his estranged Queen on the utmost deck of the Polaris, Zeus found himself virtually alone on high Olympus, save for his venerable elder sister

Nepheleid

Hestia, eternally true to her task of tending to the hearth, and august Themis, his former wife, who to this day remained his adjutant among the deathless gods. A great many of his other former brides and lovers remained, as did a small number among his children, though Zeus suspected that they had elected to stay on Olympus more out of fear of crossing their Queen's path than out of fealty to their King and to the righteousness of his cause.

With lids growing heavy and his heart sinking in despair, Zeus tried not to glance at the Nephele gleaming tantalizingly at his right. Perhaps he ought to veil the Northern skies with a blanket of clouds, he thought for a moment, before he heard Metis wordlessly calling attention to the irony of concealing in such a fashion an object named after a cloud-nymph he had created in Hera's mirror-image millennia ago.

"At least you will never leave me," the Cloud-gatherer said aloud to Metis, forever imprisoned inside the confines of his own mind since he swallowed the goddess out of fear that she would one day bear a son who would overthrow him, as he had supplanted his own dastardly father. Even now, he could almost hear Metis' voice giving him her usual wise counsel:

You could never have swallowed Hera as you did me. Hera would have fought you tooth and nail, and had you prevailed, this time Prometheus would have cut you in half to rescue his mother from your maw instead of acting as midwife as he did when Athena was born from your head. And if not Prometheus, then Hera's child would have split you asunder upon being born. You have glimpsed the girl for yourself, she and her mother are very much of the same mind. And if not Junia, then Hera would have eventually torn her way through your chest cavity with her indomitable strength, then risen from your viscera with her babe at her breast and crushed your still-beating heart under the heel of her golden slippers.

"And probably danced on whatever pile of flesh constituted my deathless remains," Zeus answered the voice inside his head. "After all, our Hera is nothing if not sanguine."

"My King," Aphrodite interjected. "Only yesterday you said Hera's heart was colder than the waters of the Arctic Ocean where she has spent her Summers of late. Surely she cannot be ice-cold and sanguine all at once!"

"I said no such thing," Zeus muttered nonchalantly, as if the goddess of love had not just caught him talking to himself. "Prometheus is the one with ice in his veins. He inherited his cleverness from Hera, of this I have no doubt. Yet unlike Prometheus, Hera's impassioned nature has always been her undoing, even in the execution of her coldest, most elaborate schemes..."

"She has stayed the course so far, my Lord, and shows no sign of changing her mind," Leto, the mother of Apollo and Artemis said. "Perhaps the wisest course to take would be to let her go on her way."

"She has my children, Leto," Zeus said without masking his growing irascibility at what remained of his Court. "And yours. She has Athena... Hermes she unwittingly acquired... she has Herakles and the children she bore me, except for our midwife daughter, who above all others had the good sense to keep away from Prometheus and his merry band of traitors! She even has my brother and sister! Demeter was not long in joining her when Persephone returned to Hades at Summer's end, and Poseidon, well, he has always found a reason to follow her when it suits him. Though for the life of me, I cannot fathom why he chose to finally join her ranks after opposing the CARINA venture for so many years."

"But once Hera brings her work to completion, surely our children will return to starry Olympus," Leto said demurely. "If not Hera herself..." she added in a far less reassuring tone.

"You are far more optimistic than I," Zeus grumbled.

"Hera has not imprisoned your children and our siblings against their will," Hestia said amiably. "Such is not her way."

"I know she is not keeping our kin under her spell," Zeus replied irascibly. "It is that fiend, Prometheus, who has poisoned their minds! Pardoning him of his crimes when Herakles released him from his rock was truly the gravest error I have ever committed during my reign."

"Surely you do not mean that, my Lord?" Leto asked meekly. "Prometheus has paid dearly for his theft of fire from Olympus to benefit mortals! All of us deathless gods, whether denizens of holy Olympus, or Oceanides and other immortals who dwell at the boundaries of the Earth, we were all of the same mind on this matter."

"And all of you, here on Olympus and at the boundaries, all of you were dreadfully mistaken!" Zeus bellowed, as thunder rumbled across Olympus' golden halls. "Long have I known that giving fire to mortals would grant them the potential to surpass the gods in cleverness and ingenuity, without giving them the wisdom required to wield absolute power over an entire world. For all their leaps in knowledge and understanding of the workings of the Cosmos, none among the countless generations of mortals that have lived and died under our auspices ever found a way to achieve the effortless excellence of the gods without exacting a terrible price upon the Earth. Certainly, there have been a few notable exceptions over the course of centuries – a handful of worthy individuals who under Hera's guidance improved their lot as well as that of their fellow mortals. And yet, these were far too few and rare to truly represent any significant hope for the whole of their wretched kind! Do you not remember that it was only a few hundred years ago that their numbers grew to such an extent as to imperil the very continuation of life itself upon the bountiful Earth? As the Fates would have it, the Earth and the rising Seas made quick work of the teeming masses of humanity, leaving us now with greatly reduced populations of all mortal kind in a ruined world."

"My King," Themis said, addressing Zeus for the first time that day. "Prometheus recruited Hera to help mortals right the wrongs committed by their ancestors. Surely you cannot fault him for such a noble undertaking, even if it meant revealing that he is her true son?"

"A noble undertaking!?" Zeus replied with utmost pique. "I granted that whelp clemency, and this is how he repays my kindness? His punishment for stealing fire from Olympus had nothing to do with him being Hera's son! I was the one who made certain that he found a caring mother in Klymene when Hera rejected him in her grief! I never faulted him for the accident of his lineage! That is something Hera would do! But still, I would not be surprised if he had been plotting his revenge the whole time by absconding with my wife and convincing her to leave with him, just to spite me, and help him bring to completion his plan to evict the Earth of its brightest minds! Just now, they are planning their exit through that abominable device above the Polaris. Do you not think that I already know Hera seeks to join those mortals aboard the Nephele, and set sail towards the stars never to return to the only world she has ever known? Hermes has confirmed to me as much, when he delivered his tidings from the Queen's travels at the heart of Turtle Island. She means to leave us forever! Even the gods of Turtle Island are troubled by this!"

"Then you need to find common cause with those of us who also wish to see Hera remain here on Earth," Rhea, the Mother of the gods, told Zeus sternly. "Even if it bruises your pride!"

"I do not see you infiltrating her retinue of Oceanides and Titanides on her final journey across the broad-pathed Earth, Mother," Zeus replied angrily.

"My sister Mnemosyne is the only Titanide accompanying Hera on her travels," Rhea answered, unimpressed. "You will need to sway her also, as well as all the goddesses, nymphs, and Oceanides you've alienated over the ages by treating them like little more than harlots to be used at your pleasure. No wonder they joined Hera at the ends of the Earth! My daughter may be an implacable battle-axe at times, but at least she will never abandon those who are loyal to her to their own devices after she's had her way with them."

"Enough!" Zeus clamoured, before he caught himself and took a calming breath. After a moment, he looked at the small crowd gathered around him, and said, "Leave me be. I need to be alone with my thoughts."

The blessed gods who remained on starry Olympus dispersed to their abodes – all save for Aphrodite, who waited to be alone with her King.

"I thought I told you to leave," Zeus said, his ire slowly returning.

"And I thought you needed my counsel, since you are given to throwing tantrums of late."

"Do not test me, Aphrodite," Zeus replied angrily. "Your stratagem failed to keep Hera by my side ten years ago. The potion you gave me to slip in her drink caused her womb to quicken, I will give you that much, but she left me nonetheless. Perhaps listening to your counsel only made things worse."

"Hera already had one golden slipper out the proverbial door, my King," Aphrodite answered coolly. "And my methods would have worked perfectly, had it not been for an impromptu visit from Prometheus on that late winter morn. Now, most of the time, women stay with their husbands upon discovering that they are newly with child. As for Hera, she never had the time to come to that realization on her own. She had barely risen from the marriage bed when her firstborn made his way to the throne room and gave her another... purpose. Had it not been for our unexpected guest, well, we would not be having this rather unpleasant exchange."

"What am I to do, Aphrodite?" The Cloud-gatherer asked, making no effort to mask his growing desperation. "She does not want to have anything to do with me. Nor does our child. Truth be told, I do not know which insults stings the most, Hera's refusal to return to me, or the child's insolence towards me."

Zeus closed his eyes and took a deep breath. Perhaps there still remained hope, he thought direly. Perhaps his blessed subjects who dwelt among the mortals at CARINA Borealis, and at Polaris beneath the Hub, would wait for other, newer monstrosities to be built before leaving the Earth, emboldened as they were by the success of their endeavour. Perhaps the natural caution of immortals could buy him more time... But time had run out, and the end had come in a constant, spectacular display of light, a hundred thousand times brighter than the weak embers Prometheus stole from Olympus when mortals had only begun to show their potential for perfidy and hubris. Overcome with bitter defeat, Zeus felt a deep pang of sorrow and hopelessness creep across his chest, far more dreadful than the heartache he had known on the morning when Hera summoned her ghastly whirlwind of stars and vacated Olympus for the very last time.

Never had he felt such disparaging melancholy, not even on the day long ago when Hera tearfully confessed her role in the creation of the monster Typhon, upon her return to Olympus after yet another one of her long absences. Never had he felt such outrage, not even on the night his beloved Queen led the blessed gods into rebellion against his rule. At that moment, Zeus could not quite determine what was worse: that Prometheus had bested him at his own game, or that white-armed Hera, destined by the Fates to rule forever by his side, had deserted him to join her firstborn son in his mission to encourage mortals to surpass themselves in finding new ways to put the gods of Olympus to shame. The latter was probably the worst, he deliberated after some time. Hera's disaffection was far more devastating than all the quarrels she had ever instigated against her lord and husband before the whole Olympian Court, her only means of retaliation, short of outright insurrection, against the acrimony his indiscretions had caused her over the course of centuries. This was more calamitous than deliberate dereliction of her duties to her King, or open treason for that matter.

This was desertion

This was divorce.

"I can join them, over there on Turtle Island, and sway their hearts towards returning to Olympus," Aphrodite said finally, as if reading the

Thunderer's thoughts. "When the blessed gods begin to leave her, one after the other, then perhaps she will understand fully the futility of her pursuit and return to Olympus with your child."

Zeus shook his head. "If you think it will do any good, then do as you will," he answered unconvincingly. "But please, I beg of you, let me be alone with my thoughts."

"My King," Aphrodite bowed gracefully, before finally exiting Zeus' presence.

Once he was satisfied that he was well and truly alone, Zeus set his gaze upon the blinding lights of the Nephele, and heaved a weary sigh.

"You must be enjoying this immensely," he told the empty space around him.

You know that it brings me no joy to see you so suffer, O Zeus, victor of Titans. I have felt all your sorrows and your triumphs, ever since the day you swallowed me whole, with our daughter still inside my womb.

"Then you know that our worst fears have come to pass," Zeus replied.

Which fears do you speak of, my King?

"Do not mock me, Metis. I am not in the mood to be trifled with."

I do not mean to mock you, my King, but even you must admit that you hold so many fears close to your heart, that is has become difficult to keep track of which you fear the worst.

"Hera has set her sights to leaving the Earth," Zeus answered flatly. "And this time, she has recruited my children to sanction her madness. I am alone in this, Metis. Even the others question my motives for dreading the outcome of her folly. And she has our daughter. She has Athena!"

And yet, I remain... You can never be alone, for I am forever in your mind. Do you not recall that it was I who gave Athena her fabled wisdom, even though mortals only remember that she was born from your head? What sage counsel could she ever give you in your hour of despair, that I could not?

"Hera has left us," Zeus replied. "And I cannot trick her into coming back. She has all but sworn to never return to Olympus, and now she has Hermes' very breath at her mercy. There are times when it feels as though even our combined wisdom counts for nothing against her cunning. And she has such a hold over Athena, and all my other children, that I cannot break!"

You chose Hera as your bride, your Queen, because of those very rare qualities she possesses. You always knew that she has the power to muster those who cannot otherwise be swayed. Besides, you must have known that Hera has had a hold over our daughter since the very first time Athena laid eyes on her. Have you never thought it strange that for all the times our daughter found herself at odds with your will, she has never once disobeyed or challenged her Queen? Such is the power that mothers have over their daughters, and we both know how direly Athena needed a mother...

"I need her more!" Zeus almost cried out. "Hera, I mean... and Athena as well."

Even after she made it abundantly clear that she wants nothing to do with you? After she's made a mockery of Olympus and its King? You've condemned others to Tartarus for far lesser offences!

"I would never send Hera to Tartarus," Zeus replied truthfully. "I once swore by the Holy River Styx that she would never dwell in the lowest places in the Cosmos, and yet now she mocks me by burrowing inside those tunnels under the forests of Turtle Island, where she and Prometheus are doubtlessly plotting to build another city-ship like the Nephele as we speak!"

She does not know about your Oath, nor does she know that you swore to your Mother that she would ever meet my fate. Your words were erased from her mind the moment she took her bath in the Lethe.

"And I cannot force her to return against her will, otherwise Hermes will serve the penalty of the Holy River Styx. You understand the quandary in which we find ourselves."

Imagine if you had never sworn your Oath by the Lethe's shore. You could have sent her to the Pit of Tartarus for one of her more treasonous offences, and once there she would have forsaken her Oath of fealty, for surely she would have led an uprising among her Titan allies, and stormed the very gates of Olympus with the army of the damned.

"And by breaking her Oath, she would have forever forsaken her position as Queen, as no Oathbreaker can ever rule among the gods,"

Zeus replied dismally. "If that had become her fate, then she would have put an end to us all, and to all life on the Earth and in the Cosmos. She never bows to defeat."

But is that not the very outcome she has tried to prevent, by leaving Olympus and joining Prometheus and his mortals in their laboratories and star-ports? Did she not claim to try to save all Earthly life, by helping all the threatened creatures of the Earth find new homes among the wanderers?

"That is what she has claimed so far," Zeus replied, feeling the weight of his defeat bearing down on him all at once.

Then you cannot say that her motives are treasonous, if she hopes to save all Earthly life, and to restore the Mother of us all to her full glory! Even if she has taken with her more than half the Olympian Court!

"Perhaps," Zeus said wearily. "But that does not matter. I want her back, as well as all the others... even Ares and Eris. I want everything back as it once was – I want to see her golden throne at my left when I hold Court, I want to hear the laughter of my blessed children within Olympus' golden halls, and I want to see the Earth teeming once again with soaring life! Hera was my last chance to reclaim what was ours; she was the only one who never once gave up hope. She was the only one who never failed to draw upon her endless wellspring of strength, whenever she had to endure the whims of Fate. She is the only one who could ever help me understand this world, which I barely recognize anymore. She always was my one true equal, strong even in defeat, undaunted, indomitable even when brought low. She is everything without me, and yet I am nothing without her... And now I fear that she means to leave this world in one of her city-ships, never to return..."

My King, there is a way to compel her to return to you, with your children.

"Please, do not taunt me, Metis. If you have any counsel to give, then do so. Otherwise, kindly leave me in peace as I grieve all that I've lost."

All that was lost can be found again, in the deep wells of memory. Do you not remember another Oath she swore to you at the ramparts of Troy, whereby you allowed her to lay waste to your favoured city, and in return she would not show any resistance should you one day do the same to a citadel dear to her heart?

"That was thousands of years ago," Zeus replied. "And I never called in this dreadful Oath. She would be forever disgusted with me if I had!"

Nepheleid

Then tell me, which outcome do you think she will find more palatable? Returning to Olympus with all your Court, her golden throne restored at your left, or would she rather see you destroy the Nephele without her intercession? As you said yourself, Hera could never again rule as Queen, among gods and mortals alike, if she were branded an Oathbreaker... Think on it, my King, but do not linger in your sorrow, for Earth's child will soon be severed from the Mother of us all once the mortals and gods of CARINA are fully satisfied that the Nephele can live and thrive in the void beyond the Heavens... You have but this one last recourse, and you must act upon it, even if you find it most distasteful.

"If I must, then so be it," Zeus replied at last to the emptiness before him, as the last rays of sunlight vanished from sight.

Chapter Five

A soft, nourishing rain heralded the arrival of Eileithya, the Life-Bringer, at the CARINA Borealis headquarters on a late April morn. As soon as the Divine Midwife's feet landed upon the blooming Earth, the clouds parted, illuminating the goddess' path towards the buildings encircling the artificial lake at the heart of the forest. Drawing near an unassuming shed a stone's throw from the tree line, Eileithya slowed her pace to make herself visible to the surveillance camera nestled above the door-frame. Within seconds the door slid open, and there stood Athena staring back at her in an uncharacteristically anxious manner, while Hermes awaited at the top of a stairway leading into the massive underground compound.

"Eily!" the Virgin Warrior said almost cheerfully. "I am so grateful that you came..."

"Do not thank me yet, Pallas," Eileithya answered. "I agreed to come here to speak to Hera, but not necessarily to convince her to return to Father's bed."

"But you must at least try to talk some sense into her," Athena replied. "She will not listen to me, not anymore. We've barely spoken since she came back from her farewell tour among the gods of Turtle Island!"

"How in the world did *you* run afoul of Hera?" Eileithya asked with genuine surprise, and some measure of amusement.

"I know, we used to be so close, once upon a time," Athena said. "And we still are. She isn't angry with me, not truly, although she has avoided me ever since the end of Winter, when she caught me telling Junia about all the wondrous things that awaited her in Olympus should her mother choose to return with us. That was when Hera evicted me from the room she set aside for me in her living quarters and sent me away to share a flat with Hermes across the lake."

"And I wager that Hermes has not fared better in convincing her to return to Father?" Eileithya asked.

Nepheleid

Athena chuckled softly, despite the look of annoyance Hermes threw at them from the bottom of the stairs, when he now stood.

"Wonders never cease," Eileithya said sardonically as she followed Athena and Hermes into the stairwell.

"You will find Hera on the other side, in the greenhouses," Hermes told Eileithya when they reached the nadir of the ALSESTIS facilities beneath the lake.

"Of course, we cannot be seen escorting you, otherwise Hera will get suspicious," the Virgin Warrior added.

"I will think of something to tell her," Eileithya replied. "Though I am fairly certain that somehow, my mother already knows that I am here."

"If you say so," Hermes half-mumbled as he unlocked the inner gate to the greenhouse with a mortal-made device and swung the door wide open.

Eileithya stepped inside the brightly lit Southward-facing wing of the greenhouse complex. Located on a gently sloping hill beyond the ridge encircling the recently thawed waters of Lake New-Agassiz, the greenhouses at CARINA Borealis harboured all manner of equipment, crates, and garden beds in neat layers and rows. In many places, there were large metal and polymer boxes stacked almost all the way to the ceiling several meters above the ground. Eileithya immediately thought that these were meant to transport the contents of the greenhouse to the Polaris, and perhaps eventually aboard the Nephele through the Hub. As she walked quietly through the rows of plants and trees and growing things, Eileithya marvelled at the sheer volume and variety of the biomass that remained within this vast indoor garden. Nodding a polite greeting to Demeter, who was busy instructing a group of adolescents on how to properly grow and keep crops alive in microgravity, Eileithya scanned the greenhouse for signs of her mother's presence.

The tales she had heard Hermes tell the Father of gods and men in recent months of Hera's new haunt did not do this place any justice. Perhaps so as not to arouse Zeus' pique, Hermes never mentioned the sheer scale of the installations, nor had he ever said anything of the mortals' actual capacity to subsist outside the realm of nature in their dwelling-places under the Earth. Turning her gaze skyward, Eileithya saw greenish water sliding down between the glass panes across the entire expanse of the ceiling. The lake obviously watered the greenhouses gravitationally, seeping from irrigation pipes crisscrossing the space overhead in mesmerizing patterns. It was all so wondrous, this place of soaring life built out of the ruins of mining and industry. These facilities, Eileithya knew, were meant to habituate mortals to environments entirely separated from the Earth and Sea and Sky, such as the vast expanse beyond the Heavens over which her parents once reigned supreme. More specifically, these facilities were designed to recreate the habitat the learned mortals would encounter aboard the Nephele, where a wide, rotating central component simulated the gravitational pull mortals experience on Earth in order for their bodies and their bones not to wither as they make their way towards new homes beyond the familiar wanderers.

And yet, Eileithya wondered how long mortals could sustain this semblance of a living, breathing biosphere in the vacuum of space, once the considerable resources required to keep their sophisticated machines aloft dried up. Though Demeter's gift had proved a most generous boon to the survival of vast numbers of mortals for untold millennia, farming still required the constant benevolence of the Earth-Mother, who provides the necessary conditions for life to thrive, as well as the goodwill of the Sky Kings, whose gentle rains replenish the Earth. Mechanical gardens such as these would carry out their mission in the space beyond the Sky for some time, of this Eileithya had little doubt. However, there would come a time when, deprived of the life-giving rays of the Sun, such marvels of human ingenuity would wither and die in the cold, dark emptiness of space if mortals failed to find home worlds in which to take root. City-ships like the Nephele, of which there would one day be an innumerable fleet, would likely end up wandering among the lifeless stars like the twilight gardens in the Elysian fields and the Isle of the Blessed, where the Mighty Dead make their homes in the Kingdom of stalwart Hades.

Ever since Hera abandoned Olympus and cast her lot with her firstborn son and his learned mortals at the CARINA citadels strewn across Turtle Island, Eileithya had grown convinced that her mother persisted in championing Prometheus' cause out of a lingering sense of alienation from her own Creation. Why else would the once universally revered Mistress of all Life give up her royal prerogatives among the gods, and plant her Widow's Garden among the machines that would artificially sustain mortals in their likely ill-fated voyages across the Cosmos? And why, for the love of all that was pure and good in this world, would Hera, who once presided over conjugal love and the conception of trueborn children, ever forsake her gift of a fecund womb, and relinquish the care of her youngest offspring to a mortal-made machine, if not to seal the full abdication of her sacred duties?

"Eileithya! How good to see you!" the goddess heard her mother say from behind a hedge. It surprised her that Hera had said these words aloud in a clear, audible voice, instead of planting thoughts directly inside her mind, as was her custom when in the presence of mortals.

"What took you so long?" Hera asked as she walked through the hedge and reached to embrace Eileithya. "I had hoped you would have joined us much sooner. Zeus didn't threaten you against coming here, did he?"

"No, Mother," Eileithya answered truthfully. "Zeus would never dare to threaten me. Not now, nor ever. Anyway, not if he wants his future children to be born alive."

Eileithya bit her lip. Perhaps she should not have reminded Hera of Zeus' countless by-blows, past of present.

"Do not concern yourself with such things, Darling," Hera said reassuringly. "I am long past caring, and very soon, none of that will matter any longer. Now tell me, why have you waited so long to come here, at Borealis? Will you be staying with us a little while, or are you here for the long haul, to board the Nephele with us at Summer's End?"

"No, Mother," Eileithya replied. "I am only here for a spell. I came because I need to speak with you, and also to see this place and judge for myself whether Father's ornery ramblings have any basis in truth."

"Is he still going on about that?" Hera asked, rolling her eyes. "Bloody, hell! When will he ever learn that the fires of mortals' ingenuity burn brightest when their prospects are at their darkest?"

"Until the lights burn out completely," Eileithya muttered under her breath.

"Eileithya," Hera said crossly. "If you have something to say, then speak plainly, and stop pussyfooting as you would with your father. What is it that you came all this way to tell me?"

"All right," Eileithya said, choosing her words wisely. "Mother, I have my doubts about the viability of purely artificial means of creating and sustaining life, and I fear that you are leading these learned mortals on a fool's errand, that will inevitably lead them to their doom."

"Is that all?" Hera replied sardonically, raising an eyebrow for effect.

"It is enough cause for concern, Mother."

"And is this purely your opinion, or is it your father's, pray tell?"

Eileithya rubbed her forehead. "My thoughts are my own, though not mine alone," she said after a moment.

Hera gave Eileithya a hard stare, though she let her daughter press on.

"And Junia," Eileithya said. "I still cannot fathom how you could have let her come into the world the way she did."

Now it was Hera's turn to rub her temple in annoyance.

"Then let me ask you this," Hera said. "Last Summer, at Polaris, you told Zeus that Junia was born of his seed, and that she was indeed my child, though she was not quite as deathless as the blessed gods who dwell on Olympus. You said that as if you had midwifed her yourself. Do you truly know the tale of how your young sister came to be?"

"I saw the circumstances that preceded her birth when I glanced upon her in her flight that evening, yes." Eileithya answered, her breath growing erratic. She shook her head slightly. "How could you -"

A pipe burst overhead, spraying the hedge with the frigid waters of Lake New-Agassiz. The leak was brief, though, as a swarm of minuscule devices coagulated around the breach, patching the tear in the pipe with near breakneck speed.

"Nanobots," Hera told Eileithya when she saw the look of confusion on her daughter's face. "They are as quick as they are useful, especially in places where mortals will have great difficulty manoeuvring in nooks and crannies on the wrong side of airlocks. So much for the shortcomings of technology, wouldn't you say?" she added sarcastically.

"That is not what I meant, Mother."

"Of course not," Hera replied. "You take exception at the prospect of mortals wagering their very survival on our life-support systems, and you seem to take a particularly dim view of the device that hosted your sister before she was ready to be born! Now, why would that be so, unless Zeus has thoroughly poisoned your mind against the inevitable prospect that one day mortals would achieve a level of astuteness that will allow them to leave the bosom of the Earth and colonize the wanderers?"

"There is more to it than that, Mother. That device in which Junia grew from a seedling is anathema to the natural order. That is all."

"Tell me, Eileithya," Hera asked in her most remarkable approximation of a neutral tone. "Do the others know about these thoughts which you claim are very much your own on the matter of Junia's birth? Our Olympian kin, I mean? Because I am quite certain that Hermes had the good sense not to say a word about the circumstances surrounding your sister's incubation to Zeus, for his own sake as well as Junia's."

"I am the only one among the blessed gods who have remained on Olympus to know about the device that safeguarded my sister until the time came for her to be born."

"It gladdens my heart to hear this," Hera replied with a smile. "Let's keep it that way, shall we? Your father would not know what to do with this knowledge, if he ever found out."

"What the hell, Mother?" Eileithya blurted, though she regained her composure when Hera gave her a look of concern as the pipes overhead began to rattle. Taking a deep, calming breath, she asked, "Why did you sever Junia from your womb upon arriving in this foreign land? We both know full well that you would have both remained unharmed had she stayed inside you until she was ready to be born... So, is it true? Did Prometheus have her removed from your flesh to conduct experiments on her as you slept?"

"Now where did that come from?" Hera asked, her cheeks flushed with annoyance and surprise. "Did Hermes tell you such a thing? Well, let me be perfectly clear, in case there was ever any doubt: no blades or needles have ever touched Junia's flesh before she was born. She was put in her artificial womb so that she would suffer no ill effects from my slumber, as I recovered from the effort of transporting Prometheus and myself out of Olympus. I fell out of the sky from a considerable height, I'll have you know. Prometheus and Asia performed a great deal of mental contortions when they explained to the mortals how I happened to be relatively unhurt from the fall. They told them some tall tale about the softening ice of the lake breaking my fall, which was not entirely untrue. But still, it would have looked dreadfully odd to the learned mortals here at Borealis had I *not* run the risk of losing my baby. They are clever, you know, the mortals who live and dwell here in these parts. They would have known something was amiss if I carried on with my pregnancy as if nothing had happened!"

"Mother... I –"

"And one more thing," Hera continued. "There is absolutely no reason for you to look upon any of these life-saving devices with suspicion. You should know better than that by now! Have you not noticed how few mortal women have died in childbirth in recent centuries, when in millennia past their deaths were legion, to the point of banality? These inventions have become a necessity, especially if mortals are ever to succeed in crossing the unfathomable void of interstellar space."

"And why in the world would mortals *need* false wombs to birth their children, out there among the stars and wanderers?" Eileithya asked frantically, almost at her wits' end.

"You poor, dear child," Hera replied. "Have you any idea how difficult it is for mortals to remain hale and strong when they leave the safety of the Earth-Mother's embrace? Even in the most sophisticated city-ships, even aboard the mining-ship Corona, far beyond the skies of Mars, mortals aloft in the space beyond the Heavens are constantly exposed to radiation and the threat of mechanical malfunctions of all sorts! Loss of gravity is perhaps the most insidious of them all. Remember, Daughter, that the mortals who first set out to dwell in the space beyond the Sky withered after some time, if only because their flesh was untethered to the gravity that ultimately gives them their strength. Unborn mortals are particularly vulnerable in the microgravity of low Earth orbit, and even more so in deep space, as they have no force to pull their essence together and create their form in the womb. This is why the mortals who will take to the stars will need to gestate their unborn offspring in specially adapted devices such as the one that nursed your sister to life. These will be placed in dedicated chambers where loss of gravity cannot harm them should some temporary disaster plague their parents' floating citadels. We will need such measures until mortals find new worlds to inhabit, where we hope the conditions propitious to life include a gravitational pull that approximates that of the Earth."

"And what of my sister?" Eileithya asked unflinchingly.

Nepheleid

"What about Junia?" Hera replied. "Your sister has spent some time aboard the Nephele. She loves it there, especially the centre of the main gravity wheel. It makes her feel as if she were literally walking on air! And keep in mind that we never allow small children aboard space stations unless the radiation shields are fully operational, and gravity simulators are functioning at their most optimal parameters. I believe Junia to be quite well suited for life up there above the skies. As would you, if only you chose to ignore the drivel your father has been feeding you for the last few millennia about the hazards of the ingenuity of mortals."

"That is not what I meant..." Eileithya muttered under her breath.

"Then what is it?" Hera asked. "And do speak up! I have little patience for tiptoeing, as always."

Eileithya took a deep breath. "Did you change her?" she said at last. "My sister, did the others... *change* her, as she grew outside your womb while you slept?"

"I've told you, *no*." Hera answered unequivocally.

"Then why do Prometheus' most trusted learned mortals dote on Junia as if she were their own creation?"

"What ever do you mean, child? The mortals here have looked after Junia and cared for her ever since they extracted her from my womb. This had never been done successfully before – Eileithya, what is the matter? You look as though you've seen a ghost!"

"You... mean to change the *mortals* somehow," Eileithya stammered, her lovely features turning a delicate shade of pale. "Oh, I am going to be sick!"

"Don't be silly," Hera chided her. "You are a deathless goddess, a scion of Olympus. You cannot get sick. Nor can Junia, for that matter. And no, we are not making a new race of deathless gods through Junia, Daughter. What we are trying to do is to make these learned mortals stronger and longer-lived, so that our goal of seeding the stars with Earthly life can come to fruition within the lifetimes of their children and grandchildren!"

"This is not right," Eileithya said in a faint voice barely above a whisper. "Zeus will not be pleased if he ever hears of this..."

"Then do not tell him," Hera replied. "He will never bring himself to understand the importance of the work we are doing here and elsewhere across the wilderness of Turtle Island. And you know full well how he often ends up seeking to destroy all that he fails to understand, lest Metis stay his hand. Now, calm yourself, and eat something from the garden. Here, have an apple…"

Hera stepped over to a nearby row of trees and picked the fruit from the orchard.

"Take this," Hera added. "You look a little pale. The mortals will be worried if they see you like this."

"But it's only April," Eileithya whispered more to herself than to her mother. "How can you have apples in April?"

Hera smiled. "This is the true purpose of places such as these, to provide sustenance to those who live beyond the reach of Earth at all times. At last, you are beginning to understand. Now, will you speak a word of this to the others when you return?"

"No, Mother," Eileithya answered. *It will not be I who will tell Zeus of all that you mean to do.*

"And for that you have my gratitude, Daughter," Hera answered aloud. "Come now, Klymene will have some lunch ready soon. There is so much more we need to discuss."

Nepheleid

Chapter Six

It takes a lot of effort to sidestep the decontamination process without being noticed, Junia thought as she hid in the locker room while the rest of her classmates underwent the hours-long process before boarding the Krios Khrysomallos passenger chamber of the Hub. It was named after the fabled flying ram with the golden fleece that the children of the cloud-nymph Nephele rode to avoid being sacrificed to Dionysus. The passenger chamber of the space elevator could house dozens of waking mortals at a time for the long ascent, and many more should a significant number of boarders choose to sleep during their vertical voyage. Junia never understood why anyone would choose to do that, for the view of the aurora borealis from the thermosphere was unlike any other that could be experienced on terra firma.

Junia did not skip the crucial and necessary decontamination process out of laziness or spite, but rather because she knew, but could not tell the other children, that her biology was far more evolved than theirs, which meant that her flesh could not host pathogens of any kind. In the span of her nine years of life, Junia had never known illness, and she knew from the tales her mothers had told her of her origins that she would probably never taste death, even if she chose to remain among mortals and forgo a blessed existence among the gods of Olympus once she came of age. Her fate still undecided, Junia had little choice but to play along when Hera told her a few days ago that she had arranged for her and her classmates to make an impromptu field trip aboard the Nephele under the pretext that the children ought to explore their new home at least once before joining their parents on the city-ship at Summer's end.

When the last of the other pupils stepped out of the decontamination vestibule, Junia snuck out of a shower stall and donned the required standard-issue CARINA thermal uniform adjusted for her small size. Tiptoeing behind Derek and Paul, whose relative height concealed her small form adequately enough, Junia set about to climb onto the highest bunk bed at the topmost level of the passenger chamber, scaling the stairs and outer ladders like a parkour champion, despite Ares' and Eris' loud objections. Junia smiled, knowing full well that her red-haired siblings' show of concern was only an act, for they had witnessed firsthand her fleet-footedness and prowess at escape the previous year aboard the Polaris, situated below their feet at the heart of the Arctic. Once she was satisfied that her selected bunk was well within eavesdropping distance of Prometheus and her other divine kin at the control deck, Junia settled in snugly within the small confines of the space that would be her living quarters for the duration of the long ascent toward the Nephele. As per Asia's request, Ares and Eris would reside on the bunks flanking hers, though they would travel under sedation, as would any young passenger deemed too unruly, claustrophobic, or anxious to comfortably spend the next several hours aboard the elevator to the topmost reaches of the Heavens.

"All right, children," Mnemosyne said from the ground level of the passenger chamber, before stepping into the inner lift to the control deck. "We will depart in ten minutes. Remember that it is perfectly normal to feel queasy near the end, as we will have lost most of our gravity by the time we approach the loading bay of the Nephele. This is why, and I can never say this enough, you are not to leave your bunks during the last three hours of the ascension, nor are you to unbind your harness. If you must go to the bathroom, push the yellow button inside your bunk, and you will be pulled to the vacuum toilet facilities on your tier, as you've been instructed."

"Ewww," said one of the children, though Junia strongly suspected Eris of impersonating one of the adolescent cohorts to break the monotony of the boarding protocol.

"And do heed the advice of your elders," Mnemosyne continued, ignoring the heckling from the peanut gallery. "Use this time to take a long, restful nap, as your circadian rhythms will be thrown wildly off course for the next few days. And if, for whatever reason, you cannot go to sleep on your own, push the blue button inside your bunk, and you will be dosed with a perfectly safe amount of our patented Hypnos mist."

The double doors to the decontamination chamber slid shut outside the Krios Khrysomallos, and the structure shook slightly and steadily for a few seconds. A few of the younger children shrieked, while many of the older ones laughed nervously.

"No need to worry," Mnemosyne said reassuringly. "This is perfectly normal. The elevator shaft is only evacuating all the remaining air before departure. Are all the little ones tucked in, Eris? Good, now you and your brother take your bunks, up there."

"Five minutes to lift-off," Asia said from the loudspeaker at the control deck.

"Your harness will lock when your names are called out," Mnemosyne continued. "You will be able to rotate your beds upwards to sit up and look outside the windows, but otherwise keep your heads and limbs within the bunk area at all times. Are you all excited to see the Nephele?"

"YES!" the children replied in unison, at a pitch that could almost shatter glass.

"All right then," Mnemosyne said. "We will call your names alphabetically. Is everyone in their bunk? Good. ARES."

"What the – " the god of war exclaimed as the harness slid shut across his chest. His surprise was short-lived, as a rather large dose of the Hypnos mist hissed audibly from above his bunk. A loud thump, consistent with a mesomorph suddenly losing consciousness and going limp, ensued.

"ARGOSI, Junia," Mnemosyne called out when the adolescent girls' giggles died down.

Junia lay still as the harness bound her in her bunk. Once snug and secure, she rotated upward and clockwise to a seated position and liberated a small device from her pocket, from which she read quietly while Mnemosyne called the other children by name.

"You will need to put that away when we reach the mesopause," said swift Iris of the rainbow wings, standing at Prometheus' right and looking down at Junia from the control deck.

"I know," Junia replied. "I've done this trip before."

"A seasoned veteran," Prometheus chuckled softly.

"Now go to sleep, little one," Asia said, before announcing the remaining thirty seconds before lift-off.

Nepheleid

The Krios Khrysomallos rose slowly at first, gaining speed as it soared high above the thawing Arctic winter ice at the very top of the Earth. In a few hours, the clear azure skies would give way to darkening hues of indigo, once the passenger chamber of the Hub reached the upper limits of the stratosphere. Sleeping through this spectacle would be out of the question, Junia thought, even if it meant staying awake for twenty-odd hours straight until bedtime the following day. After all, was Junia not also a scion of Olympus, capable of great feats of endurance and strength, as were Ares and Eris, now slumbering peacefully in their bunks under heavy sedation? Was she not also preternaturally resilient like Hephaestus, who would join them on the Nephele at Summer's end?

More importantly, napping on the way to the city-ship would entail missing all the interesting news she would glean from eavesdropping on Prometheus and his mostly deathless entourage up on the control deck. Knowing that the adults would keep silent on important matters until they believed her to be fast asleep, Junia put away her device in the pocket of her uniform and rotated her bunk to a supine position. She then pulled a blanket from the compartment beneath her feet and made a show of cocooning herself into a cozy little bundle.

About an hour later, Junia heard Iris cooing, "Look at the little Kitten napping."

Of course, this was pure provocation, for Iris knew that Junia would only ever suffer her mothers to call her by that name.

"But like a noble gas, she does not react," Mnemosyne said, also testing Junia for signs of alertness.

Refusing to take the bait, Junia unfolded herself instead in her nest of blankets until her limbs were outstretched and her belly faced the ceiling.

"Careful," Prometheus said with a smile in his voice. "She might be messing with us."

"Is that Apollo outside, in the window?" Asia said facetiously.

Once again, Junia summoned her considerable willpower, honed from many hours of daily martial arts practice and sheer stubbornness, and refrained from laughing, continuing instead to feign slumber.

"Coast is clear, as mortals say," Asia declared finally.

"Good," Prometheus replied. "Because we are scheduled for our conference call with 'Dr. Archer' about the Hesperides Protocol in about two minutes. Iris, do you have the headsets ready?"

Iris reached under her folded wings, made to look like a colourful shawl in the presence of mortals, and produced four small devices equipped with earpieces and small microphones jutting from a thin headband. She then rummaged deeper in her concealed plumage and pulled out four translucent, bowl-like items meant to dampen sound while attached to the diminutive headsets.

"Even the Kitten would have great difficulty hearing us with these," Iris said as she clasped the dampener to her own headset and fastened the contraption onto her head.

Asia and Prometheus assembled the pieces of their headsets, all the while keeping an eye on Junia.

"Settings are already on low volume," Asia remarked, nodding gratefully at Iris.

"I will take the call in the back," Mnemosyne said, leaving behind an idle headset, and taking a seat at the rear of the control deck, where she grabbed hold of a heavy receiver reminiscent of rotary telephones of centuries past.

"It's all right, Elisapie," Mnemosyne added when one of the mortal deckhands gave her a strange look. "I remember things better when I am holding an object in my hand."

As expected, within a few minutes a faint signal came through, inaudible to mortal ears, but loud and clear to Junia, who had turned her head in such a way as to be directly aligned with Prometheus and Asia, whom she knew would not take their eyes off her throughout the duration of the ascent.

"Dr. Archer," Prometheus said. "You are live on the Golden Ram. I am here with Asia, Iris, and our lovely headmistress, auntie Mnem. How are you on this fine Spring morn at Borealis?"

"All is well on our end," Apollo answered with a soft laugh, taking great delight in aping the notoriously casual manner of the mortals of Turtle Island. "We are joined by Athena – I mean, Dr. Weiss, Dr. Summers and... Eileithya? She has yet to affect a plausible mortal name. And that is all. The mortals are outside in the greenhouse, harvesting crops before the entire nursery is shipped to Polaris with our Dear Leader."

"We are well aware," Prometheus said. "And we will not need to use aliases; this is a secure line."

"Hera leaves tomorrow with a skeleton crew of my sisters," Asia added, "and not a single mortal among them. She already dismissed most of her human administrative crew at Polaris; and promoted them to better positions elsewhere throughout the CARINA network. Case in point – her personal assistant is now with us, travelling to the Nephele via the Hub."

"Good for Elisapie," Demeter said from her seat at the back of the boardroom, somewhere beyond the ALSESTIS laboratories under Lake New-Agassiz. "She has earned it!"

"I suppose the precious cargo is also secure," Athena said.

"Of course," Prometheus answered, knowing full well that Athena was speaking of the children, and Junia in particular, who had left Borealis the day before. "Everyone is accounted for, and all are in good spirits... The ones who are still conscious, anyway."

"That is good to hear," Apollo said. "Now, is the entire bridge secure for discussing the subject matter at hand?"

"It is," Asia answered. "And we are on the control deck. The elevator does not have a bridge to speak of. You are thinking of the Nephele."

Apollo laughed. "I stand corrected," he said.

"We can speak freely," Iris replied.

"So, Phase One of the Hesperides Protocol is well under way," Prometheus said. "As Asia mentioned, Hera leaves on the morrow for Polaris, to tie some loose ends with a certain Maiden who dwells at the bottom of the Sea. It is my understanding that she will remain there until the first day of Midsummer, to bid farewell to the goddess who graciously welcomed us and allowed us to build our installations for extensive testing for several years before these were implemented aboard the Nephele last Winter. You lot are to oversee the remainder of Phase One, which is the transport of the contents of the greenhouses off-world, until Hera's return. Phase Two involves the migration of key personnel in July and August, and Phase Three will entail the assembly of the Hesperides Autonomous Station from parts of the Nephele starting early September – "

"Say again?" Apollo interrupted. "I mean, the last part? The one about Phase Three? I thought I heard you say that the Hesperides Station will be crafted from parts of the Nephele. Is the city-ship not still under construction?"

"It is, in a matter if speaking," Asia answered. "Last August, when Hera resurfaced after her unplanned absence, the Nephele was near completion, saved for a few, mostly cosmetic, finishing touches. We might have exaggerated the state of completion a wee bit to avoid disclosing the contingency plan she had drafted in case a certain ex-husband of hers reared his head in these parts. But now that he has, the Hesperides Protocol is already under way, and it involves establishing a permanent ALSESTIS facility off-word, as well as building the new CARINA headquarters in low Earth orbit."

"But... how?" Eileithya asked, addressing the others for the first time. "Your citadel beyond the Heavens harbours these spare parts in abundance?"

"Again, it does, in a matter of speaking," Prometheus said. "We built additional emergency escape habitat compartments, in case we needed these as the primary infrastructure from which to assemble the greenhouses and laboratories that would house and feed our CARINA personnel tasked with continuing the Earth-based missions. The donor modules of the Nephele will be rebuilt once the city-ship reaches the Corona. And since the Corona has long begun its mining operations at the edge of the asteroid field in the far orbit of Mars, there would be no dearth of materials to fulfil this task."

"The Nephele already has several active auxiliary emergency habitat modules," Asia added. "And that includes the ones meant to be transplanted into the Corona. There are more than enough greenhouse modules to sustain the crews of both stations for decades, even centuries, even if the donor modules for the Hesperides Autonomous Station were never replaced."

"What of the seed library?" Demeter asked. "And the frozen zoological specimens that were locked up in the restricted access floors at Borealis? These are no longer here. I thought they were simply dispatched to the

Nephele ahead of schedule. Is that the case, or were they taken as part of the Hesperides protocol, to orbit the Earth-Mother, in your ALSESTIS facilities above the Heavens?"

"A bit of both," Iris replied. "You must understand, Zeus has proved himself a veritable threat to CARINA in recent years. Do you not remember the last time I set foot on starry Olympus? He would have struck me with his thunderbolt had Apollo not intervened..."

"And in the end, I all but gave away Hera's whereabouts," Apollo said.

"That may be so," Iris continued, "but finding our Queen at the ends of the Earth did not endear us, nor the importance of the CARINA venture, to our King. In fact, we have reports that he is even more distrustful of the technological advancements made by mortals in recent centuries. Is that not so, Eileithya?"

"There is truth to this," Eileithya admitted. This is also why Hephaestus has told me that he plans to leave with Mother on the Nephele, for he sees no future for craftsmen of his calibre in a world where the achievements of the clever and learned are not celebrated as they should be."

"But who will rule over the Hesperides Autonomous Station?" Athena asked.

"Asia and I will," Prometheus said. "That is, until we find a qualified and willing Director of Operations, among mortals, or perhaps immortals of other nations of the broad-pathed Earth, if any such individual makes themselves known to us. We would have been overjoyed had Mnemosyne accepted the assignment, however our dear aunt declined the original position of ALSESTIS Director of Operations years ago, opting to recruit Hera for the task instead. As the Fates willed it, her judgment proved most fortuitous, as our operations have run optimally for years with our Queen holding the reins."

"Until a year ago," Asia said absentmindedly.

"Now, that's not fair," Iris replied. "Hera never once let her restlessness compromise her aptitude at leading the ALSESTIS division until her mission was complete."

"No," Asia said, "except for that time last year when she disappeared with Junia in the Underworld. Meanwhile, we had to host and entertain

Apollo and Athena aboard the Nephele for weeks on end! Not that I'm complaining... But never mind that; now she simply acts as though she were in a hurry to leave the Earth, even though the Nephele is scheduled to remain here in low orbit for some time. Truth be told, I fear she might launch the city-ship prematurely, if only to put some distance of a cosmic scale between herself and the Thunderer."

"And that is where the four of you come in," Prometheus told Apollo, Athena, Demeter and Eileithya through the aether.

"You want us to remain with Hera to keep her calm and focused while Father whinges on Olympus and hovers above Polaris?" Eileithya asked incredulously.

"We need you to remind Hera that not all the blessed gods who dwell on starry Olympus agree with Zeus' judgment on the matter at hand," Mnemosyne answered from the rear of the control deck. "Your father has consistently mistrusted mortals for their cleverness, and in a way, he was not wrong, only insufferably ornery and at times downright detestable. Not all those who have once called ourselves his wives agree with him in all things. Hera always proved the bravest of us all, which is why I chose her to take my place as the Goddess-Queen of the countless generations of mortals to come, spread among the stars -"

"And why did you decline the role as Goddess-Queen among these learned mortals, pray tell?" Eileithya interrupted crossly.

"My goal was not to take your mother from you, child," Mnemosyne replied. "But even you must have seen that Hera had, in her own way, already left the company of the blessed gods centuries ago to cast her lot with mortals and their wilting kind. Even before I had her taste the waters of my fountain, she understood that mortals are our only means of perpetuating the memory of life on Earth long after it is gone, whether by their own hands or by the inexorable passage of Time. Hera keeps close to her heart the memory of Earth as it once was, when she was a Maiden Queen and the Mistress of the soaring Life that thrived in all the nations of the world, even if the world back then was so much smaller to the knowledge of our deathless kind. That being said, Hera needs to know that you and your siblings at Borealis support her in her endeavour, and you agree that she was right to stand strong against her bully of a King."

"We support Hera," Athena said flatly. "That is why we are all here."

Nepheleid

"No, Grey Eyes," Mnemosyne answered, her voice betraying disappointment. "You are here to stand by your brother, Hermes, who was unjustly tasked with shadowing your Queen wherever she may roam. Perhaps Demeter is here for her sister, or Hebe, Hephaestus, Eileithya, and the twins for their mother. Or perhaps not. This matters little, and I am not one to judge the motivations of others. I declined the offer to rule the mortals who are to dwell beyond the Heavens because I was loath to leave the Earth while five of my Titan brothers lingered in their prison in gloomy Tartarus, and my children remained on starry Olympus to sing the praises of the one who condemned them to that fate..."

Junia took a sharp intake of breath when Mnemosyne mentioned the Titans. Before the previous Summer, the only Titans she had known were Okeanos and Tethys, Father and Mother to Klymene and to the Rivers, as well as Mnemosyne and their sisters, all save Themis, who dwelt among the blessed gods of holy Olympus. As for their brothers, Junia had met them only once, when Hera took her to the Kingdom of Hades to hide from the gods who, on Zeus' orders, searched for them with renewed effort. While her mother and uncle were busy speaking of grown-up things, Junia had snuck off to Tartarus to meet her ancestors, who in turn had welcomed her with uncharacteristic kindness and curiosity. As far as Junia knew, the tales told of the Titans' monstrosity were greatly exaggerated, as were the stories mortals continued to believe of Hera's cruelty and pettiness towards womankind. No, the Titans were not all that bad, Junia thought. After all, had her Grandpa Kronos not gifted her with his prized scythe, with which he liberated his own siblings from his father's tyranny by relieving the Sky-King Ouranos from his manhood?

Junia knew the Titans as the original generation of immortals, born after Chaos begat Night, and in a bright explosion of light, brought about Day and Space and Earth. The Titans sired the deathless gods who dwell on starry Olympus, which was once the abode of Okeanos and Tethys before Junia's grandparents Kronos and Rhea expelled their elder siblings to the boundaries of the Earth and claimed the Holy Mountain as their own. But now that Hera, heir to Rhea and the Earth-Mother herself, had left Olympus, pledging to never return, and joined Prometheus and his ilk at the most advanced scientific enclave yet known to mortals and deathless gods, Junia wondered whether the flight of the Nephele would expand the realm of Okeanos and Tethys farther still, to the very edge of the Cosmos. Just as her mind wandered to her memories of those strange sky-rivers she had seen while making her way to Tartarus the year before, Junia felt a strong hand lightly squeezing her shoulder.

The child opened her eyes, and saw Prometheus standing by her bunk, looking at her benevolently.

"This is exactly what the flight of the Nephele, the Corona, and all other city-ships yet to come will accomplish," he told her in a soft voice.

Junia gave him a sheepish smile. Of course he had seen into her thoughts the entire time, just as Hera would have done had she joined them on this ascension.

Prometheus laughed. "You can stop pretending to be asleep now," he told her. "Besides, if you look outside, a little to the East, an aurora borealis is just beginning."

Junia heeded her brother's advice and let herself become entranced by the beauty of the dancing lights, while Prometheus returned to the control deck, presumably to finish the conference call without the distraction of his littlest sister's deafening thoughts.

Nepheleid

Chapter Seven

In the quiet town of Borealis, far from the Arctic shores, Hermes sat alone at the counter of the Café Basilea, sipping the last dregs of his flavourful bean brew that grants mortals exceptional powers of insight and concentration at all hours of the day. At some point, he would have to return to the flat he shared with bright Athena at the CARINA Headquarters to prepare for yet another journey, but for now, he was content whiling away the hours before the lunch rush inevitably put an end to his delusion of calm and solitude among the scarce late-morning stragglers.

For the moment, Hermes strove to ignore his growing despair at his exile from Olympus, as well as his festering annoyance upon hearing that he would have to accompany golden-throned Hera yet again on one of her journeys among the gods of Turtle Island. Just when he thought that Spring had finally arrived in these parts, and that life in the boreal wilderness would become marginally more tolerable for the next six months, Hermes learned that Hera sent Junia and the other schoolchildren North to the Hub, under the pretext that they ought to acclimate themselves to their new homes in low Earth orbit before their final relocation. In the meantime, while the young ones bounced around on the Nephele during their extended school trip, Hera decided to spend the next few weeks at Polaris to oversee the base's transition from remote staging ground for off-world operations into a glorified waystation between Earth and Sky for space-bound travelers.

For Hermes, whose sworn duty to the Thunderer was to follow his errant bride wherever she may roam, these latest tidings meant that he had to accompany Hera to the Arctic until it pleased her to return to the more temperate climes of Borealis in the wilderness of Turtle Island. Knowing that this Summer might be his last shadowing the Queen on the face of the Earth brought Hermes little joy, for he knew that if all went according to plan, Hera's final trip aboard the Hub doomed him to permanent exile from Olympus, or at least until Zeus rescinded his decree whereby he could not go home without his Queen and Junia. It seemed odd to

Nepheleid

Hermes that Hera should have chosen to leave for the Arctic so early in the season, as the month of May had barely begun, and it was Hera's custom to spend her Midsummers with Sedna, the Maiden of the Deep, while Junia was away with the other children at Junior Space Camp while on school break. Perhaps Hera suddenly found herself in a hurry to tie up loose ends before making her final voyage to the stars, Hermes pondered, though he thought it far more likely that his stepmother had chosen this point in time to make her impromptu journey North to avoid Aphrodite's imminent arrival at Borealis. Like Hermes, Hera likely heard Eileithya mention this to Hebe upon her own arrival in these parts, as the two sisters often spent their idle time chatting in this very establishment at all hours of the day.

Perhaps Aphrodite's forthcoming visit was the true reason why Ares insisted so vehemently on accompanying Junia and the other children to the Nephele. After all, had he not left Olympus of his own accord after growing weary of Aphrodite's ceaseless solicitousness towards his father, whom he knew hated him the most among all of his children? Or perhaps being cast into the role of protector to his youngest sister had made Ares grow fonder of Junia than he ever was of Aphrodite, or for that matter Eris, his twin and accomplice in war and mischief. In a strange way, Junia's innocence, and her endlessly curious and lackadaisical demeanour curtailed Ares' aimless anger and bloodlust as effectively as it subdued Eris' proclivity for chaos mongering. Though Hermes himself had not grown quite as fond of Junia as the other blessed gods who left Olympus to join their Queen in her self-imposed exile, he could at least appreciate that the child did not share her mother's unadulterated contempt for him and his duty to his King.

"One more before you set off on your journey to Polaris?" the lovely Hebe, daughter of Hera, asked amiably as she refilled his cup.

"You read my mind," Hermes replied dourly, while Herakles threw him a sideways glance from the kitchen beyond the counter.

"This one's on the house," Hebe said, giving Hermes a sympathetic look.

"I see what you did there," Hermes said.

"What ever do you mean?" Hebe replied innocently.

"All my coffees and meals and whatever else are a gratuity from CARINA. Prometheus decreed it out of pity when Father banished me from Olympus last Summer."

"He did it out of the kindness of his heart," Hebe corrected Hermes. "Just as he gave my husband and I this place, for us to operate as we see fit for as long as it pleases us to stay here among the learned mortals at CARINA."

"And will you be staying long, pray tell?" Hermes asked, loud enough for Herakles to also hear. "Since our Queen seems rather eager to leave the planet when the Seasons turn to Autumn."

"Are you asking if we're going to accompany Mother aboard the Nephele, or return to Father on holy Olympus once this base gets decommissioned?"

Hermes raised an eyebrow. "Are you privy to secrets that I ought to know?" he asked.

"I don't know," Hebe replied causally. "You should ask Doctors 'Archer' and 'Weiss'. They're coming up right behind you."

As soon as the divine cupbearer uttered these words, Hermes spun around on his seat and spied Apollo and Athena entering the Café Basilea. The blessed gods who had left Olympus for his sake, as well as Demeter and Eileithya who followed in their wake, looked as pleasantly stunned as Hermes felt morose and perplexed.

"Good morning!" Hebe exclaimed cheerfully, as she did to all her customers. "Welcome to Café Basilea. Would you like to see our lunch menu?"

"Perhaps in a bit, Hebe," Apollo answered.

"Right now, we've found the one we were looking for," Athena added.

"Very well," Hebe replied politely. "Whenever you're ready."

Apollo and Athena took their seats at the counter, each flanking Hermes, while Eileithya and Demeter sat at a small table nearby. Athena scanned her surroundings, then nodded at Apollo once she was certain that there were no mortals around to eavesdrop.

"What!?" Hermes asked Athena as the Virgin Warrior fixed him with her gaze.

"You missed the conference call," Apollo answered in Athena's stead.

Nepheleid

"Of course, I did," Hermes replied. "I am not to meddle in the affairs of CARINA, or have you forgotten? This means that I cannot listen in on conference calls!"

"Since when do you obey Hera's rules?" Athena asked with a soft chuckle.

"Since she's had her minions find the means to catch me intercepting her messages and her calls," Hermes answered. "Mind you, she devised such means herself long ago, and has become an expert at obfuscation whenever she senses my presence. So, I've stopped bothering."

"That's a damned shame," Apollo mused.

Athena turned her gaze to the Archer, her eyes obviously questioning whether they ought to disclose the morning's developments.

"Well, I suppose there is little point in being coy," Apollo answered her wordless query.

"How dire are your tidings?" Hermes asked dubiously.

"The Nephele is having a baby," Eileithya said brusquely, to everyone's surprise.

Hermes answered the news with a blank stare.

"What?" Eileithya continued. "That pretty much sums it up!"

"Say again Eily?" Hebe asked. "Nephele has returned, and she is with child?"

"No," Athena said. "She meant the city-ship. *The* Nephele."

"How the hell can a city-ship have a baby?" Herakles asked incredulously.

"By shedding some of its parts to constitute a new whole," Apollo said. "The Nephele will release some habitat modules and form another, smaller space station in geostatic orbit at the Hub."

"That part wasn't entirely clear, really," Athena added, "but as far as we know, it is meant to remain nearby, in low Earth orbit, indefinitely."

"Apparently Hera devised this plan long ago as a contingency measure, in case we ever found her among the mortals at CARINA," Apollo said.

"But you found her years ago!" Herakles protested. "And we've been here with her for months! Why is this only now coming to the fore?"

"Prometheus didn't say," Demeter answered, "but Asia and Mnemosyne insinuated that the new station would deploy if Hera felt that their mission were in any sort of jeopardy."

"You mean, because of Father?" Hebe asked, though Hermes could guess that all present already knew the answer.

Demeter nodded. "And they tasked us with overseeing the move of the CARINA facilities from Earth to Heaven, so to speak," she added.

"The entire Borealis campus?" Hebe asked, doling out a half dozen coffee cups to the blessed gods gathered in the Café Basilea. "Not just the greenhouses and what's left of the ALSESTIS laboratories?"

"They're moving the entire headquarters to space!" Herakles said, to everyone's surprise.

"That is what I gathered from this morning's exchange," Apollo replied.

"I as well," Athena concurred.

"And what is this new station called?" Hermes asked.

"The Hesperides Autonomous Station, if you would believe it," Athena answered.

"Hesperides?" Herakles repeated incredulously, almost dropping a tray of panini onto the polished floor.

"Hesperides, like her old garden with the golden apples," Athena said.

"Like her old *nuptial* garden with the golden apples," Demeter added emphatically.

"So what, is she is planting gardens in the Sky out of spite now?" Hermes asked fitfully.

"Please tell me that Mother has changed her mind about leaving with Junia on the Nephele, and that she will be staying up there on the Hesperides, where we can reach her via the Hub as mortals do!" Hebe implored.

Nepheleid

"I very much doubt it is so," Apollo replied. "Prometheus and Asia told us that they have begun looking for an optimal candidate to to fill the position of Director of Operations on the Hesperides. For all they know, this legacy station of theirs might be handed over to gods of other nations, or even to mortals. I believe that Hera and Prometheus devised this contingency to keep CARINA's technological treasures out of reach, where Father cannot thwart the progress of mortals, or punish them for surpassing our kind in brilliance and ingenuity."

"No," Herakles said. "She is taking vengeance against us."

"What do you mean?' Eileithya asked. "How exactly is Mother retaliating against us? We've done nothing to incur her wrath!"

Herakles shook his head. "She is getting back at us, all of us, for all that was hers that we destroyed in our collective pursuit of glory," he said. "She is lashing out for her un-mourned husband, Eurymedon, whose murder instigated Gaia's enmity towards Zeus and our blessed kin to the point where the Earth-Mother brought forth an entire race of Giants to lay waste to Olympus. She is getting back at Zeus for taking her into the fray, where she prophesied my birth and deeds, and for her unwitting complicity in her own downfall, as all that she has ever loved and protected came to ruin through the deeds of heroes such as myself. I did not know then that slaughtering her pet dragon Ladon, guardian of the tree of the golden apples, would cause the Pleiades to rob her garden of its treasure until it could no longer sustain itself. I did not know that all I have ever done, even to glorify her holy name, was truly done on Zeus' behalf to bring her low. If I could undo such deeds and bring back the world of soaring life over which she once reigned as Queen, I would. But we are too late."

Hermes bristled upon hearing those words, for he too had often undermined Hera's ascendancy over the millennia, all in the service of his King.

Hebe turned around and placed a hand on Herakles' shoulder.

"You did not know," she said consolingly. "Back then, when you were mortal, you were only performing your Labours, as the Fates decreed. You could not have known…"

"And to think," Eileithya said, "that Aphrodite got the very last one of these golden apples as her prize after the judgment of Paris. That was so terribly unfair! The apples of the Hesperides rightfully belong to Mother! No wonder she would be willing to leave it all behind, even if she does not blame us personally for all the wrongs done to her over the centuries. At least she gave us a choice on whether to accompany her aboard the Nephele."

Hermes threw Eileithya a quizzical look.

"I meant to say, some of us were given a choice," Eileithya told Hermes. "I am certain that Mother would allow you safe passage if you chose to accompany her to the stars... And if she didn't, at least Prometheus would. Unlike Mother, he is not the sort to carry a grudge. After all, he allowed Hephaestus to join him in the engineering decks of the Polaris, and Hephaestus was the one who fastened him to his rock when Father sought to punish him for stealing fire from Olympus! And now, Hephaestus is slated to assume command of the mining-ship Corona in a few decades, once the current mortal administrator either retires, or passes away from space sickness or something of the sort – "

"So, Hephaestus is definitely leaving?" a familiar, melodious female voice inquired from somewhere beyond the neat row of tables between the counter and the entrance of the Café Basilea.

All the blessed gods turned their gaze toward the store front, where golden Aphrodite stood at the door, her beauteous form framed by the luminous radiance of the noonday sun beyond the high glass windows.

"I suppose this ought not to surprise me," Aphrodite said to her stunned audience in an indifferent tone. "He left me on the deck of the Polaris to join Hera last Summer, without so much as a goodbye. Ah, well. So be it."

"How long have you been standing there?" Hermes asked, slightly ashamed for not having noticed the goddess of love in their midst, engrossed as he had been by Herakles' heartfelt testimony.

"Long enough to ascertain that Hera has all but abdicated her stature as the daughter and heir to Rhea, Mother of the Gods, and is abandoning the Earth-Mother and all that lives upon her bosom," Aphrodite answered without irony.

"That's not quite true," Demeter replied crossly. "My sister has never abdicated anything, for any reason whatsoever, during the entire course of her deathless existence. She has simply shifted her aim above the realms of Earth, Sea, and Sky! As for her purported abandonment of all earthly life, you could not be any further from the mark!"

"Oh really?" Aphrodite taunted. "Then I suppose that the mortals who struggle to live beyond these walled cities of science, in the fallow wildernesses where they cannot farm or hunt, or on the Oceans' shores where they cannot fish under pain of death through poisoning or worse, would agree wholeheartedly with your assessment that all life is on the mend across the broad-pathed Earth!?"

"You are mistaken," Demeter answered. "Hera and Prometheus and others of like mind have planted the seeds of life's renewal through the CARINA network in all the nations of the world. My sister would never abandon a ruined garden unless she knew for certain that it could restore itself, whether by caring hands or through the passage of Time. Such is not her nature!"

"I suppose you are right," Aphrodite said, "except that the Earth's and the Ocean's gardens are nowhere near the point where anyone, whether deathless or mortal, could expect to see a world rife with soaring life, as our dear Herakles put it so eloquently. So, it would seem that our Queen's imminent departure remains, at best, ill timed, and at worst perfidiously reckless."

"What are you saying, Aphrodite?" Hebe asked.

"All I am saying, dear child, is that I've got my work cut out for me, in the parlance of mortals," Aphrodite answered. "Now tell me, where is Hera? I need to speak to her at once."

"I would advise against it," Athena replied. "Right now, she is preparing for her journey to the Arctic, and does not wish to be disturbed. Klymene was abundantly clear on the matter when I spoke to her this morning. If you seek an audience now, you will only make things worse for yourself. I ought to know."

"I appreciate your counsel," Aphrodite said as she spun around and took a step outside the Café Basilea. "However, it is imperative that I speak to Hera before she dooms us all. Now, Hermes, if you would be so kind as to show me the way to her lodgings…"

Hermes looked at the blessed gods gathered around him. Judging from the expression on Athena and Apollo's countenances, the messenger thought it wise to follow Aphrodite back to the compound, lest she blunder her way to the heart of the CARINA Borealis compound.

"If you can hold off a few more days," Hermes said as he caught up to Aphrodite, "then perhaps you can seek Hera on the Polaris once she returns from her visit with Sedna. She will be saying her farewells to the Maiden of the Deep much earlier than is her custom, and this is a journey she always undergoes alone. I will send for you when the time is right, just after she returns. By then you might catch her when she is feeling wistful enough to question her decision to leave the Earth and all that she has ever known and loved. That will be your best chance to talk some sense into her, and then perhaps we can all *finally* go home."

Aphrodite gazed upon Hermes approvingly.

"I hope you are right," she said. "For Zeus' sake, as well as our own."

Nepheleid

Chapter Eight

The late-May Midnight Sun lit the dark frigid waters cradling the steel ramparts of the Polaris, affixed to the bottom of the Ocean high above the Arctic Circle. The brilliant play of sunlight on the dancing waves made for perfect camouflage as white-armed Hera emerged from the Deep, having returned from her visit with Sedna, the Maiden who dwells at the bottom of the Sea. Hidden from the sight of the few mortals who had remained at CARINA's Northernmost base of operations, Hera climbed aboard the mighty vessel, and made her way to the Polaris' water management and treatment deck, at the heart of the ship's hull. The goddess walked down the winding staircase to the very bottom of the sepulchral tiered deck, where a network of perforated water pipes fed hanging installations containing various sorts of plants, vines, and fungi, whose purpose was to filter and treat the used waters collected by the ship's crew. The only light in this place came from the translucent ceiling, which illuminated the Polaris' garden pit far more brilliantly than the artificial solar lights required during the long Arctic Winter night.

Unbeknownst to CARINA's learned mortals, this was also one of the secret places on the broad-pathed Earth, and on the Sea, where Hera expunged the filth she often absorbed within her divine form whenever she set about to heal the waters upon and around Turtle Island. She had long known that centuries of industrialization, fed by rampant greed and the disregard of previous generations of mortals for the Earth upon which all known Life dwells, resulted in a particularly severe accumulation of such miasma at the very top of the world. Though she had not planned to cleanse in such a manner the Ocean floor where Sedna dwells, she thought it a far more benevolent gift to her strange and lonely friend than simply braiding her hair with caring hands, as she had done each year at Midsummer since her arrival on Turtle Island ten years prior.

Once she finally arrived at the basement of the water management and treatment chamber, Hera discarded the few garments she had retained from her excursion for the sake of modesty, lest any mortal gifted with second sight gaze upon her true form in her wanderings from the Depths of the Ocean to the ship's bowels. She then pulled aside the heavy metal covering of a squat circular water tank at the centre of the floor and sat within the cylindrical receptacle. Once submerged, Hera scanned the steel inner lining of the tank with her fingers until she found a lever, then resurfaced and took a deep breath. With great effort, she pulled the lever as she released through every pore of her skin the effluvium of toxic waste, heavy metals, and sooty debris once trapped in the vanishing Arctic ice sheet. As the tank drained itself of the filth, Hera lay breathless, taking a moment to find her bearings before she finally sat up and climbed out of the now-empty vessel. Without a second glance, she made her way towards the stairs and climbed halfway up the chamber until she reached the mid-way tier, where Klymene greeted her beyond the heavy double doors of the Polaris' communal bathing and shower facilities.

Slowly recovering her strength, golden-throned Hera waited until Klymene finished drawing a warm bath in one of the private bathtubs upon the deck. The washrooms were completely deserted, for the mortals of the Polaris were all fast asleep in their beds, despite the brightness of the Arctic skies casting a long shadow of the Hub that reached from the topmost deck of the ship all the way to the shores of Northern Canada. At the Queen's bidding, Klymene took her leave, for she knew that it would take a long time for Hera to recover from her ordeal.

To pass the time until her breathing found its strong, steady rhythm, and her flawless, milky flesh regained a semblance of its characteristic vigor, Hera lay still in the warm bath, pondering what would become of Sedna and the gods and Manitous of Turtle Island once she left this ancient land at Summer's end. The gods of the mainland would continue to recover the ascendancy they once enjoyed before the settlers of Old Europe claimed the so-called New World for their fledgling god, of this Hera had little doubt. As for the gods of the Sea, Hera hoped that they would in turn grow in strength as Life returned to the Oceans, beyond the few protected areas that some mortals had set aside to conserve for their descendants to enjoy. As her own brother, the great Sea-King Poseidon, had come to attest, the CARINA venture and its many affiliates throughout the world had done wonders in restoring critically endangered Ocean habitats in the past few decades. Surely the learned mortals who chose not to accompany their colleagues aboard the Nephele and ships of its ilk would continue Prometheus' great work in this manner, until soaring life returned to all the shores of all the lands upon the broad-pathed Earth.

Sedna had been quite displeased when Hera told her that she would leave Turtle Island shortly before the Sun finally set in the West for the long Arctic Night. As a gesture of friendship and goodwill towards the gods of Turtle Island and its Arctic Seas, Hera declared Sedna an honorary member of the CARINA philanthropic network. Also, to remedy Maiden of the Deep's near-permanent state of isolation, for which the Queen of Olympus' yearly visits provided only a temporary balm, Hera assured Sedna that she would find mortals gifted with second sight among her employees at Polaris whose forebears hailed from Turtle Island's Northern shores. These mortals would visit Sedna often, using their ancestral skill to communicate with the spirits of the Earth and the Sea, and offer to braid her hair in exchange for wisdom and blessings, as Hera had done on that fateful day when she came to ask Sedna's permission to relocate the ALSESTIS laboratories at the bottom of the Arctic Ocean.

Loath though she was to admit it, Hera knew that she would dearly miss her reclusive and peculiar friend, who reminded her so much of the daughter of her former rival Leto upon their first meeting. The thought occurred to Hera more than once that perhaps Artemis ought to take her place as Sedna's occasional companion in these parts, and comb and braid her hair each year at Midsummer. It would do Artemis a world of good to befriend the gods of Turtle Island; perhaps then the Manitous would allow the Huntress and her virgin acolytes to hunt in their vast, convalescing woodlands once the herds attained healthy and sustainable numbers. Furthermore, Hera thought it highly unlikely that Artemis would choose to join the crew of the Nephele, if only for the lack of wilderness and prime hunting grounds aboard city-ships bound for interstellar space.

For this reason alone, Hera harboured serious doubts about Apollo's stated intent to board the Nephele at Summer's end, even while the city-ship remained in low Earth orbit for at least a few more months, if not years, due to the recent development concerning a certain contingency protocol of her own devising. By now Prometheus had surely informed Apollo, Athena, and the others about the construction of the Hesperides Autonomous Station, and how the completion of this structure would impact the launch date of the Nephele towards the asteroid belt. Though Prometheus and Asia gave a three-year estimate between the present and the anticipated time of completion, Hera somehow knew that the delay would exceed this benchmark by at least twice that length of time, best laid plans be damned. Perhaps this was the price she ought to pay for welcoming Eris into the Nephele's putative crew of immortals, Hera wondered wearily. She did not let her mind linger in such grievous thoughts, for she knew that Eris' factious chaos-mongering and mischief somehow consistently skewed the odds in her favour in the end.

If Apollo did indeed choose to stay aboard the Nephele until the Hesperides Autonomous Station became independent of its mothership, then perhaps by that time Junia would have outgrown her eerie fascination with the Lord of the golden bow. Or perhaps he would eventually grow weary of his bright but all too young darling, prompting him to return to starry Olympus to be with the rest of his blessed kin. Hera knew full well that such an outcome would devastate Junia, however she judged it far better for her beloved daughter to discover at an early age the truth about the fleeting nature of erotic love, long before she found herself abiding wistfully in its wake, heavy with child – or worse yet, married!

"Oh, come now," said a familiar female voice. "Surely you do not wish heartbreak upon your daughter? She is only a child!"

Hera sat bolt upright, splashing the now lukewarm bath water with enough force to cause a small tidal wave within the deserted facilities. She scanned the room for the interloper, until she fixed her gaze upon a brilliant yet unnatural source of light emanating from the darkened shower stalls beyond the row of private bathtubs.

"What in the world are *you* doing here!?" Hera said curtly after drawing a sharp intake of breath. "I am at my bath! Have you no shame!? Of course, you don't. Look to whom I am speaking!"

"It's good to see you too, my Queen," Aphrodite replied coyly, appearing at last before Hera in all her radiance, her feet scarce touching the streams of bath water draining from the semi-porous floor.

"Truer words have always been spoken," Hera said. "Now answer my question. What are you doing here?"

"I've come to speak with you, in private," Aphrodite said innocently, handing Hera one of the fresh towels from the pile that Klymene had left behind.

"You could have waited until morning," Hera answered angrily, ignoring the towel.

"I can hardly tell when it is day or night in these parts," Aphrodite replied. "It is bright as day at all hours. I honestly have no idea what keeps the mortals from going mad!"

"They have work to do here. As do I. That is what keeps us all on point. Now get on with it. What do you want?"

"What do you think I want?"

"You tell me," Hera replied bitingly, "Honestly, you are the last goddess I ever expected to see here aboard the Polaris. The absolute last. And by that I mean, I sooner expected Zeus to dispatch Themis, or even Leto, to spew their platitudes about royal duty or wifely obeisance, since Hermes and Athena have long given up on pestering me about retuning to Olympus. But I did not expect you. Zeus must be getting desperate, if he thought it wise that you should come here and interrupt me while I am at my bath."

"Perhaps I've come to take care of you as you recover from your exertions, while your handmaiden awaits you in your bed," Aphrodite said. "This is what you want the mortal men of CARINA to think when they see you and Klymene together, is it not? Pity that they don't know you've been hard at work all these years, tending to the River-gods of Turtle Island, though not in quite the same way you used to look after the sons of Okeanos and Tethys..."

"Oh, piss off. You did not come all this way to taunt me about the gossip of mortals with regards to my real or imagined lovers. That is sloppy, even for you. Besides, you already know that I want for nothing, and that Klymene took her leave at my behest. Why are you really here?"

Golden Aphrodite said nothing, her gaze fixed upon her increasingly irate Queen.

"You are wasting your time," Hera answered matter-of-factly after a moment. "Unless you have something you need to say, I suggest that you take your leave, as I have nothing to say to you."

"What a pity," Aphrodite said calmly. "Your absence has been sorely felt by all ever since you left the hallowed halls of starry Olympus. Why, we haven't spoken in years! I was hoping for a much warmer reception from my dear mother-in-law!"

"Don't play games, Aphrodite," Hera answered crossly. "You are lucky that I express my displeasure only with words, after what you've done on my last night on starry Olympus. Did you think I wouldn't know that it was you who gave Zeus the potion he put in my drink? The daffy brew he told me was 'medicine', as if I ever needed such a thing!"

"The brew that eased your troubled thoughts until you were calm enough to bring your guard down and conceive your favourite child, you mean?" Aphrodite asked coyly. "How could I have poisoned you, when the whole world knows that you are immune to all the poisons of the Earth, for having triumphed over the Hydra's venom?"

"Because the potion you gave Zeus that night was neither a love charm or philtre," Hera answered, slowly rising to her feet. "Instead you gave him an antidote to love. An oxytocin inhibitor. Those were the words the mortal doctors used for the strange concoction they found coursing through my veins as I slept, shortly after I arrived at Borealis. But I knew, as soon as the milk stopped flowing from my breasts on the night Junia was conceived, that some sort of treachery was afoot. And I knew you were the one responsible for what happened next. Oh, I applaud your audacity for finding a way of getting me with child, though. That was very clever. Even I did not foresee that move on your part. I always knew you were far cleverer than you ever let on, but then again, I remember you from my heyday at the court of El."

Aphrodite averted her gaze and fixed her eyes upon a point somewhere above Hera's head as the Queen stood before her, stark naked, her divine form dripping with crystalline rivulets of the purest water. Hera caught the bath towel from Aphrodite's hand and tugged hard, causing the goddess of love to wince.

"I've known for millennia that you were biding your time, waiting for your chance to take my place," Hera continued. "I've known this ever since you crawled out of the Sea and found your way to Mount Olympus. Perhaps you hoped that I would not recognize you in your new guise as the Sea-born, but you were sorely mistaken. I may have sampled the waters of the Lethe more than is advisable among immortals, but even I know my curse when I see her!"

"Your curse?" Aphrodite said, exaggerating shock and dismay. "That is truly unkind!"

"Oh, is it?" Hera replied mockingly. "All these centuries, you've done everything in your power try to bring me low by pandering to Zeus' basest desires, but you failed time and again to dethrone me as Queen of Olympus. And though I now dwell on Turtle Island, as far away from Olympus as is possible on the vast Earth, I am still very much a Queen among the mortals at CARINA and the gods of this ancient land. I am a friend to the Manitous, an honoured guest who repays their kindness and hospitality by purifying their waters and restoring Life where there was once nothing more than devastation and death. That is a gift only I alone possess, which is why Prometheus chose me to nurture and guide the learned crew of the Nephele as they set out to spread the seeds of Life beyond the boundaries of the broad-pathed Earth. I will be with them until their task has come to completion, for though there may be countless Earths across the vast Cosmos, there can be no Life without the waters."

Aphrodite stood still for a moment, taking stock of Hera's words.

Hera turned her back at Aphrodite, climbed out of the bathtub, then reached for the clean flannel pyjamas Klymene had left with the pile of fresh towels.

"Have you ever thought that perhaps I've come here to make my peace with you, before you leave on your last journey from the broad-pathed Earth?" Aphrodite asked, no longer able to contain the pique in her voice.

"Before you return to Olympus and obtain your heart's desire, you mean?"

"What do you mean?" Aphrodite said, her voice growing shrill despite her best efforts to appear even-tempered. "I am a loyal servant of Olympus, whose King is like a father to me!"

Hera let out a laugh that inadvertently resembled a snort. "Believe me, that never stopped him, but you already know that!"

"You've been alone for far too long, my dear," Aphrodite replied coolly. "Your long exile from a proper marriage bed has made you strange, and that is why you must return to Olympus at once, before you make mortals as strange as you've become!"

"Ah, there we are," Hera said mockingly. "The true purpose of your visit comes out at last! You could have saved yourself the aggravation and simply answered me when I asked you the first four times. You are truly worse than a child! No, I take that back, that last remark would be unfair to my Junia."

"If you have any thought for your daughter's well-being, then you will return to your husband at once, before you ruin her and the rest of the mortals under your care with your bloodless ways."

Hera raised an eyebrow. "Bloodless?" she said after a moment. "Well, that's different. I've been called all the worst names in the world before, but no one has ever accused me of being bloodless. If you are trying to confuse me with new and original insults, then you are in for quite the disappointment. You forget that Eris now dwells among us. I've become quite accustomed to the mind games with which she amuses herself and the children of late. But I'll bite. How, pray tell, am I ruining Junia and the mortals at CARINA?"

"Zeus thinks your youngest child might be mortal for never having set foot on starry Olympus, and for never having tasted nectar and ambrosia," Aphrodite answered.

"Yes, he said as much last year on the deck of this barge," Hera replied. "It was an inane notion then, as much as it is now. What of it?"

"I've spent some time at Borealis, at Hermes' request, before making my way here," Aphrodite said. "Our King might indeed be correct about the young Junia being mortal, but not for the reason he believes. I know why she needs the protection of all the gods of Turtle Island, and all the spirits of the Earth. You grew your daughter in a jar, outside your womb, fed and cared for by machines! Hermes told me that the mortals think it was because of the means by which you arrived at Borealis, and that Prometheus convinced them that it was necessary to extract your unborn baby from your womb to save her life, though she was never in any danger, as you were unhurt from your fall."

"I swear," Hera said, running her fingers through her dark, silky locks to expel the last remaining droplets of bath water from her hair. "You and Eileithya have always been thick as thieves… I was in a coma for a fortnight, I'll have you know! And as I told her, that incubator was a precautionary measure, and no harm came of it!"

"You were never in a coma, you were merely resting from the effort of transporting yourself and Prometheus through space and out of time for a few months," Aphrodite said. "The same thing happened the first time you opened the gates of the Seasons when we left the battlefield as we fought the Giants, after you prophesied the birth of the lion-skinned mortal who would join us in the fray and tip the scales in our favour. You were also newly with child on that day, were you not? With twins, no less, and you recovered from the effort without harming your children."

"Have you even met Eris and Ares!?" Hera asked sarcastically.

"Only this time," Aphrodite continued, ignoring Hera's retort, "you did not anticipate your unborn child being called by the Earth below, and by Father Kronos in the deepest recesses of Tartarus, which is why she grew in your womb at the rate children usually do, when you thought you had escaped the pull of Time as it passes upon the broad-pathed Earth. So you allowed the mortals to remove Junia from your womb, and in doing so, not only did you compromise her immortality, you showed mortals that children could be conceived and born without the act of love."

"No, Aphrodite, mortals devised the means to conceive children ex-utero well over two centuries ago. You truly need to step away from the golden halls of Olympus once in a while and engage with the mortal world. You might be surprised at what you will see!"

"You mean to render love and marriage obsolete!" Aphrodite said frantically.

"Again, no. What I've shown them is that a child could successfully incubate from the first trimester onward. Such a thing had never been attempted before. At least try to get your facts straight before you make accusations! As for making marriage obsolete, well, we both know you have done a fine job of that yourself! You never needed *me* for that!"

"What are you talking about?" Aphrodite asked, almost at her wits' end.

"Oh, Aphrodite, must I take back what I said earlier about your being far cleverer than you let on?" Hera replied in a gently scolding tone. "Truly, you disappoint me. I practically handed you the perfect opportunity to take your place by Zeus' side on starry Olympus, and yet here you are, spewing platitudes of your own, as if you thought I didn't know you have always done what you've done to undermine me over the course of centuries. And to think I was willing to embrace you as a daughter, when I gave you to my kind, gentle son Hephaestus as your bridegroom. Of course, you chose to take my worst son to your bed instead, and now, as I set out on my greatest journey yet, Hephaestus and Ares will both be coming with me, of their own volition, knowing full well that you will remain far behind on starry Olympus, never to corrupt either of them ever again."

"You misunderstand me," Aphrodite retorted angrily. "All I've ever done, I've done in the service of Life. But you, with your indolent ways, you would lead mortals to their deaths, and the gods to oblivion!"

Hera rolled her eyes, her weariness bearing down upon her with full force. She truly did not need to contend with this shameless wench, who persisted in interrupting her sacrosanct solitude with a species of paranoia that rivalled Zeus' own with regards to the limitless ingenuity of mortals. But such did not surprise Hera in the least. Neither Zeus nor Aphrodite had ever cared to inquire why space-bound mortals took so many measures to protect themselves from the vicissitudes of living in an environment where artificial gravity could fail at any given time. Nor did they care that unborn mortal children could not safely grow to full term if their mothers' occupations required them to spend significant increments of time in microgravity, outside the safety of city-ships such as the Nephele. Hera and Prometheus judged it far more humane to remedy the situation by implementing incubator chambers in secure areas than sequestering the women to designated quarters while pregnant. But such sound reasoning would never sway the goddess of love, who by now probably believed that Hera meant to breed out lustfulness in human beings within the span of a few mortal generations through genetic manipulation once the Nephele and other city-ships left the reach of the Heliosphere.

Hera took a deep breath. Perhaps her sheer exhaustion, or her recent exposure to Eris' whimsical problem-solving methods, took a toll on her judgement at that point, for she resolved to rid herself of Aphrodite by convincing her that her fears were justified.

"I too have done all that I've done for the advancement of Life," she told Aphrodite. "By joining with these learned mortals, I've made sure that Life will continue beyond Earth's reach. I've given mortals a chance, and if my way renders them less lascivious and foolish, then they will be better off in the end."

Aphrodite shuddered at these words. "Was it your intention to spread *your* seed to the stars," she asked after a moment, "by colonizing the mortals' incubators with your own children, and thus rival Zeus in producing innumerable progeny, in much the same way the cuckoo colonizes the nest of other bird species with their own offspring?"

"And what if it were?" Hera replied, suppressing the urge to burst into laughter. "I have more than earned that prerogative, do you not think so? My full potential was denied to me the moment the Fates bound me to loud-thundering Zeus! What if I decided that the time has come for me to beget life at the scale that Tethys, the Mother of Rivers and the Nurse of All Life, has done? What is to stop me from reclaiming my old title of Mother of Mortals, in the same way that Zeus became known as the Father of gods and men? And in so doing, spread my brilliance, courage, and strength to untold generations across the vast Cosmos? Do you think you can succeed in thwarting me, with your daft pestering and clumsy flattery, where far more astute gods have failed?"

Aphrodite stared at Hera, dumbfounded, all colour drained from her lovely face.

"Be gone from this place and from my sight!" Hera continued. "You are not welcome to join me and my crew on the Nephele. After all the work we have done to vet and acclimate the learned mortals to endure the rigours of space, the last thing I need is for them to die off from syphilis long before we reach the outer boundaries of the orbit of Mars!'

At these words, golden Aphrodite took a step back, then vanished from sight in the span of a mortal heartbeat.

"Idiot," Hera muttered under her breath once the interloper had left.

Without further ceremony, she exited the washroom and headed for her living quarters, where Klymene awaited at the dining table, with a full pot of hot tea at the ready.

"Did you catch any of that?" Hera asked her handmaiden as she took a seat at the table and poured herself a cup of the soothing beverage.

"I saw the whole exchange mirrored in the waters, yes. You've given Aphrodite the fright of her deathless life!"

Hera smiled. "Can you believe it? She thinks I mean to make the mortals as chaste as the Vestal Virgins of old!"

Nepheleid

"Right now, she's likely crying at Zeus' knee," Klymene added.

"That does not matter," Hera replied. "Aphrodite's mind was already made before she set foot on the Polaris. Since she would not have cared a whit about the truth of the matter, I thought I might as well take the opportunity to vent some of that pent-up anger that our dear friend Ptesanwin warned me against taking with me to the stars."

Klymene smiled back at Hera. "I see that Eris has begun worming her way into your mind," she said playfully.

"Why yes, my dear. That felt *good*!" Hera answered with a genuine laugh. "And as far as Eris is concerned, never forget whose womb bore her, and why."

"Will you be retiring for the night?"

"I am afraid that I cannot," Hera said at last. "I told Aphrodite the truth on at least one account: there is still much more work that remains to be done."

Chapter Nine

Aegis-bearing Athena sat uneasily on the sofa of the living quarters she shared with swift Hermes at Borealis, her grey eyes tracking the messenger as he dashed frantically from one end of the small flat to the other. Hermes returned the previous morning from Polaris in an uncharacteristically overwrought state, made worse by the copious amounts of coffee he had consumed at Café Basilea well into the afternoon. Athena collected Hermes as soon as Hebe sent Herakles to fetch her. The Virgin Warrior took pity on her former protégé when she saw the look of abject confusion on his countenance for having spent the better part of the day trying to make sense of the messenger's mad ramblings. Athena eventually coaxed Hermes into returning to the relative safety of their apartment, far from the eyes and ears of curious mortals, though the cause of her brother's frenzied rants of impending doom eluded her, other than his obvious regret at having brought Aphrodite to the Polaris to seek an audience with their Queen.

Wasting no time, Athena sent Herakles to fetch Apollo, hoping that the Archer could use his singular gifts to discern more about the source of Hermes' torment. As expected, Apollo managed to calm Hermes long enough for him to reveal what Aphrodite had told him of what transpired during her meeting with white-armed Hera in the bowels of the Polaris at the edge of the world. According to the Sea-born, Hera plotted to put an end to the reign of the gods of love and pleasure by ridding the incipient generations of mortals to be born on the Nephele and city-ships of its ilk of all carnal desires. Hermes told Apollo and Athena that he had not given credence to the possibility that Hera would resort to such preposterous measures to take her revenge upon the goddess who had routinely strained her union with the Thunderer. He did, however, believe wholeheartedly that the Queen would utter these exaggeratedly inventive threats to Aphrodite to deter her from ever interfering in her affairs on Earth and beyond the stars. And since, as Hermes put it so eloquently, Hera's legendary bravado at times betrayed her occasional scarcity of wisdom, Hermes realized that his spirited stepmother had likely not anticipated that Aphrodite would take her at her word and flee to Olympus to relate to their King another gripe to his growing list of grievances which he held against the CARINA venture.

Upon hearing these words, Athena suggested that they heed Mnemosyne's advice and seek an audience with Zeus at once, to present their father with a united front to testify as to CARINA's worth and relevance as an agent of good in the world. This excursion, Athena hoped, might soften Zeus' stance toward the venture that has taken so many of his loved ones away from starry Olympus in recent years, and enfeeble whatever claim Aphrodite would have made as to CARINA's purported threat to the recovery of soaring life upon the broad-pathed Earth. To everyone's surprise, Apollo added that perhaps they ought to ask Poseidon to join them in this journey, for the Earth-shaker had the most to gain from CARINA's existence and Hera's continued involvement in the venture. Athena and Hermes agreed, which was why the Virgin Warrior patiently waited for the Lord of the golden bow to return, all the while tracking the messenger's movements as he flew in circles around the coffee table in their shared living room.

At long last, Apollo arrived alone, materializing in the small room amidst the shafts of waning sunlight beaming through the open patio door. King Poseidon, he told them, would make his own way to Olympus with his Court, among whom there would be a vast number of Oceanides and other immortals who dwell at the boundaries of the broad-pathed Earth. At these words Hermes ceased his frenzied pacing, and before Athena could reply, he took them both to the very steps outside the throne room on starry Olympus, where neither Athena, Apollo, and Hermes had set foot since the previous Summer.

It pained Athena somewhat to gaze upon these familiar golden halls, where the blessed gods had once dwelt contentedly, even after their fall from the favour of mortals millennia ago. Nevertheless, Athena knew that her deliberate absence from her father's Court constituted the only proper means available to her to protest Zeus' decree banning Hermes from the abode of the gods until Hera returned to Olympus with Junia, the youngest among their kind. Athena could not blame Hera for reacting the way that she did all those years ago, upon finally learning the truth about Prometheus being her long-forgotten firstborn son, whom she bore to Eurymedon, her murdered first husband and King of the Giants. Athena and her siblings had been waiting outside the high bronze doors of the throne room on the morning Hera left, so she never saw for herself the startling reunion between mother and son, nor the spectacular vortex of swirling stars through which Hera and Prometheus escaped, taking with them little else than the Queen's golden throne, and the King's everlasting eminence among the gods.

Once Hephaestus breached the heavy bronze doors, Athena and the others were made privy to what had ensued, as Hermes proceeded to relate in a flurry of words all he had witnessed moments before, despite Zeus' irritated glances and the constant barrage of deafening thunder rolls outside the throne room. Of course, all among Zeus' blessed children who dwell on high Olympus were shocked that Hera's womb had borne their King's old foe, and some even scoffed at their Queen's purported hypocrisy, bemoaning her ill-treatment of her King's mistresses and illegitimate children, all in the name of defending the sacredness of the marriage bed, when she had in fact secretly produced at least one offspring before she wed Zeus. Athena quickly told these detractors to keep their peace, for obviously Hera had not known that Prometheus was, in fact, her child by a forgotten, long-ago union before she became the Queen of Olympus.

Then as now, Athena often found herself defending Hera's character against those who sought to defame their Queen. Hera had always been kind to Athena; she had treated the Virgin Warrior as a daughter since the day she emerged from Zeus' head, fully arrayed in golden armour, and uttering a battle-cry so terrible that it caused the Sun to pause his chariot for a moment to behold the birth of Zeus' eldest offspring. At the time, Athena recognized Hera as her father's sister, Zeus' favourite among the many older siblings he had rescued from their father Kronos, the bane of Ouranos, the primordial Sky-King deposed by five of his Titan sons who now dwell in gloomy Tartarus after Zeus defeated them in turn. When Athena was newly born, Hera had been a great Queen in her own right, ruling over vast territories to the South of starry Olympus, and in aeons past, so Athena had been told, in lands far to the East. Then as now, the Maiden Queen had long been the object of Zeus' ardent desire, yet Hera had repeatedly refused her brother's insistent marriage proposals, even though she sometimes took him to her bed when it pleased her.

Truth be told, Athena felt quite glad the day she heard that Hera had finally agreed to wed Zeus, for she hoped that her father would put an end for his seemingly endless search for a Queen worthy of Olympus. As the Fates willed it, Olympus itself had yet to become worthy of its new Queen. For though Hera proved herself a moderating influence on her King's excesses in most aspects of their shared reign, she could scarce abrogate Zeus' weakness for the pleasures of the flesh, a failing which golden Aphrodite often exploited to her advantage time and again, to Hera's dismay. Still, for most of her tenure as Queen of Olympus, Hera remained a force to be reckoned with. And though she lost a considerable degree of her power after the failed plot against Zeus, Hera retained much of her ability to persuade others to bend to her will, and sway seemingly random and chaotic outcomes in her favour.

It was Hera who convinced Zeus to let the gods choose sides and fight on mortals' behalf during the Trojan War, even though the Cloud-gatherer, feigning neutrality, secretly hoped for King Priam and his sons to prevail in the famous conflict. During these discordant times, Athena witnessed firsthand the extent of Hera's dedication to a cause she believed of singular worth, whether for good or ill. When Zeus reached the point where he could no longer suffer the gulf that the Trojan War had wrought between himself and his Queen, he offhandedly suggested to Hera that he ought to let her destroy his favoured city to almost the last man, in exchange for the right to obliterate a city dear to her heart in the future. To everyone's surprise, Hera agreed, and even went so far as to name the three cities dearest to her heart in those days long gone by. As far as bright-eyed Athena knew, Zeus never called in this bargain, nor would he do so unless circumstances beyond his control forced his hand.

Athena suspected that Hera, fearing this very outcome, had set into motion the construction of the Hesperides Autonomous Station because she believed that Zeus, in his growing desperation and loneliness, and in his weakened position as King among the blessed gods who dwell on high Olympus, would eventually resort to destroying all the CARINA installations across the broad-pathed Earth. And though one day the Hesperides Autonomous Station would host the most advanced, state-of-the-art ALSESTIS facilities in low Earth orbit far beyond Zeus' reach, for the moment the entire CARINA venture remained as vulnerable to Zeus' wrath as a newborn babe asleep in its crib. This was why Athena, flanked by swift Hermes and Apollo who shoots from afar, thought it imperative to propitiate Zeus with an alternative scenario that would mitigate the circumstances surrounding Hera's imminent departure without threatening the very continuation of Life upon the broad-pathed Earth.

"So," Apollo said uneasily, pulling Athena out of her meditations. "Shall we proceed unto the breach?"

Athena and Hermes acquiesced, then quietly walked up the hallowed stairs and through the open doors of the heavenly throne room. As expected, they found loud-thundering Zeus seated at his throne, presiding before Poseidon and his retinue of bedraggled, rough-looking sea-gods, sea-nymphs, and a vast gathering of the surviving sons and daughters of Okeanos and Tethys.

"It is well past time you returned," the Cloud-gatherer berated his brother before all those assembled. "In all this time since Hera left, I have not heard a single word uttered from your lips! Usually I do not mind such an outcome, but surely by now you see the folly of our Queen's absence from her rightful place among the blessed gods who dwell on high Olympus! So tell me what you have come to say after all these years, that required you to bring the entire Sea-Court to these sacred halls?"

"If I've appeared quiet with regards to the matter of Hera's exit from Olympus," the Earth-shaker replied irascibly, paying no heed to the arrival of Athena, Apollo, and Hermes inside the throne room, "it was only because I was biding my time. I had no idea it would take this long until I knew for certain that you would be ready to listen to other voices than those of your flatterers and sycophants who have remained in your midst!"

"I would watch my tongue if I were you," the Thunderer said imperiously, his gazed fixed upon Athena and her brothers. "My brilliant children have returned to me, and the three of them would make short work of you and your host of beggars!"

"I have no quarrel with this lot," Poseidon replied nonchalantly. "For we are of the same mind."

"Is that so?" Zeus scoffed, though his ice-blue eyes betrayed his faltering confidence. "And what is it that you have all come to say to me? Out with it!"

"Hera plans to set sail on the Nephele, never to return," Poseidon said flatly.

"I already knew this," Zeus replied angrily. "Although I have not seen you try to convince her of the folly of her design!"

"It is not my place to convince Hera of such things," Poseidon said. "It is well within her rights to leave you if it pleases her, and we all know that you have done everything in your power to cause her to hate you. If you truly wish for her to stay among our kind, then it is for you to beg forgiveness for all the unspeakable depravity you have wrought upon her and her children, even to those who are of your seed."

"And what is that supposed to mean?" Zeus asked, as low rolls of thunder rumbled in the distance.

"I see your firstborn daughter and your firstborn son among us, as well as Hermes, but not Ares or Hephaestus, who have as much cause to hate you as their mother. As for your daughters, could you even tell apart the ones Hera bore you from those you sired upon all the other goddesses of the broad-pathed Earth?"

"You are in no position to lecture me about marital fidelity, Brother," Zeus replied, his gazed fixed upon Queen Amphitrite, ruler of the deep waves, who stood valiantly at her husband's side. "If I am not mistaken, you have sired far more children outside the marriage bed than I have, and you wed fair-haired Amphitrite many years after I claimed Hera as my bride."

"You are right on that account," Poseidon retorted. "And yet I, unlike you, have never given my bride cause to despise me nor to rebel against my rule. Most of all, I have never humiliated my Queen by stripping her bare and binding her to the Sky, before repudiating her before all the gods, in favour of Thetis."

Athena and Apollo winced at Poseidon's words, which were clearly meant as provocation. Hermes simply bit his lip and turned pale, obviously hoping that Zeus would have the presence of mind to eat his heart and let the Earth-shaker make his point.

Thankfully, Zeus kept quiet for a moment, looking as though listening to some inner voice beckoning him to keep calm.

"If I recall," the Thunderer said at last, "you did nothing while Hera endured her punishment for her betrayal. Nor did any of you," he added, looking straight at Athena.

Now it was Athena who swallowed her rising anger and resisted the urge to react in a way she would later regret. She took a deep breath and tried to conjure the same impassive mask she had seen Hera don thousands of times before, whenever Zeus sought to silence her with unkind words and threats.

"Hephaestus would disagree," Thetis, daughter of Nereus, said from behind a row of awestruck sea-nymphs. "I should know, I was the one who nursed him back to health after he fell from Olympus for the second time."

"And yet," Zeus told Thetis benevolently, "you were the one who came to my rescue. If you thought it wise back then to uphold my reign as King of Olympus, despite consensus to the contrary, then why, dear one, have you also come to upbraid me today, among your brethren of Sea-dwellers?"

"None of us have come to upbraid you, my Lord," Thetis answered timidly.

"We thought it wise to press upon you the utmost urgency of the matter at hand," Amphitrite said, at last finding her voice. "Hera cannot leave the Earth! Our distant kin at the boundaries of the world have told us that she has cured the waters of Turtle Island! And yet, we who dwell in the inland Sea linger in waters tainted with the filth of three and a half thousand years of human civilization! We are desperate! You must do something to convince her to stay!"

"You need to beg for her forgiveness," Poseidon pleaded, looking utterly devoid of any further recourse.

Zeus pinched the bridge of his nose, as if annoyed at the absurdity that he, the King of Olympus and supreme ruler among the gods, ought to beg anyone, even his beloved Queen, for forgiveness. Poseidon ought to be the one to beg Hera for forgiveness, Athena thought, for she had long suspected him to be the reason behind Hera's unexpected decision to yield to Zeus' relentless pursuit of her hand in marriage after denying him his heart's desire for centuries.

Long ago, when the blessed gods began to make their homes upon the shores of bountiful Hellas, Poseidon fought Hera in a contest for supremacy of the rich lands of the Argolid, from which Hera emerged victorious. Forgetting his past alliances with his powerful sister, Poseidon withdrew all the rivers from the lands he had been denied, causing a terrible drought that devastated the region for many years. However, soon after Hera wed Zeus, the rains somehow returned to the parched Argolid, and partially replenished the storied land's fabulous wealth. Though Hera had never once admitted that she wed the ruling Sky-King to save her people from certain doom, Athena knew that her Queen's many efforts to aid mortals in their time of need often went unsung, whereas Zeus' indifference towards the plight of human beings, including his aloofness to the suffering of mortals, was never questioned by even the wisest of mortals. This was truly ironic, since Hera had once been known and celebrated as the one who rewarded heroes with everlasting glory and fame beyond the short seasons of their lives, yet the goddess never sought the same degree of renown for herself, no matter how selfless her deeds, or dire the consequences for her own ascendancy among gods and men.

Perhaps Poseidon deserved Hera's neglect of the waters embracing the shores of her former homeland of Hellas, as much as Zeus deserved Hera's abandonment of their marriage bed. However, all the beings of the Earth did not deserve impending doom on account of the pettiness of gods, Athena though dourly.

"What would you have me do?" Zeus said finally, his countenance betraying his bitter resignation. "Hera will not suffer my presence, and I am loath to antagonize the gods of Turtle Island, against whom I bear no ill will whatsoever, but who appear determined to guard her against my repeated efforts to speak to her. Even these three have failed to convince their Queen to return to her rightful place, by my side."

Athena threw Apollo a sorrowful glance, which the Archer answered with a grave look. "We all get what we deserve in the end, and as such we will get the version of Hera we truly deserve," Athena conveyed wordlessly to the Lord of the golden bow, knowing full well that he could hear her innermost thoughts whenever she allowed him to do so.

Apollo closed his eyes, nodding gravely in agreement.

"It is not for lack of trying, Father," Athena answered Zeus' unkind remark at last with a surprisingly even tone. "But I think there might be a way to resolve the issue at hand, that we will all find satisfactory…"

Forgive me, Hera, Athena thought finally before she proceeded to voice her proposal that would undoubtedly save Prometheus' citadels of science, and the countless lives that would benefit from CARINA's continued existence, from the Thunderer's impending righteous retribution.

Chapter Ten

Clad in a mantle of clouds gilded with the golden hues of sunset, loud-thundering Zeus awaited his bride on a mountaintop he had visited only once before. Eleven years had passed since he found his Queen in this lonely place, staring out at the starry night, yet in this inordinately short span of time his entire world had been upended, all because Hera had fallen prey to the machinations of his old foe Prometheus. Zeus had little doubt that the so-called benefactor of humanity deliberately targeted his beloved wife in her yearly wanderings across the broad-pathed Earth all those years ago, to take his revenge on the one who had rightfully punished him for his crime of stealing fire from Olympus. But now the time had come for the Father of gods and men to set things right and reclaim what was his, even if the means he would take to achieve this feat were likely to arouse Hera's wrath for countless aeons yet to unfold.

This was a risk worthy of the outcome, Zeus thought, for Hera would surely come to see the error of her ways eventually and forgive him for insisting upon this meeting in this fateful place overlooking the town of Borealis and its CARINA headquarters below. How Hermes convinced his Queen of the urgency of this parley, Zeus did not know. No matter the means through which his son achieved this feat, Zeus hoped that Hera went easy on the lad, as this reunion had been, in fact, of Athena's own devising after much deliberation in the throne room on starry Olympus only a few days ago. August Themis accompanied him from the abode of the gods to this foreign land yet wisely elected to remain at Borealis among her kin until Zeus needed her counsel. Themis waited until Zeus needed her to plead his case on his behalf should Hera choose to resolve this dispute through an advocate of her own. Such was the Queen's prerogative, or so Metis and Themis reminded their King daily, almost in unison.

While Hera was indeed well within her rights to settle the matter in this fashion, Zeus feared that his bride, in a fit of cunning vengeance, might choose Prometheus as her defender, if only to prompt the King of

Olympus into a hasty retreat lest he react in a shameful manner before his exiled Court and all the gods of Turtle Island. Even after more than a decade of estrangement, Hera doubtlessly knew that Zeus would not suffer another confrontation with Prometheus without jeopardizing a possible reconciliation, even though endless centuries had come and gone since the Father of gods and men allowed valiant Herakles to free Hera's firstborn son from his rock.

Remember, my King, a familiar voice said within the confines of Zeus' venerable mind. *At this moment, Prometheus is far away, high above the Earth on the city-ship Nephele.*

"I know," Zeus replied to Metis without moving his lips. "He would still be far away even if he had intended to return with the schoolchildren tomorrow morning. By now the young ones will have boarded the Hub, with my young daughter among them."

So this is why we are holding this meeting at this late hour? Metis inquired. *How clever of you, to ensure that Prometheus will be nowhere near this place as you present our dear Lady with your ultimatum.*

"You know," Zeus answered the wise voice inside his mind, "I sometimes manage to devise brilliant ideas all of my own. And if this allows me to reunite with my bride, and see my child again, without interference from that fiend Prometheus, then all the better."

I hope you know, my King, that Junia is not exactly fond of you, for the image she has of her father has been coloured by her brother and her mother's perceptions of you, ever since the moment she was born. And as for Hera, well, I hope you also know you have not been her favourite for quite some time …

"I am well aware of this, Metis," Zeus replied fitfully. "I fully expect this to change once Hera comes to her senses and return to Olympus with Junia. Junia... What an awful, lowly, mortal name. Remind me, Metis, to change that as well once this unpleasantness is over, and my Queen returns with me to her rightful place, her golden throne restored by my side."

Oh? Could it be true? Metis asked with some measure of excitement in her disembodied voice. *Has Hermes found Hera's golden throne at long last?*

"He must have by now," Zeus answered gaily. "Hermes has searched the whole continent for Hera's lost treasure from starry Olympus ever since

I exiled him to this faraway land. If the golden throne is not in Borealis, or at Polaris far to the North, then I shall send him to search the Nephele, among the learned mortals bound for the vast expanses between the stars. And should Hermes fail to find my bride's throne there, then I shall send him to search for it in my brother Hades' Kingdom, where Hera likely hid it on the day she tried to hide my child somewhere not in this world. Unless Hera sees reason in the meantime and acquiesces to my terms. If she is half as clever as I remember her to be, then she will not refuse my offer of clemency when I present it to her. That is, of course, if she graces us at all with her presence this evening."

Now, now, you know full well that Hera is far cleverer than even you care to admit most of the time...

"And yet sometimes I wonder," Zeus mused sardonically. "What in the world was she thinking when she told Aphrodite that all her fears would soon come to pass? Did that seem particularly clever, or sane, to you?"

Metis' voice laughed softly. *Must I remind you, my King, how absurd is the very notion that our beloved Hera would even consider ridding mortals of all carnal desire? Is she not the goddess who presides over the sacred rites of the marriage bed? Surely you understand how out of character such an outcome would be for our dear Lady. For the longest time, she was never one to shy away from your touch, unless you forgot...*

Zeus smiled inwardly at these words, reminiscing fondly on all the times he and white-armed Hera shared their sacred marriage bed, and how for millennia only he truly ever knew how beautiful she was whenever the golden rays of the setting Sun lit up her features as she lay in his arms. This was how he remembered their bridal, which lasted three hundred years, in the splendour of Hera's long-gone sunset Garden of the Hesperides. No matter how terrible their disputes had been in the centuries that followed, Zeus never forgot those blessed years, nor could he banish from his mind the great love he had felt for Hera ever since their first meeting, when he rescued her from the maw of wily Kronos. Hera might hate him now, and for many years to come, for what he had done and for what he intended to do, however he felt quite certain that some day Hera would put aside this whole sad business and willingly return to him in heart and mind, even if he had to overplay his hand and compel her to return to Olympus in the most distasteful way.

Nepheleid

Still, his heart quaked with anticipation as he imagined his estranged wife appearing before him as he had often seen her of late, whenever she chose to let herself be seen by the eyes of mortals in this place and at CARINA's other lairs across the broad-pathed Earth. Before mortals Hera usually took the guise of a beautiful yet soberly attired woman, clad in her ubiquitous white laboratory coat, her gorgeous ebony locks often loose upon her shoulders and back, or at times bound in braids in the fashion of the women whose ancestors have dwelt for millennia on Turtle Island. This was quite a departure from the way all the blessed gods of Olympus remembered their Queen, who could easily have won the title of fairest among the immortals had Zeus chosen a better judge than the shepherd-boy Paris, who famously gave the coveted golden apple to Aphrodite and set into motion the events leading to the Trojan War.

And yet, even during those dark days that ensued, at the lowest point in their marriage, Hera found a way to rekindle her King's desire by visiting him on the top of Mount Ida in ancient Anatolia, while mortals busied themselves laying waste to one another on the battlefield. Even then, Zeus knew that his disaffected Queen showed herself in her most beauteous form to distract him from surveying the carnage below, while Poseidon joined the fray and fought on behalf of the Hellenes beyond the mighty ramparts of Troy. He remembered how angry and betrayed he felt that day, going so far as to force Hera to swear an Oath by the Holy River Styx that she had not seduced him only to prompt Poseidon to disobey his orders to not interfere in the mortals' battle. To Zeus' surprise, Hera swore the solemn Oath, and to his delight, she did not keel over, deprived of breath, which meant that she had told him the truth.

Still, Metis told Zeus, *you should not have threatened Hera the way you did. That did not endear you to her, especially not after she spent those hours alone with you atop Mount Ida, unseen by mortals, in your loving embrace.*

"Perhaps not," Zeus replied, "but at least I knew that Poseidon had acted of his own volition while I was distracted by Hera's charms."

But this is not the only Oath you made her swear in those dark days…

"Mistakes were made on all sides during those terrible years," Zeus agreed dolefully. "And calling in the other Oath might prove the undoing of our marriage… But she has left us with no other alternative.

She might have eventually made her peace about the part I played in hiding the truth from her about Prometheus being her son, but for this, she might never forgive me."

Which is why you must pour honey on that old, festering wound. Remember that which you and Apollo rehearsed. There she comes…

The Cloud-gatherer lifted his pensive gaze and beheld white-armed Hera as she arrived upon the mountaintop, showing herself not in her guise as a respectable mortal woman, but rather as a true Queen among gods, who surpasses in beauty all who dwell upon the Earth, Sea, and Sky. She floated through the air until she landed upon the meeting-place, unseen by mortals, yet to those with eyes to see she appeared to fill the space between Zeus and the vast valley below, her form eerily ethereal against the reflected light of the waning Sun upon the waters of Lake New-Agassiz, her raven locks lit in hues of deep indigo against the coming Night. Zeus could not help but smile when he looked upon her, which she answered with a peeved mien, conveying her obvious displeasure at being summoned to this place at such a late hour.

"My darling," Zeus said softly as he reached to embrace her. His greeting went unfinished, for Hera dodged from his grasp by shifting her position slightly to the side, leaving his immortal eyes momentarily unshielded from the blinding light of sunset.

"Spare me the pleasantries if you please," Hera replied bluntly. "Whatever you need to tell me, be quick about it. I have to return to Polaris tonight!"

"Tonight? How will they know when Night falls, if the Sun does not set for weeks on end?" Zeus jested to lighten the mood.

Hera rolled her eyes. "This was not funny when Aphrodite said it," she answered. "So, what do you want? Tell me and be done with it!"

"I think you already know why I am here," Zeus said calmly.

"I am not returning to Olympus with you," Hera retorted curtly, "and neither is Junia."

"Will you at least let me finish?" Zeus chided her with good humour. "You've come all this way, you might as well do me the courtesy of hearing all I have to say before telling me off."

Nepheleid

This time Hera stared at the firmament for a moment, then reluctantly set her gaze upon the Thunderer.

"Surely Hermes must have told you by now what dreadful effect your words had on golden Aphrodite upon her return to Olympus," Zeus told her. "She was most frantic, making outlandish accusations I simply cannot ignore."

"We are not turning mortals into sexless worker bees!" Hera scoffed. "Are we done here?"

"I wish it were that simple, my love," Zeus replied. "I want to believe that your designs for those learned mortals bound for the stars are every bit as benign as you would have your Court of exiled gods and the Manitous of Turtle Island believe, however I will need assurances that it is so."

"Then let Apollo brief you on our genetic research, and how the protocols we've developed will prolong the mortals' lives while they travel between the stars," Hera answered. "Apollo will tell you everything you want to know, and he will tell it true."

"Apollo will placate me with wondrous tales about the ingenuity of the learned mortals in these enclaves Prometheus has built across the broad-pathed Earth," Zeus said softly. "He will tell me these things in a way he knows I will find palatable, and he will tell me nothing else. He will say nothing of the new, damning facts that have come to my attention of late, which I have found to lend credence to Aphrodite's most outrageous accusations."

"What in the world are you talking about?" Hera asked impatiently.

"I speak of the way our daughter Junia came into the world," Zeus replied. "I know that you grew our child outside your womb, and that is why Eileithya believes her young sister lacks the deathless quality that all the blessed gods who dwell on starry Olympus share."

"And who told you such a thing?" Hera asked with forced calm.

"I have my own eyes and ears on the ground, my love," Zeus answered gingerly. "Besides, the miraculous circumstances surrounding our daughter's birth is not exactly a well-kept secret in these parts..."

Hera stared at Zeus for a moment, her eyes betraying a most burning incredulity, until her features softened with the resignation that she could no longer conceal from him the truth about Junia's birth.

"Which one of my lab assistants did you fuck to obtain this information?" she said at last after a long, tense silence.

"How I learned the truth does not matter," Zeus said in the most delicate tone he could muster. "But I have reasons to believe that you intend to use the technology that brought our daughter into the world for nefarious ends. Perhaps Aphrodite was right to accuse you of planning to put an end to love and marriage as a means for mortals to procreate. At first, I thought she was being silly, but now I see she was perhaps much wiser than I had cared to consider. So, this is where we are. I cannot allow you to continue upon this path, lest you denature mortals and bring their kind to ruin."

"Oh, bloody hell! This again?" Hera interjected indignantly, turning her back on the Cloud-gatherer. That was when Zeus began to notice that the gentle ambient breeze had suddenly intensified, and that the very mountain seemed to cry out for leniency while the Earth began to tremble slightly with the goddess' ire.

"You must abandon this futile quest and return to Olympus with our daughter," Zeus continued, undeterred. "Otherwise I will have no other choice than to call in that odious Oath you swore to me by the ramparts of Troy and destroy a city that is dearest to your heart. Now, too many centuries have passed since you have given much though about the cities of ancient Hellas you offered up in exchange for the blood of the Trojans. I will not destroy these as tribute for letting you lay waste to the city I loved the most, in exchange for the promise that there would one day be everlasting peace between us. You knew back then why I was willing to exact that terrible toll, and yet you still would have hunted down every Trojan to the last man left alive, if I hadn't bribed you with the promise that their descendants would honour you more than any nation had done. So unless you see reason and return to Olympus with our youngest child, I will enforce my prerogative and repay all the heartache you have wrought upon the sons of Priam by destroying the city-ship Nephele."

Hera took a step back, her ire giving way to dismay. Zeus gave her a moment to reply, but she simply stared at him, dumbfounded.

Nepheleid

"Although," Zeus said after Hera failed to answer, "if you do agree to return with me to starry Olympus, I shall show leniency to the learned mortals of the Nephele, as well as Prometheus and his Court. I will allow all to continue their work unimpeded, for I have no proof that Prometheus, his learned mortals, as well as those immortals who dwell at the boundaries of the Earth, have any intent to do that of which Aphrodite accused you. If you return to Olympus with our daughter, I will even allow you to continue the work of planting gardens in the Heavens, in CARINA's new Garden of the Hesperides, so long as you abandon all attempts to geld the human race of lustful impulses. That is why I summoned you here."

At these words Hera's countenance grew ghostly pale, as the air around them grew unbearably humid and hot, despite the strong gale.

"All those years ago when Prometheus told me the truth," Hera said once she finally found her voice, "a truth that even my wildest dreams could not even fathom, I experienced the brightest moment of clarity I ever had in my entire existence! And to think that I used to wonder why for centuries you always treated me with such contempt, even though I knew at my very core I had done nothing to deserve it! All these years I should have known that your complete disregard for me had nothing to do with any real or imagined flaw upon my character, and that it had everything to do with the fact that I had given birth before we wed, to a son who to this day remains my only true equal in terms of brilliance and guile, one you could never co-opt because he was not of your seed! Is that why you treated him so horribly, chaining him to his rock for having performed an act of mercy towards mortals? Because he was my son, and not yours? Is that why you continue to torment me, even years after I left you!?"

"You know full well that the way I chose to punish Prometheus had nothing to do with you," Zeus answered with a hint of sadness. "I always knew that you were blameless for the way he came into the world. However, I cannot say the same for the way you chose to bring forth Junia. I almost went mad with worry when you failed to return to Olympus to give birth all those years ago. You always called to me when you endured your bitter birth pangs. Even when you were far away, you would call to me to let me know the time was near. I knew for certain that I seeded your womb before you left me, so I listened for you at the turn of the Seasons. I listened and heard nothing! I even dreaded that you might have dispatched our child into oblivion, to erase any trace that I ever lay with you, if only to punish me for what I did to your firstborn."

Unnerved, Hera turned away once from Zeus, but the Father of gods and men caught her by the shoulders before she could summon her gate of swirling stars, and escape to who knows where. He lifted her chin so that she could meet his gaze, but her eyes held nothing but anger and scorn.

"That was unrighteous of you, not returning with our daughter," he told her after a moment. "Why did you not come home? You know that I would have taken you back, that I would have forgiven your desertion without a second thought." Zeus lowered his head until his lips grazed Hera's temple, and he felt her shiver under the unwelcome touch.

"How could you hide her among mortals," he deplored. "Our beautiful child, the first one you've borne me since... *Ares*."

Zeus had not meant to utter the name of his most hated son with such bitter contempt. Even after all these centuries, he still believed that Hera conceived Ares out of spite, manifesting her long-festering animosity toward her husband in the least subtle way imaginable, by taking his seed and giving him a violent, bloodthirsty offspring in return.

"Ares was the son you deserved!" Hera hissed, divining Zeus' unflattering thoughts. She pushed him away with such force that he released her. Even so, Zeus continued to stand only inches before her, making it clear that escape from him was not an option. She froze where she stood, giving herself enough time to regain her composure, attempting with all her might to contain the magnitude of her wrath within her heart.

"You pretend to care about Junia, but what do you mean to do with her, should I return with her to starry Olympus?" Hera asked, her voice quivering with anger "Do you think she will ever bear you a son? You are out of your mind if you think I will ever let you come near her!"

"I thought we agreed to never speak of that ever again," Zeus said as he took a step towards Hera, as the mighty gale brought dark, green-hued clouds on the horizon.

Hera stepped aside to elude Zeus once more, but this time he caught her by the wrist, then reached to place his other hand around her waist.

Nepheleid

He pulled her against his chest, holding her fast to neutralize her ire with his own power before she could obliterate all that lay between them and the valley below with her wrath.

"I may have forgiven you for what you did to Persephone's child, but you are far from innocent. In fact, you have not been innocent for a very long time, my love," Zeus told her with a caustic smile despite his better judgement.

"Get your hands off me!" Hera cried out. "I am not yours to do with as you please! I was never yours..."

Zeus softened his hold when Hera began to tremble but did not release her completely.

"You had no right!" Hera continued. "You had no claim on me, you never did! I was betrothed to another, the father of my first child. And you killed him! We were deeply in love, and you couldn't bear it, so you murdered him, and then you gave my son to Klymene..." Hera pushed Zeus away once again, and this time he released her when he saw the tears welling in her eyes. "I once felt the true bliss of love," she lamented, "and now I can't even recall how it felt because you thought it just to cleanse it away from me, like a stain upon my heart! You ruined any chance I ever had at happiness, for no other reason than to satisfy your selfish desires. I was never yours to claim!"

"I see that the madness that afflicted you when you left Olympus had not yet left you," Zeus said resentfully, steeling himself and taking a step back so that Hera would not be harmed by the icy rage that had begun coursing through his entire body.

"I was never mad," Hera protested indignantly. "And if I were, I have gone sane since I left you for good! My only madness was to believe that there ever was love between us. You never loved me, you have done nothing but humiliate and undermine me since we wed. You tried to swallow me whole in your own way, but I was too strong for you, so you took everything from me, and even that wasn't enough! No, I may not be innocent, but you were the one who drew first blood. I never wanted to be your Queen, but that never mattered to you, did it? You never cared about me, you only wanted to usurp the true power only I could bestow upon my Consorts..."

"Hera, that's enough!" Zeus said reprovingly.

98

"Oh, no, you will not berate me any longer!" Hera replied, undaunted. "You have no power here! I came here to reclaim part of that which you took from me. I am here among these learned mortals because my son remembered that it is in my power to make the Earth bloom with soaring life. For this reason alone, I shall take to the stars with these brave heroes on their mighty ships, and I will bestow my blessings upon them and their endeavours. By then I will once again be the bringer and tamer of Life, as was my purpose before you ruined me. My efforts here have nothing to do with you, nor with Olympus! I have left you, and I intend to stay my new course until my labours bear fruit. And, if the Fates so will it, by that time I shall be free from you and from this world forever!'

Zeus gave Hera a stern, solemn stare.

"And what of your innumerable misdeeds against my lesser wives and the children they bore me? Those poor souls who suffered the brunt of your wrath when you were in the throes of your jealous rages?" he asked derisively. "Do you truly believe that I would allow you to sever our marital bond without facing justice for your wickedness?"

"I have been wicked at times, that is true," Hera sneered, "but being your Queen was penance enough for any misdeed I could ever have done, including all the preposterous lies that the mortals of old believed about me. All that I have done, I did to repay the harm you did to me and to the ones I loved. As for your other women, these so-called wives you took after we wed, and all your bastards, whatever suffering they endured was your own doing in the end. I only let mortals believe those slanderous tales told about me so that they would quake in my presence, as they were no longer inclined to revere me, but that was a mistake, as was our marriage, which should never have been. As for the wicked deeds I actually committed, they cannot even compare to the evil you have done in the pursuit of your insatiable lust!"

Zeus swallowed the insult calmly, refusing to be provoked by Hera's taunt.

"Return to Olympus with our child," he reiterated, "and I will forgive your desertion and impiety, as you have not been in your right mind since you swallowed Mnemosyne's vile brew. You also have my word that no harm will come to these brave learned mortals under your protection, nor to their encampments and bases in these frozen northern lands. However, should you choose to remain here, I will lay waste not only to the Nephele high above, but also to the great halls where mortals entrust their founts of knowledge which Prometheus gave to them against my wishes, and I will send storms to destroy the shipbuilding yards where they make their mighty sky vessels. Then all of their science, all their labours, all your valiant efforts to send mortal life to the stars will have been in vain."

Zeus drew closer to Hera and caught her in an artless embrace before she could attempt to flee once again.

"Should you dare to oppose me in carrying out my judgement," he continued, "you will be branded an Oath breaker, and I will have no choice but to see to it that you carry out the sentence reserved for this most loathsome crime among our kind, much as it would pain me to see you in a breathless, lifeless trance for one year, then see you shunned from Olympus for the following nine years until you expiate your perjury. During this time, I would absolutely not suffer our child to be put in the care of mortals while you endured your sentence. Should you renege on your solemn word, I shall take our daughter to Olympus where I would give her a proper Olympian name, and choose for her a suitable bridegroom among the blessed gods, as befits a maiden of her rank. Should you choose to rebuke my gracious offer, you would not see our young daughter come of age, nor have any say about how she would be brought up, as you would be an outcast from the hallowed halls of starry Olympus during those precious years..."

"You fiend!" Hera gasped, trying to wriggle herself away from Zeus' hold.

"It is a simple choice," he told her as he pulled her close, "and it is yours to make since, as you said, I no longer hold the power to command you."

"Now you have gone mad," Hera answered in a fervid whisper. "You could leave this place, and we would never see each other again. Marry whomever you choose, I no longer care! You've always done as you please anyway. Why have you come here to torment me? Haven't you got the decency to leave me be?"

Zeus felt a pang of pity at the sincere despair in her voice, but he did not budge.

"I will do no such thing," he said wistfully. "I've already told you long ago, I will never again seek to replace you as my Queen. I have kept my word, and for that reason alone I will not suffer your absence any longer. Come home with me, return to our marriage bed, and all will be forgiven. Our child will live as one of the blessed gods of Olympus, and you will see her blossom until the time comes when she is ready to wed and have children of her own."

Hera trembled in anger, while the Cloud-gatherer closed the distance between them one last time before he told her, "I shall hear your answer when we meet again on this mountaintop tomorrow at Sunset. And by that I mean the Sunset at this latitude, not at Polaris. I do hope you have the presence of mind to bring our child this time, as she will have returned from the Nephele by morning. Until then, my love."

Zeus leaned over to give Hera a kiss on the cheek before he disappeared from sight, leaving an abortive storm, and an irate goddess, in his wake.

Nepheleid

Chapter Eleven

The Krios Khrysomallos arrived at Polaris at exactly seven in the morning, jolting to a halt as the passenger chamber touched down upon the best imitation of Terra Firma mortals had engineered at the topmost deck of the great ship in the middle of the Arctic Ocean. The tremor rocked Junia awake, and for a moment she resisted the urge to join the wags wailing fretfully about feeling pinned down in the confines of their bunks. As this was not the first time she had travelled up and down the reaches of the firmament, Junia rested lazily in her bunk instead, and waited for the Hub novices to finally acclimate to their natural planetary surroundings. After a moment she pulled the blanket over her face to hide her widening grin, trying her best not to laugh at the delicious absurdity that a large group of supposedly advanced schoolchildren could ever be surprised upon feeling the full force of gravity once newly returned to the surface of the Earth.

Junia had fallen asleep almost as soon as the Krios left the Nephele the previous evening, blissfully unaware that Prometheus, Asia, and Iris had also boarded the elevator at the very last minute without announcing their presence to their fellow passengers. Junia only found out that her kin had joined her and her classmates on their Earthbound trip when she awoke in the middle of the night and took a quick glance at her surroundings under the pretext of needing to use the vacuum toilet behind the column of passenger bunks. Due to her peculiar biology, Junia never needed to use such facilities – on Earth or in low orbit. However, as her mothers, Prometheus, Asia, Iris, Grandpa Okeanos and Grandma Tethys, Auntie Mnem the Headmistress, and every other immortal who dwells at the boundaries of the Earth reminded her time and again, it was paramount that she frequent washrooms for the sake of appearances, lest the other children discover that she was not human, at least not in the conventional sense.

When Junia saw Prometheus' likeness reflected against the great Earth-facing window of the Krios, she felt a knot tighten in the pit of her stomach, which she had thought quite strange, given her fondness for her older brother. No, something definitely was amiss. Prometheus, Asia, and Iris were not due to return to Polaris until shortly before the ember days of Autumn, when the remainder of the CARINA personnel not yet transferred to the Nephele would bivouac at the base of the Hub before departing for their new home high above the Earth. And yet, there they were, at the topmost deck, whereas Auntie Mnem appeared to have remained on the Nephele after decreeing an early end to the school year moments before Junia and the other children boarded the Krios. Though she knew not why that had come to be, Junia suspected that the reason behind this recent development had something to do with the grim look Prometheus' reflection gave her when the benefactor of humanity spied her milling about the rows of sedated pupils in a chipper manner. Before Junia could climb the stairs to interrogate her kin on the upper deck, Iris appeared by her bunk, and told her gently to go back to sleep. At this point Junia knew that she would not be able to rest while so many questions stirred inside her forebrain, so she sat back on her reclining seat, pressed the blue button overhead, breathed in the Hypnos mist, and promptly drifted off to sleep.

The surreal dream that followed almost had her longing for the halcyon days before the past Summer, when life appeared simpler, and half the Olympian Court had not yet joined Hera at the various CARINA locations where their Queen reigned as ALSESTIS Director of Operations. Back then Junia had not yet encountered her other siblings, except in the tall tales Hera and Klymene told her of their former home in a faraway realm. Junia only knew these tales to be true because at the dawn of her consciousness she had already made a habit of visiting Apollo in her dreams for reasons she still did not fully understand. The last time Junia encountered him in this fashion, she ended up inadvertently prompting the spirit-world of Turtle Island into guiding him straight to Sedna's lair deep below the Polaris, where he found Hera combing and braiding the Sea Maiden's hair as was her custom each year at Midsummer. Since that fateful day, Junia had not once dared to seek Apollo's company as they both slept, nor would she need to do so, as he had been the first among the blessed gods who dwell on holy Olympus to join Hera and Prometheus at CARINA shortly thereafter.

As the active ingredients of the Hypnos mist coursed through her tiny, preternatural veins, Junia found herself in an oddly familiar dreamscape of starlit meadows with huge rivers crisscrossing the land and Sky, though at the time she could not quite recall where she had seen these before. Annoyed at the obvious mind-addling side effects of the sleep aid, and hedging upon the likelihood that none of her deathless kin were listening in on her dreams, Junia uttered a very grown-up profanity that echoed throughout the vast emptiness of the phantasmagoric Sky-River world surrounding her. Partially satisfied that she had escaped a scolding for her verbal misbehaviour, Junia set her mind to willing herself awake, until she felt a warm hand land upon her shoulder. Looking up behind her, she saw Apollo's image framed by a swirl of stars, though once again she could not recognize with any degree of certainty the galaxy formation illuminating the Archer's golden hair like an elaborate halo. It could not be the Milky Way, she remembered thinking in her dream, for no mortal had ever seen or photographed the double spiral arms of stars of the only galaxy in the Cosmos known to harbour Life. Driven to distraction by her slumbering mind's obsession with identifying the mysterious star formation above Apollo's head, she barely heard what the brilliant Lord of the golden bow said to her. She did register, however, the gentleness in his tone, which in hindsight led her to believe that the news he had tried to break to her had something to do with why Prometheus and the other adults boarded the Krios earlier that night.

"Junebug, wake up! We have to go, eh?" she heard a familiar, albeit less otherworldly voice calling out in the passenger chamber.

Lifting the blanket off her face, Junia saw a youth looking down at her, his handsome face and golden hair framed by the light of the Arctic Sun outside the window. It took Junia a moment to realize that this was the mortal boy Derek, and not Apollo, who had come to wake her as the other children were filing out of the Krios long after it reached its destination.

"I'm coming! Give me a minute..." She answered with a much higher pitch than she had intended.

"Only *you* could sleep through a Hub landing!" Paul, Derek's perennial companion, remarked sardonically as he untethered his duffel bag from underneath his bunk. "What? Couldn't you hear all the other little kids crying for their mommies?"

"Yeah, gravity really sucks!" Junia said, giggling despite herself. "Anyway, I'll see you guys back at Junior Space Camp in a couple of weeks?"

"Uh, sure," Paul replied, giving her a strange look, while Derek tried his best to suppress a smile.

Nepheleid

Junia rose from her bunk and retrieved her own luggage. For some reason, she never seemed to need help lifting the heavy duffel bag, her small stature notwithstanding. This was probably why she heard Paul call her a "weird little kid" behind her back for the thousandth time as she exited the Krios, though today she distinctly heard Derek reply, "Nah, she's all right; Eris is much weirder."

Feeling somewhat vindicated, Junia stood an inch taller as she stepped into the vestibule and expertly evaded detection while the other passengers and their belongings underwent a cursory decontamination protocol. Sneaking up to the front of the line at the exit, she flashed a grin at Ares and Eris who awaited her outside on the utmost deck of the Polaris.

"There you are," Ares told Junia as she stepped into the sunlight. He grabbed her heavy bag and carried it effortlessly with his own while Eris took her hand and led her down a flight of metal stairs.

"Iris told us to let you sleep," Eris said. "So we did."

"Did Prometheus or Asia or Iris tell you why they're here?" Junia asked her older siblings.

"They did not," Ares answered. "Although you can ask them yourself when they return to Borealis with us in Mother's shuttle. Iris also mentioned that Hephaestus will be joining us on the return voyage as well."

"This should be fun!" Eris said in her spirited manner that always implied an undertone of mischief.

Junia found Hera nowhere near the Henokhie when they reached the Southward-facing launch pad of the Polaris. Instead she spied Hermes, ever her mother's shadow since his exile to Turtle Island, looking slightly hung over as he stood idly by the shuttle while awaiting his fellow travellers. Hermes greeted Junia and the red-haired twins without much ceremony, though he did help Ares load the duffel bags in the vast cargo compartment at the very back of the Henokhie without being asked. To Junia's surprise, the shuttle's cargo hold was filled almost at half-capacity with the entirety of Klymene and Hera's possessions at Polaris, and the other half with a number of smaller, portable, high-tech devices and other equipment, as well as mundane luggage and sundry. These, Junia guessed, must belong to her older brother Hephaestus, a kind, gentle fellow she had met only a few times before who mostly kept to himself, and whose most distinctive feature was the slight hobble with which he walked, for reasons that almost always brought Hera to tears whenever Junia inquired why this was so.

Once the luggage was secure, Junia stepped into the passenger compartment of the Henokhie, and found Klymene engaged in fitful conversation with Hephaestus, who occupied two seats in order to elevate his perpetually injured leg. Both ceased to speak as soon as they saw Junia. This left little doubt in the child's mind that something had indeed gone terribly awry during her short stay aboard the Nephele in the past few weeks, though by now she had already guessed that no one would tell her what happened until more unpleasantness came to pass.

"Kitten," Klymene said at last with the saddest of smiles. "Come, sit next to me. Have some food. You must be famished, what with your mandatory fasting before the descent. We will be in Borealis by the time you finish breakfast. Here, eat this. I've prepared meals for all of us to eat while we wait for the others." She handed a covered tray to Junia, and another to Hephaestus, as well as to Eris and Ares, who eagerly welcomed the sustenance. When offered a tray, Hermes declined, muttering something about having already feasted well into the wee hours of the evening the night before with the other blessed gods of Olympus at Borealis.

"But Mama, it takes at least 240 minutes to fly to Borealis, even if we don't stop to refuel along the way," Junia replied. "And where's Mom? She told me she'd be right here when we got back!"

"She wanted to be here, little one," Klymene answered. "Believe me, she would rather be here with us than at Borealis right now, but she got pulled away by a matter of some urgency. Now eat your breakfast. Iris and Prometheus and Asia will be here very soon."

Junia took the covered tray from Klymene and ate her breakfast in silence. With every bite she hoped to neutralize the unease she had felt earlier when she saw Prometheus' reflection aboard the Krios, but she already knew that mere food could not offset that sinking feeling in the pit of her stomach. After a few tense minutes, Iris greeted Hermes outside the Henokhie, and took a seat at the co-pilot chair of the cockpit, where she set about to prepare the teleconference screen for an incoming call. Moments later, Prometheus and Asia climbed at the front of the passenger compartment. Neither three appeared to have brought luggage from the Nephele.

Nepheleid

As Hermes took his place at the pilot's chair in the cockpit and prepared the Henokhie for takeoff, Iris' voice could be heard while she put the call through to the passenger compartment. "Incoming call from CARINA Borealis, Dr. Argosi's office," she obviously said for the benefit of the call log voice recognition database. "You are live on the passenger shuttle Henokhie."

"Thank you, Iris," Hera replied, her voice as strong and clear as though she were standing among her kin in the shuttle. "Prometheus, please turn the screen so that I can see Junia."

Without being told, Junia put aside her long-gone breakfast, and climbed over Hephaestus' seats, carefully so as not to rattle his elevated leg, and reached the front of the passenger compartment.

A jolt went through her entire being when she saw the look on her mother's face.

"Mom? Is everything okay?" she asked in a hopeful voice, though she feared she already knew the answer.

"Kitten, I will see you very soon," Hera answered truthfully. "Do you remember last Summer, when we returned from our visit at Uncles Hades' palace? Do you remember how quickly we all got back to Polaris, without stepping into the vortex? That's because Hermes has the power to travel at fantastic speeds without detection. It will be the same with the Henokhie, so do not be frightened. The land and Sea will disappear and reappear around you before you know it. And it will be nothing like the ascent or the descent on the Hub. You won't feel a thing. Now be a good girl and sit next to Mama, and try not to look outside as it happens. Can you do that for me?"

"Yes, Mom," Junia replied, more stupefied than complacent.

"I will be waiting for you all at the old launching grounds at Borealis. Argosi out."

Junia allowed Hephaestus to lift her off the floor and pass her back to Klymene, who then proceeded to tether her to her seat for the voyage.

"Mama," Junia asked Klymene while Hermes punched the coordinates to their destination onto the onboard computer. "We're not going to live on the Nephele, are we?"

Before Klymene could answer, Hermes spun around and said, "We will be home very soon, little one. Home. At last. At fu – "

The rest of his words were lost in a loud rush of wind as the Henokhie sped from the centre of the Arctic across the length of the Quebec peninsula at unimaginable speeds. Even so, Junia immediately understood their meaning. Despite being told all her life that she would one day call the vast expanses of the Heavens home, she never imagined in her wildest dreams that this would not be aboard a city-ship fashioned by the most learned mortals of their time.

Home, Junia would soon find out, was a place far stranger than even the cleverest mortal minds on Earth could ever imagine.

Nepheleid

Chapter Twelve

The Henokhie appeared through parted clouds above the natural promontory overlooking Lake New-Agassiz, where the previous evening loud-thundering Zeus met his estranged wife and heedlessly floundered Athena and Apollo's best-laid plans to save the CARINA network from impending annihilation. Apollo watched in silence as the shuttle touched down upon the landing pad. Like the other immortals gathered at the open door of the underground hangar housing CARINA's ample fleet, the Lord of the golden bow waited for Hermes to emerge from the craft with the rest of their kin, hoping that the messenger had kept his composure during the voyage. At long last, Hermes opened the door from the pilot's side of the cockpit, while swift Iris exited from the other side and walked towards a side panel on the Henokhie, where she punched in a lengthy code to unlock the outer door of the passenger compartment. As soon as the passenger door slid open, Hera emerged from the centre of the assembly by the open hangar door and strode towards her shuttle, no doubt to greet Iris, Klymene and Junia, as well as Hephaestus, her red-haired twins, and Prometheus and Asia as they deplaned. For some reason, Apollo already knew that Hera would not say a word to Hermes, who now took staggered steps, bracing himself against the bright sunlight as he gradually recuperated from last night's revelry.

Apollo motioned to follow Hera but halted when a strong hand took hold of his shoulder, gently holding him in place. Without being told, he knew that august Themis would advise against joining Hera while she discussed the matter at hand with Prometheus, just as the Titanide had thought it unwise that Apollo should appoint himself the Queen's champion in Prometheus' absence after learning about the mess Zeus had made of his own counsel the previous evening. At Themis' insistence, Apollo and bright-eyed Athena gave Hera a wide berth, to better avoid unleashing the Queen's legendary wrath should she ever find out that they shared the blame for instilling in Zeus' mind the idea of leveraging a city dear to her heart to negotiate the terms of her return to starry Olympus. Instead the Archer remained with the crowd of deathless gods, standing by his mother, Leto, who had come to Borealis under the pretext of visiting her children. Beside Leto stood Artemis, looking slightly pale and unsteady from having imbibed too much of Dionysus' brew the night before, when many of the blessed gods exiled at CARINA prematurely celebrated their imminent return to starry Olympus. Apollo held his tongue when he saw the pitiful state of many among his brethren this morning, for he suffered no such ill effects, having remained, as always, true to his nature of espousing moderation in all things.

The Archer and the Virgin Warrior had hoped to meet Hera's gaze and speak to her this morning, however the Queen's entourage, consisting today of her daughters Hebe and Eileithya, her sister Demeter, her usual bevy of Oceanides and Titanides, as well as her foster-parents Okeanos and Tethys, kept any interlopers well at bay. Apollo had little doubt that Themis instructed them earlier that morning to shield Hera from any attempts on his part to explain what he and Athena had done, even if they had only the best of intentions. Even fair-haired Rhea, who also came to Borealis with Zeus and Themis, strove to intercept her eminent daughter' would-be advocates, while her elder siblings thwarted the Titan Queen's own efforts to comfort Hera following yet another indignity wrought upon her by Zeus, her favoured son.

"Look, there's Ares and Eris, with Junia!" Hebe exclaimed gleefully, oblivious that her cheery voice had a temporarily unsteadying effect on her stalwart husband, and on others with far less formidable constitutions than that of the mighty Herakles.

Apollo smiled. Having seen Hebe imbibe as much wine as Dionysus the previous night, he now had irrefutable proof that the goddess of youth possessed at least some of her mother's preternatural immunity to the poisons of the Earth, including intoxicants resulting from the fermentation of fruit and grain. Perhaps one day, when all this unpleasantness would be but a distant memory, Apollo will witness Hera drinking Dionysus under the table, in the same way Dionysus once famously out drank Thor of Asgard following a heated disagreement with the Queen of Olympus long ago.

"Right," Artemis said groggily. "Where are they going?"

"Ares and Eris are likely taking the child away from here while Hera and Prometheus devise a plan to respond Zeus' ultimatum," Themis answered. "Our King has made it quite clear that the fate of CARINA now rests solely in her hands."

"Thus, we have achieved the sum of our fears," Athena said.

Themis threw Athena a grave look.

"Are you implying that Hera would sooner blow up the Nephele herself than return to her husband at this juncture?" the Titanide asked crossly. "I would not even think such thoughts if I were you. In fact, I think it would be best if all of you held your tongues, until Hera formulates her decision... And Hebe – you and Herakles would be wise to keep Dionysus hidden away at Café Basilea and see to it that he does not cross the Queen's path until the fate of CARINA is known."

"So, you expect us to wait, and do nothing, while Hera surmises that Apollo, Hermes, and I each had our part to play in this clusterf– unfortunate turn of events?" Athena muttered under her breath with undue irascibility, which Apollo knew had more to do with the lingering effects of ethanol poisoning than guilt at the unfolding catastrophe they now faced.

Not that there was any cause for culpability or regret; even after Zeus threatened Hera with that which she feared the most, Apollo contended that he and his siblings had counselled the Thunderer sagaciously on their last visit to Olympus, and that their father's preposterous blunder, born of his chafing desire to be reunited with his bride, remained his alone. While Apollo would have liked to spend the remaining hours before Sunset counselling Hera on maximizing her bargaining position, the Queen evidently favoured conferring with Prometheus and Asia. This made sense, Apollo admitted, for the benefactor of humanity and his bride had much more at stake should Hera consider returning to Olympus a far more egregious fate than seeing the city-ship Nephele destroyed.

And yet, how Prometheus knew to board the Hub the previous night to return to Polaris even before Zeus met with Hera, Apollo could not say. On second thought, Prometheus likely divined this outcome with his gift of foresight, an ability few immortals mastered so proficiently, except perhaps for Apollo himself, whom Themis instructed in the prophetic arts, and of course golden-throned Hera, who undoubtedly bestowed upon Prometheus this aptitude while he grew in her womb. None of this mattered at the moment, Apollo thought, turning his mind instead to what needed to be done to convince Zeus that it was in everyone's best interest to accept all of Hera's proposed terms in exchange for her return to Olympus. If Apollo had his way, Zeus would graciously agree to Hera's continued involvement in the affairs of CARINA's off-world operations, whether on the Nephele, on the Corona, on the Hesperides Autonomous Station, or other ships of their ilk yet to be built.

After a few minutes, Hera, Klymene, Prometheus, and Asia headed towards the hangar, trailed by Hephaestus, Iris and Hermes. When Apollo saw the look on Hera's face as she walked towards the open doors of the building, presumably to reach her office on the top floor above, he spontaneously placed himself between Athena and the Queen. Hera gave him a strange look, as if amused that the Lord of the golden bow believed that it was within his power to shield the Virgin Warrior from her ire, when in the past entire cities were obliterated off the face of the broad-pathed Earth by her wrath.

Instead, Hera paused before Apollo and Athena.

"You impudent wench!" the Queen told Athena before Prometheus and Klymene could collect her. "You sold me out, again! What have I ever done to you, to be treated so poorly!?"

"We were trying to stop Zeus from obliterating the CARINA network," Apollo said. "Neither of us advised him to do as he did!"

"Be quiet you!" Hera replied angrily. "Athena is more than capable of speaking for herself! Answer me! Why have you so casually cast aside our friendship to placate your father, when you know full well that he is not the one that can be reasoned with! He is fickle and self-absorbed as a child! He cares for nothing and no one but himself! Why did you think it wise to sell me out to this… monster, when all you needed to do to safeguard the CARINA network was to distract him until Summer's end, when none of our strategic assets and laboratories would have remained in these parts for him to strike down!?"

"We all thought he might better inure himself to your imminent departure if he thought that there was some glimmer of hope that you might consider taking the reins of the Hesperides Autonomous Station for a while," Athena answered. "At least for as long as the Nephele lingered in low Earth orbit for a few more years, until it was ready to set sail towards the Corona."

"It's true," Apollo concurred. "We almost had him convinced that you considered it your duty to keep watch over the Earth and oversee the recovery of Life until you knew that Gaia had become whole once more!"

"We were merely trying to undo the harm that Aphrodite's words had done to compromise the integrity of CARINA's mission," Athena said.

Hera pinched the bridge of her nose, as Klymene patted her arm lightly. "Have you young ones learned nothing after all these centuries?" she asked exasperatedly. "Zeus only sees what he wants to see and believes whatever he thinks will justify the ends he strives to achieve! His so-called wisdom, which mortals inexplicably vaunt as often as they unjustly vilify my character, was never his own! You should have stayed the course, until Summer's end! Now your actions have doomed CARINA and undone all of our work."

Hera took a deep breath to regain her composure, however Apollo saw that the Queen was now on the verge of tears. Klymene and Prometheus drew closer, flanking her protectively against those who had unwittingly caused her untold harm.

Okeanos, the venerable Father of Rivers, looked at Athena. "You need to give us a moment," he told her with a gentleness Apollo would never have believed possible from a son of Gaia and Ouranos. To Apollo he said, "come meet us in the large conference room on the administrative floor. There we will discuss terms with Lady Themis, our noble sister, and emissary to loud-thundering Zeus."

Apollo and Athena watched as Okeanos, Prometheus, and Klymene took Hera through the inner doors of the building, with Tethys, Rhea, Demeter, Iris, Eileithya, and Hephaestus following closely. Hermes, Hebe, and Herakles had long since taken their leave, as had Leto and Artemis for that matter, presumably to recover Dionysus from behind the sofa in the posh lounge of the administrative wing, where the blessed gods banqueted merrily the previous evening until the first light of Dawn. Once Hera and her entourage had fully vacated the hangar, Athena wisely elected to join her siblings in their quest to conceal Dionysus until Themis or Iris gave them tidings of the fate of the CARINA network.

As Apollo exited the elevator upon reaching the highest floor, he spied his father waiting on a sumptuous and expensive-looking couch in the anteroom of the executive boardroom, where Themis likely instructed him to wait while she negotiated a palatable agreement with Hera and her retinue. To his surprise, Ganymede was also there, manning the wet bar on the far side of the hall, as far away from the boardroom doors as the building's peculiar architecture allowed. The Trojan prince nodded politely at Apollo, offering him a beverage of his choice, which the Archer promptly and courteously declined. Apollo uttered a quick greeting to Zeus before heading into the boardroom, taking great care to close the sound-proof doors behind him as he entered the fray.

The Lord of the golden bow found Hera seated at the head of the table, with Prometheus at her right, and Klymene at her left. Asia and Iris sat beside Prometheus, while Okeanos and Tethys sat by their daughter Klymene. Hephaestus, Demeter, and Eileithya sat closest to august Themis near the middle of the large, oval table, while Rhea stood by the wide window overlooking the promontory and landing pad. Beyond the hill Apollo glimpsed the dark green bowl of Lake New-Agassiz, the only recognizable feature hinting at the presence of the broad underground complex that once housed CARINA's ALSESTIS laboratories.

"My dear," Apollo heard Themis say, "you have the word of our King that no harm will come to the learned mortals at all the CARINA cities across the vast and bountiful Earth, as well as in those that they built beyond the Heavens, if you see to it that Junia returns to Olympus with you. He will agree to whatever else you ask, so long as you celebrate the marriage rite upon your return, and have your daughter join her blessed kin to be raised as a proper princess of Olympus."

Hera closed her eyes, looking as one who had spent the previous night cleansing a waterway without subsequently expelling the offending miasma through every pore of her being. Apollo banished the very thought out of respect for his embattled Queen, for he knew full well that she had, in truth, spent the night sleeplessly fretting over her encounter with the Cloud-gatherer, while her ungrateful Olympian stepchildren mocked her anguish with their revelries in the lounge two floors below.

"He will strive to do with me what he will upon my return," Hera replied flatly. "Of that, I am quite certain. Perhaps I am partly culpable for the troubles I now face, but Junia bears no such blame. These are my terms: I will return to Olympus with Zeus, on the condition that I retain my position as Director of Operations at ALSESTIS, as well as my stake in the ownership of the Nephele, whereas Junia will relocate to the aforementioned city-ship at Summer's end with Klymene. I will bestow to my dear and loyal friend full custody of our child until Junia comes of age and decides for herself whether to join the learned mortals on their voyages to the stars."

Rhea gasped audibly, while Klymene reached for Hera's hand.

"You cannot mean this, Daughter!" Rhea said. "You would give up your own child, just to spite your husband?"

"I would spare Junia the indignity of growing up under the yoke of that fiend," Hera answered without looking at Rhea. "I would spare her the horror of witnessing her father humiliate her mother as he always has, and of using her as a pawn to flatter his own sense of self-importance. Junia can never see her mother treated so wretchedly, nor ever think this to be customary or just. Junia will continue to thrive among her people, the learned mortals of CARINA as well as the boundary-dwelling offspring of Okeanos and Tethys, whose dominion will extend into the farthest reaches of the Cosmos under the guidance of brilliant minds such as hers. My daughter will leave for Junior Space Camp will her friends after the Sun reaches its apogee in two weeks and join her class on the Nephele when Summer turns to Autumn. If safeguarding the happiness of my daughter means that I must send her far away, as you sent me away to dwell in the House of Okeanos and Tethys when I emerged from the River Lethe all those centuries ago, if securing her future means that I ought to leave her in the care of another, until I become no more to her than a cherished memory, then so be it."

Apollo cleared his throat, an affectation he learned from mortals, for no phlegm could ever take hold his deathless trachea, nor mar his divine singing voice.

"What do you want?" Hera asked crossly, guessing his intent to draw attention to himself.

"Great Lady, if I may," the Archer replied. "It appears that your negotiations have reached an impasse. If you will allow it, Themis, I wish to speak to the Queen in private, in her office perhaps? We will meet you here in an hour with our answer."

Hera looked at Apollo with a combination of outrage and admiration at his boldness. August Themis acquiesced to his request, rising to her feet to leave the boardroom, followed by all the others, save for Prometheus, Asia, and Iris. When Apollo glanced at the benefactor of humanity, Hera, as if divining his thoughts, told him simply, "Though I appreciate the sentiment, Prometheus and Iris will be the ones who will give my answer to Themis and to Zeus. I have no intention of speaking to your father until that becomes absolutely necessary. On that note, we will be taking the private corridor to my office… I am well aware of whom awaits on the other side of those doors."

Apollo nodded, and waited as Hera and Prometheus led the way through a door hidden behind a panel on the wall adjacent to the wide panoramic window overlooking the grounds of CARINA Borealis. As they stepped into Hera's cavernous office, Apollo marvelled at how much at ease his stepmother appeared in this environment designed by learned mortals in this citadel of science at the heart of the wilderness of Turtle Island. This place was as alien to the glorious halls of starry Olympus as was the landscape of the dream he once shared with golden-throned Hera a decade ago, on the night Junia was conceived. Apollo smiled, recalling his mother's gentle taunt last night about bearing as much responsibility for Junia's creation as the girl's mother and father. After a few sips of strong wine, Leto even had the audacity to ask him whether he had summoned Junia into being from the far recesses of the Cosmos, to become his bride once she came of age.

"Tell me, Phoebus," Hera said as she took a seat at her imposing desk, while Prometheus waited for Asia and Iris to cross the threshold to close the door behind them. "Was this your plan all along, to have me return to Zeus after I set my mind to leaving him forever? I cannot help but notice echoes of that night when you put me in his bed, shortly before I left Olympus the following day with my newfound son Prometheus."

Apollo was astounded. Only a few minutes ago, he could have sworn that Hera had seemed at her wits' end, yet she now gave him the most curiously amused look, which made her look even more lovely and youthful than she already allowed herself to appear under her mortal guise. This gave Apollo the proof he had always sought as to whether Hera possessed the ability to hear the thoughts of others as they formed in their minds, a skill even august Themis never taught him when he was her pupil.

"I assure you," Apollo replied, biting his lip in a vain attempt to conceal his own amazement. "What Zeus did then on starry Olympus, as well as what he did yesterday on the hilltop above Borealis, had nothing to do with my counsel. Then as now, he listened to my words, but did as he pleased.'

"And so, here we are…" Prometheus said, his voice rife with sarcasm and exhaustion in equal measure.

"I am truly sorry for the way this all turned out," Apollo said.

"The sad part about all this is, I believe you," Hera replied with utmost sincerity.

Iris and Asia nodded slowly in agreement.

"How seriously must we consider Zeus' threat, really?" Asia asked after a moment.

"As seriously as can be imagined," Hera answered. "It is exactly as I had feared. He has called in the Oath I swore by the ramparts of Troy, yet he claims that he will abandon his pursuit of CARINA's obliteration if I agree to return to Olympus with him. I am afraid I will have little choice but to comply on that account, but I will not let Junia suffer for my sins of long ago... I never could fathom uttering these words, but it now appears as though I owe Rhea an apology for being angry with her for ever sending me away to dwell at the House of Okeanos and Tethys at the boundaries of the Earth. I now know that she did so to protect me from Zeus' unrequited attentions, though that did not do any good in the end."

"Mother," Prometheus said, causing Hera to wince slightly. "Zeus' threats have no teeth. Borealis is already almost empty of its staff and ALSESTIS facilities, and the other locations are well protected by the gods of Turtle Island. Zeus would not be so foolish as to start a quarrel with them, for he does not know their weaknesses or strengths!"

"There are still many ways he could influence the course of events," Hera answered, shaking her head. "He could command the Sun to send a geomagnetic storm that would damage the Nephele due to its proximity to Earth! He could compel Poseidon to withdraw all the rivers of the fertile lands of the Earth, causing the last remaining strongholds of humanity to abandon their lands and wander the Earth in search of hospitable places to call home, many of which are no more... There are so many ways he could bring our great work to naught, limited only by the extent of his considerable and perverse imagination..."

"The only part of the CARINA network he could threaten is the Hub at Polaris," Prometheus said. "Even then, thunderstorms almost never reach the Canadian High Arctic. That is why we chose that location to harbour the Polaris and build the base of the Hub. You do not need to sacrifice yourself on account of his empty threats! Unless..."

Hera looked up at Prometheus, her countenance betraying her dread. "Unless what?" she asked cautiously.

Nepheleid

"Unless... There remains a part of you that longs to be reunited with your husband," Prometheus replied. "Is this so, Mother? Is your voluntary act of atonement, for laying waste to the Trojans aeons ago, a mere ruse to be reconciled with the one who has tormented us both for millennia?"

Apollo cringed at Prometheus' words. Were the benefactor of humanity half as insightful as Apollo believed him to be, then he would already have surmised that Hera's enmity towards the Trojans had nothing to do with the city-state, and everything to do with taking her revenge on Zeus for how poorly he treated her in those dark days long gone by.

"I can forgive you for thinking such thoughts, Prometheus," Hera replied dolefully, her tone almost apologetic. "We have only come to terms with the truth about our filial bond ten years ago, which for our deathless kind constitutes a measure of Time far too brief to consider. You have become proficient in knowing my mind and my thoughts, but not when it comes to bringing to light the secrets of my heart. No, I must face the consequences of what I've done, if only to buy the Nephele some time until it soars freely towards the vast expanses of the Cosmos. This is what I must do, to give these learned mortals, my trueborn children through your sacrifice, a fighting chance against encroaching oblivion, borne by the rule of fools such as the King of Olympus... Though in the past I may have failed, however unwittingly, to protect you as your mother, today I shall not fail you as your Queen. Iris, Apollo – tell Themis that I am ready to have her hear my terms."

Chapter Thirteen

Autumn came to the woodlands of Turtle Island in a kaleidoscope of colours, painting the vast continent beneath the Arctic Gilded Coast in a patina of yellows, reds, and oranges mixed with the lingering greens of the Northern Summer. For all her short life, Junia had anticipated to glance upon this spectacle from her new home on the Nephele at the very top of Earth's axis, before all the hues were gone by the time she celebrated her tenth birthday. However, as the Fates willed it, she would not be joining all the people, mortal or otherwise, she had known since infancy on the city-ship high above the Earth. Instead she would relocate with her mothers to starry Olympus, where her brother Prometheus' troubles began after he stole a spark from Hephaestus' forge to gift mortals with fire, back when the gods were as young and foolhardy of mind as mortals who have yet to live past their prime.

Glancing at the denuded walls of her small bedroom, Junia came to terms with the knowledge that today would be the last day she would arise from her bed in her mothers' Autumn and Winter flat at Borealis. Junia and Klymene had already packed up the rest of their worldly possessions over the last few days, while Hera busied herself with overseeing the return of the CARINA compound to the local people whose ancestors allowed Prometheus to use this land decades ago to build his enclave of science in the sleepy wilderness. These mortals, Junia was told, heeded Prometheus' counsel and intended to repurpose the vast, underground facilities into a hybrid solar and wind energy generating and storage plant. All that remained on-site, including the CARINA-issued bedding and pillows Junia now placed in the open storage crates for processing at the nearby laundry, would return to the local tribe of mortals, for the learned mortals at CARINA Borealis had no need for such things on the Nephele, or on starry Olympus, as Hermes was fond of reminding Junia of late.

Nearly all the learned mortals at CARINA Borealis left for Polaris a few days before, save for a skeleton crew of those who chose to forgo their welcome on the Nephele and instead dwell forever on terra firma. Though Hera always spent her Summers at Polaris, when the weather proved less inclement to most of her crew than during the long Arctic night, this year she insisted on staying in the sweltering woodlands of Borealis until her time among the learned mortals of CARINA ran its course. This was one of her terms in the agreement she devised with the Thunderer on the day Junia and her kin returned from Polaris at the end of the previous school year. Junia mostly remembered from that day the look of grave concern on all the adults' faces, except for Hermes, who despite looking rather out of sorts also seemed quite relieved for a change, as if suddenly freed from a burden he had borne for far too long.

Junia also recalled how quickly Ares and Eris ushered her away from the administrative building after Hera greeted them briefly by the landing pad, and later, shortly before Sunset, the bizarre commotion following Zeus' defenestration from Hera's office window, while Apollo, Prometheus, Asia, and Iris deliberated with Themis in the adjacent boardroom. Ares and Eris had not tried very hard to shield Junia from the most recent development in the interminable battle of wits between their parents. Without being told, Junia already knew that Zeus would never leave the skies of Turtle Island until all the exiles among his Court, including his Queen and their progeny, returned with him to Olympus when the Seasons turned to Autumn. And yet, for reasons Junia did not quite fully understand, Hera finally acquiesced to Zeus' demands, under certain conditions that took an inordinate amount of time to cogitate among the grown-ups.

Perhaps Zeus grew impatient of the proceedings by the end of the afternoon and hoped to conclude the negotiations by meeting Hera directly to hear her terms. Perhaps he wished to celebrate his victory before the appointed time. No matter his reasons, Junia saw from her vantage point on the plaza overlooking Lake New-Agassiz her father step into her mother's office. She then saw Hera rising to her feet as Zeus walked briskly toward his quarry and reached to embrace her, while the room filled with a golden mist of some sort that blocked everything from view. A split-second later, Junia saw her father projected through Hera's high office window, exploding the entire span of so-called shatterproof glass, and land upon the ground, causing a small earthquake and a spiderweb crack on the cement. Junia then saw Hera at the window, looking rather angry, before she stepped back inside as the drones began filling in the opening with liquid polymer.

What happened next was truly the strangest thing Junia had ever seen, stranger still than that time she visited the Titans in gloomy Tartarus the previous year, after Hera brought her to Hades' Kingdom to lay low for a few days. As Junia remembered it, Zeus rose to his feet, shook off the small shards off his shoulders, and adjusted his cufflinks. Once he was done pretending he had not been cast out of a window off the top floor of the highest building in the CARINA Borealis compound, the Thunderer walked straight towards Junia, Ares, and Eris, and said in a gleeful tone, "Tell your mother that I agree to her terms – all save for one." Turning to Junia specifically, he added, "I expect to see *you* on high Olympus at Summer's end."

Then he disappeared.

The plaza had been nearly empty that day, and yet Eris had no other choice but to confound any mortal unfortunate enough to have witnessed this utterly random and outlandish event. Even hapless Derek, newly returned from Polaris, did not escape this fate. Moments before, he had found himself in their midst, teasing Eris innocuously about purportedly taking the name of the goddess of Chaos. Junia barely registered Derek's taunt about Eris' vanity for appropriating dominion over "the guiding principle of the Universe", until they all saw an imposing figure leaping through the air and landing on his feet, seemingly unhurt.

After Zeus left, Derek turned to Junia and asked, "Was that your dad?", to which Eris answered, "Gaze into my eyes for a moment, young one." Derek became very quiet, staring intently into Lake New-Agassiz, until his older sister came to collect him for supper.

When Junia saw Derek again at Junior Space Camp, he mostly remained with Paul, though at times Junia could have sworn that they both studied her whenever they thought she was not paying attention. Three months had come and gone since Derek unwittingly met and then forgot about the King of Olympus, yet with each passing day Junia hoped that the beautiful mortal boy who always found an excuse to spend time with her did not suffer permanent brain damage from this misadventure.

Hera was in a foul mood ever since that day. She spent all her time on the grounds at Borealis, working late into the evenings, as if she could not bear to witness the spectacle of the setting Sun each night. It was perhaps a mercy that Hera and Klymene sent Junia to Junior Space Camp shortly thereafter, where she remained for the duration of the

Nepheleid

Summer, even though most of her classmates left for Polaris by the middle of August. Whenever Junia asked Prometheus and Asia why she ought to continue attending Junior Space Camp if she and her mothers would relocate to Olympus, they answered that she and Hera and Klymene would remain part of the crew of the Nephele, albeit remotely, as per the agreement between Hera and Zeus. They never truly told Junia why she and her mothers and her immortal kin, all save for Iris, Auntie Mnem, and many of the sons and daughters of Okeanos and Tethys, had to join Zeus at his Court on starry Olympus.

Before her return from Polaris at the end of the school year, the adults used to tell Junia everything, and in return Junia never once questioned Prometheus and Hera's motives for hiding her from the rest of her Olympian family before the previous Summer, nor Hera's sudden change of heart in welcoming all those who sought to join her efforts to bring the work of CARINA to completion. Before the end of the last school year, Junia did her best to obey Hera's command to ignore Zeus whenever she saw him looking down upon her from his Heavenly perch, for she knew that none of her classmates could see him – unless they possessed the gift of second sight or had some minuscule amount of divine ichor flowing through their veins.

Until she met her father on the topmost deck of the Polaris a year ago, all that Junia knew about him came from the tales Klymene and Prometheus told her since long before she could walk. At that very tender age, Junia already knew to never ask Hera about her biological father, as her mother often grew uneasy at the very mention of his name and left the room until someone kindly changed the subject. Over the course of several years, Hera grew increasingly confident that Zeus would never find her, and at last opened up to Junia about the children she had borne besides Prometheus. These included a sister who turned out to be a barista of sorts, another who was as an obstetrician, a brother who worked as a master craftsman, another who was a warrior, and another daughter, the latter's twin, who proved herself quite the trouble-maker among the blessed gods of holy Olympus.

In the span of one year, Junia met them all, in addition to her aunt Demeter and many other half-siblings, or *cousins*, as Hera insisted Junia call them. They all returned to Olympus after that strange day spent with Ares, Eris, and Derek on the plaza at Borealis. Hebe and Herakles closed Café Basilea and left with Athena, Eileithya, and Artemis that very afternoon. In early July, after Hera relieved Ares and Eris of their duty to shadow Junia when their charge left for Junior Space Camp, the pair spent some time at Polaris with Hephaestus, until all three returned to Olympus together. Hermes later told Hera and Klymene that it had something to do with helping Hephaestus carry some of his things back to Olympus, but Junia remembers that Hera did not believe a word of it. But then again, Hera seldom took Hermes' words at face value.

Apollo resigned from his post at CARINA in early September, whereas Demeter left two weeks later after her daughter Persephone, who visited Borealis while Junia was away, returned to her husband when the Seasons turned to Autumn. Of this lot only Hermes remained, as Zeus' decree that he could not return to Olympus without his Queen and her youngest child still held, even after Hera agreed to end her exile and return to the abode of the gods at Summer's end.

"Kitten? Are you dressed?" Junia heard Klymene say from behind the closed door of her bedroom.

"Yes, just a minute!" Junia answered. She quickly grabbed a folded shirt on her otherwise empty nightstand, pulled the garment over her head, then grabbed the pair of loose-fitting trousers underneath and donned them as Klymene slowly opened the door.

"It's time to go, little one," Klymene said wistfully as she reached to straighten Junia's tangled hair. "Now, have you checked behind the dressers to see if there is anything left?"

"I looked yesterday, Mama," Junia replied. "I made sure of it. Everything is in the crates."

"Then take one last look," Hera said, appearing unexpectedly a few paces behind Klymene. "Because this building will be turned into office space starting next month."

Hera looked down at the carpeted floor, and grabbed a trio of small, elaborately bedecked dolls in a heap behind a crate.

"Why have you left Kweetoo, Kadlu, and Ignirtoq behind?" Hera asked. "Do you not want to bring keepsakes from the Arctic with you to Olympus? Or have you outgrown your fondness for Thunderers?"

Nepheleid

Junia bit her lip but did not reply. She honestly did not know what to tell Hera as they set out to leave Borealis for the very last time.

Hera gave Junia a wan smile. "We might be leaving the woodlands of Turtle Island," she said, "but that does not mean we are leaving CARINA forever. Remember, you will continue to attend school with your friends on the Nephele, through virtual means, at least for the next few years. Once you come of age, you will be free to decide whether you wish to join the crew or stay among your kin on Olympus. This was one of my most explicit terms. Zeus knows he cannot bind you to Olympus until you decide otherwise. Now, do you want to bring the Thunder Sisters with you, or should we place them properly in the donation crate?"

Junia took the dolls from Hera and placed them in the backpack Klymene held out for her.

"What about you?" Junia asked. "Are you free to leave Olympus and join the crew of the Nephele after I grow up?"

Hera gave Junia a look of alarm but did not answer.

"We really ought to go," Klymene offered mercifully, taking Junia by the hand as Hera closed the door of the bedroom. "Hermes brought us your queenly chariot for our return to Olympus."

"Aren't we taking the Henokhie?" Junia asked meekly.

"No, Kitten, we are not taking the Henokhie," Hera answered with a soft chuckle.

When Junia saw the "queenly chariot" Hermes brought to the landing pad, she did a double-take, which elicited a good-spirited laugh from Klymene and Hermes, as well as a genuine smile from Hera. To Junia, this contraption looked nothing like the CARINA shuttle Hera flew from Borealis to Polaris and back again over the course of the last decade as ALSESTIS' Director of Operations. Indeed, the vessel looked like something far too beautiful to have been crafted for purely utilitarian purposes, a gold-and-silver hued oblong spearhead of sorts, splendid to behold.

"You got a new shuttle?" Junia asked Hera, her voice barely above a whisper.

"No, darling," Hera answered. "This is my old chariot, made to resemble a contemporary vehicle for mortal eyes. It will look as it always has the moment we land upon starry Olympus. Until then it will look like this golden, aerodynamic canoe with wings. That ought to make a memorable entrance, don't you think? I thought it fitting to bring something of Turtle Island to Olympus as well." To Hermes, she asked, "Will Hebe be ready to take my chariot to the stables?"

"She will, my lady," Hermes answered casually. "The entire Olympian Court will be awaiting your arrival. I believe some are placing bets as to the guise you've chosen for your chariot."

"I have no doubt," Hera muttered under her breath as she walked towards where the pilot's side door should have been on a long-distance shuttle craft.

"I think Ares wagered that you'd disguise your chariot as an Apache helicopter," Hermes said. He made to enter through the pilot's side door first, but Hera blocked him with her right hand.

"I will drive," she said. "You can sit at the back with Junia."

"That's all alright, my lady," Klymene said. "Hermes can sit beside you; I will sit with Junia."

Junia looked a Klymene quizzically. She had never heard her call Hera "my lady" before, nor had Hermes addressed her in this manner in the last year as he dwelt in Borealis with Athena on the other side of Lake New-Agassiz.

"You will have to get used to this, Kitten," Hera said, as if reading Junia's mind. "The ways of Olympus are quaint and atavistic, as you will soon discover once we leave this place. How I will miss Turtle Island, with all its gods and Manitous who have ruled this land since long before Mother and Father cast Okeanos and Tethys from high Olympus to dwell at the boundaries of the Earth!"

Nodding solemnly at these words, Klymene took Junia by the hand and led her inside the aircraft that was not truly an aircraft. There the Oceanid fasted Junia to her seat and sat beside her, while Hera sat at the pilot's seat and Hermes took the place of co-pilot. In a matter of seconds, the mighty vessel rose from the ground, in a smooth, elegant motion, then rapidly ascended at a high altitude, without ill effect, until the vast colourful woodlands of Turtle Island gave way to a wine-dark sea of stars.

"Look ahead, Junia," Klymene said as a bright, golden city appeared before the chariot. "This is Olympus."

The abode of the gods appeared lit from within the heart of an impossibly high mountain range, taller by many magnitudes than the Mount Olympus of Northern Hellas, or any mountain upon the face of the broad-pathed Earth. This was no place on Earth, Junia concluded, in the same way she had determined that the Kingdom of Hades could not have been contained under the surface of the planet, so vast were its perceptible dimensions to one as keen-eyed as a trueborn daughter of Zeus and Hera.

"This is the most wondrous sight you will ever see, bar none," Hermes told Junia beatifically.

Hera looked at Hermes crossly for a moment, then guided the vessel to a wide empty landing before a high stairway that led to an imposing edifice at the centre of Olympus.

"That's the throne room, Kitten," Hera said as she proceeded to land her chariot at the base of the stairway. "To enter Olympus, one must first meet the gods where they rule. We will climb those stairs, then make our way inside, where your father will await us. When we enter, he will be holding Court at his throne, and you will be brought before him so that he can officially claim you as his child. As I've told you, he will likely ask you if you wish for a boon of some sort. Do you remember what you are to say to him if he asks this of you?"

"Yes, Mom," Junia replied. "I know what to say to Zeus."

"Good," Hera said as the vessel touched down upon hallowed ground.

Without further ceremony, Hera stepped off the vessel, followed closely by Hermes. Klymene unfastened Junia and bade her to follow Hermes, assuring her that she would meet them all once Hera's palace was ready to receive them. When Junia stepped off the vessel, she glimpsed at the vehicle that had transported them from the Earth to this strange realm and smiled at the gold-and-silver hued horses at the very front of the most elaborately lavish chariot she had ever seen. A queenly chariot indeed, she thought, as Hermes tapped her on the shoulder and led her towards the massive bronze doors at the top of the stairway. To her surprise, Junia did not tire from climbing the stairs, nor did she feel any fright creeping upon her from the sheer height of Olympus' ramparts, as she had sometimes experienced looking down upon the Earth from the Nephele. The high bronze doors of the throne room opened before they reached the top of the stairway, which gave Junia some measure of apprehension.

Hera immediately turned around and took Junia by the hand. "Remember what we've practiced back at Borealis," she whispered before crossing the threshold into the cavernous throne room. "Remember Protocol Olympus, and all will be well."

The throne room consisted of a high, seemingly circular wall, capped by an immense cupola that reflected the movement of the stars outside the confines of this world. And yet, the entire span of the broad-pathed Earth appeared beyond the walls around them, from the slumbering Night at the edges of the firmament, to the bright Day at the centre of the horizon.

How was such a thing even possible?

"Stay close, Kitten," Hera said, squeezing her hand almost as hard as she had done on the topmost deck of the Polaris, on the evening Junia met Zeus for the very first time.

As Hera forewarned, the entire Olympian Court gathered in the throne room to greet their Queen upon her arrival. Though Junia saw many familiar faces beaming welcoming smiles at her, there were many more blessed gods there whom she did not know. This frightened her more than she cared to admit. Gathering her courage, Junia stopped dead in her tracks and pointed at the zenith of the cupola above them. ' Is this where Zeus tied you up and hanged you from the Sky?" she asked her mother innocently.

"No, Kitten," Hera answered with undue calm. "It was over there, before that high palace on the highest peak. He hanged me in full view of his dwelling."

Hermes cringed visibly at these words, and the blessed gods gathered in the throne room on high Olympus murmured uneasily. At last, rising from his seat at the highest point in the chamber, loud-thundering Zeus addressed the recent arrivals, hushing the crowd into silence.

"There is no need for such theatrics, little one," he said placidly. "Today is a happy day, for you and your mother have come home, where you truly belong. There is no need to be reminded of any unpleasantness that took place long ago. Now, come closer, and let me take a good look at you."

Junia took a step closer to Zeus but stopped some ten paces away from him.

"Closer, child, until you are right in front of me," Zeus added patiently, patting the arm of his throne as if summoning a pampered house cat to take a seat beside him on a sofa.

As she walked irritatingly slowly towards her father, Junia noticed that Ares, Eris, and Herakles stood sentinel at his left, in a way that appeared uncharacteristic of this lot. Junia scanned Eris' face for clues as to the meaning of this configuration, but her older sister simply exhibited an unmistakably mischievous grin. Turning back to face Zeus, Junia stopped once more, and waited for her father to address her first.

"Usually when I welcome my progeny among the blessed gods on high Olympus," he said ceremoniously, "I offer them a gift as a token of my love. However, given the strange circumstances preceding your homecoming, I will grant you an audience much later, after this evening's banquet, as I tuck you into bed. I am certain your mother will allow this, will you not, my love?"

Hera answered with the most inscrutable look she could muster, though Junia and most of the blessed gods assembled within Olympus' hallowed throne room could tell that she was rather irritated at the King. Hera managed a semblance of an indifferent shrug, her mind undoubtedly racing to remember whatever contingency plan she had devised should Zeus divine her schemes and delay granting their child a boon, with all the blessed gods of holy Olympus bearing witness.

"And since you have returned with our child, as we agreed," Zeus continued, "I have prepared a gift for you..."

With a wave of the Thunderer's hand, Ares, Eris, and Herakles moved aside to reveal Hephaestus kneeling on the floor, tightening some bolts at the base of what looked like a sumptuously ornamented golden chair, which Junia guessed must have been her mother's famous golden throne. This puzzled Junia somewhat, as Prometheus told her some time ago that Hera kept her golden throne in a vault somewhere on the Nephele, as collateral for her stake in the ownership of the city-ship and her share of the CARINA venture. Though slightly confused, Junia kept silent and looked up at her mother, who in turn stared dumbfounded at the golden throne. For some reason, this appeared to amuse Hermes a great deal.

"Do you like it?" Zeus asked her earnestly, trying his best to conceal his own mirth.

"What... how... that's my throne..." Hera stammered. After a moment, she turned to Hermes and asked, "How did you find it!?"

"With a little help from my friend," Hermes replied, looking appreciatively at Hephaestus. "I admit that I spent the better part of the last year looking for this treasure, which you hid rather well. I almost despaired of never finding it, but Hephaestus said something about your being far too clever to actually hide your throne anywhere even half as secure as in plain sight, so I searched your garden shed on your yard at Borealis last Spring, while you were away tending to your mermaid friend in the North, and found it behind the patio furniture. Very ingenious thing you did, hiding under the big blue tarp with the snow removal equipment. The hardest part was getting the duct tape to come off..."

"The hardest part was to carry the damned thing," Herakles interjected. "You must have been truly pissed off when you grabbed it and carried it all the way to the Turtle Island by yourself all those years ago. That thing is heavy as shit!"

Hermes burst into laughter, while Ares and Eris helped Hephaestus to his feet.

"The bolts are secure," Hephaestus said. "No one should be able to move it, not even Herakles, unless he intends to rip off half the floor!"

Zeus drew closer to Hera and nudged her on the elbow. "Go sit on it," he told her.

"And if I do, will I be able to get up?" Hera asked sardonically, crossing her arms across her chest.

Nepheleid

Hephaestus gave Hera an amused look. "Mother," he told her, "I swear, by the Holy River Styx, that I have not booby-trapped your throne this time."

Hermes let out a giggle, which annoyed Hera even more. She pondered the object at Zeus' side for a moment, then glanced upon Hephaestus, who gave her a complicit look. Hera softened her gaze and took a step towards the golden throne. At last she pointed towards Hermes and said, "You, smart mouth, you go sit on the throne."

Hermes immediately stopped laughing and threw Hera an incredulous look. When he refused to move, Hera gave Herakles a silent command, prompting the demigod to lift Hermes off his feet and force him to sit on Hera's throne.

"See? There is no trap," Zeus told Hera after Hermes rose from the seat indignantly.

The Cloud-gatherer closed in on Hera, wrapping his arms around hers to push her gently towards her throne. Hera spun around, finding herself face to face with her estranged bridegroom, who in turn took this as a cue to embrace her before the gathered crowd. Junia saw the utmost look of alarm on her mother's face and took a sharp intake of breath. In the span of a mortal heartbeat, Hermes began gasping for air before the incredulous assembly. Zeus looked at his messenger with some measure of concern, yet he continued to hold Hera in his grasp.

As Hermes' complexion began to turn a delicate shade of purple, Athena stepped up and tried to help Hermes to his feet, to no avail. After a few moments Apollo walked towards Junia and lightly grabbed her by the shoulder. "Stop it," he told her gently. "You made your point."

When Junia distractedly turned her head to face the Lord of the golden bow, Hermes instantly regained the ability to breathe. In the confusion, Hera broke free of Zeus' embrace, and ran towards Junia to comfort her, flanked by Klymene, recently arrived into the throne room, and Demeter, who had remained close to Hera during the entire proceedings.

Junia glanced up at her father, who despite his expression of mild dismay was staring intently at a very beautiful blonde goddess that had evidently shielded herself from Hera's sight since their arrival on starry

Olympus. This must be Aphrodite, Junia thought, pondering why her mother's foe looked as though she had just experienced a breakthrough, to which only she and Zeus were privy.

"Daughter," Zeus said at last, his countenance inexplicably cheerful. "I want you to meet Aphrodite."

"Look away, Kitten. Look away and go with Mama. I will see you tonight before bedtime," Junia heard Hera say, before Klymene took her in her arms and ushered her away from the throne room.

Nepheleid

Chapter Fourteen

Cued by the glorious light of the Autumn Sunset, the blessed gods concluded the Feast celebrating their Queen's return to high Olympus and made their way to their dwellings to welcome the restful embrace of Night. Loud-thundering Zeus would soon do the same, however he first needed to see about a child. Most of all, he needed to see about the child's mother, who all but made a spectacle of avoiding him throughout the evening's festivities. Although Hera deigned to remain in the banquet hall until the revelry came to a close when the Sun listed towards the horizon, she quickly took her leave thereafter, under the pretext of putting her young daughter to bed.

This was, of course, pure fabrication, Zeus thought as he made his way to the luminous palace neighbouring his own, for Klymene, the child's nurse, had stayed behind with the girl in Hera's dwelling while the Queen graciously attended her homecoming banquet among the eminent Olympian Court. There was much work to be done to bring the child in line with the ways of Olympus, Zeus pondered, recalling his young daughter's eager participation in the Queen's theatrical display of resentment at being made to return to her King's side. The child's earlier tantrum, which almost caused Hermes to begin serving the penance reserved to those who break the sacred Oath of the Holy River Styx, indicated that she had not yet accepted her fate as a rightful scion of Olympus.

At least there was some hope for true reconciliation as far as her mother was concerned. It had taken no time at all for Zeus and golden Aphrodite to notice that Hera had not, in fact, instigated the child's eagerness at projecting her anger at her current circumstances upon Hermes, who had otherwise faithfully carried out his duty to his King. Surely a show of goodwill needed to be made before the child, if only to dispel any chance of reiterating what occurred in the throne room shortly after Hera arrived with her diminished retinue on holy Olympus. If the child was half as clever as her kin believed her to be, then she would undoubtedly see the error of her ways and show gratitude to her father for putting an end to her lifelong exile among the strange and alien gods of Turtle Island.

As for Hera, this would not be the first time the Cloud-gatherer found himself on the verge of renewing his union with his beloved wife after a long estrangement, although in the past she never withdrew from him for quite so long, no matter how angry their words, and how dastardly her offences against those she believed threatened her position as Queen of Olympus. For this reason alone, Zeus never thought that Prometheus, of all beings, would prove the instigator that jeopardized their love, which had so far endured for several thousand years. Though Hera's terms demanded that no harm come to Prometheus and his mortal and immortal coterie at CARINA and elsewhere upon and beyond the broad-pathed Earth, Zeus feared that the benefactor of humanity's very existence would continue to imperil the integrity of his union with white-armed Hera for as long as the Nephele remained aloft above the Heavens.

Fortunately for the King of Olympus, the Fates had granted him a few years' grace to win back his Queen's heart and their young daughter's unquestioning loyalty. The very thought filled him with the sort of sanguine optimism that he felt when he first set his mind to winning Hera's affections all those centuries ago, when he was the newly crowned Sky-King and she a powerful Maiden Queen in her own right, the heir to Gaia, the Earth-Mother, and fair-haired Rhea, the Mother of the gods. His heart lingered in joyful anticipation as he climbed the steps of Hera's palace, until he reached the threshold of the heavy doors, where the venerable Hestia greeted him warmly.

"I did not expect to see you here, Sister," the Father of gods and men told his elder congenially. "Is Hera hosting an exclusive after-party with her intimates?"

"She is comforting little Junia," Hestia answered. "The child had been in quite the bellicose mood all evening, and Klymene has not been able to calm her down completely."

"Does her disposition remain a threat to Hermes?" Zeus asked with some measure of apprehension. On the morrow he would have to remember to put an end to Ares and Eris' tutelage of the girl, lest she become yet another harbinger of War and Chaos among the blessed gods.

"I think not," Hestia replied. "That was one victory Klymene managed while Hera was at Banquet. Junia knows that Hermes was not to blame for their return to starry Olympus. I should think that he no longer needs to fear her on that account. Klymene also explained to her that dwelling among the gods is not a fate that warrants sorrow."

"That was kind and generous of Klymene," Zeus said. "I ought to commend her for this at once."

"She has retired to her bedchamber," Hestia replied. "Hera told her to get some rest while she spoke to their daughter."

"Now all that we have left to do is to convince her mother," Zeus muttered under his breath, trying not to sound annoyed at Hestia for reminding him, however innocuously, that Hera somehow convinced legions of mortals on Turtle Island that Klymene had been her lover and co-parent to the child that was rightfully his.

"And for that, I wish you the best of luck," Hestia said with the warmest of smiles, turning her gaze to the small bedchamber where Klymene and Hera had presumably put up the little girl, before taking her place by the hearth.

Zeus immediately recognized it as the room where Hera put up Hebe when she was a maiden, long before she wed the mighty Herakles and produced children of her own. The Father of gods and men thought this rather fitting, as he had every intention for the bedchamber's newest occupant to take her sister's place as Princess of Olympus and attend her mother and all the other gods whenever they would have need of her. As he drew near the half-closed door, the Cloud-gatherer noticed that not a sound could be heard from within.

Stepping inside, he saw Hera seated on the bed, still clad in the sumptuous garments she had worn during the Feast, and holding the sleeping child's head against her breast. Hera was surely fast asleep herself, for she did not stir when Zeus grabbed hold of a chair by the far side of the room and set it next to the bed. Zeus took his seat beside his wife and daughter, intending to let them rest until Hera would inevitably detect his presence and awaken, hopefully without rousing the child.

Hera's exile among the gods and mortals of Turtle Island had done nothing to dull her senses, as she awoke before Zeus shifted his weight completely onto his seat.

Nepheleid

"I am tucking my daughter in," Hera protested, looking rather peeved at Zeus' intrusion inside the child's bedchamber.

"Our daughter," Zeus corrected his wife casually. "And I can see that you cannot stay awake to see the task to completion."

"She is treading on unfamiliar ground," Hera replied, stifling a yawn. "She may well be the cleverest among us, but she is still a child... and she is a very light sleeper."

Zeus took Hera by the shoulders and pulled her ever so gently away from the slumbering girl. Hera sat up slowly, offering no resistance, though she still held on to her daughter's hand. Despite her mother and father's best efforts, the little girl woke at the commotion.

"Mom? What's going on?" she asked drowsily. She opened her eyes and froze when she saw her father sitting beside Hera.

Zeus could not tell whether the child was frightened or surprised to see him, or both. He stood up, pulling Hera slowly to her feet, then leaned over their daughter.

"I told you earlier that I would come see you before bedtime," he said softly. "In the meantime, I hope you have given some thought to whatever gift you would ask of me. So tell me, Daughter, is there something I can give you to make you feel more welcome in your new home?"

The little girl looked incredulously at Zeus, then said, "I want you to promise me. I want you to give me your word that you will never make me swear an Oath."

The Thunderer considered her words for a moment, then looked at Hera, who now stood right behind him. The Queen affected a deliberately impassive mien, however Zeus knew that she and the child had likely rehearsed this exchange sometime before they left the shores of Turtle Island.

"Hush now," he said softly, placing his hand on the little girl's forehead. "This has been a long day for us all, and your mother and I need to talk. Go back to sleep. Hestia will be in the other room if you get frightened. Won't you, dear sister?"

Hestia peeked through the open door. "I will," she answered with a smile and a nod, before resuming her place by the hearth.

The child was now wide awake. She gave her mother a look of alarm.

"It's all right, Kitten," Hera told her. She gave the little girl's a squeeze, then tucked it in under the covers. "I will be in the other palace, the big one next door. I will find you in the morning."

"But Mom..." the child muttered, before suddenly losing consciousness.

Hera gave Zeus an annoyed look. "You used a sleep charm on my daughter?" she asked him disapprovingly.

"Our daughter. And yes, I did. She needs to sleep soundly through the night," Zeus answered calmly as he released his hand from the little girl's forehead. As expected, the child resumed her peaceful sleep, and would not stir until sunrise at the very earliest.

"I have given your request some thought," Zeus told his wife as he rose from his seat. Hera turned her gaze from the little girl and looked up at the Cloud-gatherer, who gave her a benevolent smile when he glimpsed the creeping unease upon her countenance. "But I think, and I know you agree, that we ought to discuss such matters elsewhere," he added.

Hera did not move. Zeus looked at her longingly, and closed the distance between them, placing his hand on her lower back, then nudging her towards the door. To his surprise, she obliged, but stopped when they exited their daughter's bedchamber. Near the centre of the main hall, Hestia tended to the fire, feigning disinterest in her siblings' reunion.

"I know what you are thinking," Zeus said when Hera threw a hesitant glance at her sleeping child from the open door. "You are wondering if you can trust me, and if so, whether you can trust me as far as you can throw me, in the parlance of mortals."

Hera tilted her head incredulously but did not reply.

"If this is so," Zeus added with a half-smile, "then you need not worry, for we have both seen how far you can throw me from a high window when you find yourself on your own turf, even if the land upon which you tread is borrowed from those who dwell at the boundaries of the Earth."

Nepheleid

"That was not meant to become fodder for your own amusement," Hera said crossly, though keeping her voice low.

"What choice did you give me?" Zeus asked, placing his arms around her waist and gently nudging towards the side door that led to his own dwelling. "I came to offer you a truce, and –"

"And you went too far," Hera said flatly.

"Yet here we are," Zeus replied. "Our daughter is well cared for; you must not worry. Now, come, we have a lot to discuss."

Zeus took Hera by the hand, and this time she offered no resistance as they exited her palace. Once outside, the Thunderer lifted his bride off the ground and carried her over the threshold of his own dwelling and into the luxurious bath, yet he promptly put her back down on the polished marble floor when she instinctively pushed a knee against his chest.

"I kept my end of the agreement," she protested, finding her voice once their daughter was presumably out of earshot. "That was completely unnecessary!"

"That you did," Zeus answered with a smile, though he rubbed the place on his ribcage where Hera had pushed him. "And I will stay true to my word and keep my end of our agreement. But as for releasing you from your Oath..." Zeus placed his hands lightly on Hera's shoulders and let his words linger between them for a moment, in part to see if she would try to interrupt him.

She bristled at the unwelcome intimate touch but said nothing.

"I have come to a decision that should bring us both satisfaction," Zeus continued. Leaning closer to kiss her cheek, he whispered, "bathe in the pool, filled to the brim with the waters of the Kanathos spring, then join me in our marriage bed to bring the nuptial rite to completion. Once this is done, then shall I release you forever from the dreadful Oath you swore at the ramparts of Troy, all those centuries ago. This is not open to negotiation."

Hera gasped and tried to turn away from Zeus, but he caught her and spun her around and held her fast against his chest.

"That was *not* part of our agreement!" she said in a heated whisper.

"Calm yourself, I am only proposing an amiable truce," Zeus told her as he slid his hands onto her upper arms and pulled her tighter in his embrace. "I offer release from a hateful debt you created when you made that unrighteous bargain, in exchange for a bond sealed in love."

"You dare to speak to me of love!?" Hera said indignantly. "Now you are the one being unrighteous!"

"You are mistaken, my love," Zeus replied placidly. "I agreed to your terms because I was made to understand the importance of your work among the learned mortals who gaze at the stars. That is why I tolerate your continued involvement in their endeavour. But in agreeing to your terms, I have done you a great injustice. I allowed you to persist in your delusion that we are no longer bound by our sacred marriage, and that will not do." Zeus brushed a strand of hair away from Hera's face and tucked it behind her ear, as the goddess stood motionless, as if paralysed with rage and dread. "Your acquiescence to my request for your return was polluted by the toxicity of your anger when you left me," he continued. "You let that anger fester, and it left a stain on your heart that must be wiped clean with the ichor from your maidenhead."

Zeus grabbed Hera's wrist and kissed her fingers. Hera was too livid to blush, and too angry to speak. The Father of gods and men then kissed her in the middle of her forehead.

"Come now," he told her softly. "The Horai drew your bath in my palace while our young daughter fretted in yours. Surely you remember that pool I gifted you for our nuptials upon your return from your journey, all those years ago before all this ugly business with Prometheus began? I found it to be a fitting place to end our enmity. I will attend you as you bathe and restore your maidenhead, then relieve you of it. That is what I ask of you if you desire release from that ugly Oath. That, and one more thing. You must sleep in my arms tonight, and every other night thence, as well as whenever you find yourself on holy Olympus, as we have always done. This will never change."

Zeus spun Hera around to face the bathing pool, which lay once a few paces from where they stood. To his delight, the waters had the same luminous glow as they did on that night eleven years before, when Zeus found Hera on the mountaintop overlooking CARINA Borealis as she concluded her annual journey at the boundaries of the broad-pathed Earth.

Nepheleid

"You cannot be serious!" Hera said as she glimpsed towards the bath. "You truly expect me to bathe in… that? Why?"

Zeus gave Hera a solemn look. "To renew – "

"I hope you did not expect me to wed you again after all that's happened!" Hera interrupted him. "I returned to Olympus as per your request, which was actually more of a threat, but this is overreaching!"

"You've shown no reluctance in bathing in the innumerable rivers of Turtle Island during your exile, or so Aphrodite told me," Zeus replied calmly, barely concealing his growing irritation. "You never were afraid of water, or of anything else for that matter. Why are you now acting like a cat about to be dunked in a pond? This is a splendid pool with the purest waters of the Earth – "

"It's a virginity bath," Hera said crossly. "Let's not mince words. You want me purified for some reason-"

"I want your maidenhead restored for our wedding night, as is our custom," Zeus interrupted in turn. "There is nothing strange in this, save for taking your bath in the comfort of my palace, here on starry Olympus, instead of faraway Nauplia. And if memory serves me right, this was your custom long before we wed." He slid his hands on her hips and gently pushed towards the bath. "Get in the pool," he said, almost with a purr.

Hera pondered his words for a moment. "It's true, I used to take my Maiden bath every Spring at the confluence of rivers," she said as if thinking aloud. "But it's not as though the bounty of the Earth actually depended on you making me bleed in our royal marriage bed once a year!"

"Perhaps not," Zeus replied, sliding a hand onto Hera's back to loosen the girdle holding her dress in place, then realizing that she had kept her flight suit under her queenly raiment all evening. "But it is our custom," he continued, ignoring this rather off-putting discovery. "It is a custom for which I have developed a great affection, which is why I ask this of you, as a show of goodwill to put all this ugly business behind us. Get in the pool."

Hera spun around to face the Thunderer. "You go first," she said in the most deadpan manner.

Zeus raised an eyebrow. "I think we've been through this before," he said, amused. "You would find me rather disappointing as a virgin, as most women find inexperienced males, I suppose. But the same is not true with blossoming maidens, and I know from experience that is especially not so with *you*. So, if you please, get in the pool."

"After you," Hera replied without a hint of humour.

"Must I repeat what I said earlier?" Zeus asked, struggling to stifle his laughter at the absurdity of Hera's request. "My prowess in bed took many centuries to perfect. You will be glad of it by morning. Now get in the pool."

"You first."

"No, I insist. This is for you alone," Zeus said as he began to lift Hera off her feet once more.

To his surprise, Hera used his lifting motion to her advantage, leaping onto his back, and wrapping her arms and legs around his chest. Zeus almost fell backwards, but regained his balance quickly, while Hera ceased moving as soon as she was confidently stable astride her would-be bridegroom.

"Is this a new courtship custom you learned on Turtle Island?" Zeus asked incredulously. "Perhaps you do need a virginity bath, if you thought our union no longer held while you were gone all these years. At least this time, you refrained from telling everyone I was dead, like you did back when you withdrew from me and hid on the Island of Euboea, until you revealed yourself when you fell into my trap and pounced on a wooden dummy I had attired as my new bride." He tried to tug Hera's hands apart, but she held fast as if holding on to dear life. "You are worse than a child, you know."

"Am I?" Hera replied. "Even if I had brought others to my bed while I dwelt on Turtle Island, I think we both know you are far more in need of a purification bath than I."

"Get off me and get in the pool!"

"I will, but only after you do. I promise I will climb off your back and bathe in the waters of the Kanathos Spring once you're in the pool yourself. Or better yet, you can sit at the bottom and I will swim off.

Then we'll know you have truly been cleansed, as you will have submerged yourself completely."

Zeus heaved a weary sigh and without warning dropped to the floor, rolling on his back to dislodge his bride from her improvised perch. To his dismay, Hera anticipated his manoeuvre, and leaped off him before he hit the floor, then pounced onto his chest as would a house cat demanding breakfast from its slumbering keeper.

Zeus looked up at Hera and smiled. "I've missed you," he said softly.

Hera gave him a cold stare.

"Must I worry about finding Hermes without breath when the Sun rises?" Zeus asked.

"That depends on you," Hera answered flatly. "Is it safe for me to get up without being tossed in the pool, or any other insanity you've devised while I left you alone to think on all that you've done?"

"You have nothing to fear, I promise," Zeus answered.

"Good," Hera said as she rose to her feet. "Speaking of promises, Junia asked you for something today, and you knocked her unconscious without answering. That will not endear you to her in the slightest, I'll have you know."

"She is only a child," Zeus replied, reclining to face Hera, who had begun to walk away from the bath. "I would never compel a child to swear any Oaths until she is of age. When she decides to stay on starry Olympus with us and the rest of our blessed kin, then, of course, I will have her swear the Oath of fealty that you swore to earn my forgiveness, after your failed attempt to depose me."

"What makes you think she will choose Olympus over her glorious destiny on the Nephele?" Hera asked haughtily.

"The same reason that will compel you to stay as well," Zeus answered, rising slowly to his feet. "Love."

Hera scoffed. "I think you might have hit your head just there, and knocked Metis unconscious," she said sardonically.

"But will you stay the night?" Zeus asked hopefully, taking slow, measured steps towards Hera. "I see you are not ready to renew our marriage. The pool will remain here until you are willing to seriously consider my generous offer. But until then, please. I've missed you dreadfully."

Hera gasped. For a fleeting moment, she looked at Zeus as if at an old friend.

"Metis…" she whispered almost inaudibly.

Zeus smiled, and gestured for Hera to accompany him to the front hall of the royal palace.

Nepheleid

Chapter Fifteen

The early Autumn Dawn gently stirred white-armed Hera from her peaceful slumber, caressing the Queen's heavy lids with its pale light as she came to full wakefulness. Divested of her many layers of clothing, Hera opened a wary eye and felt a momentary twinge of panic upon finding herself enfolded in her saviour's arms. It took her a moment to remember that it was not Zeus but wise Metis who lured her into the royal bedchamber the previous night, when sleep began to overtake the Queen's weary limbs. Hera grinned, knowing full well that it would take Zeus far longer to realize that his first wife had assumed complete command of his mind and flesh the previous night, after his own efforts to take Hera to his bed ended in spectacular failure.

Hera rose slowly, careful not to rouse the King of Olympus, lest his keen senses detect her proximity and her nakedness and react accordingly as was his custom, even before regaining full consciousness. Perhaps it was just as well that he ought to wake up alone, Hera thought, for she had no intention to indulge him this morning. Nor did she feel inclined to arouse his pique by admitting at long last that for all the years of their long marriage, Metis had been the only part of him she had truly loved, the only saving grace residing deep within an otherwise uncaring and self-indulgent tyrant. In Hera's estimation, Metis alone was responsible for Zeus' success in rescuing her and her siblings from Kronos' belly, for without the Oceanid's aid, Zeus would have surely joined his brothers and sisters in their prison. Hera remembered Metis as kind, loyal, and peerless in her cleverness, and often saw echoes of Metis' cunning and benevolence whenever she gazed upon grey-eyed Athena, though she often pitied the Virgin Warrior for her unabashed confidence in her father's competence as supreme ruler of Olympus.

Before Metis was swallowed herself by the Cloud-gatherer days before Athena's birth, Zeus' character had been much like that of their son Ares, though he somehow found a way to temper his heedlessness and brazen conceit with his considerable charm. However, the spell Zeus cast over

Nepheleid

Hera's heart in the days and years following her rescue broke the moment she learned of the fate that befell Metis, prompting the Maiden Queen to seek her lovers and Consorts in remote lands for untold centuries, far from Zeus' lascivious gaze. Had Hera also known that Zeus murdered her long-forgotten husband Eurymedon and gave her newborn son away to another, and subsequently removed all her memories of his evil deeds, she would never have agreed to become his bride, even after he ravished her and shamed her into granting him that which he desired most. She would have forever forsaken Olympus, as well as her native Hellas, and made her home beyond the farthest boundaries of the broad-pathed Earth where Okeanos and Tethys dwell, to never again cross paths with the Thunderer, despite knowing that whatever remained of wise Metis yet lived within the confines of her dastardly brother's mind.

Even so, Hera found it difficult to believe that Zeus alone devised the stratagem of leveraging the Oath she swore to him at the ramparts of Troy in exchange for her return to Olympus. At the time, Hera determined that agreeing to let Zeus destroy a city dear to her heart in exchange for the annihilation of Troy would so outrage him that he would never speak of it again. As expected, Zeus kept his peace for over three millennia, until his desperation compelled him to call in an Oath he had otherwise deemed too odious to consider in the past. Hera took one last look at Zeus' slumbering form before she slowly stood up from the bed and gathered her discarded clothing strewn across the floor. She then exited the palace silently, thinking it best to let Zeus and Metis believe they prevailed in the never-ending battle of wits between the King and Queen of Olympus. She had known that spending the night in Zeus' bed would prove risky, however her bold move allowed her to obliterate all doubt from her mind concerning Metis' culpability in her current predicament. In the span of a few short years, none of this would matter, for Hera who would finally get her due and become a Maiden Queen once more, restored in her proper role as protectress of untold generations of learned mortals yet to come, their worthy ancestors soon to set out to spread Life across the Cosmos.

Hera quietly made her way across the shared garden between Zeus' palace and her own, careful not to appear too conspicuous should Junia happen to rise early and gaze upon the grounds beyond her bedroom window. As expected, Hera found Klymene waiting for her by the side door of her palace, a lovely silken robe delicately folded in her arms.

"My lady," Klymene addressed her in a soft voice, barely above a whisper.

Hera did not reply, for she already knew from Klymene's demeanour that Junia still slumbered under Zeus' sleep charm from the previous night.

"I was unsure when you'd return," Klymene continued. "But I drew you a bath nonetheless. Here, take this robe. I will take your clothes."

"Thank you, my dear," Hera said. "I think I will need to marinate in the bath for a while."

"Dare I ask?" Klymene inquired timidly, failing to stifle her grin.

"Your sister sends her regards," Hera replied, to which Klymene's smile broadened. "You needn't bother with changing the bed sheets, though. No ichor was spilled last night… none from me anyway. There might have been some from where Zeus likely hit his head when I pinned him to the bathroom floor, but I did not see any. No matter. Let Ganymede deal with it. The boy will know how to pacify Zeus, of that I am quite certain."

"Perhaps I should go," Klymene said," if only for the sake of appearances."

"Perhaps you're right," Hera answered. "Here, give me the robe. I will take my bath shortly and then take care of Junia's breakfast, but there is something I must do first. I've arranged to have Eris come by in an hour to set up Junia's remote classroom conference hologram, or whatever it is mortals call it. Junia's missed enough school as it is, with all this nonsense of relocating to Olympus. I will not have her fall behind the rest of the class."

"Very well, my lady," Klymene replied before taking the bundle of Hera's discarded clothes inside the Queen's palace.

Hera donned the silken robe. The garment felt light and cool against her skin, a welcome change from the heavy fabric of the flight suit she had worn the previous day under her royal attire. She walked toward her private garden at the back of her palace, where a grove of ancient trees lined up against the horizon like a palisade safeguarding Olympus against the void beyond the edge of the world. Hera smiled, knowing full well that the ravine beyond her garden was an illusion concealing a gateway towards the Heavenly vaults of faraway worlds. Wily Kronos had told her this once, when her brothers and sisters were fast asleep in the confines of his belly, but she remained awake, listening to his thoughts, and gazing upon the Cosmos through his eyes. Kronos told her that his siblings Okeanos and Tethys, the original denizens of Olympus, had opened this doorway in the vast expanses beyond the summit where her palace stood, but hid it when Kronos and Rhea claimed Olympus for themselves and banished their elders to the boundaries of the broad-pathed Earth. To Hera's knowledge, no one ever found the doorway since, nor had she given it much thought, believing it a fanciful tale her father told her to ease his guilt from his ill-treatment of his children.

The goddess made her way to a small rise at the centre of the garden, where a massive willow, the largest among the ancient trees in the goddess' garden, held court. Hera planted this willow many centuries ago in memory of the sacred tree under which she was born on the Island of Samos, before Rhea surrendered her to Kronos to be devoured. Hera sat at the base of the willow between the upraised roots crisscrossing its trunk in serpentine patterns, reaching all the way to a small stream that flowed toward the garden she shared with the Cloud-gatherer. How strange that Zeus had not ordered Hephaestus to build his palace on this side of the summit and told him instead to build the Queen's dwelling beside his own in this beautiful place. Perhaps this was Zeus' fanciful way of making amends for being such a terrible husband and an even worse father to her children, Hera mused. For a fleeting moment, she became keenly aware that she would forever leave this place after she departed for her final flight to the Nephele with Klymene and Junia a few years thence. Shaking off her creeping melancholia, Hera resolved to undergo a final journey among her primordial forebears to bid farewell to the ancient powers of the Earth who had been her allies before her embattled reign as Queen of Olympus. This would be far more difficult than abandoning this hallowed corner of the world, which had remained her home even at the worst of times.

As her mind lingered on such thoughts, the goddess straightened her spine, and aligned her back along the length of the willow's trunk. She took a deep breath and released all the restless vigor awakened in her belly after spending so many hours in the arms of loud-thundering Zeus the previous night. At the end of her exhale, Hera felt a slight tremor beneath her golden-sandaled feet. The Queen smiled, knowing that her release jolted Gaia herself, at a time when the Northernmost lands of the broad-pathed Earth prepared for their long yearly slumber.

Hera took another, deeper, calming breath, this time mindfully focusing her thoughts on the task that lay ahead. For the next few years, she would have to feign surrender and beatitude, and even occasionally share the bed of her hated Consort and King for the sake of maintaining their tenuous peace, all the while shielding young Junia from the cesspool Olympus had become since Zeus declared himself the supreme ruler among the gods after Hera's insurrection failed aeons ago. Their presence on starry Olympus constituted a temporary setback, an inconvenience to be endured in the pursuit of a far grander destiny than that which the Fates had ever granted the favoured daughter of wily Kronos and fair-haired Rhea. Yet Hera had suffered far worse affronts at the hands of the Thunderer in the years leading up to the Trojan War, when the state of their marriage reached its nadir, and Zeus' treatment of his Queen devolved into outright malevolence. At the time Hera found herself forced to share Zeus' bed to avoid facing his formidable wrath, fuelled in part by his humiliation at Thetis' repeated refusals to replace her foster-mother as Queen of Olympus. Though she reluctantly yielded to Zeus' summons, Hera experienced the full brunt of his abuse nonetheless, until she laid waste to Troy to show him where her rage would lead when pushed to the brink.

Another, stronger tremor jolted Hera from her grim reminiscence. Though the sacking of Troy at the hands of her beloved Aegean warriors was far from her proudest moment, she could never allow herself to show any iota of remorse, for doing so could easily be construed as a sign of weakness. Troy had to burn, lest Hera become consumed with rage and devour the Earth, and all its creatures, whole. Such had been the sombre and storied legacy of her marriage to the King of Olympus. At least Hera succeeded in shielding her youngest daughter from this inanity long enough for Junia to mature past the age of reason and become far wiser than a child of almost ten years ought to be. Hera deeply regretted bringing Junia to Olympus, however she knew that their stay in this accursed place would remove any doubt from her daughter's mind about whether to join the crew of learned mortals aboard the Nephele once she came of age. So far Junia proved the brightest among her children, cleverer than even Prometheus and Hephaestus, Hera's stalwart sons and true heirs in courage, ingenuity, and grit. Surely Junia would not fail to notice how things stood on starry Olympus, and wisely vow to leave the Earth with her eldest brother and his learned mortals to spread Life among the wanderers of distant stars as soon as she could.

And once Junia made her choice known, Hera would forever leave the Earth and join her children in their worthy endeavour.

The Earth trembled for a third time, prompting Hera to rise to her feet to face the willow. I must bid a proper farewell to Gaia, she told herself. I must pay my respects to the Earth-Mother in the confines of the Garden of the Hesperides, long hidden from the view of her immortal kin, before the ground opens and swallows Olympus whole, and with it some of the blessed gods Hera still loved. Hera smiled, remembering the time when august Themis hosted a gathering in her garden upon her return to Olympus after her yearly journey circling the Earth, at the time appointed by the Seasons. This was the day after Hera's fateful encounter with Prometheus on the promontory overlooking the CARINA Borealis campus, when the last cargo rocket bound for the Nephele's sister-ship Corona took to the Heavens for the very last time. Hera remembered telling the goddesses gathered in Themis' garden that should she ever decide to leave Olympus to never return, she would surely take them all with her, if they so desired. Perhaps Hera ought to remind her allies of this promise and take them with her aboard her mighty ship bound for the stars, before Gaia inevitably took her revenge against Zeus for his countless offences against her and the ancient powers of the Earth.

Hera took another, deeper, calming breath. She still had a few years to dwell on such matters before the time came for her to eat her heart and bid farewell to the Earth-Mother and those among her kin who would choose to remain on Olympus instead of undertaking the long voyage to the stars on the Nephele. Until then, she needed to focus her mind on the task at hand. Once all her labours came to fruition, she could take the time to grieve all that she stood to lose.

Hera lingered in silence before the ancient willow for a few moments, resolute in her purpose, until her senses detected a familiar presence walking a few paces behind where she stood.

"Mother?"

The voice was soft and feminine, disconcerting in its familiarity, and conveyed disquiet and desperation in equal measure. Hera knew that the voice did not belong to Hebe, Eileithya, Junia, or Eris, or to any other child her womb had ever borne. She turned around to answer her visitor's greeting, steeling herself for the madness that the next few hours would bring.

"Thetis," Hera said at last to her foster-daughter. "What a strange time for you to have come."

Nepheleid

Chapter Sixteen

Junia awoke to the sound of spirited chatter in the hall beyond the private quarters of Hera's palace on high Olympus. Her senses muddled by the preternatural sleep charm her father had bequeathed her the previous night, the child lingered in bed for a moment, until she realized that her arrival in this strange place was not, in fact, a chimerical deception concocted by her own imagination. As the outrageousness of her predicament dawned upon her consciousness, that she would dwell among her own kind for the foreseeable future, she remembered that some of her siblings would doubtlessly remain her allies in this place, which until yesterday she had known from her mothers' tales as one of both boundless wonder and unfathomable treachery.

Sliding off the bed slowly, still unused to seeing her feet float above the ground like the other blessed gods who make their homes on starry Olympus, Junia instinctively reached for the pile of folded clothes Klymene usually laid out for her every morning. To her surprise, her garments consisted of several sheets of diaphanous fabric, which she recognized from her lessons as chitons, worn by the mortals of Hellas in aeons long gone by. Unskilled at garbing herself with such strange vestments, Junia wrapped the layers of fabric around her small form like so many blankets, tying whatever loose ends she could find over her shoulders in awkward knots. Satisfied with her efforts, she stepped out of her bedroom and followed the sound of the voices of those who had gathered in the Olympian abode of their Queen.

As soon as she reached the hallway, Junia caught a glimpse of Klymene attending Hera at her bath through an open door adjacent to the master bedroom, hidden from the sight of the others in the front hall. Both her mothers had their backs to the door, and though she could not quite tell for certain, it seemed to Junia that Klymene was holding a vessel to Hera's torso. Junia took a step towards the open door, and before she even reached the threshold, she heard Hera call out to her in a bemused voice.

"Come inside, Kitten," Hera said. "Before I take my bath."

Nepheleid

At that moment, all the voices in the palace became silent. Junia obeyed, closing the door behind her. The din of voices resumed shortly thereafter.

"Don't mind them," Klymene told her gently, putting the vessel she had been holding on the tiled floor by the warm, fragrant bath. "I've told our guests that their Queen is at her bath. They will wait for as long as they need to. What are you wearing!?"

Hera stifled a laugh.

"I did not put these robes by her bedside," Klymene continued, almost in protest.

"It must have been the Horai," Hera replied. "I suppose Zeus gave the order that his new little Princess ought to dress the part."

"Oh, come here, and I will fix your dresses," Klymene told Junia. "This is far less complicated than it looks. It might take some getting used to –"

"No, let her wear her own clothing," Hera declared in a strong, confident voice that could have carried to the farthest reaches of the Cosmos, which Junia believed possible in this place that defied all the laws of nature known to mortals. Somehow, Junia also knew that Hera was not addressing Klymene.

"My daughter can wear Olympian robes when she is not seated before a camera broadcasting her likeness in a classroom on the Nephele," Hera continued. "During school hours, she will dress as mortals do. I expect that my daughter's clothing that was packed away and put into crates on Turtle Island will be returned to her at once!" To Junia, she said, "In a few moments, you can go get changed in your room. But first, you must have some breakfast. Klymene, darling, could you take care of that? I need some time alone."

"At once, my lady," Klymene answered, picking up the vessel from the floor. "Come now," she told Junia, nudging her by the elbow as she carried the vessel with both hands and exited through the open door.

"Please close the door behind you, Kitten," Hera said. "Mommy needs her quiet time."

"What were you doing in there just now?" Junia asked innocently as she followed Klymene down the corridor towards a hallway that circumvented the front hall entirely.

"Grown-up things," Klymene answered. "Nothing you need to concern yourself with. You have a big day ahead of you. First day of classes -"

"And I am starting three weeks late," Junia lamented.

"Through no fault of your own," Klymene replied. "Auntie Mnem knows what happened. No one will give you grief for starting late, or for attending classes remotely, for that matter. Besides, you are not the only one currently taking lessons at a distance. Other pupils remained on Earth while their parents continue their work on the various CARINA campuses across the world."

"Right," Junia said. "But we are not exactly on Earth, are we?"

Klymene halted a few paces from the entrance of a large, open room facing a vast garden. Junia figured this must be what passes for a kitchen on Olympus, where no one truly needs to eat, or sleep, or poop for that matter, to keep themselves alive.

"You know what," Klymene said, in a tone that suggested she was not asking a question. "I think I hear the crates with your belongings being moved back into your bedroom. Why don't you go get changed, and meet me here afterwards? Demeter has not yet returned from picking the veggies and berries in the garden for your breakfast shake. It shouldn't be long, though. Go on."

Junia took the hint, and retraced her steps back to her bedroom, careful not to let her thoughts linger on the closed door behind which she imagined Hera hard at work scrubbing away the cooties from having spent the night with Zeus. Junia knew that Klymene, Demeter, Hestia, and the other adults would try to shield her from her parents' nocturnal activities, but she already knew that her father's visit last night had nothing to do with tucking her into bed. The previous afternoon, Klymene tried to explain to Junia that they moved to Olympus for a few years because Zeus and Hera needed a lot of time to work out their differences before finalizing their divorce, however Junia had long figured out that Zeus meant for Hera to abandon Prometheus, CARINA, and the Nephele, and get back together with him forever. Junia also knew that Hera would never willingly return to Zeus and was likely placating him with hate-sex until Junia was old enough to leave Olympus and join her eldest brother and classmates on the Nephele. But still, the thought of her mother kissing Zeus, and worse, filled Junia with a particular species of trepidation she had never experienced before in her short life. Hera must be really brave, she thought as she entered her bedroom and closed the door to change into her school clothes.

Once attired in the fashion of mortal children, Junia made her way back to the room by the garden, where she found her morning meal in a large lidded cup on a low table. Klymene was nowhere in sight, likely gone to the front hall to attend to Hera's visitors. Junia stuck a metal straw in the opening of the lid, grabbed the cup, and joined the small gathering of deities arguing loudly at the front of Hera's palace. There she found Eris seated in a corner, hard at work testing the connection between a small, lightweight computer to the Nephele. This was no small feat, Junia thought, for she knew of no satellite linking starry Olympus to any space station circling the Earth in low orbit. Junia walked towards Eris and sat beside her, then smiled when she saw the CARINA logo on the screen mounted at eye level on the wall. She made a mental note to inform Derek that Eris did, in fact, rule over Chaos and quantum mechanics, whose principles lay behind the ascent of even the most primitive, twentieth-century computing technology.

"The Golden Apple is online," Eris said in a low voice, returning Junia's smile. "Though the Nephele is still on standby."

"That's because class has not started yet," Junia replied. "We're early. School should start in about ten minutes. Why is everyone arguing?"

"Do I look like a subject matter expert on interpersonal conflict to you?" Eris asked with a sardonic smile.

Junia nodded emphatically as she sipped her morning meal through the thick straw.

"All right then", Eris answered with an amused grin. "That one," she said, pointing a finger towards august Themis, whom Junia met upon her return from Polaris when the school year ended, "that one, you will recall, is Father's herald and emissary, though not quite like Hermes. She came here this morning to gauge whether Mother and Father reconciled and renewed their union, as per their custom."

"So she wants to know if they had sex," Junia inquired casually.

"Pretty much," Eris replied, unfazed by her younger sister's words. "Aunt Demeter, who brings forth gifts, is politely telling her to fuck off and leave Hera alone for the moment, though of course not in so many words. Klymene came to tell them both that there is nothing yet to tell, but since Mother is still at her bath, even I have my doubts on the matter. Those three, Eunomia, Dike, and Eirene, they are the Horai, the Seasons, and handmaidens to Mother when she dwells on Olympus. They are here to tend to Mother whenever she has need of them. They don't really say much, which is a pity, for I am certain they have many interesting tales to tell."

"They're the ones who stole and returned my clothes," Junia said, putting down her empty cup by a low table. In the span of a mortal heartbeat, the cup disappeared, as did one of the Horai. Junia made a mental note to learn the names of Hera's many handmaidens, grateful that none among them were named Thalia – a name already shared by one Muse and one of the Charites, handmaidens to 'that wench' Aphrodite.

"Presumably," Eris answered with a wink. "But yes. They tried to replace your clothes."

"What about that one?" Junia inquired, nodding towards a lovely stranger warming herself by the hearth.

"That one," Eris said, "is Thetis, daughter of Nereus. A long time ago, long before Ares and I were born, Mother raised Thetis like one of her own children, and Father, he lusted after her as if she were... well, you know the story."

"Oh," Junia said, deducing that this innocent-looking goddess was indeed the cause behind the animated chatter.

"You haven't met Thetis yet, have you?" Eris inquired.

"No, but I've heard all about her," Junia answered.

"So you can understand why her presence here is making everyone... nervous," Eris added.

"But why?" Junia asked. "Most of what happened between her and Mom and Zeus was, like, literally thousands of years ago! Besides, she rescued Hephaestus after he fell both times from Olympus, at his birth and that time he tried to help Mom when Zeus chained her to the Sky."

"She's also responsible for stopping Mother from becoming the sole sovereign of Olympus, when she went to get the creature Briareus from the Gates of Tartarus to help free Zeus from his bonds that day," Eris said.

"She didn't know Zeus would react the way he did, otherwise she might not have done it," Junia replied.

"No, little one," Thetis said casually from across the room, prompting all gathered to halt their animated chatter at once. "I would do the same thing again, because at the time it looked as though Olympus was on the verge of turning into a battlefield. I deeply regretted that Zeus almost repudiated Hera afterwards and tried to make me his bride, however you must remember that by refusing Zeus' repeated marriage proposals, I ensured that Hera maintained her position as Queen of Olympus in the end."

"That's a fair point, Demeter told Thetis. "Yet if Prometheus had not told Zeus about the prophecy that you would one day bear a son destined to surpass his father in might and deeds, he would never have relented his advances. Just ask my sister."

"And Olympus did turn into a battlefield, didn't it?" Junia said. "I mean, after Zeus made you marry a mortal, and Eris wasn't invited to your wedding, and she threw a golden apple and watched the world burn for ten years."

"Once again, I never meant for any of that to happen, child," Thetis told Junia, half-amused at the little girl's gumption. "Besides, the whole world knows the story. There is nothing new to tell on the matter."

"Iris told me once that Zeus gave you her twin sister Arke's wings as a wedding gift," Junia added, then paused to gauge Thetis' reaction. "Arke lost her wings when Zeus threw her in the pit of Tartarus, because she took the side of the Titans in the War. I met her once, a year ago. She's kind of crabby, but given her circumstances, I don't really blame her. Anyway, you gave the wings to your son, Achilles, the greatest warrior to fight on the side of the Greeks during the Trojan War."

"That is true," Thetis replied. "Not many mortals know this. But are you mortal as they say, for having been born after the Deluge? I can scarce believe it. You are like a small, copper-haired twin to Hera. I cannot fathom anyone bearing her likeness as capable of tasting death."

"Nephele was mortal," Junia answered. "And she was Mom's mirror-twin, fashioned from a cloud. I was *not* fashioned out of clouds."

"From the tales I've heard told of your birth, you might as well be," Thetis replied.

"No one knows for certain," Klymene interjected, visibly annoyed at the turn the conversation had taken. "Nor does any of this matter at the moment; Hera decreed that Junia will choose whether to embrace immortality when she comes of age, and that is the end of it. But right now, Junia, you are late for class. The lesson has already begun As for the rest of you, unless you seek an audience with Hera after her bath, I suggest you return later, after Junia has finished her lessons for the day. Thetis, I strongly urge you to wait until the evening banquet to discuss –"

"Klymene, if I may," Thetis interrupted.

Junia did not catch the rest of Thetis' statement, for Klymene placed the headphones upon her head and turned on the volume loud enough to drown out any conversation beyond the monotone of the teacher's voice across the vast expanse separating starry Olympus from the Nephele in low Earth orbit.

Eris looked at Junia and smiled, shaking her head slightly.

"Tell me later," Junia mouthed to Eris, before the sensor caught her words on camera.

"What was that, Junia?" the teacher asked on-screen.

"Oh, uh, nothing. Just signing in, sorry," Junia stammered into the microphone embedded onto her headgear.

"That's all right," the teacher said. "But do try to be on time. You are not our only remote student, you know."

Junia nodded and noticed the likeness of two of her classmates in-set on-screen, their countenances set apart from the rest of the students assembled in one of the Nephele's boardrooms. On the upper-left corner sat Junia's long-time classmate, Jennifer Cohen-Tugaalik, whose parents elected to remain at Polaris. To Junia's surprise, on the lower-left corner she saw Derek's perennial companion, Paul Red Buffalo, who had remained at Junior Space Camp almost as long as Junia did, until his Anishinaabe mother decided to stay indefinitely near the town of Borealis as their people reclaimed the grounds of the now decommissioned CARINA Headquarters. Though their parents had since left the employ of Prometheus' space-faring venture, Jennifer and Paul, like Junia, were granted the option to join the crew of the Nephele upon graduation, which was why they remained enrolled in the school for spacefaring students from the comfort of terra firma.

After a few minutes, Junia realized that she had already studied the contents of today's lesson in the latter weeks of her prolonged stay at Junior Space Camp, when she found herself alone among the camp counsellors who had to come up with new ways to entertain their bright, precocious charge. Junia smiled, knowing that her mothers would be pleased to learn that she had not fallen behind the rest of her class after all.

Despite Klymene's less than subtle intimation at Hera's guests that they ought to leave, Themis, Demeter, and Thetis lingered in the front hall, while Eris remained by Junia's side, under the pretext that she ought to be near in case the connection to the Nephele terminated abruptly. Junia discreetly muted her headgear and gave Eris a complicit smile. It was now obvious to Junia that Eris meant to eavesdrop on the goddesses gathered in Hera's palace, and that Eris also knew that Junia shared her intent.

"You are wasting your time," Junia heard Klymene tell Thetis. "You can wait for Hera to finish her bath, but I know exactly what she will tell you. She will refer you and your King to the many CARINA satellite locations dedicated to restoring the Oceans, and to the networks of coastal sanctuaries, kelp farms, and the like as loci of marine resurgence. Restoring Life in the Oceans is an achingly slow process, but it is ongoing,"

"You know I cannot tell Poseidon such things," Thetis protested. "He is wary of mortals, even more so than loud-thundering Zeus! He can scarce understand Hera's faith in those whose ancestors imperilled his Kingdom, and only two centuries ago brought it almost to the brink!"

"Very well," Klymene replied. "If you insist on acting as ambassador to King Poseidon on high Olympus, then so be it. We will prepare a room for you in this palace, but since we arrived only yesterday, and are still retrieving and unpacking some formerly missing luggage, you might need to share a room with young Junia until your own quarters are ready."

Junia did not react, for she knew that Klymene was probing whether she was following her lesson. Besides, if Hera ever found herself lacking the rooms to accommodate a large number of guests within her palace on Olympus, she would probably open a rift in the space-time continuum and house the entire crew of the Nephele in her living quarters if she wished it so.

"Thank you, Klymene," Thetis replied calmly. "But if I may, I will stay in my old bedchamber, the one across the hall from Hebe's, when she was still a maiden. I would have settled in sooner, but someone stacked a pile of luggage crates up to the ceiling, and I did not quite know what to make of that."

"Do what you will," Klymene sighed. "In the meantime, I must see about our Queen. I will find you when she is ready to see you all in turn. Ladies." Klymene bowed courteously and took her leave without a second glance at Junia and Eris, who did their best to stifle their mirth in the corner of the wide front hall. Thetis rose to her feet moments later, presumably to settle into her newly vacant bedchamber.

Once both were well out of earshot, Junia looked at Eris, who squatted beside her, careful not let her likeness get caught by the small camera embedded in the screen monitor. Eris gestured at Junia to look at the camera for a few seconds, then punched some keys. Satisfied that the machine executed her command, Eris tapped Junia on the shoulder, and pantomimed for the child to remove her headgear completely.

"How long until teacher notices you are on a loop?" Demeter asked Junia, amused at her nieces' coordinated tomfoolery.

"Who knows?" Junia replied, holding back her grin.

"As long as her image moves ever so slightly in the corner of the monitor on the Nephele," Eris answered, "no one will be the wiser. I've programmed the loop to be completely random and slowed the five-second footage at a third of the speed."

"So I'll look like I'm swaying very slowly instead of fidgeting," Junia said.

"How ingenious," Demeter replied, almost laughing.

Themis raised an eyebrow. "It's a wonder Zeus never acknowledges your cleverness," she told Eris. "I bet he would, if only you used your genius for less mischievous purposes, instead of corrupting your young, impressionable sister."

Nepheleid

"What would be the fun in that?" Eris asked innocuously.

Themis shook her head.

"I already learned the material in today's lesson," Junia explained.

"What if teacher asks you a question?" Themis asked in a grave tone.

"She won't," Junia said. "Teachers at the CARINA-Borealis school have avoided asking me questions since I first started attending. Because when they do, I start answering in excruciating detail. Auntie Mnem has since told all her staff not to probe me, ever, unless they want answers in dissertation format. So, I'm good!"

"It's a downright conspiracy!" Demeter exclaimed, laughing riotously while Eris grinned from ear to ear. "And to think," she added, "most of the pupils there are already highly adept. I've taught a lesson or two at that school, while I was in their midst."

"Very well," Themis said, resignedly. "Zeus does not need to know you are neglecting your school work. He would be much displeased, since your attendance at the school among the children of the Nephele was a point of contention during the negotiations for your return to Olympus. If he had his way, the Muses would have been your tutors, but Hera would have none of it. So I will advise you to keep your truancy to a minimum."

"Okay," Junia replied, biting her lip. "Aunt Themis, can I ask you a question?"

"Of course, child," Themis said, surprised at the sudden inquiry.

"Why is Thetis supplicating my Mom? I mean, if she's here on official business as ambassador to Poseidon, then shouldn't she be talking to Zeus? Or you?"

"Your mother is the Queen of Olympus, child," Themis answered bluntly, then softened her tone. "Your father chose your mother as his Queen long ago, because she cares deeply about the world and all the creatures that live, perhaps even more so than he does. And for that, all the blessed gods who dwell on Olympus are endlessly grateful, and willing to see past her temperamental outbursts whenever her King misbehaves. Surely a clever girl such as yourself understands the importance of the resurgence of Life in the Seas for the Earth-Mother to recover from the wounds inflicted upon her by generations of mortals, since the day Prometheus stole fire from Olympus and gifted it to their unworthy kind. Or is that a lesson too advanced for one so young?"

"No, I know all about the origins of Life in the Oceans, Aunt Themis," Junia replied. "I learned about the cyanobacteria in the shallow pools at the Waterton-Glacier Nature Preserve, at the heart of Turtle Island, belching out massive quantities of oxygen millions of years ago in the biosphere, and making life possible for complex, multicellular organism and All My Relations. Even before I learned that in school, my moms already told me that Grandpa Okeanos and Grandma Tethys, the Father and Mother of Rivers, are the Origin and Nurse of all Life. But that wasn't my question. If mortals are making inroads in fixing the mistakes of their ancestors, then why is Thetis asking my Mom, specifically, for help?"

"Oh dear," Demeter whispered, looking warily at Themis. "Should we tell her?"

Themis nodded. "Your mother, our Queen," she said, "is beloved of Gaia, the Earth-Mother. Hera has always been like an ambassador of Gaia here on Olympus. That is why Gaia gifted your mother with her tree of the golden apples upon her nuptials to your father, our King."

"The tree in the Garden of the Hesperides," Eris told Junia in a stage whisper.

"That's right," Themis continued. "Now imagine, child, if Hera were to remain as indifferent to the recovery of the Seas as Zeus has become. Imagine if the lifeblood of the Earth-Mother grew too weak to sustain Life, what do you think would happen?"

"Life on Earth would end," Junia answered. "Unless humans set up additional technological enclaves in special places on the Earth where Life could thrive and gradually reintroduce species. That's what the people at the CARINA networks have been doing, though. My Mom is already doing her part!"

"But Gaia might not see it this way, little one," Demeter said. "Right now, she is as an old mother nearing her death throes. Have you seen what happens to mortals when they are very close to death?"

Junia shook her head.

"Of course, you haven't," Themis said. "Your mother has been fiercely protective of you all these years. This we know all too well. What Demeter is trying to say is that when one is close to death, one becomes either placid, and slips away benignly across the River Styx, or one becomes enraged, as if on the verge of violence. Knowing Gaia as I do, for having been imprisoned within her vast form for many aeons with my Titan brothers and sisters, I can assure you that when Mother awakens from her torpor, she will try to rid the world of all the creatures that have ever caused her harm, or undermined her supremacy, unless one as powerful as Hera takes the initiative to find a way to appease her."

"And if she doesn't?" Junia asked meekly, dreading august Themis' answer.

"It is as you said," Themis replied. "All Life on Earth will perish. And do know what would happen to our deathless kind, should mortals expire from this world?"

Junia shook her head.

"All the blessed gods who dwell on starry Olympus," Themis said, "as well as the other immortals who make their homes at the boundaries of the broad-pathed Earth, will follow them into oblivion."

"I see," Junia said calmly, her eyes wide with alarm.

"But Hera will find a way out of this predicament before we all face catastrophe," Demeter assured her. "She had been a powerful Queen and ally of the Earth-Mother long before she wed loud-thundering Zeus, longer still than she has served as Director of Operations at CARINA-ALSESTIS, and become known to the gods of Turtle Island as –"

"Sky River Woman," Junia said.

"Sky River Woman," Demeter repeated, nodding and smiling benevolently.

"I think I'll go back to my class now," Junia said flatly.

"That would be best, child," Themis told Junia, as Klymene returned to the front hall.

"The Queen is ready to hold Court," the Oceanid declared. "Oh, that sounded high-handed. Apologies. Iris was so much more skilled at this, when she served as Hera's messenger before joining Prometheus on the Nephele. I do miss her dreadfully."

Themis and Demeter gave Klymene a charitable smile, then followed her somewhere down the corridor at the very end of Hera's palace.

"So that's the real reason why we're here?" Junia asked Eris once they were alone in the cavernous front hall.

"I'm afraid so," Eris replied. "In the meantime, do you want to help me set up Mother's computer? Hera is still on the CARINA payroll, you know."

Junia smiled. "I thought you'd never ask," she said, leaving her headgear upon the stool before her randomly swaying likeness on the wall.

Nepheleid

Chapter Seventeen

Girdled amid towering rose bushes, and clad in the soft, pleasant hues of Spring blooms, golden Aphrodite held court alone in her luxuriant garden, patiently awaiting tidings from swift Hermes. As the hour was early, and the dewdrops still clung to the delicate, fragrant petals of the many rows of flowers within the enclosure, Aphrodite knew not to expect Zeus' messenger until he attended to his morning duties to his King. And since Hermes' unwitting exile from Olympus lasted more than a year, Aphrodite surmised that she would not see him until the Sun arced much higher in the Heavens. She did, however, suspect that whatever intelligence Hermes conveyed to her on the day after Zeus and Hera's long-awaited reunion would only serve to corroborate the dread news her handmaidens gave her shortly after Sunrise that very morning.

The Charites, whose sweet gifts of joy, beauty, and grace uplift the spirits of mortals as much as they gladden the hearts of the blessed gods who dwell on high Olympus, took an inordinate amount of time debating on how to break the disappointing news to their mistress. As they told the tale, the Horai, daughters of loud-thundering Zeus and august Themis, after relieving loyal Klymene of her burden of changing the royal bed sheets following the King and Queen's bridal, found no trace of Hera's maidenly ichor upon the linens. Still, the Horai related to the Charites, Ganymede insisted that he saw Hera slumbering contentedly in the Cloud-gatherer's arms that morning, though the Queen absconded from the marriage bed long before the King awoke. As for Zeus, so the Horai told the Charites, Ganymede found him confused and distraught at the empty space beside him in his bed, and it took him quite some time console his lord, until Hermes appeared at the royal palace to receive his orders for the day.

That Hera found a way to sidestep renewing her marriage to Zeus, while riding his thunderbolt nonetheless, displeased the goddess of love more than she cared to say, given the undue time and effort it took for her to win the Queen's everlasting devotion for the King of Olympus. Millennia ago, when golden Aphrodite first came to the shores of Hellas, she quickly befriended Zeus, who at the time had only recently won the throne of Heaven against his father, the Titan-King Kronos. As proof of their abiding amity, the newly crowned Sky-King requested that Aphrodite grant him the heart of his beloved Hera, the powerful Lady of the Argolid, who so far refused all his repeated marriage proposals. By that time, Hera was a Maiden Queen whose vitality was bound to the life-giving Earth, whose Consorts were many, and whose unions were as brief as the Seasons. Unbeknownst to the Thunderer, the venerable Aphrodite, older by far than her aspect as the Sea-born who dwells among the blessed gods on starry Olympus, already knew white-armed Hera quite well, though under a different name.

Aeons ago, long before laughter-loving Aphrodite rode the waves Westward to foreign shores, she knew the favoured daughter of Kronos as Asherah, one of the two wives of El, the once mighty ruler of the gods in the ancient lands between the two rivers far to the East. Renown as the Mother of the gods and the Queen of Heaven, Asherah nonetheless had to share her power, and her husbands El, and later the usurper Baal, with another. Still, Aphrodite, then called Astarte in storied Mesopotamia, never challenged the Queen's power, nor was ever her rival. Asherah's co-wife was instead a virginal, sanguinary goddess named Anath, who so resembled grey-eyed Athena in face and limb that Aphrodite wondered whether Hera sampled the waters of the Lethe for a second time upon meeting Zeus' eldest child.

After much deliberation, Aphrodite surmised that Hera somehow lost all recollection of her tenure as El and Baal's Queen by the time she made her home in Southern Hellas. This was the only explanation Aphrodite could find as to how Hera could ever forget the seventy sons she bore El, or the countless godlings she nursed at her breast in the desolate expanses beyond the fertile lands of the Levant and the two mighty rivers. Among the few clues by which Aphrodite discerned that the old Queen Asherah yet lived within Hera was the goddess' propensity to adopt, nurse, and raise children who were not born of her womb, such as Thetis, daughter of Nereus, the Old Man of the Sea, long a friend to Asherah and her son Yamm, the Sea-Prince. Another indication was Hera's fondness for planting gardens to commemorate her many unions with her favoured divine bridegrooms far and wide across the broad-pathed Earth.

Once satisfied that Hera and Asherah were one and the same, golden Aphrodite set about to find a way to help Zeus win the affections of the reluctant Lady of the Argolid. Remembering Asherah's formidable maternal instincts, and noticing Hera's fondness for all living creatures, Aphrodite instructed Zeus to take the form of an injured cuckoo, which the Maiden Queen took to her breast, unwittingly embracing her ardent bridegroom and sealing her own fate forevermore. Though loath to admit it, Aphrodite quickly realized that forcing the outcome in the Thunderer's favour constituted the most egregious blunder she ever committed since her arrival upon the shores of ancient Hellas, as this indulgence to her King forever transformed Hera into a someone even the goddess of love could scarce recognize as the years went by.

Aphrodite long inferred that her powers to set men and gods ablaze with desire did not always hold as much sway over the hearts of women and goddesses, who were often more easily won over by an appeal to their survival instincts as well as their intellect. This, she believed, made many females frustratingly impervious to seduction, not to mention uncommonly difficult to manipulate. Though she fancied herself an agent of Eros, the most powerful being in the Cosmos, and the driving force behind the renewal and perpetuation of all Life, Aphrodite preferred to favour those who understood the urgency for gratifying their innate appetites for the pleasures of the flesh as the utmost act of devotion. Despite her many dalliances with innumerable suitors over the span of many centuries, Hera, like most mortal women and goddesses, favoured the bonds of affection for kin and community over the act of love itself. Even after Zeus succeeded in seducing Hera on Mount Thornax through his clever stratagem, the Maiden Queen remained reluctant to wed the King of Olympus. Aphrodite begged Eros to drive Hera's bridal chariot and bring the goddess to her bridegroom before Zeus truly obtained his heart's desire.

For millennia, Aphrodite assuaged her creeping guilt for her complicity in ending Hera's reign as Maiden Queen by convincing herself that the once all-powerful Lady of the Argolid would inevitably fall in love with Zeus, especially after experiencing the intensity of his ardent lust during their three-hundred-year bridal. However, once the King and Queen returned from their nuptials, Zeus resumed his libertine ways, whereas Hera remained faithful to the marriage-bed in the hopes that Zeus would see the error of his ways and do the same. As Zeus bestowed many stepchildren upon his increasingly embittered wife, Hera grew angrier by the day and gradually divested herself of her maternal and nurturing impulses, which were once Asherah's most lauded qualities. Why else would Hera stand by idly as Zeus cast their newborn son Hephaestus from Olympus, or worse yet, why would she arrange Aphrodite's marriage to Hephaestus if not to punish her son for ensnaring her upon her golden throne? Surely Hera devised this ill-conceived marriage out of spite for both the bride and groom, for she must have known that the goddess of love would make a most unsuitable wife for the god of the forge.

As the centuries went on, Hera became increasingly obsessed with preserving whatever prerogatives she had left as Queen of Olympus and as the lawful bride of loud-thundering Zeus, which gave Aphrodite some hope that Hera, at the very least, still loved her King above all others. There were times, however, when the Queen herself shattered this cherished perception – most notably in the last year of the Trojan War, when Hera came to seek Aphrodite to borrow her girdle, an object endowed with the power to make its wearer irresistible to one's intended paramour. At the time, Hera told Aphrodite that she needed this love-charm to help her dear-foster parents, the elder Titans Okeanos and Tethys, reconcile and return to their marriage-bed. Aphrodite immediately saw through the ruse, for the Father and Mother of Rivers had never once required any prompting to surrender to their carnal desires. Guessing that Hera meant to encounter Zeus and make an attempt at salvaging their imperilled union, Aphrodite gladly gave her Queen the device, all in the service of Eros and the continuation of Life, or so she wanted to believe. Aphrodite later realized that Hera likely used the love-charm on herself, since in those dark days the Queen appeared to despise the very thought of sharing Zeus' bed, even though she complied to his desires every evening when the Heavens became aglow with the golden light of Sunset.

Millennia came and went since Troy fell and Rome later rose, and yet Hera, newly returned to her husband once more from a long ten year estrangement at the very ends of the Earth, appeared to care not a whit for the legitimacy of her union with the Thunderer, nor her wifely duties to her King. Instead she occupied her mind with ruling over cities in the Heavens, the newest of which, in a fitting and ironic allusion to her abandoned marriage and neglected bridegroom, bore the name of her long-derelict nuptial Garden of the Hesperides. Such pursuits, in Aphrodite's estimation, were better left to learned mortals than the deathless Queen of Olympus, heir to Gaia and the Titan-Queen Rhea, once known as the Mistress of all Life and loved by all, even long before golden Aphrodite came to the ancient shores of Hellas.

At least Hera cared somewhat for her progeny, and to a lesser degree for her kin, for she gave the blessed gods shelter in her various homes on Turtle Island for as long as it took to convince her to see reason and return to Olympus. As for Junia, whom Aphrodite helped the King seed unto the Queen through covert means, there remained the mystery as to why Hera chose not to bear this precious child in the safety of her own womb. Had she done this out of spite as well? Had Hera's heart truly grown so cold that she no longer cared about the means through which Life must perpetuate itself? If this were so, why on Earth did Hera spend the previous night with Zeus, yet refused to bathe in the waters of the Kanathos Spring to renew their marriage, unless she meant to further confuse and destabilize the Thunderer in order to humiliate him, in much the same way as Zeus had brought Hera low throughout the course of their union?

The Queen's brazen effrontery towards the act of love also beckoned Aphrodite to wonder to whom, exactly, did the noble Hera make love on the night of her return to starry Olympus. Surely Hera knew of the fate that befell Metis, Zeus' first wife and grey-eyed Athena's mother, and where the goddess of wisdom dwelled since the days before Athena's birth. Had Zeus at last aroused Hera's enmity to the point that the goddess who once presided over marriage and the birth of legitimate children now actively shunned the ardent desire of men, preferring instead the wiles of clever women? Had Hera not raised her youngest daughter with her loyal handmaiden Klymene, naming her foster-sister, the daughter of Okeanos and Tethys, her co-parent and lover among the learned mortals at the CARINA network upon the broad-pathed Earth? The goddess of love hoped direly that this was not so, for if Hera's heart were ever to grow cold to her Lord and to all men, then perhaps all the lands and rivers and Oceans of the broad-pathed Earth might as well turn to ice until the Queen of Olympus and Mistress of all Life abandoned her bloodless ways.

"Apologies for the lateness of my visit," Aphrodite heard Hermes say as he made his way to the centre of the garden. Grey-eyed Athena stood beside him, as if safeguarding him from invisible foes, while the blushing Charites followed a few paces behind them. To Aphrodite's surprise, the lovely Thetis, daughter of Nereus, trailed in their wake.

"But you must understand," Hermes continued, looking a little pale but otherwise unharmed. "The situation at the royal palace proved quite... interesting this morning. Why so glum, my dear? You look as though your favourite mortal pet suddenly died of unnatural causes!"

"Hera did not take her virginal bath before her bridal last night," Aphrodite replied flatly.

Nepheleid

"I know," Hermes answered. "Though Thetis assures me that our Queen took a very long bath after the fact. And the Horai told *her* that the Earth shook this morning –"

"This bodes ill," Aphrodite said.

Hermes pinched the bridge of his nose in annoyance, but said nothing, which was enough to give Aphrodite pause. Had he not yet recovered from the Junia's spectacular tantrum the previous morning? Surely by now Hera and Klymene had explained to the child why she ought not to antagonize Zeus' messenger by threatening his very breath and consciousness. Truth be told, Aphrodite was glad that it was Junia, and not Hera, who expressed her displeasure at suddenly finding herself among the blessed gods who dwell on starry Olympus. This meant that there was indeed a glimmer of hope for a true reconciliation between the King and Queen, or so Aphrodite direly wanted to believe.

"I know why you would think such things," Athena said. "But have you considered that perhaps you are being a tad over dramatic? A day has barely passed since Hera returned to Olympus. In fact, we ought to consider ourselves fortunate that she returned at all with the girl, and without making much of a fuss. This is quite the achievement considering the mess you made after your encounter with our Queen at Polaris. Is this not in itself a victory worth celebrating? Is anything ever *enough* for you?"

"We do not have the time to wait until she stops sulking from her momentary defeat," Aphrodite replied crossly. "She needed to return here, for her own sake, and for the sake of us all! And now she needs to take her bridal bath, return to Zeus' bedchamber, and kiss and make up at once! If Hera fails to renew her marriage, then the entire order of the Cosmos – the Seasons, the renewal of Life itself – all are in dire jeopardy!"

"Have you even considered that perhaps she means to wait until the actual time appointed by the Seasons to take her bridal bath?" Athena inquired. "Autumn has barely even begun; and though she might not undergo her journey to circle the Earth this year, she might yet choose to wait until the Ides of February to do the... deed. Even at her worst, Hera has always prided herself on her propriety. Why would this be any different?"

"Hera will surely have left by then, you wait and see," Aphrodite answered.

"She cannot leave Olympus until her daughter comes of age," Hermes retorted, as a shadow of worry darkened his features. "And if she does undertake her yearly journey when the Seasons turn to Winter, Zeus insists on either accompanying her, or have me never leave her side. So until Junia's flower comes to bloom, Hera will remain bound by the terms of her agreement with Zeus, which means we will be enjoying the pleasure of her company for at least a few years."

"Until then, we must convince her to stay of her own free will," Aphrodite muttered, more to herself than to her guests.

"That would be preferable," Hermes replied, his countenance turning a delicate shade of pale.

"We must find allies," Aphrodite continued. "We must find common cause with the old powers of the Earth, such as the Titanides and the immortals who dwell in the Sea! They have much to lose if Hera were to leave, never to return!"

"I think that Mnemosyne, the other Titanides, and the immortals who dwell at the boundaries of the Earth had already cast their lot with Prometheus long before Hera left Olympus a decade ago," Hermes said. "Zeus ordered me to find evidence of Prometheus' designs for our Queen the day after I found them both speaking amicably on that mountaintop at Borealis when this strange business began. I cannot yet prove the extent of the conspiracy, but I doubt that the Titanides would grant us much assistance – all but august Themis, of course."

"Aphrodite, my lord Poseidon already means to beseech Hera to stay on Earth, even if she were to leave Zeus forever," Thetis interjected. "That is why he sent me to dwell on starry Olympus, to better sway his dear sister the Queen. When I spoke with Hera this morning, she did not even mention spending the night with Zeus, which I though quite strange. And when I relayed to her my King's pleas for help, she told me instead to take a position at the marine reserve at CARINA-Atlantis, in the South of Spain! It was as though she has bequeathed the work of restoring Life on Earth entirely in the hands of mortals!"

"That is exactly what she means to do," Hermes replied. "Having spent the better part of a year in exile among her learned mortals, I can assure you that she has every confidence that the few mortals left on the Earth, learned or otherwise, possess the means to do what they must to restore the Earth to what it was before greed became their ancestors' defining virtue."

"Which is why we all had to go behind Hera's back to undo the damage you've done after your little stunt at Polaris last Spring!" Athena added irascibly. "Do you not see the value in what Prometheus and his learned mortals are trying to achieve? Are you truly so single-minded that you cannot perceive how important it is for mortals to spread the light of civilization beyond the boundaries of the broad-pathed Earth?"

"I do see the value in their work," Aphrodite answered. "And I will thank you to not project your guilt onto me for selling out Hera in exchange for the survival of the CARINA venture. I would have been content to see Hera return to Olympus upon discovering that she was with child, and to leave the work of resurgence to Prometheus and his learned mortals. There was no need to have her reassigned to the Hesperides station as a compromise! Why could she not leave the smaller garden-ship in the care of one of her cleverest mortals, or even one of the gods of Turtle Island? Oh, why did Zeus not follow my advice and show Hera the nursery he built for the child as soon as they landed on Olympus? Perhaps then she might have softened her heart and reconciled with our King at that very instant! And now, I'm afraid she plans on merely humouring him by occasionally sharing his bed, all the while planning another escape. We've waited too long to act!"

"I fear Aphrodite is right," Thetis said. "From what I gleaned from our encounter this morning, Hera is hedging her bets that Junia will choose to leave once she comes of age. And when she does, Hera will follow her to the city-ship in the Heavens without a second glance at Olympus, or all that she has ever loved and protected on the broad-pathed Earth"

"There must be another way to make them stay," Aphrodite lamented.

"A nursery?" Hermes asked after a moment, looking confused and amused in equal measure. "You told Zeus to build a nursery to show Hera? How would our Queen not see through the ruse? I mean, Junia is almost ten years old! Soon enough she will be breaking hearts as she packs up her crates once more before joining Prometheus on the Nephele."

"It is as I told Zeus yesterday, while we all waited for Hera's craft to arrive," Aphrodite replied. "But I think we have our answer. Little Junia must elect to stay, of her own free will."

"How so?" Athena asked.

"There is only one power, one being in the entire Cosmos who can overpower Hera's acquired antipathy towards Olympus," golden Aphrodite said, a luminous smile brightening her lovely features. "And that is Eros – the most ascendant force in the Cosmos, more powerful that even Zeus himself! Love can sway even the most reluctant hearts, and if by some dark trick Hera proves as impervious to the power of Eros as she is to the effects of all the poisons and venoms of the Earth, then surely one as pure and untested as her virgin daughter can be easily subdued, as the hearts of the very young often succumb to the first stirrings of love."

"That is quite a tall order," Hermes said, "considering that Hera keeps a tight leash on the girl at all times. When she and Klymene are not with her, Ares and Eris follow her like a shadow. I have no doubt that Hera intends for them to continue to do so, even on Olympus."

"Then we have our work cut out for us, as mortals say," Aphrodite stated at last, as the ground beneath her feet erupted with a thousand blooms, as if the Earth herself laughed with fragrant flowers before the long slumber of Autumn.

Nepheleid

Chapter Eighteen

In the perpetual twilight of the thermosphere, golden-throned Hera stood alone upon the observation deck of the Hesperides Autonomous Station, CARINA's fully operational, state-of-the-art ALSESTIS laboratory headquarters in low Earth orbit. Soon, the Nephele's daughter station would sever its ties with the city-ship, once the latter detached from the Hub and left its current position high above the Polaris in the Arctic Seas. Though newly completed, the Hesperides Autonomous Station was far from autonomous, the goddess mused lightheartedly, for the laboratories remained embedded at the bottom, Earth-facing tier of the Nephele, giving both structures the look of a mother bird nesting upon her unhatched egg.

Paying no heed to the scores of Oceanides and learned mortals on the decks below going about their business, Hera scanned the inky expanse for the incoming meteor shower headed towards the world she would soon leave behind as well as the city-ship she hoped her young daughter would favour as her dwelling-place once she came of age. If the learned mortals told it true, the incoming barrage of space rocks would soon sail harmlessly past the Nephele and burn out brightly within the cerulean glow enfolding the soft curvature of the broad-pathed Earth. These objects, Hera knew well, posed little threat to the Nephele for the city-ship's thermal and anti-radiation shields consisted of several protective layers, each thicker than the next. Though unlikely, any breach in the Nephele or the Hesperides' ramparts would trigger the release of a veritable army of nanobots to coagulate around and within any wound that the chaotic realms beyond Earth could inflict upon the two stations. Even so, the Queen gazed intently at the firmament as if daring the seemingly indifferent Cosmos to aim a missile at the Hesperides Autonomous Station nestled safely at the subjacent axis of the Nephele's collection of interconnected concentric rings.

Hera bit her lip at the absurdity of such a thought. Far be it for the Mistress of all Life to tempt the Fates with the safety and survivability of the Nephele and its daughter-station, especially after going through the trouble of negotiating with Zeus this yearly tarriance in exchange for forgoing her seasonal journeys at the ends of the Earth. At first, the Cloud-gatherer refused to let either his estranged bride or their youngest child leave the gilded halls of starry Olympus for any reason whatsoever, under the pretext that the former had been absent for far too long and the latter denied her birthright of divinity and immortality through the vindictive machinations of her brother Prometheus.

So committed was Zeus to rehabilitating his wife and daughter from their alienation from Olympian splendour that he tasked august Themis and Leto with throwing a lavish party for Junia's tenth birthday, caring not a whit that the child would rather have celebrated this landmark event with her friends and boundary-dwelling kin aboard the Nephele. Zeus often tried to compensate for this confinement by consoling the child with bribes of dolls and impractical regal attire – something he had never done with any of Hera's other children, including Hebe, who held the title of Princess of Olympus for centuries until her marriage to Herakles.

To Hera's relief, in the three years since she and Junia arrived on starry Olympus, the child grew to dislike her father a little more each day for reasons of her own. Junia took a dim view of Zeus' particular brand of hypocrisy whenever he touted his boundless love for his estranged wife and her legitimate children, despite the obvious misery his philandering caused Hera over the course of millennia as well as his varying degrees of ill-treatment towards Prometheus, Hephaestus, and Ares. Junia also found Zeus' shameless attempts to gain her approval singularly egregious in light of the neglect he habitually accorded her sisters Hebe, Eileithya, and Eris above all others.

Hera often wondered how Junia would react if she knew about the times Zeus succeeded in coaxing his Queen into spending the night in his neighbouring palace since they returned to the abode of the gods. Surely Junia knew how much Hera loved Metis, her mother's true saviour who remained, quite regrettably, embedded within Zeus' mind. Should Junia ever catch her mother in the act of sneaking back inside her palace in the wee hours, Hera instructed Klymene to explain to the child that such indiscretions would never imperil her future as a crucial member of the Nephele's crew. At first, Hera agreed to placate Zeus' ardent desire as a ruse to manipulate Metis into convincing their shared bridegroom to let her substitute her journeys at the boundaries of the Earth with brief sojourns aboard the Hesperides Autonomous Station. Once Metis convinced the Cloud-gatherer that Hera ought to be intermittently present at ALSESTIS' laboratory station as consolation for relinquishing the helm of the Nephele, he also agreed to allow Junia to accompany her mother, if only to attend school in the company of her classmates a few weeks at a time. Since Junia's first Winter on starry Olympus left the child feeling increasingly isolated and disaffected towards her blessed kin, Zeus thought it best to acquiesce to this compromise.

It was just as well that Hera spent her Winters aboard a mortal-made city-ship at the edge of the Heavens on CARINA business, for she already bade farewell to all the beings of the Earth, though not Gaia herself, shortly before her return to Olympus, a place she once thought as her rightful home. At least Zeus no longer required Hermes to accompany his Queen on her travels. Hera smiled, grateful for Junia's memorable tantrum upon her arrival in the holy throne room on starry Olympus. Hera stifled a laugh at the memory of that day when Junia proved before all the blessed gods assembled that she could bring low Zeus' enforcer with the force of her displeasure at having her fate momentarily co-opted by her unworthy father. Ever since that day, Hermes somehow proved expertly adept at avoiding Hera and her youngest daughter altogether.

Most of all, Hera remembered the smug look on Hermes' face upon declaring that he stole back Hera's throne from its purported hiding-place in her garden shed at Borealis last Spring. At times, she genuinely wondered how she conjured up the willpower not to call him out on his blatant lie. Hermes could not possibly have stolen the throne now ensconced beside Zeus' own at the end of Spring while Hera was away bidding her farewells to Sedna below the Polaris because Hephaestus had not yet finished fashioning this exquisite replica while stationed in the bowels of that very ship. Hera knew that Ares and Eris planted the fake in her garden shed later that Summer while Junia was safely away at Junior Space Camp, then took their mother's true seat of power to a secure vault aboard the Nephele through the cargo hold of the Krios. Hera almost regretted that she would never see the look on Hermes' countenance when he eventually discovered the truth. She bit her lip and let a momentary pang of guilt pass over her for wishing the whelp were here with her right now, if only so she could throw him out of the airlock after he invariably, and deliberately, began to irritate her.

So far, only two of Hera's children, Hephaestus and Eileithya, chose to resume their employ among the learned mortals of CARINA, the former aboard the Nephele and the latter as part of the roster of immortals assigned to the Hesperides Autonomous Station. It was only a matter of time before Hebe, Herakles, Ares, Eris, and Thetis joined the Queen on the city-ship on a more permanent basis. Curiously, at the same time Hera began her work on the Hesperides Autonomous Station, Apollo resumed his post as a high-ranking scientist at CARINA aboard the Nephele proper. When Zeus asked him why the timing of his visits to the city-ship coincided rather suspiciously with Hera's, Apollo answered that his work with Prometheus and his learned mortals at CARINA was far more beneficial to the gods and to humanity than his leisurely travels to the land of the Hyperboreans, his mother's fabled homeland. Hera stifled her laughter the first time she heard him utter those words for she knew that the Lord of the golden bow's motives had very little to do with manifest altruism.

Though magnanimous in his own peculiar way, Apollo rarely worked and dwelled so intimately among mortals unless ordered to do so by Zeus, usually in the course of serving penance for some grave offence against his King. Hera knew of two instances where Apollo served as bondsman to mortals for this very reason. The first time, he incurred his father's wrath by slaughtering the Cyclops who forged the lightning bolts Zeus used to execute Apollo's son Asclepius, at Hades' behest. When Asclepius became so proficient in the healing arts that he habitually brought mortals back from the brink of death, Hades came to Olympus to complain that his Kingdom would soon be devoid of shades if Asclepius were allowed to continue unabated. Fearful that Asclepius' prowess would upend the balance of the Cosmos and wary of upsetting his formidable brother, Zeus agreed to smite Asclepius, leaving Apollo in a state of unspeakable anger, a sentiment Hera later exploited to recruit the Archer as co-conspirator in her rebellion against the Father of gods and men. This complicity in turn led to Apollo's exile from Olympus for a full year in the service of King Laomedon to build the ramparts of Troy, a city close to Zeus' heart whose destruction Hera gleefully sanctioned decades later and the cause of her current asperity.

When Apollo first slew the Cyclops with his golden arrows in a blind rage, Zeus condemned him to the pit Tartarus where the Titans dwell, however, Leto begged her King to reduce their son's sentence to a year of servitude among mortals to atone for his crime. Swayed by his former paramour's distress, Zeus agreed to let Apollo serve his penance among a mortal of his choice. The Archer selected as his master the mortal King Admetus, known far and wide for his justness, kindness, and hospitality. For a full year, Apollo served as shepherd to Admetus' flocks, and over the course of his servitude he and the King became close friends, some even say lovers. Hera never paid much heed to the lurid gossip of the Olympian Court, however, she knew that Apollo showed his gratitude towards his mortal overlord by causing each of Admetus' ewes to bear twins for a full Season and by helping him win the contest that would grant him the maiden Alsestis' hand in marriage. When the appointed hour came for Admetus to die, Apollo got the Moirai drunk, and they agreed to let Admetus live if someone else volunteered to take his place among the dead. To Admetus' chagrin, the virtuous Alsestis offered to die in her husband's stead, leaving the King inconsolable. Fortunately, Admetus' grief was short-lived for Herakles rescued the mortal Queen from death's cold embrace shortly thereafter, and returned her to her overjoyed husband.

At the time, Hera thought Apollo quite bold for daring to intervene in the decrees of the Fates, even though the Archer since swore to Zeus to never do so again. At times, Hera wondered if the Lord of the golden bow chose to take part in the affairs of the learned mortals aboard the Nephele to absolve himself from the part he played in forcing her to return to Olympus three years prior. Though this did not seem out of character for the Archer, Hera doubted very much that sheer guilt lay behind his motivation to continue his work at CARINA. Despite all that had come to pass since her return to Olympus, Hera remained convinced that Apollo would eventually decline to take his place among the crew of the Nephele once the city-ship left the safety of Earth's orbit a few years thence. Alternatively, she suspected that he, like many among the blessed gods who dwell on starry Olympus, began a veritable contest to win the favour of the young, nubile Junia who grew in godly beauty with each passing day.

Though no longer a stranger to the denizens of starry Olympus, Junia had yet to join the blessed gods in their evening banquets lest one of her deathless kin trick her into tasting nectar and ambrosia, thereby rendering her immortal before she came of age and, worse of all, claim her as their bride. Until Junia grew to full womanhood, Hera would not suffer her cherished daughter to become another barely pubescent bride to one of the decadent gods of Olympus – her brothers of seed and ichor. So far Junia fed on the fruits and grains and all the other gifts of the Earth as well as the milk from Hera's own breast, which Klymene collected each morning while Hera was at her bath. The divine milk ensured that the child would grow as strong and impervious to any sort of natural death as was Hera and the rest of her kin whether on Olympus or at the boundaries of the broad-pathed Earth.

Nepheleid

Though Hera trusted Ares and Hephaestus to defend their young sister's virtue if the need ever arose, she had no such faith in the other sons of Zeus or in the Cloud-gatherer for that matter. Prior to her tenth birthday, Junia blossomed with Prometheus as a paragon of kindness and compassion, a far more laudable father figure than the Father of gods and men himself. This was why Hera insisted that Junia accompany her on her travels to the city-ship: to spend more time with her eldest brother, if only to be reminded of what good men could aspire to become, far from the corruption of Olympus' gilded halls.

With her thirteenth birthday fast approaching, Junia's flower would soon come to bloom, whereby she would surely choose to undergo the nanobot fallopian occlusion procedure, the most benign and reliable form of birth control yet devised by mortals. Such a procedure was offered freely to each female member of the Nephele's crew for as long as they chose not to bear offspring in any conventional manner. Mortal men, on the other hand, often opted for another temporary, reversible contraceptive measure akin to the vasectomies of old, however adolescent boys were discouraged from undergoing the procedure until they grew to full manhood. And yet, though cleverer by far than her divine siblings on holy Olympus, Junia needed this procedure as a preventive measure from being claimed for she remained unseasoned against the pangs of burgeoning lust so pervasive in the very young.

Heaven knows how many centuries it took Hera to master her own lascivious impulses, long after she gave up trying to measure her worth by her capacity to satisfy the appetites of a Sky-King whose prurience knew no bounds. Whereas the Queen of Olympus once thought of herself as a devoted emissary of Life, not unlike golden Aphrodite who delights in laughter, in recent centuries Hera began losing her fondness for the act of love, having suffered for far too long the ramifications of her bridegroom' insatiable gluttony for the pleasures of the flesh. Having spent ten continuous years among the gods and Manitous of Turtle Island, Hera became familiar with the tale of the Wendigo, those monsters who, as told by the People of the Eastern Woodlands, lost their full humanity upon resorting to cannibalism to temper their quenchless hunger. Though the Wendigo were once mortals whose hearts turned to ice whenever the dearth of the boreal Winter became too great a burden for them to bear, Hera sometimes wondered whether the same sort of psychosis could affect deathless gods in warmer climes, especially those whose weakness of character rendered them prone to licentiousness and overindulgence of any sort.

More than once the gods of Turtle Island heard Hera tell the tale of how her father, the Titan-King Kronos, swallowed her and her siblings until they were rescued by Zeus, the only child their mother Rhea spared from their father's maw, and Metis, the Oceanid who devised the scheme to force Kronos to relinquish his children. The gods of Turtle Island told Hera that her father was likely a Wendigo, whose madness was motivated by fear instead of hunger. In that regard, Hera asked them whether Zeus, who in turn swallowed Metis out of fear for the male offspring she would bear, and who subsequently ravished his own daughter Persephone to produce a son after his previous wives had borne him only daughters, was a Wendigo of a more sordid kind? The gods and Manitous of Turtle Island, who had seen their peoples decimated by the greed of European settlers over the course of half a millennium, told Hera that they could absolutely envision such a possibility.

Though it truly pained her to leave her friends who dwell on Turtle Island, Hera was relieved that the place that had briefly been her home would remain in good hands under the care of its many eminent gods and goddesses. Among the latter, Sedna safeguarded the North from her underwater lair below the Polaris, while the White Buffalo Calf Woman nurtured the vast Plains of the continent, as did Changing Woman in the Southeast, and many others in the vast landmass to the South. Regrettably, many gods and goddesses of Turtle Island no longer watched over their traditional territories for the Wendigo lunacy of past generations of mortals caused the Eastern shores and the Great River intersecting the heart of the continent to disappear beneath the rising waves. Bereft of their turfs, these exiled gods joined the fray with those whose homelands withstood the folly of the very few, to the detriment of the many.

Despite the unquestioned benevolence and stalwart resilience of the gods and goddesses of Turtle Island as well as others of their ilk across the world, Hera still hoped direly that Junia would choose not to remain anywhere on Earth once she became old enough to decide her own fate. The world below the clouds now held few opportunities for one as brilliant as Junia, and for this reason alone, Hera took a dim view of Apollo's thinly veiled attempts to begin courting her young daughter, even if there were objectively far worse outcomes for a maiden than to become the Consort of the bold, dashing Prince of Olympus. So far, the Lord of the golden bow proved that he possessed the good sense to avoid incurring his Queen's ire by withholding his attempts to ensnare her precious child. Not that it mattered, Hera mused, for Apollo, like the Cloud-gatherer himself, had not yet learned Junia's true name without which neither the son nor the father could fully claim the girl or take over the reins of her fate.

And what a brilliant fate her daughter will have as she sails between the stars, keeping watch over the mortals born above the clouds while they slumber for centuries in their cryogenic chambers. She, too, will be the Great Mother and divine protectress to countless generations yet to come as Hera once was, aeons ago upon the ancient shores of Hellas and beyond. Even if her lips never touched nectar and ambrosia, Junia will be as deathless as her Olympian kin, even though she had yet to show any emblematic signs of divinity, such as the ability to shapeshift at will, for instance. Hera did not remember possessing such abilities at such a young age, either. However, the Queen spent her entire childhood within the belly of King Kronos in the company of her siblings, then had her memories of her earliest years of her maidenhood after her release erased by an involuntary bath in the Lethe.

Upon reflection, perhaps it was best for Junia not to develop just yet the trappings of godhood. Hera and Prometheus already anticipated the inherent difficulties that would arise when the time came to explain to their mortal crewmates why their leaders never age, especially in the decades before they would begin using hibernation technology during interstellar travel. Still, many mortal lifetimes yet remained until such irritants needed to be addressed. At the moment, Hera busied her mind with the innocuous meteor shower headed toward Earth, hoping to try her hand at knocking the speeding missiles off-course through sheer will, even if the meteors posed no threat to the Nephele and to the world below. Before she spied the first bolide above the blue glow of the horizon, she saw a bright flash of light precisely where it ought not to be, on the near side of Earth, far from the trajectory of the meteor shower.

In the span of a mortal heartbeat, Ares barged through the doors of the observation deck of the Hesperides Autonomous Station, trailed by his twin sister Eris. Both looked rather startled and breathless. Ares did not need to utter a single word before Hera knew what had come to pass.

"Mother," Ares panted, bracing himself for a possible outburst of maternal wrath. "Junia, she's – "

Hera raised a hand to silence the god of war and took a deep, steadying breath, then removed the communication device holding her hair in place and pushed a hidden button.

"Iris," the Queen told her unseen messenger through the small device. "Tell Elisapie to add Ares, Eris, and myself as priority-one passengers on the Krios tonight. Twenty minutes? Yes, we can be ready by then. Very well. No, nothing too worrisome, at least not yet. Tell Prometheus and Asia that Junia recently developed the ability to leap through the Nephele's thermal and anti-radiation shields. No, I saw exactly where she landed. Yes, Olympus. I know, it's only November. This will be a year without Winter, I suppose. Thank you, Iris. Argosi out."

Hera looked at the device in her hand for a few seconds, then turned her gaze towards Eris. "Can you hack into the passenger roster for the Krios and add Junia's name somewhere?" she asked. "You will have to also remove Junia's likeness from her classroom's video feed for the last eight hours, and possibly confound her teacher and a few of her classmates for good measure. Can you do this quickly, or from the Krios if need be?"

Eris nodded slowly, her eyes wide with alarm.

Hera took a long look at her red-haired twins and gave them a reassuring smile.

"It looks as though our little Junia is growing up," she said wistfully as her right hand inadvertently crushed the small communication device into a fine powder, quickly whisked away by a wispy swarm of nanobots.

Nepheleid

Chapter Nineteen

"Nicely done," Apollo told Artemis as a melodious note rang from the string bound to the Huntress' silver bow. "Although I do hope that none of the learned mortals aboard the Nephele saw your arrows knock the meteors off course,"

"They most certainly did not!" Artemis protested with mock indignation. "I put a glamour on my arrows to make them look like space debris. For all the mortals will ever know, space litter shielded their city-ship through pure, random chance. You're welcome."

"The Nephele was not on a collision course with the meteor shower, Sister," Apollo said. "Unless you were trying to confuse the mortals who dwell above the clouds, I would hazard a guess that you did it all for show. Did a pious devotee remember to make an offering in exchange for some exotic fireworks?"

"I'll never tell," Artemis replied with a grin. "Besides, you're not the only one who protects mortals from impending catastrophe. It is in my purview to protect the young, and the Hesperides Autonomous Station is still a child, in so many ways."

"When you're right," Apollo said with a soft chuckle. "Are you off on your hunt?" he asked after a moment.

"Soon," Artemis answered.

"Where to this time?"

"Central Africa," Artemis answered as she loosed another arrow. "Off to hunt poachers and feed their corpses to the wildlife."

"Didn't you do that last week? That made the news in every nation on Earth!"

"I did, and I will do it again!" Artemis declared. "Really, mortals these days are few and far between, and they have the means to feed their families without encroaching upon sanctuaries for imperilled wildlife. Those who fall to the arrows of my huntswomen fully deserve the indignity of their fate!"

"You should tell Hera," Apollo replied with a grin. "Your words would be like music to her ears."

"She would say that she finally got through to me," Artemis griped. "I'm not giving her the satisfaction!"

"Oh, come now! It's been years since we all returned from Turtle Island. Hera has left you in peace since then. She has more pressing matters to contemplate than her lingering influence on your behaviour!"

"Yes, she has to contend with taking the reins of the Hesperides while Junia takes her place by Prometheus' side on the Nephele in a few years," Artemis retorted. "I cannot fathom that this outcome will ever grant her any measure of peace of mind or happiness. No more than her marriage to Father ever did."

"You cannot imagine anyone happy once they're wed!" Apollo replied. "It happens every now and then, I'll have you know. Just think of Persephone. No one ever thought she could have found her happiness with Lord Hades, and yet she did."

"That's because they only see one another for a third of each year," Artemis said. "They have time to miss each other. Whenever Hera leaves Father on her seasonal journeys to the Nephele, she is gone for almost as long, yet invariably returns almost under protest. If Hera herself no longer cares for the virtues of being wed, how does that look to those among us who care not to be yoked into marriage?"

You never cared for the virtues of being wed even when Hera willingly reigned as Queen among the blessed gods of high Olympus, Apollo wanted to answer. He wisely elected to keep his thoughts to himself, lest he irk his capricious twin.

"Are you not soon to leave on your own journey, Brother?" Artemis asked.

"In a few days," Apollo said. "When the days grow too short and the nights intolerably dark before the snows blanket the broad-pathed Earth."

"And before Junia begins to miss you as she awaits you on the Nephele."

"Junia is still a child," Apollo replied, expertly masking his annoyance at the Huntress' unflattering insinuation.

"Junia is almost a maiden," Artemis said. "Her flower will soon to come to bloom and then she will be beyond my help. So it is with all little girls."

So it is with you still, Apollo considered, once again letting his retort trail off in the breadth between himself and his twin. Though his elder by a single day, Artemis of the silver bow remained quite unfledged in so many ways, unlike Apollo, and all the blessed gods across the broad-pathed Earth. As for Junia, Apollo deemed her unnaturally wise for one so young, even more so since the Father of gods and men compelled Hera to return to Olympus from Turtle Island almost three years prior.

At the time, loud-thundering Zeus fully expected Junia and Artemis to become fast friends, however Apollo already knew this would never come to pass. In days long gone by, children were presumed to be as wild and unfettered as the beasts of the woodlands, as was Artemis and her maidenly coterie of virgin huntresses. In recent centuries, though, Artemis found herself increasingly bereft of unripe protégés as mortals across the broad-pathed Earth had little choice but to raise their young to become dependable, competent members of their societies as soon as they came into full consciousness. For most children, this occurred long before the first flowering of adolescence.

Like all the children born in these interesting times, Junia knew more about science, mathematics, the arts, and the workings of the Cosmos than even the wisest philosophers of old ever did. Moreover, since infancy Junia proved startlingly skilled in other uncommon abilities of the mind, such as bridging the vast distance between Turtle island and Olympus to visit Apollo in his dreams as he slept. At first, these nightly forays into his slumbering mind left the Lord of the golden bow confused and intrigued in equal measure. However, by the time Apollo reconciled this strange dream-child with the daughter Hera bore Zeus during their long estrangement, he grew to suspect that Hera's spirited daughter had already surpassed her classmates, and perhaps even most of her Olympian brethren, in astuteness. And yet, even during those earliest encounters the child reminded Apollo of the exiled Queen of Olympus, leading him to wonder whether Hera could once have been exactly like this rambunctious little girl, if only she had ever been given the chance to be a child.

Nepheleid

Perhaps Hera understood better than most why her youngest daughter sought Apollo in shared dreamscapes before their first official meeting on the Polaris all those years ago, on the day Zeus first attempted and failed to force his wife to return to with him to the abode of the gods. Apollo himself witnessed the first stirrings of Junia's self-awareness shortly before she was conceived on the night the Archer sought Hera in a shared dream to console his Queen after prompting her to reveal to him her darkest, half-forgotten secrets. In spite of all this, Hera wasted no time in forbidding Apollo from spending any time with Junia without a chaperone, a role for which Eris happily volunteered. In the years since, Apollo honoured Hera's wishes to keep Junia at a distance, save for the occasional private music and science lessons made all the more interesting by Eris' very presence.

In his eagerness to indoctrinate his youngest known child to the ways of Olympus, Zeus insisted that all the blessed gods take turns spending time with the little girl. However, under Hera's orders Eris and Ares made certain that Junia never remained alone with anyone other than themselves and their mother, as well as Klymene, Junia's co-parent, whom Zeus only barely tolerated in this role, preferring to view the Oceanid instead as Junia's nurse-maid. If their father had his way, Apollo knew, Junia would remain a child for many more years, perhaps to delay Hera's inevitable departure once their daughter came of age and the Nephele became ready to detach from the Hub. Perhaps this was why Zeus never chided Hera for keeping Junia confined in her palace during the evening banquets on high Olympus. Had the child tasted nectar and ambrosia as Apollo did on the day of his birth, she would have instantly grown to full strength and become immortal. As neither outcome can be undone, even at the hands of the wiliest immortals, Zeus had no choice but to eat his heart each night as Hera recused herself at the earliest hour to mind the young Junia while he and the other blessed gods feasted in the banquet hall on high Olympus.

As far as Apollo could tell, Zeus did not fully appreciate why Hera insisted on keeping their youngest child innocent of the trappings of immortality, at least until she became old enough to decide her own fate. Having spent a fair amount of time with Prometheus and his learned mortals aboard the Nephele in recent years, Apollo became cognizant of Hera and Prometheus' plans to extend the lifespan of mortals yet to come, so that they could travel the unfathomable distances between the stars within single generations. For this to come to pass, Prometheus would need to improve the very integrity of the building blocks within the mortals' living tissue,that which the learned mortals called DNA, and the philosophers of old called the "clay" from whence all men and beasts were fashioned. If Zeus ever learned that Prometheus meant to splice Junia's clay, obtained by harvesting her embryonic stem cells while she developed in her artificial womb all those years ago, with that of the learned mortals aboard the Nephele, then no one would be able to spare the benefactor of humanity or his prized city-ship from the Thunderer's wrath.

Just as Zeus smote Asclepius without a second though for the wonders Apollo's son could have bestowed upon the Earth after finding a way of curing mortals from death, the Cloud-gatherer would obliterate the Nephele and all that dwell within, deeming Prometheus' spacefaring venture a threat to the natural order of the Cosmos. This time no one, not even stalwart Herakles, could protect Prometheus from whatever sentence Zeus would inflict upon him, which Apollo knew would far surpass his previous ordeal of being chained to a rock as an eagle devoured his ever-regenerating liver each day. As for Hera, Apollo shuddered at what Zeus would do to her as punishment for her complicity in Prometheus' designs, despite her repeated admissions that she only returned to Olympus to safeguard the Nephele against any impediment to its mission of spreading Earthly life to worlds yet unknown. Somehow, Apollo knew, Zeus would find a way to overrule Hera's lawful acquiescence to his terms of surrender and force her to witness the Nephele's destruction while he devised other heinous ways to retaliate for her habit of reciprocating his affections only sporadically, while their daughter matured at the tedious pace of mortal children.

Perhaps this time, instead of chaining his Queen to the sky, Zeus would also deliver on his threat to arrange Junia's marriage to one of his sons without Hera's counsel on the matter of the chosen bridegroom. By now, the Thunderer likely knew that Hera would sooner choose to suffer the penalty of the Oath of the Holy River Styx than see her brilliant child sold into marriage to any scion of Olympus, even though Zeus doubtlessly loathed the very thought of another lingering separation from his wife. Though Apollo long supported Hera's efforts to see Junia join the crew of the Nephele, he grew increasingly apprehensive about the continued survival of CARINA' city above the clouds. For this reason, he often considered preemptively vitiating his father's abhorrence towards Prometheus and his spacefaring mortals by proposing a truce sealed through the sacred bond of marriage as Zeus and Hera's nuptials forever sealed the alliance of Earth and Sky millennia ago.

Nepheleid

Surely Hera would find the Lord of the golden bow worthy of Junia, once the child grew into a maiden of acceptable age. The Queen had long respected Apollo for his intellect and for the measured justness of his deeds, in the same way that the Archer admired Hera for her cleverness and strength beyond measure as well as her boundless courage in the face of impossible odds. Had the time not come to further endear himself to the Mistress of all Life by proving a fitting suitor to the child she obviously considered her heir and successor, at least among the learned mortals yet to be born above the clouds in city-ships yet to journey across the vast Cosmos? If Hera's plans for her daughter came to fruition and Junia ascended as Queen in her own right among CARINA's learned mortals, then Apollo needed to prove worthy of his bride by learning Junia's true name, which as far as the Archer could tell was a secret only Hera, Klymene, Prometheus, and Asia knew.

Even Zeus, for all his imperious bluster, could not command Junia's fate without this crucial information, which of course Hera would never disclose to her King, not even in the throes of her most regrettable moments of carnal longing. Apollo had little doubt that Hera would admire him even more if he somehow uncovered the secret of Junia's name. He also imagined that his Queen would become grateful to him for sacrificing his cherished bachelorhood to ensure that the Nephele fulfilled its mandate, at least until Zeus found a way to make his peace with Hera and Junia's inevitable departure from Olympus and the broad-pathed Earth. Once that day came, Apollo would join his bride and the Queen dowager on their heavenly sojourns, and they in turn would crown him as the Sky-King he was inevitably born to become. For this outcome to come to pass, Apollo would need to act quickly, for Junia grew in beauty and strength ever more each day, and soon his brothers would take notice and also vie to claim the unwitting Princess of Olympus as their bride.

A pang of unease crept over Apollo momentarily, as if the thought of Hera leaving Olympus forever were somehow forbidden, heretical, despite the Archer's soft complicity in the success of her mission with CARINA. If the Fates granted Apollo his heart's desire just this once, then perhaps Hera would at last abandon her quest to sever her unbreakable bond with her King, sealed by the Fates themselves on her wedding day, and make her peace with her lot to reign forever as Zeus' Queen among the blessed gods on high Olympus. Of course, Apollo knew better than to voice these thoughts to anyone, at least not now. Not even to august Themis, his mentor, or Artemis, his twin and confidante, and especially not to the incorrigible gossip, Hermes – as any talk of marriage at this point in time would doubtlessly stoke the embers of Hera's perennial wrath.

Apollo closed his eyes, lest his gaze betray his brazen musings. He opened his eyes again when he heard Artemis loosing a final arrow into the dusk.

"And now the Sun has gone," she said, "and my hunt begins. Good night, Brother."

"Good hunting, Sister," Apollo told his twin as the goddess nodded her farewell and disappeared into the starlit night.

Apollo rose slowly to his feet, intending to join the other blessed gods feasting in the banquet hall, when a flash of light somewhere behind him, followed by a faint sonic boom, distracted him from his task. The Archer turned around and walked toward the edge of the parapet, expecting to see the trail of a small meteor arcing across the firmament. Instead he spied a small figure in the distance, at the farthest boundary within Olympus' heavenly citadel. Apollo stood still as the figure sat up, shook the dust from her tattered, slightly singed, form-fitting CARINA-issued uniform, and set her gaze towards the stairway leading up to the throne room.

Before the figure took her first step, Apollo appeared before her, blanket in hand.

"Junia," he greeted her. "What in the world are you doing here? *How* did you get here on your own? Did something happen on the Nephele?"

The child gave Apollo a strange look. "I can't believe that worked," she whispered incredulously.

Apollo draped the blanket across Junia's shoulders, putting out the last embers upon what remained of her clothing. "Let me guess," he said. "You leaped from the airlock?"

"Please don't tell my Mom," Junia replied with a sheepish smile and a shrug.

Apollo let out a laugh. "When Hephaestus fell from Olympus and into the Sea," he told her, "it was from a lesser height, and he still broke his leg. How did you-"

"I looked down and I saw you and Artemis," Junia answered.

Nepheleid

"Did you get frightened by the meteor shower?" Apollo asked with a hint of humour in his voice.

"No, of course not!" Junia squeaked. "We weren't on the collision course!"

Apollo laughed again, though this time he waited until the child spoke first.

"I was looking straight down from my favourite spot above the Hub," Junia said. "I was looking at Turtle Island, then I felt kind of bad. I looked away towards Olympus and I saw you and Artemis, and I... really needed to talk," Junia said after a moment.

"All right," Apollo replied, beckoning Junia to follow him towards the stairway. "Come now, before Father sees you and starts asking questions. But still, what possessed you to dive back to Earth that could not wait a few days until I returned to the Nephele myself?"

"I've been thinking. About when the Nephele is ready to launch towards Mars."

"Go on," Apollo replied, his breath catching slightly in his throat. "You were looking down at Turtle Island. Why did you feel bad? Are you homesick?"

"Kind of, but no. I mean, I miss it, but Mom always told me that the Nephele would be our home once it's built."

"And now you are not so certain about the Nephele being your home?" Apollo asked.

Junia sighed. "Yeah, I mean no. That's not it. It's just –"

"And you thought I could give you clarity?" Apollo interrupted. "You know, the Nephele's launch is still years away. You do not need to burden yourself with deciding your fate until then, so why are you –"

"I think we're leaving for the wrong reasons!" Junia blurted out at last.

Apollo said nothing, eager to hear more.

"When we first got here, Aunt Themis told us, Eris and I... in a roundabout way that we're here on Olympus because the other immortals who live in the Oceans and at the boundaries want my Mom to stick around. And Thetis keeps telling my Mom that she can help the Earth and the Oceans and the other fragile ecozones in a way that Zeus can't – or won't. I know my Mom really wants to do more than what she does on the Hesperides, but she doesn't want to stay there once the Nephele launches because she hates Zeus so much. And I *want* to go on the Nephele with Prometheus and Asia and Iris and Auntie Mnem, but I don't want the Earth to die a slow death if we can help it! I don't blame my Mom for wanting to leave, it's just – I need to figure some things out, you know?"

"I understand completely," Apollo said truthfully. "But tell me this, what would you have me do?"

"I don't know! I just thought maybe you could do something like that time you got the Fates drunk and got them to change their minds, and you spared your friend Admetus from his appointed hour of death? You can do things like that!"

"I have done such things," Apollo confessed, "But I cannot longer interfere with the decrees of the Fates. Even though my will prevailed that time you speak of, I had to swear an Oath to Zeus to never do that again."

"Ugh! What is it with him and Oaths! Jesus Christ! No – not you." Junia stammered almost comically to a robed, bearded figure lounging placidly by the bottom of the stairway, cup of wine in hand.

"That was Dionysus, little one," Apollo said, trying with all his might not to burst into laughter. "One would have thought you'd be able to tell your fellow Olympians apart by now!"

"Mom told me not to bother getting to know that one," Junia replied casually. "She said that if she has her way, the kind of worlds that the learned mortals will build across the Cosmos will be so awesome that gods like Dionysus won't be needed at all."

"And I meant every word, Kitten," Hera said flatly as she appeared before Junia and Apollo in a bright whirlpool of light.

"Mom!" Junia exclaimed, clutching her chest in surprise.

"Oh dear," Apollo muttered softly as the figures of Ares and Eris materialized within Hera's rapidly fading swirl of stars.

Nepheleid

Chapter Twenty

"And what were you thinking? Diving to Earth from the Nephele." Hera scolded Junia in her stern, motherly voice. "Did you think at all at how awkward it would look if you turned up missing... on a SPACE STATION!? You are lucky that I saw your smouldering trail upon re-entry, and that Klymene wasted no time telling your teachers that I took you with me on an urgent trip to Polaris. Speaking of which –" Hera turned her gaze toward Eris.

"The mortals on the Krios will see our likenesses on the top deck during the overnight descent," Eris said. "All four of us, nicely sedated in our bunks. No one will question this."

"Good," Hera replied, looking somewhat relieved.

Junia stared at her mother in disbelief. She could not fathom how a goddess as ancient and capable as the Queen of Olympus could teleport so seamlessly from low Earth orbit to terra firma, with two of her adult offspring no less, without leaving any visible trace across the firmament.

"Oh, don't be so melodramatic!" Hera chided Junia as the child continued to clutch her chest. "You are a scion of Olympus. You *cannot* suffer a heart attack! Now let me take a look at you." Pulling the blanket off Junia's shoulders, Hera and inspected her daughter for signs of trauma. "Now look at your uniform!" she said upon noticing Junia's tattered clothes. "Ah well, you are due for a growth spurt, so I suppose there is no harm done."

Junia made an undecipherable noise, somewhere between a groan and a whimper, as Hera spun her round to assess the extent of her wounds. Finding none, Hera turned her gaze to Apollo.

"Was she injured from her fall?" the Queen inquired imperiously, addressing the Archer for the first time since her sudden arrival on holy Olympus.

Nepheleid

"No, my lady," Apollo answered. "Not that I could see, although she left a small impact crater where she landed."

Hera shook her head and handed the blanket back to Junia, as the heavy bronze doors creaked open behind them. Before she turned her gaze towards the throne room, Hera already knew that Hermes stood at the threshold, staring at them with his usual coy grin. Hera took a deep breath, steeling herself for the inanity that she knew would follow. To her surprise, Hermes said nothing, and instead handed his Queen a yellow, maidenly dress, and a pair of gilded slippers, far too small for Hera's dainty, gold-shod feet. Hera nodded, took the garments and handed them to Junia. Without prompting, the child hid behind the blanket Apollo had given her, held aloft by Ares and Eris to guard her modesty, and changed out of what remained of her charred school uniform.

Hermes opened the door wider and gestured for his Queen to step inside. Satisfied that her youngest child no longer looked as though she recently discovered atmospheric friction experientially, Hera entered the throne room, followed by Apollo, with Ares and Eris flanking the newly presentable Junia.

"Wipe that ash off your forehead, Kitten," Hera muttered to the child as they crossed the threshold. "It's unseemly."

Once inside, Hera saw all the blessed gods who dwell on high Olympus assembled in the throne room, all save Hephaestus and Eileithya, who were hard at work on the Nephele, and Artemis, likely gone on her nightly hunt somewhere on the broad-pathed Earth where such offences were still permitted. All appeared in various stages of inebriation, as was their custom at this late hour on long Winter nights when Hera journeyed far from the abode of the gods to the very ends of the broad-pathed Earth. They made quite a spectacle, these illustrious denizens of starry Olympus, many wandering around the throne room in a haze, quite visibly longing for the informality of the banquet hall. Hera suddenly felt a pang of regret for taking Junia inside the throne room, as she had so far done all that she could to shelter her child from the notorious pit of debauchery Olympus had become ever since the gods welcomed Dionysus within their ranks.

To Hera's dismay, Junia scanned the cavernous room intently, her face a pale imitation of the notoriously placid gaze her mother perfected long ago in order to feign serenity whenever inner tempests roiled within her very being. Though Junia's almost decade-long martial arts training rendered her adept at affecting a reasonably calm demeanour in times of upheaval, the child still had much to learn in keeping her gaze neutral. Junia took in her surroundings, her eyes comically wide as she doubtlessly struggled with her dissonance at the memory of her first arrival in this very room, when she was first introduced to the august company of the gods. Though visibly reeling with disbelief, Junia maladroitly averted her gaze whenever the sons of Zeus by mothers other than her own looked upon her with lascivious intent, obviously undeterred by the menacing countenance of Ares and Eris guarding her closely.

At least Dionysus possessed the good sense not to join his brothers in gawking at the child, Hera thought, as the son of Semele raised his cup to his Queen in such a way that Hera could not quite guess whether he did so out of reverence or mockery. Knowing him, it was probably the latter, Hera thought while grabbing hold of Junia's hand. For reasons known only to himself, Dionysus made a sign of the cross of sorts in the manner of mortal priests when Junia threw an uneasy glance in his direction, and laughed boisterously when Hera looked upon him in utter confusion. When the Queen looked to the Archer for an answer, Apollo fixed his gaze upon the polished floor and bit his lip as if to stifle a giggle.

At the far end of the throne room, loud-thundering Zeus held court, looking slightly less anaesthetized than the other blessed gods who dwell on high Olympus. All cheerful chatter came to an abrupt halt when he rose to his feet to address the newcomers.

"Well, then," Zeus said as he addressed Hera, though his gaze lingered upon Junia.

The child quickly released her mother's hand and took a sideways step towards Apollo, grabbing the Archer's arm. Annoyed, Hera gave her daughter a reproachful look, then turned her full attention back to the Cloud-gatherer, who watched the scene unfold with visible amusement.

"I see that our Queen and young daughter have returned to us much earlier than expected," Zeus continued, as a grin crept across his face. "Tell me, young one, have you grown bored of your city-ship, where you have nothing else to gaze upon but a dreary mass of ice below your feet during the endless wintry night? Is this why you've chosen to join your blessed kin at last on high Olympus?"

Nepheleid

Hera turned her head back towards Junia, who looked upon her father incredulously.

"Um, actually, no –" the child stammered unsteadily.

"And I see you've chosen your bridegroom for your own matchmaking," the Thunderer added, ignoring Junia's denial.

"Junia did no such thing," Hera interjected curtly. "And we were just about to take our leave."

"I very much doubt this, my love," Zeus replied, as the blessed gods began to disperse to the edges of the throne room to avoid the wrath of their increasingly irate Queen. "Why else would our daughter leap out of the Sky, if not to initiate a tryst with a most worthy suitor? I suppose the time has come for our little girl to wed. Now, does anyone dare to challenge Apollo for the hand of the Princess?"

Hera threw a quick glance at Junia, who took looked rather distressed as Apollo momentarily left her side to stand before Zeus, while Ares and Eris paced around in wide arcs to keep the crowd at bay.

"Father," the Archer protested. "This is not why Junia came to Olympus. She came here only to seek my counsel."

"It is good that a bride should learn to listen to her future husband," Zeus said, pretending not to notice the air begin to roil with growing intensity within the throne room. "Now, if only her mother had bothered to teach her the virtue of feminine vanity. Athena! Bring some proper bridal robes for the Princess to wear, as tonight's banquet has become an engagement party."

In the corner of her eye, Hera spied Athena grabbing hold of Hermes, as if to shield him from the Queen's line of sight.

"ENOUGH!" Hera bellowed, while the blessed gods cowered at the sonic boom reverberating across the golden halls of holy Olympus. "We are not here to entertain your delusions," the Queen added with forced calm. "As I've told you, we were just leaving. Junia, Ares, Eris, come with me. We must make an appearance at Polaris before the Krios makes it ascent back to the Nephele."

"Now, now, don't be such a sore loser," the Father of gods and men told Hera in a patronizing tone. "You know full well the terms of our agreement. If the young one chooses to stay, so must you. And while we're at it," he continued, his eyes locked on Junia, "it is high time to give you a true and proper Olympian name. Like perhaps... Nepheleis? It means Daughter of the Cloud. I find that it suits you quite well, since all those gathered here have taken to calling you the Cloud Born, whether you know it or not. Or what about Apollonia? It does seem like the Fates bound you to our most illustrious son before you were even born... or hatched, or whatever it is mortals call those who come into being inside fish-bowls."

Before Hera could retort, Junia somehow gathered her courage and blurted out the most colourful string of anatomically inspired profanities ever to befoul the hallowed halls of holy Olympus. Despite her tender age, Junia managed to describe with utmost precision through which orifice the Cloud-gatherer ought to impale himself with his thunderbolt, in a manner that elicited both shock, and a quantum of pride, from white-armed Hera, as well as audible gasps from august Themis, gentle Demeter, and Leto, ever the proper courtly lady. Even golden Aphrodite blushed at the child's lewdness, as did swift Hermes, while Athena covered her mouth. Dionysus spat out his wine, Ares bit his lip, Eris grinned beatifically, whereas Apollo's usually stoic and self-assured demeanour betrayed amazement and dismay in equal measure.

To Hera's surprise, a fierce gale suddenly spiralled with untold fury from the edge of the throne room towards its centre, where now Junia stood. The impending tempest, Hera noticed, grew in intensity with every breath Junia took, as the child stared upon the Thunderer defiantly with her half-feral gaze.

Drained of his good humour, Zeus looked down upon his youngest daughter with a frown that shook the Earth to its very core.

"What did you say?" he spat out furiously.

"You really don't listen, do you?" Junia answered. "I told you to go f–'

"Junia," Hera interjected with impeccable timing. "Did I not tell you long ago that your father would never pay heed to your wishes, if he believed these contrary to his own designs? But now that he's put you on the spot, so to speak, tell us what it is you wish to do, now that he's declared you ready to determine your own fate."

Junia took a few deep, calming breaths. "Mom, I want to go home!" she said, without ever taking her eyes off Zeus.

Nepheleid

"Very well," Hera replied, her heart swelling with gladness and relief. To the King of Olympus, she said, "Junia has made her choice. As per our agreement, I am free to leave with her as I please. And as I've said on the deck of the Polaris, those among you who wish to join us on the Nephele and beyond are welcome to do so." Scanning the throne room, Hera's gaze fixed upon golden Aphrodite, who stood beside Dionysus.

"Except for you two," Hera added, addressing the pair. "Your... services will not be needed where the brilliant generations of mortals yet to come will make their homes across the stars. To the rest of you, I will wait until the end of the polar Night to hear your answer. Otherwise, farewell."

Hera took Junia's arm and motioned the child to follow her towards the tall bronze doors of the throne room. As mother and daughter turned their backs to the Father of gods and men, a loud thunderclap reverberated across the hallowed halls of starry Olympus.

"Halt!" Zeus thundered from where he stood. "I forbid anyone from leaving our presence! And this one," he said, pointing at Junia, "this ungrateful little brat dares to speak such filth to her own father! I suppose I am partly to blame, for allowing her mother to choose Eris as her mentor, but nonetheless, the urchin must be chastised for her impudence. Hermes, seize her!"

"If you don't mind, Father," Hermes said uneasily, as Athena raised her shield between her King and his messenger, "I'd rather not."

"I see. Afraid of a little girl, are we?" Zeus asked derisively, shaking his head for effect. "All right then, suit yourself. Ganymede! Seize the brazen wench!"

Before the hapless cupbearer could even register his master's command, Hera took a step towards the centre of the throne room, staring right at the mortal-born Trojan Prince.

"Let me be perfectly clear," she declared gravely, "If *anyone* even dares to lay a finger on my daughter, I will make them yearn for an end to their deathless existence in a way that made the destruction of this one's city seem like a dream."

"Know your place, bugger-boy!" Eris growled, taking great care to let the blessed gods see that she now stood at Junia's side, ready to pounce on whomever threatened her charge. In response, Ares stepped in the space between Zeus and Hera, drawing his weapons as a warning to anyone who would thwart his mother and Junia from exiting the throne room.

"Eris," Hera said, her gaze steadily fixed upon Zeus, "take Junia away from this place. Take her to those whose interests are aligned with our own, whose fate depends on her true name remaining known only to those who would pledge themselves to her, as she fulfils her destiny to spread Earthly Life across the vast, empty Cosmos. Kitten, go with your sister, and have faith that I shall see you very soon."

As Hera held Zeus in place with her implacable gaze, the furious spiralling tempests grew increasingly opaque, until they swallowed Eris and Junia whole, and collapsed into a singular point of light.

Surprisingly, Zeus remained where he stood, looking rather unimpressed.

"Why do I get the inkling that you did not dispatch them to the Nephele?" he asked nonchalantly. "Answer me truthfully, otherwise I will take certain measures, lest you break your Oath."

Hera took a deep breath, refusing to take the bait. Ares looked uneasily at Apollo, who somehow maintained a composed demeanour, despite having also just witnessed Eris and Junia casually vanish into thin air.

"Do you think I care if I break my Oath?" Hera said after a few tense seconds. "I would actually welcome the respite of spending a year without breath and consciousness, if it meant that my path never crossed yours ever again! I would gladly slumber for a thousand years in such a manner, along with the mortals of the Nephele in their chambers of ice, if it meant that I should awaken far from this place, as a Maiden Queen once more, in a world I can truly rule as my own. Now let me ask you this, *Brother*. Do you think I care that I should be branded an Oathbreaker among the blessed gods who dwell on high Olympus, if my dearest wish is to never grace its golden halls ever again?"

"You would choose to spend your endless days with mortals, spreading Life to new worlds, knowing full well that their kind will bring to ruin to whatever semblance of hospitable wanderers remain to be found in the Cosmos, as they have done far and wide across the broad-pathed Earth!" Zeus replied, without concealing the sadness in his voice. "You would send our child on this fool's quest, dooming her, as you are dooming the best and bravest among mortals, and their offspring yet to come. Do you not see the folly in this!? How could I even call myself your King, if I did not stop you from committing this gravest of error? Do you not see that I seek only to thwart your madness because I alone love –"

"Oh, piss off, you vainglorious windbag!" Hera scoffed. "If you truly wanted to ask me why I would choose mortals over Olympus, over *you*, then here is my answer. While it is true that the greed and folly of mortals have brought the Earth to near death, their descendants have long since proven willing, and able, to be better and do right by their children and the offspring of all living things upon this world and the worlds yet to be seeded with Earthly Life."

Hera paused, scrutinizing the Thunderer's mien to determine whether he heard her words and gave them due consideration. Once she saw the realization dawning behind his ice-blue eyes, she said finally, "In all my years, in all these centuries ruling by your side, it has become unequivocally clear that you do not share this most noble quality."

"What the hell are you saying?" Zeus whispered loudly, the tremor in his voice audible to all who dwell on starry Olympus.

"What I am saying, *Brother*, is that you are unwilling, and therefore unable, to change, especially for the better," Hera answered with eerie calm. "And this is why you, unlike the mortals Prometheus rescued from utter wretchedness with his gift of fire stolen from Olympus, will never be worthy of the throne of Heaven, just as I have always known that you were never worthy to be my King."

And with a spiral motion of her graceful hand, golden-throned Hera transmuted the newly tranquil air around her into a brilliant swirl of stars, into which she stepped gingerly. She waited for Ares to follow her, but the god of war stood transfixed in place, as if the prospect of following his venerable mother into the unknown was far too terrible to contemplate.

Recognizing with some measure of disappointment that she would undertake this journey alone, Hera motioned to collapse the whirlpool, her eyes lingering upon Apollo's placid countenance, his cerulean eyes staring back at her intently.

Thank you, my Lady.

These were the last words white-armed Hera heard in the confines of her mind upon dispersing into the Aether, while the other blessed gods gasped in awe at the spectacle of their Queen exiting the throne room yet again in a swirl of stars, this time for all of Olympus to see.

Nepheleid

Chapter Twenty-One

Swift Hermes bit his lip, thinking it prudent to keep his peace while the blessed gods gathered in the throne room took a moment to fully grasp what had come to pass before their very eyes. Though Eris had since made her own exit with the young Junia, many immortals looked upon one another in utter dismay. Evidently, no one knew what to make of Hera's latest theatrics, nor what these would mean to the tenuous peace of holy Olympus, and for the most mindful among the venerable assembly, to the future of the Nephele and the resurgence of Life upon the broad-pathed Earth overall. Whatever the Fates decreed for either, Hermes dared not venture a guess. Instead his gaze fixed upon his half-brother Ares, sword in hand, looking up in abject confusion at loud-thundering Zeus.

For all anyone could tell, the Cloud-gatherer might finally take this as his longed-for opportunity to strike down his most hated son, now that his Queen no longer stood in his way to protect her young. However, Zeus made no move against valiant Ares, standing instead in silence before his throne, as if listening to wise counsel only he could hear. Once Ares fully realized that his mother was well and out of danger, he lowered his weapon and looked at his brethren for clues as to what to do next. Finding none, the god of war withdrew from the centre of the throne room, taking his place beside Apollo, who looked as shocked and confused as all the other gods who dwell on starry Olympus.

Curiously, Zeus abstained from ordering his messenger to fetch Hera and their daughters, yet Hermes knew it was only a matter of time before his father issued the command. The certainty of it left Hermes quite ill at ease, and he detested the prospect of undergoing another ceaseless search for his runaway Queen. Hera had seemingly grown even more proficient at disappearing through the cracks between realms, to places unknown even to the cleverest of gods and mortals. Perhaps the time had come for Hermes to follow the example of his spirited stepmother and unwitting nurse-maid and at last refuse to take part in Zeus' inane designs lest the Father of gods and men learn to face the consequences of his own intransigence. Before Hermes had the chance to voice his brazen thoughts, august Themis mercifully spoke up to everyone's relief.

"My King," the Titanide said. "Before you act against the Queen and the Princess for their show of displeasure and insolence, I must advise you to consider your deeds very carefully."

Zeus raised an eyebrow but kept silent, allowing his trusted advisor to speak her piece.

"Until anyone can produce demonstrable proof that Hera broke her Oath," Themis continued, "you do not possess the lawful prerogative to take punitive measures against the city-ship Nephele or any other mortal settlement in the Queen's care. These were the terms you devised to secure Hera's return to Olympus, to which she justly acquiesced."

"Very well," Zeus conceded, before turning his gaze towards Hermes. "Find our Queen at once," he told the messenger. "Later you may bring the Princess before us as well. With or without Eris. That one is of little concern to us."

"As I've said earlier, Father," Hermes replied, gathering his courage, "I'd rather not."

Zeus gave Hermes a cold, hard stare, the corner of his eyes twitching ever so slightly at the provocation. "You dare defy my order?" he asked crossly.

"No, Father," Hermes answered, his voice unwavering, surprising all gathered and himself above all others. "I do not dare, I simply object to bringing Hera and Junia back to Olympus against their wishes, for reasons you would surely understand, if you had any care about my continued well-being, and that of Olympus."

As grey-eyed Athena raised her shield once more and pulled Hermes behind her, Zeus turned his irate gaze towards Themis, gesturing in the direction of his insubordinate offspring.

"And what am I to make of this open display of defiance, pray tell?" Zeus asked the Titanide.

"Hermes has a valid point," Themis replied. "If he executes your order, then he might risk suffering the penalty of those who perjure against the Oath of the Holy River Styx. Surely this is an outcome you would rather avoid, is it not, my King?"

Zeus threw another glance at Hermes, however this time the Virgin Warrior stood between both, as if daring the Thunderer to strike down his messenger before the blessed gods assembled in the throne room on high Olympus.

"And you, Pallas?" Zeus said, addressing Athena. "Are you in league with your Queen, as she seeks to undermine my rule once more!? Perhaps I was too lenient with you the last time, but now I see that you are as capable of sedition of the highest order as Hera was when she had me bound in chains all those centuries ago! At least then she had the decency to avow her own treachery!"

"I swore obeisance after her insurrection failed," Athena declared. "As did Hera, and all those who dwell on starry Olympus. But as even wise Themis will attest, neither her absence nor Hermes' conscientious objection constitute demonstrable treason, Father."

"Then why do you stand before me with your aegis raised?" Zeus asked.

"Truth be told," Athena answered coolly, though her demeanour suggested otherwise, "I am of the mind that you are not being entirely rational at the moment."

"Athena is right," Apollo agreed. "Only moments ago, Hera and I tried to explain to you why Junia came to Olympus on a whim, but you would not hear our words nor Junia's for that matter. Instead, you falsely insinuated that she already chose her own fate, even though she is still far from mature enough to make that decision. Even so, you sought to put words in her mouth, and manipulate her to attain your most desired outcome –"

"*My* most desired outcome?" Zeus asked mockingly. "You speak to me as though you did not want Junia to stay here on Olympus for you own selfish reasons! And to that I say it's about bloody time you wed the girl properly, given that you staked your claim upon her shortly before she was even conceived! Do not think that I was ever unaware of your presence inside Hera's consciousness that night after I woke her to bring solace to her troubled thoughts."

"What?" Apollo inquired in a voice barely above a whisper as a glimmer of confusion and disgust momentarily marred his otherwise perfect features.

Nepheleid

The blessed gods watched the scene with baited breath, perhaps unsure of what to make of their King's preposterous accusations.

"You heard me, you little pervert!" Zeus continued. "Although I must admit, it takes a peculiar breed of voyeur to hide in the shadows of an unquiet mind and watch as your own father quickens his wife's womb with his seed! I only hope you did that to witness your bride-to-be come into being and not for more lurid ends!"

"Ew," Artemis said as she took her place by her twin brother's side.

Hermes did a double-take. He had been so distracted by the absurd spectacle before him that he had not seen nor heard the Huntress return to Olympus. Perhaps the commotion compelled her to return to the throne room, Hermes speculated.

"Oh, grow up, you!" Zeus scolded Artemis.

"Perhaps you should mind your own behaviour before saying such things to the Archer and the Huntress!" gentle Demeter, who brings forth gifts, blurted out angrily at the Cloud-gatherer.

Hermes suppressed a grin, wondering how long Demeter had waited to snipe at her King with this retort.

"Be that as it may, Father," Athena said, at last, cringing visibly as she lowered her shield, "the fact remains that you would gamble Hermes' very breath and force Apollo to wed an unready child if it meant that you could force Hera to remain on high Olympus, an outcome she clearly abhors."

"You're one to talk!" Zeus griped defensively. "You and this lot have done more than your share in accelerating her return! And yet, I have not seen any of you making any effort to persuade her to stay in our midst of late – *And what in Tartarus is this*?! HERMES!"

As the Father of gods and men grew increasingly agitated, swift Hermes spun round and saw Thetis, daughter of Nereus, open the high bronze doors of the throne room, with King Poseidon and Queen Amphitrite trailing closely behind her. Following in the Earth-shaker's wake Hermes saw the vast Sea-Court, composed almost entirely of the surviving offspring of Okeanos and Tethys who had not joined Prometheus and his learned mortals in their city-ship. In their midst the Titanides

Phoebe, mother of the demure Leto, Theia, bride of Hyperion, and Rhea, Mother of the gods, stood apart, as did their Titan elders Okeanos and Tethys, the Father and Mother of Rivers, accompanied by a host of Sea-gods and Sea-nymphs from oceans and rivers and lakes far and wide across the broad-pathed Earth.

"And what's all this, then, Brother?" Loud-thundering Zeus asked Poseidon before Hermes could welcome the newcomers to the throne room.

"A little bird told me you needed help persuading your Queen, our sister, to remain among her blessed kin," the Earth-Shaker replied.

"Thetis!" Demeter cried out in exasperation. "You are such a little tattle-tale! What have you done this time?"

"You leave her alone," golden Aphrodite retorted to the goddess of the furrows. "It was I who requested her to come before us with the Sea-Court, the Daughters of Gaia and Ouranos, and the other immortals who make their homes at the boundaries of the Earth."

"But why?" Artemis asked, her curiosity genuinely piqued.

"If wise Zeus cannot convince Hera to stay," Aphrodite answered, "then perhaps the ancient powers of the Earth, the Sea, and the most venerable among our kind, will help her see reason."

"Well done, little dove," Zeus said with a self-satisfied grin, though Hermes could not tell for certain whether the Thunderer was speaking to Thetis or Aphrodite. "Although your timing... leaves something to be desired. Hera's already left –"

"Do not thank her yet," the Lord of the Deep interrupted curtly. "We did not come all this way to convince Hera to stay with you and your children on starry Olympus. That duty fell to you, and it looks as though you failed at this simplest of tasks."

Zeus pressed the space between his eyebrows with his fingers. "Then why the hell are you here?" he asked, unamused. "Since Hera was not alone in swearing fealty to her rightful King after your insurrection failed, I doubt very much that you came all this way to co-opt Thetis' loyalty to Olympus and stage another coup."

"We are not here for that," Poseidon replied with a mien of annoyance.

Nepheleid

"Ah, so my sister truly is alive and well in that head of yours!" Amphitrite said sardonically. "I find it comforting that at least one of you pays attention to the world beyond the gilded halls of starry Olympus!"

Zeus turned his gaze towards Aphrodite, whose milky complexion turned veritably ashen in the span of a mortal breath. Perhaps it had never occurred to the goddess of love that her intervention could backfire so artlessly, Hermes thought.

In the time it took for Thetis to gaze upon Aphrodite with unabashed panic and for the latter to reach out to Ares while affecting a swoon, Hermes saw through the open bronze doors a familiar shape drawing near in the starry Heavens beyond high Olympus. The object's muted lights grew brighter as it approached the spot where the young Junia fell to terra firma in the midst of the meteor shower, seemingly a century ago. Drawing closer to the entrance of the throne room, Hermes stepped outside and immediately recognized the sleek craft as the Henokhie, the CARINA-issued chariot which Hera used to pilot when she dwelt among the learned mortals under her protection in the wilderness of Turtle Island.

The messenger took a deep breath and resisted the urge to chuckle aloud. At times such as these he enjoyed the memory of his older brother Apollo blatantly refusing to teach him the prophetic arts when he was a small boy, before loud-thundering Zeus expelled him from Olympus for the first time for stealing his lightning bolt. Hermes did not need the gift of second sight to divine the identity of the travellers nor the purpose for their awkwardly-timed arrival, for he already knew that the deathless denizens of the Nephele and its daughter-station high above the Earth could see all that came to pass among the blessed gods of holy Olympus.

The Lord of the golden bow likely sensed Hermes' mirth at the outlandish turn of events, for he also made his way beyond the high bronze doors to glimpse upon the newcomers deplaning from the shuttle.

"Are you certain that Eris left with Junia earlier?" Hermes asked Apollo flatly.

"I'm beginning to wonder about that myself," Apollo replied in an attempt to maintain levity.

The entire company of immortals assembled within the throne room on high Olympus grew eerily quiet as Hermes and Apollo climbed down the stairs to welcome Prometheus, Asia, Klymene, and Mnemosyne as they exited the shuttle first, while Iris opened the door at the rear of the passenger compartment from whence Eileithya and Hephaestus emerged. Behind them, Hermes spied a small retinue of other Oceanides milling about the Henokhie as well as a few foreign gods whom he had met only once during his exile on Turtle Island, mostly during Hera's farewell tour among those who kept her daughter safe from Zeus' messenger and enforcer for almost ten years.

By now all immortals, including those who came to starry Olympus with Poseidon and the Sea-Court, fixed their gaze upon the benefactor of humanity and his own entourage as they climbed the stairs purposefully and made their way towards Zeus' royal throne. As Hermes heralded the newcomers, his previous amusement gave way to apprehension, for there was no doubt in his mind that the Cloud-gatherer would remain in a foul mood as long as this latest throng of uninvited guests lingered within holy Olympus' gilded halls. It brought him a small measure of comfort to see Athena, Herakles, Hebe, Apollo and Artemis flanking Prometheus protectively as if their very presence could safeguard their lofty-minded kinsman against their father's ire.

Once Prometheus stood before the throne of Heaven, he waited respectfully for the King to address him. Hermes could tell that he and his entourage had not come to Olympus to exchange pleasantries with Zeus.

"I suppose I ought to thank you for interrupting my brother and his Court from berating me," the Father of gods and men told his old foe without humour. "Though perhaps I ought not to expect you to argue with Poseidon on my behalf."

With a decorous wave of his hand, Zeus bade Prometheus to state his business.

"I have come for my sister," Prometheus said in a sombre tone.

Zeus snorted at these words. Hermes raised an eyebrow. The evening had definitely taken a turn for the preposterous, he pondered as he tries to guess how long it would take Themis to scold her King for greeting his guests so indelicately.

"Your sister is right behind you," Zeus answered, gesturing towards Eileithya who stood beside Hephaestus behind Asia and Klymene.

Nepheleid

Prometheus did not reply. Hermes wordlessly lauded his kinsman for possessing the wisdom to first let Zeus air his grievances fully before all the blessed gods gathered in the throne room. Prometheus must have divined Hermes' thoughts, for he threw him a quick glance, followed by a subtle, almost imperceptible wink.

"You've come for your sister," Zeus said, more to himself than to Prometheus.

The benefactor of humanity answered with a small nod, but otherwise kept silent.

"The last time you were here," Zeus continued, "you came for your mother. And now you've returned before my very throne with Klymene, your mother of the breast, and your wife, and other children of mine you've taken from my Court. Let me ask you this, Prometheus, was it not enough that I agreed to let Herakles release you from your rock all those centuries ago as a show of benevolence, of willingness to let bygones be bygones? And still, you waited three thousand-odd years to come here and abscond with my wife, my Queen, from her rightful place on holy Olympus, to spite me! Hera never knew the truth, because I judged it better for her peace of mind, given the grief that preceded your birth. I gave you to Klymene when you were born, that is true, but only because I knew she would prove an excellent mother to you, having seen her raise the children she'd borne the Titan Iapetos. Was Klymene not enough as your mother? What in the world possessed you to come here and open old wounds and turn my beloved Queen against me? And now you've come for your *sister*!? You've come to poison her mind as well and turn her against me and forsake her deathless kin here on holy Olympus! Well, I hate to be the bearer of bad news, but they both left, just moments before this Sea-dwelling lot arrived on my doorstep."

Fair-haired Rhea took a step towards Zeus, placing herself between Prometheus and his former tormentor. "You leave him be!" the Mother of the gods scolded her royal son uninhibitedly.

"Be quiet, Mother!" Zeus spat out, making no effort to mask his growing irritation. "This does not concern you."

"Be mindful to whom you speak, you little whelp!" Rhea retorted sharply. "I will speak whenever I damned well please! And I'll have you know that this matter concerns me as much as it concerns all of us who dwell upon the broad-pathed Earth. It so happens that Gaia, the Earth-Mother herself, is in her death throes, and we cannot remain idle while you continue to threaten to destroy the city-ship that harbours a vast laboratory for Life, which at the moment constitutes her only hope at resurgence."

"I've not threatened Prometheus, Mother," Zeus replied with forced calm. "At least not yet. Nor have I harmed the Nephele and the learned mortals who dwell therein."

"Ah, but you did!" Rhea replied. "You threatened them all on the day you blackmailed Hera to return to you, all because you were denied your favourite toy for a few years, which is a ridiculously brief span of time for our deathless kind!"

"Are you quite done?" Zeus asked his mother flatly.

"Oh no, child," Rhea answered. "I'm only getting started."

"What the hell do you want from me?" Zeus inquired indignantly.

"I want you to admit that you are the sole reason why Hera plans to leave the Earth-mother, never to return!" Rhea spat back.

"All this because one bride was never enough for you," Tethys, the Nurse of All, said as she took her place next to the Titan Queen. "Hera never wanted to be your bride. Even after Rhea sent her away to dwell with us at the boundaries of the Earth, you came for her. That is why she left the shores of Hellas and made her homes and planted her gardens far and wide across the world as we once knew it."

"Hera knew that taking you as her Consort would mean the end of her supremacy as the Mistress of all Life," Okeanos, the Father of Rivers, interjected. "In much the same way that your greed and insatiable lust cost our daughter Metis, the wisest among our children, her life."

"And that of my father," Prometheus said. "Hera would have forgiven you for this misdeed in the end, as she has forgiven the countless offences you've committed against her, if you'd accepted that she only loved you as a brother, which was far more than you deserved!"

"I saved her from the maw of Kronos!" Zeus cried out, on the verge of losing his temper.

"That you did," Prometheus replied coolly. "And perhaps there was a time when she thought she owed you a debt of gratitude, but you were not worthy of being her husband. To this very day, you cannot bring yourself to revel in her triumphs, and you've done everything in your power to undermine her ascendancy at every turn. To this very day, whenever you look upon the starry Heavens, you do not see the Nephele, a living city-ship that Hera midwifed into being. Instead you see a constant reminder that your dastardly deeds against her first husband, my father, usurped any chance that I, firstborn grandson to the Titan-King, would ever have at succeeding Kronos as Ruler among the gods! That is the only reason why you gave me to Klymene. As for Hera, even then, she knew why you slew the doomed Eurymedon, King of the Giants. She knew that you desired her above all others, and also that you would never consider her debt repaid even, if she secured your rule among the blessed gods who dwell on high Olympus by becoming your Queen –"

"And giving birth to your legitimate children," Eileithya said accusingly, unafraid of her father's ire.

"Even the ones you refuse to acknowledge as rightfully yours," Hephaestus added, standing tall beside his sister.

It took Hermes a moment to notice how straight Hephaestus stood. He then realized that he had not seen the smith god limp on his trek between the Henokhie and the throne room. Hermes looked up at Apollo, who also looked as though he had already inferred the true reason behind Hephaestus' relocation to the Nephele. Somehow, the learned mortals found a way to heal his perennially broken leg with means unimaginable to the wisest among their kind a mere few centuries before. It was brave of Hephaestus to appear before Zeus so restored, Hermes thought, since the King of Olympus might interpret such a change as yet another challenge to his authority, like the time Hephaestus came to his mother's aid aeons ago, and was condemned to walk with a limp ever since.

"Truth be told," Prometheus said finally, "Hera was most prescient, as always, in her reluctance to marry you. Even so, she has since given you everything you ever wanted, and you took it all and gave her nothing. This is why we have come here, from the many nations of the broad-pathed Earth, and the newly born cities in the Sky, to petition, on Hera's behalf, that you release her from any and all Oaths that bind her to a King she would never have crowned, unless forced to do so under extreme duress."

Zeus stood motionless, answering Prometheus' words with his characteristic icy stare, though his fingers reached for his thunderbolt in the folds of his tunic. To the consternation of all the blessed gods assembled in the throne room on high Olympus, golden Aphrodite joined Hermes, Athena, Herakles, Hebe, Athena, Apollo and Artemis beside Prometheus and his retinue, bidding the Thunderer to withhold retaliating against Hera's firstborn son.

Hermes braced himself, for he knew Aphrodite's unexpected show of solidarity could very well prompt Zeus to declare all those gathered before him guilty of high treason, in the same way he condemned Hera to be chained to the Sky for rebelling against his rule.

Before Apollo could interject with his predictable, conciliatory words. Zeus simply addressed the crowd of immortals with a most disappointed look upon his countenance.

"It appears that the entire deathless race across the vast Earth has taken leave of its senses," he said gravely. Turning his gaze towards Hermes and his other children, he simply shook his head in disappointment and disappeared in a flash of lightning, followed by a stentorian sonic boom that reverberated across the gilded halls of starry Olympus.

When the loud ringing ceased to stupefy all those gathered within the throne room, Iris looked to her fellow messenger god and asked, "Where in the world would he even begin to know where to look for Hera?"

"Hera mentioned something about making an appearance at Polaris tomorrow morning," Athena said, "or at least some time before the Krios ascends back towards the Nephele."

Klymene looked at the Virgin Warrior with the warmest of smiles. "Our sister truly lives in you," she said in an almost breathless whisper.

"It's a damned shame that Metis lives in him as well," Asia retorted, though without a hint of malice. "At least *she* knows better than not listen to Hera when she speaks!"

Hermes took a deep breath, trying not to balk at the thought of undertaking yet another journey to Turtle Island, this time to retrieve both his Queen and his King. As he spun on his heels and made for the open bronze doors, Hermes heard Prometheus calling out to him.

"Do not waste your time following Zeus to Polaris," the benefactor of humanity said. "He will not find Hera there. Our Queen went to a place where no one can find her, unless she wills it so."

Nepheleid

"You know where she went?" Apollo asked in an uncharacteristically eager manner.

"I will bring you to her," Prometheus answered, "if you help me find my sister."

"Hera told Eris to take Junia someplace where she has allies," gentle Demeter said. "She also said something about taking her to those who know her true name, and whose very future depend of it remaining a secret? It was all so very cryptic. What else did she say, children?"

"Eris did not take Junia to Turtle Island either," Apollo said, as if in the throes of a revelation.

Prometheus nodded, as a knowing smile widened across his face.

"I know where Eris took her," Apollo said excitedly, his gaze locked upon the benefactor of humanity. "Demeter, you might prefer to remain here on starry Olympus."

"Absolutely not," Demeter replied sharply.

"Then promise you'll behave," august Hestia called out from her seat at the hearth. "And give our dear brother my best regards."

Hermes looked at Prometheus and Apollo quizzically, though he quickly realized what the goddess of the hearth had meant.

"How many can you bring across the realms under your power all at once?" Prometheus asked him.

"I can bring the entire Olympian Court, and the rest of this lot, unless some of you wish to wait for us here," Hermes replied.

"Shall we, then?" Prometheus said finally.

Hermes nodded cheerfully.

Before anyone could declare themselves unwilling to join what promised to be a very entertaining adventure, all disappeared from the throne room, all save for Hestia, who dutifully remained behind, to keep the fires burning on starry Olympus.

Chapter Twenty-Two

Junia opened her eyes, willing herself awake from what she hoped had been the most elaborately bizarre dream she ever had in her short life. Instead she found herself immersed in a seemingly endless swirl of stars stretching in all directions above and beyond. Undaunted by this apparent foray into lunacy, Junia sought the familiar Sky-Rivers crisscrossing the inky expanse between the worlds whereas a small child she always knew peace. This was the secret place where she met the Lord of the golden bow for the very first time, when he brought solace to her mother's restless mind while the blessed gods feasted in the banquet hall on high Olympus. But Junia did not find herself in the dreamscape of the Sky-Rivers. This was a different sort of pathway between realms altogether, through which her sister Eris flew, expertly guiding her towards random flashes of blue light as they forged ahead, leaving crimson-hued fractal trails in their wake.

After an unfathomable span of time, which Junia truly could not measure, having lost all bearings in what she perceived to be a quantum dimension of sorts, the sisters touched down upon a surface that looked and felt as though they landed on the hardest bedrock at the foundation of the Cosmos. There, Eris released Junia from the gravitational force she effortlessly conjured to pull her young charge across this chaotic realm and folded her wings neatly around her shoulders. Junia looked at Eris in utter bewilderment, for she never noticed until this moment that her minder possessed wings.

"Oh, you've seen these before," Eris said, grinning at Junia's dazed expression. "You just don't *remember* them. Mother was always very peculiar about showing signs of divinity around mortals, so I had to confound you and the other children every time I deployed my wings. But there are no mortals here, at least, none that are alive."

"Where *are* we?" Junia asked, willing her legs not to buckle at the knees.

"Take some time to remember," Eris replied. "If Hermes told it true, then you've been here before. Think!"

Nepheleid

Junia took a deep breath, but the air in this place was unlike anything on the surface of the broad-pathed Earth. She knew Eris had not brought her to a faraway asteroid, or anywhere else beyond the boundaries of Earth's atmosphere, otherwise her skin would tingle at the chill of what mortals call absolute zero, the coldest temperature imaginable.

"We're not in space," Eris said, divining Junia's thoughts. "Otherwise you would have floated off the ground!"

"Not if the gravity is equal to or greater than... Wait, are we even still in the same universe!?" Junia retorted fitfully.

Eris let out a throaty laugh. "Getting warmer," she said breathlessly.

Junia looked up, hoping to orient herself by the stars, but saw only pitch blackness above and beyond. "Tartarus?" she asked at last.

"There's my clever girl!" Eris answered. "Although we are nowhere near the gates. But we are in the Underworld."

"I've never been to this part of the Underworld," Junia said.

"Not many have," Eris replied. "This is a doorway into the Kingdom of Hades through which I alone enter. Even swift Hermes never passes through here."

"Why do you come to the Underworld?"

"There are times when I need to take my leave from Olympus," Eris answered. "And Hades is the Host of Many, not only of the shades of the dead. He is a most gracious Host and lets me dwell here as long as I have to, before I return to the company of the gods on starry Olympus. Mother understands this, and I think you do as well."

"Okay, so why are we in the Underworld, right now?" Junia asked with a hint of impatience.

"This is where our allies dwell," Eris said flatly. "Were you not listening when Mother spoke to us before we left Olympus?"

"Yeah, well I thought she meant that we had to go back to Turtle Island," Junia replied.

"Why would you think such things?" Eris asked.

"Because of All My Relations? You know, the Manitous and gods and spirits of place that looked after us and protected us since I was a baby?"

Eris raised an eyebrow.

"Okay, since before you and Ares started following me around like a shadow!" Junia added. "You know what I meant. All My Relations made sure that Hermes never got too close to us while we stayed on Turtle Island."

"Little one, Hermes always knew where you and Mother made your home," Eris pontificated. "He cut a truce with Prometheus years ago, and agreed to leave you and Mother in peace while the immortals who dwell at the boundaries of the Earth did their great work among the learned mortals. Athena and Apollo knew as well, and perhaps Father suspected as much, though he held out hope that Mother would return to him in time. Hermes only came to seek for you at the steps of Hades' palace because Father threatened him with exile if he did not return with you and Mother. But you already know this."

"Eris, that's exactly why we should go back to Turtle Island! Never mind the deal Hermes made with Prometheus! All My Relations will still protect us if I wish to not be found!"

"All Your Relations, as you call them, are deeply divided on the matter," Eris asserted. "Mother promised the gods of Turtle Island that she would not bring her feud with Father to their shores. She promised not to burden them with her troubles, even if she knows many would gladly offer their help. All *our* relations, at least the ones who dwell in the farthest reaches of this Kingdom, on the other hand –"

"Would rather see you consider your plans carefully before doing anything you might regret!" a deep, disembodied voice reverberated in the gloom surrounding Junia and Eris.

Though still thoroughly disoriented from her voyage through the realms, Junia immediately recognized the voice as belonging to her uncle Hades, the Lord of the Underworld. Junia had met Hades only once before, when she was eight years old, and remembered him as a kind, magnanimous fellow who offered Hera shelter for as long as she wished after Apollo visited his Queen in a dream to warn her that Zeus would soon discover her whereabouts. Junia also recalled that Hades possessed a helmet that could bend the light around him, rendering him undetectable and invisible to all, whether mortal or otherwise.

Nepheleid

"Uncle Ninja!" Junia cried out cheerfully, setting her gaze in the direction from whence she gauged Hades' voice originated.

"Well, that's a new one!" Hades replied with a chuckle as he took off his helmet directly behind Junia. "I appreciate your perceptive nature young one, but that never works. Just ask your sister."

Eris snorted. "Lord Hades' helmet scatters the sound of his voice!" she said. "You cannot find him with echolocation!"

"How about a heat-sensor?" Junia inquired innocently as she turned around to face Hades. "Or X-rays, or a Geiger counter!"

"He is the Lord of the Underworld, not radioactive!" Eris replied.

"Was your mother right about when we would meet next?" Hades asked, ignoring Eris' retort. "I see that you are not quite yet grown, and still have much to learn about the art of stealth, since I could hear you and your sister from the steps of my palace. But did your mother tell it true? Does your prowess in combat put your brother Ares to shame?"

"I kick his butt all the time!" Junia answered cheerfully, forgetting for a moment that she had only recently set into motion a chain of events that could tear Olympus asunder.

"He lets you because he's the one who now teaches you such things!" Eris replied. "He has to let you prevail lest he run afoul of Mother!"

Hades chuckled softly. "That is good to hear," he said benevolently. "However, I am of the mind that you both did not come here, through the secret entrance of my Kingdom known only to the very few, to play that game of invisible laser tag that I was promised when you were a small child."

Junia bit her lip. She had all but forgotten that part about her last farewell to Hades, though not her wistfulness at leaving her newfound kin in this strange place.

Hades set his gaze upon Eris. "What sort of trouble have you conjured up this time?" he asked her casually, as if for the thousandth time.

"Not I, Lord Hades," Eris replied. "And Mother foresaw this particular trouble long ago. Now that it has become manifest, I ask that you keep my sister safe in your care, while I seek out Mother's allies in your realm."

Hades sighed, shaking his head slightly. "It seems as though I've heard these very words spoken from Hera's lips only a few short days ago," he said. "But that's because Time goes by at a different pace here in my Kingdom than that of the world of the living."

"We're here to seek the Titans!" Junia whispered aloud, understanding at last Eris' meaning. Junia sat down on the bedrock of the Cosmos, as the full brunt of the realization hit her all at once.

That long-ago Summer, when Hera petitioned Hades for his protection from Hermes and other agents of Olympus, Junia took the initiative to seek the wisdom of the Titans by herself while her mother and uncle conversed in the royal palace overlooking the Elysian Fields. To everyone's surprise, Junia found the gate of Tartarus with relative ease, and entered the prison of the damned in much the same way as a small cat crosses the space between the slats of a picket fence. Once inside Tartarus, Junia met the Titans, who were all too eager to welcome her as a favoured child of Hera. Of course, Hera quickly divined Junia's whereabouts and sought to bring her back to Hades' palace, fearing that the Titans would devour her as King Kronos once devoured five of the six children fair-haired Rhea bore him. Strangely enough, the Titans also greeted Hera as an old friend. Later, as Hades brought Hera and Junia back to his palace, Hera admitted that she had made her journey to Tartarus many times and always knew how to find her way back out of the darkness.

Junia also remembered what Kronos told her when he gifted her with his sickle, all the while boasting that she would one day avenge him by naming the new Sky-King among the gods, though Junia herself would never ascend to the throne of Heaven: *When the time comes, little moppet, this mighty weapon shall cut away all that hinders you in fulfilling your destiny. When you do use it, remember us five, who have been waiting for you at the gate of gloomy Tartarus, and have shown you kindness, when some of your kin had no such luck.*

Hades gave Junia a sagging look. "Where is Hera, pray tell?" he asked.

Junia looked at Eris, who said nothing.

"Before I even consider your request to journey to the Pit," Hades pressed on, "I insist that you follow me to my palace. Now, if you please –"

With a gesture of his hand, The Host of Many bade his guests to follow him.

225

Nepheleid

Eris took Junia by the hand and pulled her to her feet. "Mother will not be joining us here today," she told Hades flatly.

"I was afraid you'd say that," the Lord of the Underworld replied. "All the more reason for us to discuss a few things-"

"We know the rules, Uncle," Eris interrupted. "We will return the Titans unharmed."

"We've been through this, Eris," the Lord of the Underworld said patiently. "No one journeys to Tartarus until we've spoken in my palace. Now remember, this is the time of year when my Queen shares my Kingdom. You *will* mind your manners."

"Yes, Uncle," Eris mumbled sullenly, following Hades aboard his chariot, with Junia at her heel.

Before Junia released Eris' hand to grab the railing of Hades' swift chariot, the trio arrived at the stables upon the grounds of the royal palace. Junia remembered this place well, though this time the grandiose dwelling of the Lord of the Underworld looked smaller than it had all those years ago, when Junia was so little, and soon to catch a glimpse of how immense, and stranger still, the Cosmos would prove to be.

"Look, by the doors!" Eris whispered to Junia as she led her off the chariot. "There is someone you need to meet!"

Junia followed Eris' line of sight, and spied a beautiful goddess looking down at them from the top of the stairs leading into Hades' palace. Clad in regal attire that reminded Junia of the sophisticated raiment Hera wore whenever she attended her queenly functions in the company of the blessed gods, the lady looked inordinately young, even for a deathless scion of Olympus. In fact, the goddess looked barely older than Junia, though she was, in fact, almost as old as grey-eyed Athena, firstborn daughter of loud-thundering Zeus.

"Do you know who that is?" Eris asked Junia.

"Persephone?" Junia asked in a voice barely above a whisper.

"Have you two met before?" Hades inquired, genuinely curious and amused at Junia's reaction.

"Uh, no, I haven't," Junia answered truthfully. "I was gone at Junior Space Camp the entire Summer when Persephone came to visit Aunt

Demeter at Borealis, and I don't think I've seen her on Olympus since then. At least I don't think so."

"Why not?" Hades asked.

"Mother and Father have a bet as to what fate Junia will decide for herself once she comes of age," Eris explained. "For this reason, Father ordered that Junia ought not to meet Persephone within the gilded halls of holy Olympus until after she'd made her choice. Because, you know. ."

Hades raised an eyebrow, while Junia threw Eris a strange look.

"Well, my dear," Eris told Junia with a knowing smile, "if any hesitation lingered in your heart as to the righteousness of your decision, and as to whether Zeus deserves the full brunt of your scorn, then the time has come for you to cast all doubt into oblivion."

Junia sought Hades' gaze for some quantum of guidance, but the Lord of the Underworld no longer stood by her side. A sinking feeling settled in the pit of Junia's stomach as she recalled what Hades told her mother shortly after they arrived in the Underworld all those years ago. The Host of Many gladly offered Hera his hospitality, however, he refused to take sides in her quarrels with the Thunderer. Was that the reason why Hades later left Hera and Junia alone on this very landing after they returned from Tartarus, disappearing behind the stables under the pretext of putting away the sickle Kronos had given Junia as a parting gift? In doing so, had Hades deliberately left Hera and Junia vulnerable to Hermes' ambush, knowing that Zeus' messenger would return to collect his Queen and her young child and bring them back to Olympus? Junia banished such thoughts from her mind, as none could explain why Hades later insisted that Hermes swear an Oath by the Holy River Styx to not take Hera and Junia anywhere against their will.

"Hermes won't find us here," Eris said reassuringly, in a way that Junia found thoroughly off-putting. "Not this time, anyway. Zeus likely told him to find Hera first, and I assure you that Mother is nowhere near this place!"

"But where is she?" Junia asked.

Eris said nothing, placing instead her index finger upon her lips to beckon Junia to remain quiet, then she made a small gesture with her head towards the top of the stairs. Junia did a double-take as soon as she saw Hades escorting Persephone on the way down to greet their guests. Junia wondered when he climbed the broad steps, then took a mental note to pay more attention to Hades' practical lessons in the art of stealth.

"Back so soon, Eris?" Persephone said as she and King Hades reached the bottom of the stairs. "What mischief have you wrought upon the Cosmos this time?"

Eris gasped theatrically and clutched her chest with both hands, while Junia did her best to suppress a giggle at her sister pantomiming outrage.

"Hi," Junia said gaily, wagering that she could compensate for her lack of stealth by feigning confidence. "We haven't officially met before. I'm Junia, your cousin –"

"You're my sister, little one," Persephone interrupted disdainfully. "You are more my kin than you would ever care to know. And your name is not Junia. All the gods know this, and many of us find this rather disingenuous of you to uphold your mother's charade!"

"My darling!" Hades said, visibly flummoxed by Persephone's response. "You are being rude to our guests! And be kind to this one, she is only a child!"

"I am not here for anyone's charade," Junia answered cautiously.

"Then why are you here, Junia?" Persephone asked with a hint of pique.

"All My Relations," Junia managed to answer, perplexed by Persephone's hostility towards her.

"Ah yes, the girl from Turtle Island, unblemished by the miasma of the Olympian Court," Persephone continued. "Come to seek the Titans to wage Mommy's wars on her behalf?"

"Persephone!" Hades protested. "Why are you berating our guests?"

"No, that's a fair question," Junia replied. "Yeah, I guess I'm here to see the Titans, to help us solve a delicate matter."

"Against whom?" Persephone inquired.

"Who do you think?" Eris snapped back, while Hades lowered his face in one hand, visibly dismayed at the exchange.

"So, Hera sent a child to the Underworld to fight her battles?" Persephone taunted. "Wonders never cease!"

"Uh, well, my Mom can't outright sick the Titans on Zeus because of that stupid Oath he made her swear," Junia said with an edge to her voice. "You know, after he tortured her by chaining her to the Sky? So yeah, I've come to seek our allies... What?"

Persephone scoffed at Junia's words.

"Darling, please!" Hades blurted out, looking more annoyed than Junia thought possible.

"What's your problem, Persephone?" Junia asked, growing increasingly vexed by the goddess' enmity.

"Do you know what your mother did, the last time she sought the help of the Titans?" Persephone asked at last.

Junia paused, trying to remember what exactly Hera had told Hades about the true purpose of her visit when they last set foot in the Underworld. "Mom wanted to know where Eurymedon was," she answered after a moment.

"Eury-who?" Persephone said, confused. "No, child. That's not it. The last time she came to seek the help of the Titans, she released them on starry Olympus so that they could murder my son!"

"If you mean Dionysus," Junia rebutted, "then you should know he's doing just fine! I saw him just before we left."

Persephone sighed theatrically.

"I know the story," Junia continued, undaunted. "Zeus wanted a son so badly that he had his way with you, and then Demeter sought Hera's help to give you a post-natal abortion, because you gave birth to a mutant baby with horns or something."

"And what else?" Persephone goaded Junia sarcastically.

"Mother had you take a bath in the Lethe," Eris interjected, 'so you would not remember what Zeus did to you, and so that you would carry on, unblemished by the stain of his dastardly deed!"

Nepheleid

"But Zeus brought your son back," Junia added. "Just to spite my Mom. He brought him back by impregnating a mortal, promising her that she would be his next Queen, even though she proved too daft to not ask Zeus to appear before her in his true form. It did not end well for the mortal. And I get it, my mom did to you what Zeus did to her when she had Prometheus, but what she did to you she did because she cared about you and Demeter, because she wanted to help you and protect you. She did it even though she knew that your son would come back eventually, because even when gods get dismembered or eaten, they come back because they can't stay dead."

Hades heaved a weary sigh.

"What, too soon?" Eris asked facetiously.

"Oh, you poor, naïve little child!" Persephone said, shaking her head. "You think this is all such a simple matter?"

"There are five Titans in Tartarus," Junia replied. "And one Zeus. And then there's me, and all those who agree with me that my Mom deserves better than to remain Zeus' prisoner."

"Hera has tried to defeat Zeus before with an oversized monstrosity," Hades said. "When Gaia, the Earth-Mother, told Hera what Zeus did to her first husband and her firstborn son, Hera midwifed the creature Typhon for the sole purpose of bringing Zeus low. But Zeus prevailed in his battle against the monster, and imprisoned Typhon in gloomy Tartarus with the rest of his enemies."

"Husband!" Persephone protested. "Do not give the child ideas!"

"Look," Junia said. "I know my Mom has done things in the past that she's not proud of, but whatever these are, they pale in comparison with what Zeus did to her over the course of centuries. Whatever the Titans end up doing to him, he's got it coming."

"How so?" Hades asked coolly.

"For one," Junia answered, "he threatened to destroy the Nephele if my Mom refused to return to him. So, she did. She didn't want to, but she did anyway, because she didn't want anything bad to happen to Prometheus and to all the mortals in his care. So yeah, we need the Titans' help to stop Zeus from retaliating against the Nephele, at least, until it's out of low Earth orbit and out of his reach."

"And why would the Titans do this, Junia?" Hades asked with genuine concern.

"Uh, because they hate Zeus and love Hera?" Junia said in disbelief. "Because Hera is the only one from the world above who comes to visit them? They know how horrible Zeus is to her. That's why Kronos gave me his sickle, and by the way, I need that thing, so if you could give that back, that would be just great."

"Before I do that," Hades said patiently. "You ought to know that the Titans never do anything without ulterior motives. Do you truly think they would help you without asking for something in return?"

"Like what?" Junia asked, her eyes growing wide with the realization that she had not thought this through.

"Like dominion over Olympus," Hades said. "We fought and won the War against the Titans for a very good reason, child. Would you have our efforts all be for nought? Even Hera, your blessed mother, took our side. Do remember, Junia, that Kronos devoured his own children for fear of being replaced as King, and after Zeus rescued us, Kronos still sought to destroy us."

"But, my Mom... she wouldn't--"

"I was once just like you, Junia," Persephone interrupted with a sigh. "In fact, I was exactly like you, the Princess of Olympus, long before your sister Hebe was born and eventually succeeded me in that role. I was sweet and innocent and believed the best in everyone. I was also the fairest maiden there ever was, so fair that my mother feared for what would become of me. She went to consult old Astraeus, the god who scries the stars to learn of things that are to come, and the ancient one foretold that an unworthy bridegroom would steal into my bedchamber and ravish me. So my mother spirited me away to a cave in Sicily, taking flight on chariot pulled by serpent-dragons, and then had the creatures guard the entrance to my cave while I spent the scorching days toiling away at my loom. But Zeus took their form and stole into my cave, then coiled around me in an amorous embrace, and from this unholy union I bore Zagreus, the dismembered, to whom Zeus would have ceded the very throne of Heaven! That is the truth of the matter."

"Zeus hasn't done that to me yet," Junia replied. "And if I get the Titans to help me, he will never do that to anyone ever again! And then Mom and I can go home to the Nephele and spread Earthy Life to the stars."

Nepheleid

"You would dethrone Zeus to secure the release of one who would then abandon the Earth, leaving the rest of us immortals with the bloody aftermath?" Persephone asked. "I believe that you truly do mean well, but perhaps you belong off-world, or better yet, in Elysium among the shades of the blessed dead, and all the other poor souls who proved far too callow for the world of the living."

"Hey, wait a minute –"

Hades took a deep breath. "Then let me ask you this," he said, choosing his words carefully. "If you were to depose your father as King, who would you place on the throne of Heaven in his stead? Because you are far too noble and conscientious to overthrow the Thunderer only to leave and watch the world burn from the lofty heights aboard your city-ship. So who would it be, then, if you should somehow succeed in your plot against my brother, your King? The Titans? King Kronos?"

"I don't know!" Junia muttered unhappily.

"Kronos was once a great King," Eris said gallingly. "When he ruled the world, the Earth was rife with soaring Life. Mother told me so."

"Your mother saw this from Kronos' own eyes," Hades replied. "I know this because I saw her tap into his consciousness countless times, when we were prisoners inside our father's belly."

"How about you, Lord Hades?" Eris asked. "You are a far worthier ruler than Zeus ever was. Why can't you take the throne of Heaven?"

"I already rule a Kingdom far greater than any realm of Life and matter," Hades answered, irked at Eris' persistence, before turning his attention back to Junia. "Say you do succeed in rallying the Titans to your cause, no matter how just or foolish it may be," he pressed on. "Say that they defeat Zeus. What then? This would create a power vacuum on high Olympus, which none of the blessed gods can fill, lest they suffer the penalty of those who perjure the Oath of the Holy River Styx. If you do this, then you must see it through and find a successor to the throne of Heaven. You mother failed in her insurrection because there was no consensus on who would replace Zeus as ruler of the gods. And you will fail if you do not find one that is truly worthy of the throne –"

"Prometheus," Junia said defiantly. "I will crown my brother Prometheus as King. He was supposed to be Kronos' heir, before Zeus usurped my mother's ascendancy and gave her firstborn son to Klymene. And

Prometheus is more than worthy, and you all know it. All that he's done he did to benefit humanity, and he paid a terrible price for it!"

"Now I know you're being sarcastic," Persephone said.

"Maybe I'm not!" Junia protested moodily. Looking up at Hades, she said. "I want my sickle."

"Come again?" Hades replied with some measure of surprise.

"My sickle. The one Grandpa Kronos gave me," Junia answered. "I know you took it when you and Mom came to find me in Tartarus. You grabbed it and then you hid it somewhere around here when we got back. I remember like it was yesterday! It's rightfully mine, and I want it!"

"You are correct," Hades answered patiently. "Father did give you that cursed thing. You can have your sickle back, but I cannot, in all good conscience, allow you or your sister to visit the Titans in Tartarus."

"That's not fair!" Junia protested.

"You will do as you are told, child!" Persephone snapped back.

"That's enough, you two!" Hades declared in a tone that elicited a stunned, awed silence from both Junia and Persephone.

After an unfathomable span of time, impossible to measure in this realm beyond human reckoning, magnanimous Hades softened his gaze as he looked upon his bride and young niece, respectively.

"Where is Eris?" he asked in a gentle yet slightly apprehensive tone.

Neither Persephone nor Junia offered an answer, though the Queen of the Underworld gasped when she saw the empty space where her King left his chariot upon his return.

Before the Host of Many could reply, Eris' stentorian maniacal laughter echoed insolently, and triumphantly, across the entirety of the dark Kingdom.

Nepheleid

Chapter Twenty-Three

Aloft on his golden chariot drawn by winged horses, loud-thundering Zeus sped towards the place where his torment came to an end four years before, when his estranged Queen emerged from hiding on the topmost deck of a floating city at the highest point upon the broad-pathed Earth. The darkening late Autumn skies trembled as bright flashes of lightening sundered the azure expanse in the King's wake. As the Cloud-gatherer closed in towards his journey's end, every beast in the Air, Sea, and upon the distant shores of Turtle Island trembled at the terrible spectacle unfurling in the Arctic twilight. Before reaching striking distance of the blasphemous mechanical umbilical cord connecting the bright Nephele to the Polaris below, Zeus halted, taken aback by the absence of sea ice that should have begun to enfold the tethered ship at the turn of the Seasons.

Circling his quarry above the wine-dark Ocean, Zeus wondered momentarily whether he had somehow lost his bearings and made his way instead to a mortal city-ship anchored near storied Hyperborea, the land of eternal Spring at the Northernmost reaches of the world. The Thunderer's confusion was short-lived, for he remembered that too many years had gone by without Autumn properly turning to Winter at the time appointed by the Seasons in these latitudes, far from the familiar Aegean Sea at the centre of his world. This, he knew, was the doing of long-dead mortals who laid waste to the Earth in their relentless pursuit of riches beyond anything dictated by need or logic. The Father of gods and men almost pitied the mortals alive today, eking out a precarious existence in the confines of their learned and mechanized enclaves scattered across the broad-pathed Earth, their numbers greatly reduced after centuries of rapid decline.

For all his benevolence and unwavering faith in the goodness of humankind, lofty-minded Prometheus failed to foresee that his theft of fire from Olympus would render mortals so incomprehensibly destructive in their avarice that the Earth-Mother would fall ill with a high fever for many centuries, from which she had yet to recover. Perhaps, Zeus pondered, this constituted all the pretext he needed to obliterate the CARINA network from the face of the Earth, as Prometheus' latest project in defiance to his King aimed to ultimately funnel the best and brightest mortals to cities beyond the Heavens, away from the dying planet where they were needed most urgently.

Remember, my King, that if you do this without the due process sanctioned by your own laws, under the aegis of those tasked with implementing Justice within and beyond the gilded halls of starry Olympus, then our dear Lady will surely never forgive you, wise Metis whispered in the deepest confines of Zeus' mind. *Once you do that which cannot be undone, she will rebuild her city-ships and sail away forever, never to cross our path.*

"She plans to do this no matter what course of action I choose to undertake," Zeus replied aloud. "What cause has she to cast her lot with these ungrateful whelps, whose ancestors have long sullied her name and deeds to mask their own weaknesses?"

What good can come of this, my King, other than dealing the death blow to the Mother of us all? And these mortals, whose fragile existence endures against all odds, and those of learned minds who dwell aboard the Nephele and other city-ships yet to be built, what offence have they wrought against you, other than trying to undo the sins of their predecessors? How are they any different from what we once were, before we fought and won the War against the Titans, and later against the Giants? Neither you nor I were ever guilty of devouring your siblings. But if you destroy the only hope humanity possesses in these dark times, do you not think that Junia, the youngest among your legitimate offspring, would gladly declare you guilty of far worse crimes than those committed by King Kronos against the children fair-haired Rhea bore them before you were born?

"The ranks of the CARINA venture are rife with deserters among our kind," Zeus answered. "An example must be made, even if doing so displeases me to the very core of my being."

Remember, my King, that our deathless kind no longer dwells in any CARINA base beneath your feet or beyond these shores. Any act of aggression against the Polaris could be construed as a provocation against the gods of Turtle Island, to whom Hera entrusted these mortals and their floating and flying cities of science. I would not be surprised if she entrusted the command of the nascent Hesperides Autonomous Station to one among their kind as soon as the Nephele is ready to sail the stars!

"What, then, would you have me do, now that we have come this far?" Zeus asked Metis unhappily.

Absent our kin, we ought to seek the counsel of those who are most like ourselves in this desolate place.

Zeus heaved a weary sigh. For all his puissance as supreme ruler among the blessed gods of starry Olympus, he possessed no such clout in this strange land at the boundaries of the world. Nor did he know any of the gods of Turtle Island whom Hera had doubtlessly befriended during her stay upon these distant shores. If Metis told it true, then only mortals dwelt within this preposterous metal barge, for the deathless gods from all the nations of the world in the employ of CARINA had either long since left to make their homes on the Nephele, or scattered beyond Hyperborea and all the other lands he never bothered to visit in the course of his deathless existence.

As the Cloud-gatherer's heart sank in acrimonious despair, he spied three small girls, perhaps barely older than the young Junia, standing by a pebble-covered beach on a small island due South of the Polaris. Upon second look, Zeus recognized the island as the place to which Junia fled upon their first meeting on the topmost deck of the Polaris a few years before. Prompted by her mother, Junia leaped off the Polaris into the cold Arctic Ocean, and improbably swam to shore, disappearing in the thick forest blanketing much of the continent. Stranger still, the three girls wore garments much like those Zeus had seen upon a trio of dolls among Junia's possessions, glimpsed on the night he found Hera asleep by their daughter's side, purposefully delaying their inevitable reconciliation in their marriage-bed.

Unsure whether the girls were mortal or otherwise, Zeus cast a thunderbolt across the twilit skies, causing the girls to stop what they were doing and look up at the strange newcomer in the Heavens above the Polaris. Without flinching, two of the girls responded by each picking up some rather large beach pebbles and striking them against one another until a spark of lightning emerged from the stones, narrowly missing the Father of gods and men as it arced from the Earth to the Sky. The third girl began leaping up and down, but the noise she made was quieter by the order of several magnitudes than the thunder with which Zeus had called their attention only moments before.

I think they saw you and heard your call, my King, Metis said flatly as Zeus resisted the urge to let out a victory cry so close to the unsuspecting mortals of the Polaris.

Nepheleid

Instead Zeus drew his chariot closer to the Heavens above the island where the three girls stood, affecting a cheerful mien as he addressed them.

"Young ones," he said. "There can be no doubt that you are no ordinary children. I am Zeus, King of the gods of Olympus. Who are you three, pray tell?"

At once the girls ceased their playful frolicking, and stared right at the Thunderer. After a few moments of stunned silence, one of the girls who had summoned the lightning bolt from the rocks stood straighter, and said, "I am Kweetoo, and this is Ignirtoq. We are the sisters who make lightning. Over there is Kadlu, the one who jumps on the hollow ice to make the thunder rumble, but the ice has not returned yet. It has been years since we had ice on which to play. Now we have to stay upon the shore. The stones are nice, but it's not the same."

Zeus simply stared at the girls, probing Metis wordlessly for the right words to say to these strange children. Hermes would have known what to reply, he pondered with some measure of regret at the haste with which he exited Olympus, for surely his messenger and herald never found himself at a loss for words, even in the company of alien gods in the farthest reaches of the Earth.

"I have travelled from far away," Zeus said at last, "and I seek whoever passes for a King or a ruler in these parts. I am looking for my wife and daughter who used to live on that big boat over there. Have you seen either? One is tall and lithe, with long, curly black hair, big brown eyes, and breasts like a wet-nurse. The other is almost thirteen years old –"

"Cow-Eyed!" Ignirtoq interrupted casually.

Zeus' breath halted at the sound of Hera's ancient epithet. "You... know her?" he asked the child, feigning calm.

"Everyone knows her," Kadlu answered. "She's that pretty lady who brought the People who put the machines under that boat and who used to comb Sedna's hair when the Sun stands still!"

"She had to leave years ago and we haven't seen her since," Kweetoo said.

"This Sedna you speak of," Zeus inquired. "Is she a friend to my wife? Would she know where I can find her?"

"You can always ask her," Ignirtoq said. "But you'd have to go to the bottom of the Sea, right under the boat. That's where you will find her cave."

"But you might have to wait until she's alone," Kadlu added. "I think one of the People from beyond Nanuk Bay is with her, braiding her hair."

Zeus threw a glance at the tenebrous waves surrounding the Polaris, and considered the three sisters' words. It ought to be simple enough to dive to the depths to meet this reclusive Sea-goddess, this Sedna, who he only knew by reputation. For the first time in his deathless existence, Zeus felt as an intruder upon a foreign shore, with its strange thunder children and this temperamental Sea Maiden who, as far as he knew, never graced the Court of his brother Poseidon. Zeus closed his eyes, awaiting to hear the counsel of wise Metis. How he wished his eldest brother and his children accompanied him to this place in search of his errant Queen who at least possessed the good sense to befriend the gods of every land upon which she trod in her journeys circling the Earth at the time appointed by the Seasons.

"Cow-Eyed is not here," he heard an unfamiliar voice reply from the depths, which he guessed belonged to the mysterious Sedna. "Yes, it's me. Cow-Eyed is not here. She has not come by to visit, not since she returned from her journey to the land of the White Buffalo Calf Woman. You might have better luck asking her. Now go away! You are the reason Cow-Eyed left and for that I will never forgive you!"

The Father of gods and men took one long look at the stygian waters surrounding the Polaris. He glimpsed finally at the Hub, rising like a menacing dark scorpion sting into the coming Night, until he finally came to terms with the knowledge that he would not find his bride in this desolate place, the unlikeliest doorway to the worlds beyond the Heavens. Grabbing hold of the reins of his swift chariot, he left the Arctic shore without further ceremony and sped towards the lands of the Lakota at the heart of Turtle Island, of which he had heard whispers as the place where the White Buffalo Calf Woman made her home.

Zeus cared not to start a war with the gods of Turtle Island, whom prior to Hera's desertion he had barely known, except for the tales Hermes sometimes told after his travels to this faraway land. As Hermes told it, Turtle Island was one of the last places on the broad-pathed Earth whose peoples had loved the gods before their conquered descendants were forced, some on pain of death, to embrace the worship of the Nazarene, forsaking the Manitous and other spirits of the land who had protected their mortal children for millennia. This was a fate the Father of gods and men knew all too well, for he and the blessed gods who dwell on starry Olympus also felt the terrible misery of being cast aside by legions of mortals, when for political reasons the Emperor of Rome did away with the piety of his ancestors and embraced a new, alien fate, that in turn proved the ruin of many nations. This was why Zeus, the King of Olympus and bane of the Titan-gods of old, felt as though he needed to tread upon the ancient land of Turtle Island with great care, for the gods and Manitous of this long-isolated continent had suffered enough at the hands of those who came from the Old World under the pretext of beginning their civilization anew.

As the Cloud-gatherer's thoughts lingered on the many ways he ought to avoid hostilities with the ancient powers of this land, his swift chariot reached the vast Plains at the heart of the continent. Landing upon a sleepy meadow bathed in the golden light of Sunset, he unfastened the reins and let the horses graze freely as the Earth-Mother sprouted ambrosial grasses to feed the deathless beasts. Before long he spied the silhouette of a woman high on the meadow, backlit by the rays of the setting Sun. She looked oddly familiar, yet the Father of gods and men remained unsure whether he had even seen her before. He dared to hope that this was Hera in disguise and that his Queen assumed a foreign form to hide her true self from the mortals of Turtle Island.

Like Hera, the woman possessed a regal bearing and stood straight and very still, as if studying her visitor with great interest. Though Zeus could not see her face, he noticed most of all her graceful, shapely form enfolded in a long white gown, fringed with baubles and feathers, her hair bound in a single braid that ran past her full breasts. Behind her stood a great white heifer, larger by far than anything he had ever seen on the fertile plains of the Argolid before the mighty aurochs of old passed from the Earth. For a moment Zeus was reminded of Io, a priestess of Hera he once seduced by appearing before the girl in the form of a mist, then transformed into a cow to spare her the wrath of his Queen. This could not be Io, Zeus thought, for though the mortal travelled far and wide across the broad-pathed Earth to escape the gadfly Hera sent to torment her in her bovine form, she ended her journeys in the ancient land of Egypt. There Io bore Zeus a son, and lived the remainder of her days in relative peace, far from the shores of Hellas. Through her son she became the ancestress of a long line of heroes, culminating in Herakles, the greatest hero to ever have lived.

Perhaps Hera took this guise to taunt Zeus, to remind him that she always thought him an unworthy suitor, taking particular umbrage at the affront he caused her by co-opting her mortal priestess, whose descendant brought everlasting glory to the Queen of Olympus, whether or not she wished it so. Whoever she was, this lady could not possibly be a mortal woman, as her moccasins did not touch the ground where she stood and a soft light lingered around her form long after the Sun began to disappear beyond the meadow.

"Hera!" Zeus called out, throwing caution to the wind.

To his delight, the lady answered by walking purposefully in his direction, though the Cloud-gatherer soon realized that this was not his Queen. As the lady closed the distance between them, Zeus saw that her skin was of a far darker complexion than Hera's milky flesh and her hair shone in ruddy hues, which the Thunderer thought rather unexpected for a trueborn daughter of Turtle Island.

The lady stopped a few paces away from where Zeus stood, as if allowing the newcomer to fully see and recognize the one who came to greet him.

"Buffalo Woman?" Zeus said, unsure whether it was proper to address the lady by the name he had heard her called from the depths of the Arctic by an unseen Sea Maiden.

"I am Ptesanwin, the one the People call the White Buffalo Calf Woman," the lady answered. "I've been expecting you, Sky-Father."

"You know who I am?" Zeus inquired, barely concealing his surprise.

The lady smiled. "You are the husband of Sky River Woman, the one who purifies the Waters and helps the People spread Life to the stars."

"Sky River Woman?" Zeus inquired. "I have never wed anyone of that name, at least none that I can remember."

"The one the foreign Sky-people call Hera, and the People of the Northern woodlands call Ella, and their spirits call the Cow-Eyed," Ptesanwin replied. "It is because of you that my dear friend has come to Turtle Island, and for that we are grateful... Sky Father?"

Zeus bit his lip, momentarily ashamed for letting his gaze linger upon the White Buffalo Calf Woman's supple bosoms.

"Right," he muttered. "That is not what the Sea Hag told me. She made it quite clear that I was not welcome at the Northernmost boundaries of this land or in the Sea."

Ptesanwin laughed. "Sedna is temperamental as are all the Sea-dwellers," she said.

"So, you've met my brother as well?" Zeus jested, relieved at this foreign goddess' amiable nature. He could not help but notice how the Buffalo Woman's tremendous beauty almost matched that of his Queen. Under different circumstances, he would have shown no misgivings about seducing her, but for all he knew this goddess could have already been claimed by the King of the gods of Turtle Island in the same way he had claimed Hera as his bride millennia ago.

You do not even know if there is a King of the gods in this land, Metis admonished him gently. *Tread carefully, my King, for you know nothing of these people, and they seem to know much about you. And remember that you are here to find Hera not to beguile her friends and give her greater cause to hate you.*

"I have not," Ptesanwin answered, "but we met his wife's sisters, the Ocean-born. They came to see the Sun Dancers a few years back, when Sky River Woman came to say goodbye."

"Has my wife come by in these parts since... Tessa?"

"You can call me by that name if your foreign tongue cannot abide by my Wakan name, Sky-Father," Ptesanwin said with good humour. "And no, Sky River Woman has not returned to this holy ground since she returned to the Sky-people far to the East."

"That's a shame," Zeus replied. "The Sea Hag said you would know where she is."

"I did not say otherwise, Sky-Father," Ptesanwin answered flatly.

"Then you do know where she is!" the Cloud-gatherer exclaimed joyfully. "You must tell me! I have come all this way across the world to find my beloved. Surely you would not deny me that which I have come to seek?"

"Say that I do know the whereabouts of Sky River Woman," Ptesanwin replied solemnly. "It seems to me as though she does not wish for you to find her at the moment. I can't say that I blame her, what with the way you looked at me just now –"

"I meant no disrespect, Tessa," Zeus interrupted remorsefully.

"– and yet you almost failed, just now, the very first challenge I gave the People when I was sent by the Wakan to heal the land, so many years ago," Ptesanwin continued. "Do you know the tale, Sky Father, of how I brought the Peace Pipe to the People?"

"I do not," Zeus said truthfully, as a pang of shame struck him at the core of his being.

I told you, you should have at least tried to learn something of these people before coming to these shores, Metis chided him softly inside his head.

"Long ago," Ptesanwin said, "where the Land hungered and thirsted, when the People were at war, the Creator sent me to teach the ways of peace to the People. I first came upon two hunters, right here on this Plain, on that very spot where you stand. One hunter recognized me as one of the Wakan and lowered his eyes out of respect. The other looked upon me with lust, just as you did, and intended to take me away and make me his woman. So I looked upon the second man and I gave him a choice: I told him that he could do as his friend did and revere me as one of the Holy People or live an entire lifetime in my presence, but that would mean his life would be shortened to only a moment. He chose the latter so in the blink of an eye his entire being turned to dust and where he stood there was nothing left but his bones. Then I told the other young man, the one who showed reverence, to return to his People and to prepare to receive me as I would then entrust them with the sacred Peace Pipe and teach them the seven sacred ways to pray. Since that day I've kept watch over the People and once every Age I return to them in the guise of a buffalo born with a white coat, then changing to red, then yellow, then black. That is how the People know that I am here and that the Wakan will forever guide those who live with respect and in harmony with the Land."

Zeus remained quiet for a moment, pondering the White Buffalo Calf Woman's words.

"So you see, Sky-Father," Ptesanwin continued. "You almost made the same choice as that long-dead hunter who did not show reverence. You almost let greed and lust take hold of your mind. If this is how you greet me, a stranger to you on my own turf, then I now understand why Sky River Woman sees you as unworthy to be her husband."

"You said a moment ago that you were grateful to me for bringing her to your lands," Zeus replied with great sadness. "Can you not forgive my moment of weakness, when I see such beauty before me? I almost envy that hunter for having lived an eternity in your arms and died in glory and bliss after a short Season!"

"Flattery will not loosen my tongue, Sky Father," Ptesanwin answered sternly. "We were born in very different worlds, I where words and deeds count more to measure one's worth than what your descendants call the Divine Right of Kings. Now I understand why Sky River Woman scorns you. And yet we share a common cause. We both want very much for Sky River Woman to stay on the face of the Earth. We of the Wakan need you to make this happen, otherwise the Earth will be as before the Time when this Land first breathed the air for all to thrive, at the heart of Turtle Island, when the Earth-Mother was very young, and the creatures that crawl and swim and walk not yet born!"

"Hera was always fond of the Earth-Mother," Zeus replied dejectedly. "And you are right, she's grown angry with me. And yes, if she leaves, that may spell doom for the Earth and all that lives, even the deathless gods such as ourselves. Tessa, if there is anything you know about my wife's whereabouts, I humbly beg for you to help me, in any way you can! This is a matter of utmost importance!"

"I will help you if I can, Sky Father" Ptesanwin replied. "But first you must know that it is not Sky River Woman's anger that threatens to end us all. The Earth-Mother is far angrier; she is waiting to strike down all those who live today, whose ancestors threatened her, leaving the People in greatly reduced numbers, far fewer than yet live. Sky River Woman stayed her hand first by purifying the Waters, then by showing everyone that the bright People who work with her son can continue her great work, so that Life could return to Turtle Island, where Life began, and elsewhere, beyond its ancient shores."

As the White Buffalo Calf Woman spoke, Zeus remembered something Hera told him centuries before, upon her return after one of her journeys circling the Earth at the time appointed by the Seasons. Though he seldom paid attention the tales of her travels upon her return, preferring instead to prepare for the nuptial rite in their marriage-bed, he did recall one rare instance where she mentioned her encounter with a herald of the Wakan, the foreign gods at the heart of Turtle Island. Hera told him that her new friend, who was very much like herself, brought her to the place where complex Life on Earth began, at the bottom of a long-gone Sea, of which only a dried, elevated plateau remains. Zeus remembered the tale because at the time he scoffed at the notion that Life could have begun anywhere else on the broad-pathed Earth than at the very bottom of the Aegean Sea, where King Poseidon dwells. On second thought, perhaps this was the storied land of Pallene, whence Gaia birthed the Giants to take revenge on the gods of Olympus for imprisoning the Titans when the Earth was young, and the gods even younger.

Overcome with despair, Zeus let his gaze drop to the meadow grasses beneath his feet, which his immortal companion probably noticed also hovered slightly above the surface of the Earth. Before his heart sank further into the deepest abyss of self-defeat, he heard the White Buffalo Calf Woman address him once more.

"There may be hope yet for you, Sky Father," she said. "Even we, the Wakan, have heard of your valiant battles against the Unktehila in the lands where you are from. Are you not one of the Wakinyan, the Thunder Beings, born to guide and protect the People against the destructive forces that threaten us all?"

"Unktehi-what?" Zeus asked, looking upon Ptesanwin with mild confusion.

"The water-serpents, Sky Father. Monsters who threatened to lay waste to Life itself wherever they roamed."

"The gods of Olympus triumphed over these monsters in the old world, Tessa. I mean… you know, the world whence I came. But yes, after my son Herakles joined the fray, we rid the Earth of these monsters once and for all. But perhaps this was a mistake, for they could have kept mortals from laying waste to the Earth by keeping their numbers more manageable, before they became too many and-"

"Do not let your thoughts linger on what should have been, Sky Father," Ptesanwin interrupted the Thunderer's ramblings. "Life will return to the Earth, as it always does after great calamities. Our duty is to protect the People from vanishing into dust until there is nothing left but their bones, like that hunter that lived a lifetime in the span of a heartbeat. For that you must convince Sky River Woman to stay, and to do that you must prove your worth, so that she will choose to stay of her own free will, and not because of your threats."

"You know about that?" Zeus said haltingly, his voice uncharacteristically hushed.

Ptesanwin nodded but said nothing else.

Zeus took a deep breath. "What would you have me do?" he asked. "How can I find my wife and appeal to her own sense of honour and duty to protect the People against annihilation, if you do not tell me where she is?"

"I will tell you where she is, Sky Father, once I am satisfied that you will do right by her."

"I will do whatever you ask, Tessa," Zeus pleaded, for the first time in aeons, or so it seemed. "My beloved Hera is lost to me, and without her I am also without recourse in this world. If you have any counsel to give me, I will humbly accept."

"To find Sky River Woman," Ptesanwin said at last, "you must prove your worth, as her husband and as a Chief among your People –"

"Yes!?"

"– by finding her where her troubles began. You must remember where her world first turned sour, and there, you must find her and do right by her. Only then, do we all have a chance to see the Earth and her People restored in all the nations of the world. That is all the Wakan wish to tell you."

Before Zeus could reply, the beautiful White Buffalo Calf Woman vanished from the meadow, her bovine counterpart disappearing in the mist of the coming Night.

The Cloud-gatherer stood alone for some time, trying to make sense of all he had seen. At last Zeus turned around and saw a large vessel hovering above the dark blades of grass, a few paces away from where he stood. The vessel drew nearer, and after a moment Zeus noticed that it was some sort of watercraft, built with wood and bark, with which the sons of Old Europe likely explored Turtle Island with the guidance of its native inhabitants.

Utterly perplexed, he begged for wise Metis to help him gauge whether he had, in fact, gone mad.

A gift from the gods of Turtle Island, my King. Would you prove an unworthy guest and refuse such a boon?

"What about my chariot and my horses?" Zeus said aloud. At these words the vessel grew wider and longer, until it became large enough to accommodate the Cloud-gatherer's conveyance.

Taking the hint, Zeus summoned his horses and drew his chariot onto the vessel. To his surprise, the flying watercraft remained preternaturally steady in mid-air.

Now you must infer Hera's whereabouts. Where do you think her trouble began, my King?

Zeus lowered his gaze, and heaved a weary sigh. "By the Lethe's shore," he answered. "Where she gave birth to her firstborn son after following her lover's shade to the Underworld, after I smote him with my thunderbolt. By the Lethe's shore, where my deeds caused her to lose her memories of the bliss of her first love, after which Mother sent her away to dwell in the House of Okeanos and Tethys –"

Well then, Metis interrupted Zeus' train of thought. *Shall we pay a visit to Lord Hades?*

Nepheleid

Chapter Twenty-Four

Stalwart Hades donned his trusty helmet, determined to remain unseen as he retrieved his father's sickle from its hiding place, concealed from the innumerable denizens of the Underworld under his care. He made no sound as he headed towards the stables, already devising a plan to retrieve his chariot from Eris. Hades knew that the goddess of chaos had likely reached the gates of Tartarus by now, having traveled faster on his stolen conveyance than her powerful wings could allow. At times like these Hades regretted giving Hera's children full immunity from the laws governing his Kingdom, however so far Eris seemed to be the only one among Hera's brood to have gained full knowledge of this privilege. The Host of Many also knew that Eris had visited the Titans with increasing frequency of late, beginning shortly before Hera left Olympus all those years ago to cast her lot with Prometheus and his learned mortals on Turtle Island.

Or so it seemed to King Hades, as the passage of Time differed greatly in the Underworld when compared to the surface of the broad-pathed Earth. Time beyond the shores of the Holy River Styx, by which the blessed gods who dwell on starry Olympus swear their most binding Oaths, was not bound by the rhythms of the Seasons and the orbits of stars and wanderers across the Heavens as it was in the realms of the living. Here Time slowed incrementally as one traveled from the bright Elysian fields towards Tartarus, the pit of the damned. Perhaps Eris would linger among the Titans for a spell, until Hades instructed Junia to use Kronos' sickle to cut a gate across the expanse between his palace and Tartarus. By the reckoning of the most learned mortals, the distance between Hades' home overlooking the Elysian fields, where the shades of the dead dwell until they are reborn, and the abyss at the very nadir of the Cosmos, rivalled those which kept galaxies apart beyond the Heavens. If the Fates were kind, then perhaps Hades would have enough time to bring Eris back to his palace before Hermes eventually came to retrieve her once she was welcome to return to starry Olympus

Nepheleid

Though peeved at Eris' bold theft of his chariot, Hades could not help but smile, for the misdeed had the merciful effect of halting Persephone and Junia's bickering, at least until the Lord of the Underworld found himself well out of earshot behind the stables of his grandiose palace. There he pulled Kronos' sickle from under a tarpaulin of sorts beside his flower-garden lit by the perennial light of the nearby Elysian fields, where too many shades of the countless dead milled about, perhaps unwilling to take a plunge in the Lethe before returning to the desolate wastelands that awaited them after their births. If Hermes told it true during his many visits to his Kingdom since resuming his duties as Zeus' messenger on high Olympus, then this state of affairs would only worsen should Hera choose to leave the Earth and sail towards worlds unknown aboard the Nephele and city-ships of its ilk.

With Kronos' relic in hand, the Host of Many returned to the steps of his palace, where his bride and her maiden sister-cousin resumed their squabble. Hades' smile broadened as he gazed upon his loyal hound Cerberus, whose three heads kept watch over Persephone and Junia, his six eyes darting from one to the other as they debated whether Zeus or Hera were the worst with regards to their treatment of any poor soul who ran afoul of the King and Queen of Olympus. Hades removed his helmet once he regained the ability to affect a neutral demeanour, grateful that Eris at least did not abscond with Cerberus in her flight, unlike that oaf Herakles, whom he had yet to forgive for stealing his faithful companion centuries ago while completing one of his storied Labours.

At long last, Persephone turned her gaze towards her husband with the look of someone who had utterly failed to convince a young girl of the flaws in her mother's character.

"First of all," Junia said animatedly, "my mom could not have thrown Hephaestus off Olympus when he was born. Think about it. Back in the day, even goddesses delivered their babies vaginally. Can you imagine *anyone* getting up after having half their guts spill out, then walk over to the balcony, and toss a baby like a football? Seeing how much trouble my mom went through just to make sure I was born without any fallout from... falling out of the Sky, I find it very hard to believe that she would do that to any of her children for any reason."

"But what if Hephaestus truly was as ugly as they say?" Persephone pursued.

"Okay, we really need to stop saying that Hephaestus is ugly, because he's not," Junia protested. "He gets messy from his work in the forge, but that's about it. And *all* babies are ugly and gross when they're born. All newborns look like unfinished fetuses, because that's essentially what they are. Hera would have known this as she gave birth to my brother, because she was a midwife to Grandma Tethys when she used to live in their House way back when she was in foster care. And Grandma Tethys had, like, a thousand babies or something during that time! So, as I've told you, it's far more likely that Zeus was the one who threw my brother off Olympus, because he's a proven jerk. Mama told me stories of how weird he got whenever my mom got pregnant, even when her children were his!"

Persephone looked momentarily confused.

"She means Klymene," Hades said. "Her *other* mother."

"Right," Persephone replied disdainfully. "Hera told all the mortals of Turtle Island that her handmaiden was her spouse after forsaking my father, so that the men there wouldn't pursue her. That's rather rich, coming from the goddess of marriage! Now, what about poor Tiresias?"

"What about him?" Junia said.

"When Zeus and Hera asked him whether the man or the woman felt the greatest share of pleasure during the act of love," Persephone continued, "knowing him for one who had lived as both a man and a woman, he revealed that women feel nine-tenths of the pleasure! Hera did not like that one bit, so she struck the poor bastard blind. Father, on the other hand, gave him the gift of second sight as compensation for his terrible loss!"

"I heard the story before," Junia replied. "Tiresias was a great seer. So great, in fact, that he could divine the future by watching flock of birds in flight! Come on, Percy! He *couldn't* have been blinded permanently if he could see flocks of birds! That's a crock of shit, and you know it!"

"Perhaps he saw the birds in flight through his gift that Zeus granted him as a mercy?" Persephone inquired.

"That's totally redundant," Junia answered. "And since you know my mom so well, surely you're aware of how much she hates inefficiency and redundancy. She hates it almost as much as she hates disloyalty. Your argument is invalid. And that wasn't funny, Uncle Hades!"

Hades paused. "I was not laughing," he said in an exaggeratedly sombre tone.

"Oh, please! You were grinning ear to ear before you took off your helmet!" Junia replied. "You might as well have been rolling off the floor!"

"How would you know such things?" Persephone asked, this time without any spite. "No one can see my King when he dons his helmet."

"Yes, Junia," Hades said. "How could you tell I was nearby and that I was smiling?"

Junia shrugged. "I don't know," she said truthfully. "It's like the air itself was screaming that you were there, and you were watching, and you thought this whole exchange was hilarious."

"And here I thought only Hera and Kronos could sense my presence when I am wearing my helmet," Hades said calmly. "But one was born with a powerful gift of prophecy, and the other has dominion over Time itself. How long have you had the ability to see beyond Time and Matter?"

Junia gave Hades a stunned look, as if unsure how to answer. After a moment, she said, "Pretty much since forever."

"What's it like?" Persephone asked, genuinely curious to hear such things from another of her kin gifted with second sight.

"Sometimes," Junia explained tentatively, "it's like there's a shimmer in the air, just outside of my field of vision. Like right now, over there, by the shore of the Styx, do you see that? There's a whirlwind where there should be nothing at all, but there it is. Want to bet that it's... oh, hi Eris!"

Before the Host of Many could fully register the child's words, a pitch-black gash sundered the bright firmament above the royal palace, growing wider until Eris appeared, holding the reins of the stolen chariot. To Hades' dismay, the goddess of chaos was not alone; five immense figures towered behind her, their countenances rapt for their first taste of freedom in aeons since they were last released from their prison to make short work of Zagreus, Persephone's twice-born dismembered son. When the chariot touched down before the steps of Hades' palace, Eris looked up at the opening and muttered something until it disappeared completely, leaving no trace above the Elysian fields.

While the minx busied herself in this manner, the Lord of the Underworld lay the sickle flat behind Persephone, where none could see it easily and walked stoically towards his chariot. This time, he would see to it that all parts remained secure in the stables, lest one of his newly arrived uninvited guests decide to escape the Underworld and wreak havoc on the broad-pathed Earth. Taking hold of the reins, he gave the Titans a hard stare as they stepped off the vehicle and lingered by shore of the Holy River Styx. As Hades hurried to put away the horses and chariot, Persephone rose to her feet, keeping a watchful eye over the newcomers while holding fast to the tether restraining Cerberus where he stood.

"Easy," the Queen of the Underworld whispered soothingly in the hound's six ears, while the beast's three heads snarled furiously at the interlopers. "They haven't done anything… yet!"

"Grandpa!" Junia exclaimed upon recognizing the mighty form of wily Kronos standing directly behind her sister and protector.

Why Eris would bring this cannibalistic monster to greet such a vulnerable child, Hades could not say. However, as Hera reminded him more times than he could count, Eris' actions only seemed at their most outrageous when she set her mind to right egregious injustices. Hades also knew that Eris was sworn to never let her young sister come to harm, and for this reason alone he kept his composure when he glimpsed Kronos heading towards the young girl, greeting her with a warm embrace.

"Moppet!" the Titan King said aloud to Junia, looking sincerely happy to see the child again after almost five years. "You came back! I always knew you would. You remembered us! When your sister fetched us and told us what your father means to make you do, I almost went mad at the injustice of it all! You poor, darling child!"

"No young girl should be made to wed Lord Apollo," Koios said as he and his brothers caught up to their King. "It matters not how handsome my grandson has become. A maiden of your calibre ought not to wed one who favours youths over pretty girls –"

"What?" Junia asked.

Nepheleid

"It does not matter," Kronos replied. "We will not let anyone get in the way of that which the Fates intend for you to become."

Hades donned his helmet once more and made his way back to the steps of his palace. As soon as he did so he realized the futility of this gesture, as he now knew that Junia and Kronos could detect his presence by means which he hoped to fully understand someday. Heaving a silent yet weary sigh, the Host of Many braced himself for the litany of flattery and lies that would soon follow. He pitied the young Junia, for she did not yet know how far Kronos would go to earn her favour if he thought she could secure his release from Tartarus. As Hades suspected, Kronos perfected the role of doting grandfather, in a way that almost made the Lord of the Underworld forget that this was the same villain who devoured him and his siblings to prevent one of his offspring from usurping his ascendancy among the gods. It would not be long until Kronos tried to convince Junia that she was fated to fulfill the prophecy against which he once warned Zeus, that one day one of his own children would take his place as supreme ruler among the gods, just as Kronos' youngest trueborn son relieved the Titan-King of the throne of Heaven.

"Do you not realize that your presence among us changes everything?" Kronos continued. "Now that you are here, everything that was lost will be found again! My darling child, there is nothing you will ever need to fear ever again. Now, where is your mother, pray tell?"

"We would like to know the same," Hades heard a familiar say as another rift opened by the shore of the Holy River Styx.

Hades removed his helmet and took a long look at the latest newcomer, who brought with him a multitude the likes of which the Underworld had not seen since the last great wars of centuries past, when the dead converged on the shores of the Holy River Styx by the thousands.

"Hermes!" Persephone cried out, still holding Cerberus' tether. "Where the bloody hell have you been? I've been summoning you for –"

"Seventeen hours," Hermes answered casually. "That's how long it was on Earth. What in the world –"

"Hermes," Hades said calmly as he stepped between the messenger and the Titans gathered on the steps of his palace. "We've got a bit of a situation."

"There are Titans with little Junia!" Hermes blurted inelegantly, as the remainder of the Olympian Court, all save for Hestia, as well as the Sea-Court and some foreign gods whom Hades did not know, stepped off from the rift and onto Hades' Kingdom.

"I know," Hades answered. "As I said, proceed with care."

"Why? What happened?" Hermes asked.

"Eris," Hades replied, to which the messenger simply nodded.

Kronos gazed upon the throngs of deathless gods as they crossed over from Olympus into the Underworld, his eyes settling upon the form of fair-haired Rhea, flanked by their daughter Demeter, who brings forth gifts, and their son Poseidon, the Earth-shaker. It seemed as though all the denizens of the Olympian Court, as well as the immortals who dwell in the Sea and at the boundaries of the broad-pathed Earth, gathered on the shore of the Holy River Styx. Even the elder Titans Okeanos and Tethys, the Mother and Father of Rivers, whom Kronos and Rhea expelled from Olympus millennia ago, milled about with their kin. All seemed rather confused as to what course of action they ought to undertake now that they arrived in the Kingdom of Hades.

The Host of Many also scanned the crowd, looking for his brother Zeus.

"Where is your King?" Hades asked Hermes after failing to find the Thunderer's familiar form among the crowd.

"We were told... I was led to believe we would find him here!" Hermes replied tentatively.

"By whom, pray tell?" Hades asked.

"It was I, Lord Hades," a voice answered somewhere behind Herakles and Athena. The crowd parted, revealing Dionysus putting away a small flask in the folds of his robes.

"No, not him!" Apollo said, stepping to the fore. "I divined that Junia would find herself here, among the Titans. I was led to believe that Hera and Zeus would soon follow."

"But why?" Hades asked patiently.

"I led him to believe as much," Prometheus answered, standing beside the Lord of the golden bow.

"Prometheus!" Junia exclaimed, leaping off Kronos' lap and running towards her brother.

The child's enthusiasm reminded Hades of the time he witnessed Zeus and Hera's first encounter, after their release from the prison of Kronos' belly. Hera was the last to emerge, for the Titan-King refused to relinquish his favourite child to his would-be usurper, even though she was her third-born. When at last Kronos released Hera, the maiden goddess embraced Zeus with genuine gratitude and yet, despite her unmatched gift of foresight, she never imagined that her innocuous and endearing display of sisterly love would inspire unrelenting lust in her saviour, which would one day bring an end to her innocence and happiness by the Lethe's shore.

"What the hell!?" Junia shrieked upon releasing the benefactor of humanity from her embrace.

"Junia, listen −" Prometheus said.

"Mama," Junia told Klymene, who stood behind Prometheus. "Mom's not here! She said we'd see her soon, but she didn't say where! And Eris went to get the Titans −"

"Hera is not in the Underworld," Prometheus declared, his voice loud enough so that all the deathless gods gathered by the shores of the Holy River Styx could hear. Turning his gaze towards Apollo, he added, "I apologize for the deception, but to find Hera we must pass through here and wait for another."

"What is this?" Kronos boomed from where he stood by the steps of Hades' palace.

"Isn't it obvious?" fair-haired Rhea answered flatly as she walked towards her husband from the middle of the crowd, with gentle Demeter following her closely. "We've come here to wait for Zeus!"

"I hope you did not come to my Kingdom to settle a score, Mother," Hades said calmly, his eyes fixed on Demeter as the goddess of the grain helped Persephone restrain Cerberus, who had the frightened look of a hunting hound about to be stampeded by a herd of cattle. "Eris, I am warning you," Hades added upon identifying the cause of his hound's distress.

"Leave the girl alone," Kronos said. "She brought us here to mind the child."

"Junia will be perfectly safe with us, King Kronos," Hermes said diplomatically. "Now, if you please, could you be so kind as to hand her over to us, and we will see her safely home."

"To which home do you mean to take her, pray tell?" Kronos asked Hermes.

"Prometheus," Athena asked, while Hermes continued negotiating with the Titans. "Why did you think Zeus will meet us here? Did he not set off to Turtle Island to find Hera on the Polaris?"

"That was seventeen hours ago," Asia said before Prometheus could reply.

Prometheus nodded in assent. "Ptesanwin should have sent him on his way by now," he said.

"White Buffalo Calf Woman?" Junia asked incredulously. "Eris! I told you we have gone to Turtle Island!"

"No, Kitten," Klymene said. "The gods of Turtle Island would have sent you here to seek shelter among the Titans."

"Now really," Hermes protested. "I am more than capable of protecting a child –"

"Then why did you bring reinforcements?" Kronos replied.

"Because of *him*!" Junia interjected, pointing somewhere above the gloomy waters of the Lethe, far from the light of the Elysian fields.

Hades followed Junia's line of sight saw a preposterous shape materialize in the firmament above the assembly of deathless gods gathered by the shore of the Holy River Styx. At long last, Eris' presence in his Kingdom had rendered him completely mad, Hades thought as he stood transfixed before the form of loud-thundering Zeus drawing near upon his chariot, nestled inside a rather large flying watercraft better suited for travelling narrow rivers across on the broad-pathed Earth than those of the Underworld.

"Is that the *chasse-galerie*?" Junia asked, sounding as confused as Hades felt.

"Father returns from Turtle Island," Apollo said casually.

"You've seen this before?" Hades asked, somewhat relieved that the vision was not his alone, and that he had not, in fact, gone stark raving mad.

"I have," Apollo answered. "In a dream, though. Years ago. The canoe is a sign of favour from the gods of the Eastern Woodlands of Turtle Island."

Hades nodded emphatically. "That is good to know," he muttered under his breath, confident in the knowledge that he had now seen everything that the living and the deathless could invent in the realms beyond his own.

As Zeus meandered towards Hades' palace, Kronos stood up and quickly took hold of his sickle, then made his way towards Junia and casually handed her his mighty relic.

"Remember the true purpose of this weapon, Moppet," he whispered in her ear as the canoe alighted a few paces away from the front of the assembly.

To everyone's surprise, the watercraft disappeared as soon as it touched down upon the bedrock of the Cosmos. None looked as surprised as the Thunderer himself, although Hades pondered that perhaps his brother had not anticipated to find the entire Olympian Court assembled in the Underworld at this very instant.

Hades walked towards the edge of the crowd to hail his brother, who in turn threw him a look of utmost scorn.

"What is this, Hades?" the Cloud-gathered inquired imperiously instead of greeting his elder as his equal. "Why are my subjects gathered here in the Underworld, and why in Tartarus are the Titans here, frolicking among my children on the steps of your palace?"

"Are you going to allow him to speak to you this way, in your own Kingdom, Son?" Kronos quipped a few paces away.

When Zeus reached for his thunderbolt, Hades raised his hand in a halting gesture. "There is no need for this, Brother," he said. "I sometimes take the Titans from the Pit to air them out when they get stale," he added, hoping the jest would mitigate his own growing annoyance at having all the gods of Earth, Sea, and Sky take turns appearing at the steps of his palace so soon after Eris stole his chariot and returned it laden with the sworn enemies of Olympus.

"And what about the other?" Zeus asked, undeterred.

"They came here to wait for you," Hades answered with and edge to his voice. "And why have you come here, pray tell? I have not seen hide nor hair of you in my Kingdom since Hera – "

"I have come to find my wife by the Lethe's shore," Zeus replied truthfully. "But she is not here. Now answer me, why the hell are the Titans –"

The Father of gods and men paused when he spied the young Junia flanked by both Kronos and Prometheus and frowned when the child raised the Titan's sickle defensively, albeit with great effort on account of the relic's imposing size. At least the ground held steady when Zeus furrowed his brows in this realm, Hades thought, relieved that that this corner of the Cosmos remained one of the few places left where his brother, and father-in-law, did not reign supreme.

While Zeus and Junia duelled silently with their gaze, the blessed gods who dwell on high Olympus, as well as the other immortals who dwell in the Sea and at the boundaries of the broad-pathed Earth remained silent, waiting breathlessly to see what would happen. At that moment Hades almost pitied Zeus, for he knew the Thunderer must have felt as hopelessly cornered as the Roman legions did when the Italic League, headed by the fearsome Samnite warriors allied with the Etruscans, the Umbrians, and even the Gauls, faced their regional overlords in battle. On that day, more than thirty thousand dead soldiers crowded the shores of the Styx, until the very last stragglers crossing the holy river brought news of Rome's victory to their fallen comrades. To make matters worse, Apollo and Athena rallied around Junia and Prometheus, flanked closely by Herakles, Hephaestus, Artemis, and Ares. Hades closed his eyes, hoping that the Fates had not chosen his peaceful Kingdom as the stage upon which another terrible battle was to unfold.

Of all the immortals assembled by the shores of the Holy River Styx, only Kronos appeared to revel in the strange and chaotic turn of events. "It looks as though Time has come full circle," the Titan-King said sardonically, placing his hand protectively upon Junia's shoulder.

"Oh, piss off!" Zeus replied, undaunted by the imposing figure his father continued to cast over him. "You were wrong about everything. No son of mine has yet defeated me, and none ever will!"

"I never said the child who would take your throne would be a boy," Kronos replied, his grin widening. "And as you well know, girls mature faster than boys," he added, casting a glance upon fair Persephone, now cradling Cerberus in her arms.

"Why are you here, Brother?" Hades asked again, hoping that Zeus would take this as his cue to take his leave from his Kingdom, and that his Court would follow suit.

"I've told you, I came to find Hera, but since she's obviously absent from your realm, I will take my daughter home, as well as the rest of this lot," Zeus replied, gesturing across the multitude gathered before him.

"I'm not going with you," Junia said, holding fast onto Kronos' sickle as if holding on to dear life.

Zeus frowned again, this time setting his gaze upon Prometheus.

"And I have come here for my sister," the benefactor of humanity said. "I have come here to these shores, where I was born, to bring Junia home, by which I mean the Nephele, high above the broad-pathed Earth."

"And why would I ever allow you to spirit away my child as you did with her mother all those years ago?" Zeus asked flatly, keeping his composure as the young Junia stepped between her father and her eldest brother, sickle in hand. "Stop that," Zeus told the child. "That weapon weighs more than you do."

The young girl took a deep breath. Gathering her courage, she looked up at the King of Olympus, and said, "Fuck off, and let us go!"

"Those are very grown-up words," Zeus replied condescendingly. "I will overlook your insolence just this once, however Prometheus ought to know better by now. And since I am now in my beloved brother's Kingdom, I will defer to his authority and only ask you once to come with me and help me find your mother. So be a good girl –"

"Our dear Sister is not in my Kingdom," Hades reiterated. "If she were, I would be the first to know, in the same way I become cognizant of all the creatures that cross into this realm–"

"I have no quarrel with you, Brother," Zeus interrupted. "Though seeing the Titans gathered around my children fails to inspire confidence in your abilities to rule the Underworld. Perhaps I was also wrong about your suitability as a husband to my dear Persephone –"

At these words, fair Persephone ran down the steps of the royal palace and took her place beside Junia, Prometheus, and Kronos. Trying to pry the sickle from the little girl's hand, she muttered, "if you don't use this, then I will!"

Ignoring Persephone's display of anger, Zeus gazed upon his Court with a demeanour of disappointment. "What is this?" he said. "None of you come to stop this ungrateful brat from what she means to do? Why are you not standing by my side, in solidarity with your King? Is this the mutiny I've been promised, after all these centuries?"

"We are here to collect Junia and Hera and see them safely aboard the Nephele," Athena said at last. "We are here to honour their choice to return to the city-ship. The same holds true of Prometheus, Asia, Klymene, and anyone else who wishes to join them."

As the Virgin Warrior uttered these words, Hades noticed the Titan Iapetos wringing his hands in distress, as if the very notion that his Oceanid bride could leave with Hera and Prometheus' learned mortals aboard a mortal-made city-ship troubled him in untold ways. The Host of Many also saw his brother pause, as if listening to an inner voice only he could hear, telling him to keep his peace for a while.

"Be that as it may, Daughter," Zeus said after a moment, "I would rather hear this from Hera's lips."

"Who told you our Sister was here?" Hades asked.

Nepheleid

"The Hera of Turtle Island told me I would find my wife where her trouble began," Zeus answered sincerely. "And I know that her trouble began by the Lethe's shore, when she gave birth to this one," he added, pointing a finger at Prometheus, "then promptly forgot through no fault of her own. So tell me, if the white cow goddess of Turtle Island deceived me by luring me here, then where is Hera, really? I will not ask again," he said, reaching once again for his thunderbolt.

Kronos took a step towards Zeus, as did the other four Titan brothers gathered by the steps of Hades' royal palace.

Athena raised her shield, prompting Ares to raise his spear, while Artemis and Apollo lifted their bows, Hephaestus raised his hammer, Herakles raised his club, and somewhere in the middle of the crowd Dionysus raised his cup.

Only Okeanos, Tethys, and the Titanides remained perfectly still, keeping a watchful eye over the proceedings, as if expecting Zeus to make a move to draw first blood.

After a few tense moments, which likely lasted several days on the surface of the broad-pathed Earth, Zeus took a long look at the five Titan brothers formerly imprisoned in Tartarus and lowered his thunderbolt.

"You would stand by and let this lot escort your most diligent champion far away from the surface of the Earth, purely to spite me?" he told them at last. "Think of all that would come to pass if I allowed the little one to have her way. My daughter claims that she's chosen her path, however she is far from old enough to make such a choice. Look at her, she is only a child! As for Prometheus, he is the true instigator in all this! He is the one who broke the truce won by my stalwart son Herakles, the greatest hero that ever lived, whose very name brings everlasting glory to my Queen! Prometheus is the one who must make amends and bring me satisfaction!" Turning his gaze towards the benefactor of humanity, he said, "All this time, all you ever wanted was the child, even on the day you came and spirited my beloved Hera from her loving husband's arms! All this time, you meant to take the child to Turtle Island, far from her father's watchful gaze, and turn her against me for you own ends!"

Athena said nothing, throwing an uneasy glance towards Prometheus.

"You got me," the benefactor of humanity said as a grin crept across his face.

"I knew it!" Zeus cried out. "You never cared a whit about Hera! You wanted the child all along!"

"That is not true," Prometheus replied. "I needed my mother then more than I ever needed her since she gave me life, which was why I came to collect what was rightfully mine!"

"You will not strike my grandchild!" Kronos said in a tone resembling a growl. "Have you not already done enough to Prometheus since you murdered his father, as if he was to blame for Hera choosing another to be her husband? So what if Hera had known many lovers before you wed. Was it not enough that you took her happiness away when you slew my brother, the King of the Giants and then erased all the memories of her bliss, all so you could have her all to yourself? Have you no shame!?"

"You have no right to say such things," Zeus told Kronos flatly. "You were the reason why Hera never fully trusted men, and never suffered their presence for long when she grew weary of her Consorts!"

Kronos gave Zeus an icy stare and remained quiet for a very long time. After a veritable eternity, he said in a low voice: "If you care about Hera, if you love her even half as much as you claim, then let my true-born heir leave this place with the little one and let the others go back to their homes wherever they choose to go. If you do this without spilling precious ichor upon the ground and promise to release us and ours from our prison in Tartarus, then we will help you find Hera."

Junia looked up at Kronos in alarm. "What the fuck, Grandpa?" she shrieked.

Prometheus leaned over and whispered to the child, "It's all right, let them negotiate a truce."

"You would sell her out just to get out of here?" Junia asked Kronos. "We can beat him! We have your sickle! We... you five, and these guys – we can kick his ass! Let me show you – "

"Junia," Prometheus whispered gently to his young sister. "This outcome has been foretold long before you were born. You must trust me. Hera will prevail, and we will see her soon." To Zeus, he said, "I assure you that you will not find my mother here, or anywhere in the Underworld, even if you were to send your entire Court, and the Sea-Court, to search for her in Hades' Kingdom! To find her you must prove worthy – "

Nepheleid

"No!" Junia pleaded. "Don't do it! Don't sell her out! Don't –"

"Trust that I am telling you the truth, little sister," Prometheus replied patiently. "Hera will prevail! On that I will bet my restored liver!"

"You mean *my* liver," Junia replied indignantly. "Restored with *my* stem cells..."

"Not now, Junia," Prometheus said.

"You're not the boss of me!" Junia said. "That's not my name!"

"Not here!" Prometheus continued.

"Enough!" Zeus hollered, visibly piqued at Prometheus and Junia's bickering. To Kronos he said, "Prometheus may take Junia to the Nephele on the condition that you lot will take me to Hera, for the sake of the Earth and all the dwells therein! What now?"

"You never called me by that name before," Junia told her father as her fingers drained of colour from the force of her grip upon Kronos' sickle.

"And what would you do if Hera refuses to return to starry Olympus with you?" Kronos asked Zeus.

"If that is the outcome Prometheus foretold," Zeus said reluctantly, "Then so be it! I want to see her stay as much as you do, and if she chooses to remain on the surface of the broad-pathed Earth, shunning the company of the gods, then at least we can rest assured that Life will continue to thrive upon this world. But tell me, if she is not here where her trouble began, then where has she gone to hide?"

"Let the Moppet open the way," Kronos answered.

"What?" Junia asked, genuinely confused.

"The sickle!" Eris said from her hiding-place behind the now slumbering Cerberus.

"Think of your mother and the sickle will open the way," Kronos told Junia gently.

"That's not what this is for!" Junia protested, casting a sideways glance at Zeus.

"Junia!" Prometheus scolded the child gently. "You now wield the sickle of Kronos. Put it to better use than its previous master!"

"I can't let you betray her like that!" Junia insisted, on the verge of tears. "And I *can't* believe you would do this to her!"

"Kitten, please!" Klymene cried out. "You must trust that Mommy will make all this end well!"

"It's true, child," Thetis, daughter of Nereus, said, standing between golden Aphrodite and King Poseidon among the Sea-Court. "When Aphrodite failed to compel Hera to stay with Zeus, we had to find another way!"

"This is our only chance," august Themis said, standing beside her Titanide sisters as well as Okeanos, the Father of Rivers. "Do you not care about the Earth-Mother surviving this ordeal?"

"The rhythms of Time and the Seasons have come undone across all the nations of the world where mortals were once innumerable," fair-haired Rhea said. "This, we all know, was the doing of mortals who have died long ago, however Hera has the power to reassert synchronicity of the Seasons across the broad-pathed Earth. Forget about your father for a moment, *we* need you to take us to her! Call out to your mother, child, and she will answer! And when she does, all that was lost can be found again!"

"No harm will come to Hera," Apollo assured Junia, addressing her for the first time since crossing over into Hades' Kingdom. "I will swear it by the Holy River Styx, if my Uncle will bear witness –"

"No!" Junia exclaimed. "Okay! Fine, I'll do it! Jesus!"

Junia took a deep breath and closed her eyes. In the span of another eternity, she looked as though she were searching the entire Cosmos for signs of her mother, until she finally raised the sickle and pointed towards somewhere above the distant Lethe River.

At last, Junia drew a line with the mighty blade across the firmament high above the royal palace. As expected, another rift tore the placid twilight of the Underworld above the Asphodel Meadows beyond the Elysian fields. On the other side there appeared a derelict garden bathed in the golden light of Sunset, at the centre of which stood an ancient apple tree, it branches bare and grey. As the rift grew wider, all the immortals assembled in Hades' Kingdom saw Hera sitting by the base of the tree, her eyes shut and her form unmoving.

Aphrodite let out an audible gasp. "Look to the middle," she said with alarm. "Someone bound Hera to the trunk!"

The blessed Olympian Court ran headlong towards their Queen with Junia and Zeus leading the charge followed by the Titans and Sea-Court.

Trailing the crowd, Hades turned towards Persephone and gave her a rueful look. "Stay here with Cerberus," he told her. "I will try to return quickly, however cannot tell you how long I will be gone, for I fear that Hera relocated the Garden of the Hesperides in a realm far from the surface of the broad-pathed Earth.

Persephone nodded. "See that Hera prevails," she said as stalwart Hades crossed over towards the very last of Hera's nuptial gardens.

Chapter Twenty-Five

Heartened by righteous anger at the Thunderer, golden-throned Hera sped in a swirl of stars towards the Garden of the Hesperides, hidden for centuries beyond the boundaries of the House of Okeanos and Tethys in a place that could not be found anywhere by ordinary means on the broad-pathed Earth. So well-concealed was the goddess' sacred garden that even the most sophisticated instruments crafted by the astute minds of learned mortals could not detect it from their lofty heights above the Heavens. Even the gods of Olympus and their mortal-born children could not hope to find it, for the three Hesperides nymphs who once tended the garden fled shortly after stalwart Herakles slew Ladon, the serpent-dragon tasked with safeguarding the Tree of the golden apples, during another of his storied Labours. Led by their sister Maia, who was visited in her cave by Zeus one night and then bore him swift Hermes, the daughters of Atlas robbed what remained of the garden's treasure, emboldened by the insolent slaughter of its guardian. In their haste they left a single golden apple which Eris took and turned into a prize in an infamous beauty contest for which Hera herself vied against bright Athena and Aphrodite, lover of smiles, for the title of the fairest among the goddesses.

Of all the Queen's nuptial gardens scattered on the ancient shores of the inland Sea, the Garden of the Hesperides was once the most beautiful and most precious, a gift of the Earth-Mother herself upon the goddess' wedding to loud-thundering Zeus. As she made her way towards her now derelict haven, Hera found it rather fitting that she should bid her final farewell to Gaia in this place and declare her intent to seed Earthly Life across the Cosmos with at least some of her children, as well as eldest son's crew of learned mortals. Hera also took a perverse delight in the irony that she would soon formally sever her bond with the King of Olympus in the garden where their marriage began with a three-hundred-year bridal, the decree of the Fates be damned.

Collapsing the whirlwind of stars, Hera landed above the dried, cracked leaf litter cast by what remained of her once blooming Tree of the golden apples. The goddess could almost feel the faint aura of Life clinging to the treasure, now completely devoid of fruit from its struggle to remain alive despite centuries of neglect. A pang of sorrow took hold of Hera's heart at the sight of the moribund Tree, followed by a deep regret that she never once kept the seeds of a single golden apple in the past, never once imagining that Zeus could show her such contempt by standing idly by as his bastard son murdered the Tree's guardian and his paramour plundered its riches. In centuries past, this very thought would have driven Hera mad with anger and grief, however today the Mistress of all Life resolved to see her withering Tree bloom again, if not by planting its offspring in the soil of another world, then by cutting it down to rescue its last living root.

Hera closed her eyes, summoning her prodigious reserves of strength for the unpleasantness about to transpire. She told herself time and again that snuffing out the Life from her beloved Tree of the golden apples constituted a mercy, bringing a dignified end to the opprobrium her treasure suffered over the course of her ill-fated marriage to the King of Olympus. If Eris remained true to her nature, at some point Hera's misfit daughter would find her way to this place with Junia and bring Kronos' sickle, the only blade in the Cosmos the Queen considered worthy to cut down her Tree. She did not, however, possess any inkling of how long it would take for Eris and Junia to make their way to the Garden of the Hesperides, as Time unfolded at a much different pace in the Kingdom of her brother Hades.

Bracing herself for a long wait, white-armed Hera walked solemnly towards the base of the Tree and placed her hands delicately, apologetically, upon its brittle bark. She took a deep, melancholic breath and bowed her head before taking a seat with her back to the base of the trunk. She dug her fingers in the soil between the Tree's dying upraised roots and steeled herself for her final farewell to Gaia. Closing her eyes, Hera called out to her oldest friend and ally, the Mother to her murdered husband Eurymedon and to all that lives. As soon as Gaia's consciousness reached her own, Hera fell into a deep, powerful trance, overriding all cognizance of her surroundings, which reminded the Queen of the time she intercepted the Earth-mother's admonishments to the Giants during the interminable War they waged against the blessed gods who dwell on starry Olympus.

This time, however, Hera did not hear Gaia tell her children about the herb of invulnerability that could grant victory and ascendancy to the side that found it first. Instead she felt the burden of the Earth-Mother's grief at the tremendous loss of Life during the great extinction of countless beasts of Earth, Sea, and Sky in the last few centuries alone, born of the folly and greed of recent generations of mortals. Hera felt the full brunt of Gaia's outrage at the ingratitude of these feckless mortals, who owed their very lives and the flourishing of their successive civilizations to the clemency of the Earth's Seasons after the last glacial maximum ebbed some twenty millennia ago, when Kronos, Rhea, and their Titan siblings yet dwelled confined within Gaia's womb. Most of all, Hera felt the Earth-Mother's steadfast determination to eradicate humanity's last vestiges by burying what remained of the habitable world in a blanket of ice and lie dormant for untold aeons until it pleased her to bring Life anew upon her bosom.

Hera gasped, recalling august Themis' admonition that Gaia might one day elect to rid herself of the gods' mortal descendants to maintain a semblance of Life upon the broad-pathed Earth. Mnemosyne, the Mother of the Muses, also told the Queen a similar tale once, adding that if this eventuality were to come to pass, all that would remain of the memory of the gods and their deeds would consist of ruins and skeletons buried in the sands of Time. Hera took a deep breath, resolute in her perennial purpose to protect mortals against the whims of all hostile powers of the Cosmos, be they loud-thundering Zeus in his obstinate refusal to fully absolve lofty-minded Prometheus for his past kindness to humankind by stealing fire from Olympus, or the Earth-Mother herself in her calamitous attempts at self-preservation.

Do not take me for a fool, young one, Hera heard Gaia say inside the confines of her mind. *I know you mean to leave me in my death throes. You claim that you want nothing more than to seed the stars with the Life I have borne after primordial Chaos brought forth all Matter and Light, but I know your mind more than you care to admit. I've known you even before your blessed mother bore you into Life! You will not abandon me here to wither and die, as you have abandoned your marriage to the Cloud-gatherer, and all your previous Consorts who preceded him!*

Before Hera could reply, a cluster of small vines sprouted from the ground beneath her feet, coiling upwards around her graceful limbs, until they enfolded her waist. Though her keen senses told her to quickly raise both her arms to avoid becoming completely trapped by the snare, by the time she did so the vines had bound her completely to the trunk of the doomed Tree.

Of all the deathless children my daughters have borne, you always stood apart for your courage and indomitable will to prevail. That is why I chose you as my heir, by my daughter Rhea, to carry on the sacred task of caring for and ensuring the continuity of all Life upon the broad-pathed Earth. But now, it saddens me more than I can bear to know that you have grown cowardly in my hour of need, and that you would run from me as my very Life-force ebbs away. Do not take me for a fool, for I already know why you hid for ten years on Turtle Island while your King sent his emissaries to find you in all the corners of the known world. In truth you were hiding not from him, but from me, for fear of what I would do once I knew that you meant to leave! You may run from loud-thundering Zeus as often as you would like when he displeases you, but you cannot run from the Earth!

"Then I fear you will find the tidings I've come to bear somewhat upsetting," Hera replied bitingly, pulling at the bonds with all her formidable strength.

You may be a powerful Queen among your kind, but you cannot hope to spare your mortal children from my judgment. I am old as the Cosmos itself, second only to primordial Chaos in age. You are no older than –

"I am old enough," Hera snapped back, no longer reining in her anger. "I have borne witness to all the whims of Time through my father's eyes, and I *know* that you are as mortal as the beasts and humans that walk upon the Earth, as are we all in the end, albeit at a different scale. Your demise is as inevitable as what the mortals call the heat death of the universe, however mine and that of my kind is not! My children and I have the means, and therefore, the choice, to spread Life to the Cosmos, in worlds new and old and in worlds yet to come until the stars wink out into darkness, and even we immortals are no more. You think you can restrain me with your cheap tricks? Others have bound and imprisoned me before, yet every last one of them ultimately failed to keep me confined for all time!"

And how do you expect to stop me from that which I must undertake, young one? You wasted the gift I've given you upon your wedding to the young Sky-King, and yet you never understood the full power of that which you were given! And for all your years and all your battles, for all your cleverness and unfailing versatility and resilience, you remain as unwise and naïve as a child. You let yourself be bound to a dying Tree, as you wait for others to come to your rescue. Countless times you've been bound, that is true, however your precious others have always failed to liberate you!

"You're right," Hera replied. "I was the one who had to find ways to liberate myself in the end. This will not be different!"

Zeus was always the one who came to your rescue, without fail, except for that time your son bound you to your throne, and then freed you when you were reconciled. How can you hope to conquer the stars and seed Earthly Life, if you cannot unbind yourself unless it pleases the one who binds you to release you?

"I never turn down a challenge," Hera retorted, "and now, as always, I will find a way."

Believe me, child, when I tell you that it brings me no pleasure to restrain like this. But since you insist on staying my hand, I will have to mitigate your stubbornness by feeding it to the Tree you have failed to nurture. Perhaps if you fail to free yourself, I will bestow the newly revived treasure to the next Goddess-Queen I will choose as my heir!

Now seething with unspeakable rage at the threat to her sovereignty and her continued existence, Hera slowed her breath once more and set her venerable mind to the task of freeing herself from her predicament. In the span of a few interminable moments, Hera drew inspiration from the unconventional genius of her daughter Eris and devised a stratagem which even the canniest prophetic minds among her ancient and deathless kind could ever foresee. Surmising that Gaia had grown increasingly vulnerable to poisons born of mortal folly and greed, Hera conjectured that the Earth-Mother would reconsider draining her Life-force to feed her doomed Tree if her essence somehow became tainted with a venom far more terrible than the one Herakles collected from the slain Hydra during yet another of his storied Labours.

Steadfast in her resolve to delay summoning her children to rush to her aid, Hera delved deeply within her heart for the wellspring of miasma she had buried long ago when she still held hope to redress her eminence among mortals, reminding them of her great deeds in keeping their kind on the path of virtue despite the temptations of hedonism born of egregious injustice. Throwing caution to the cosmic wind, Hera out-manoeuvred Gaia by fully allowing herself to feel, for the first time in centuries, the familiar, white-hot asperity from millennia of defamation by ignoble men set on belittling her power. Mustering her nigh boundless anger, pain, and rage at the undeserved abuse at the hands of wicked and unimaginative poets and storytellers who exaggerated her jealousy towards her rivals for Zeus' affections and the children born of these illicit unions, the Queen then turned her almost palpable effluvium of spite against her captor.

"You know," Hera said aloud with a caustic chuckle, "in all my years, mind you I am well aware that they are by far fewer than yours, in all the centuries that I have borne witness to the passage of Time, and counselled the best among mortals in the betterment of their kind, I thought I had heard all the insults anyone could throw at me. I've been called far worse things than a coward, though never for the right reasons. I've been called a shrew for having wed an uncouth lecher; I have been called a monster for embodying the innate power of women to give Life, in all its wondrous and terrifying aspects. But never have I ever believed *you* would turn against me as mortals have in great numbers, even before they crowned the Nazarene as their new God-King!"

Hera tugged at the vines to see if they loosened at the vitriol in her voice, but they held her fast against the trunk. Undeterred, she let her boundless anger marinate inside her heart and continued her tirade.

"Was I not your most stalwart ally since the day I left the prison of my father's belly, and shortly thereafter wed your son Eurymedon? Had you not already elected me as your heir when I followed his shade into the Underworld to bring him back to Life, determined though I was to see the injustice rectified? Was I not your most loyal ambassador when I planted the seeds of my nuptial gardens across the ancient shores of the inland Sea? Was I not a more effective steward of Life than the Sea-born, who from the first sought to dethrone me from my rightful place as Queen of Heaven, long before I wed loud-thundering Zeus? Did I not seek to avenge the doomed Eurymedon when you told me of the fate that befell my husband and firstborn son, by serving as midwife when you brought forth Typhon to bring Zeus low? Have I not, time and again, paid a terrible price for tempering Zeus' judgment when his hubris would have swallowed the Earth whole?"

Hera dug her fingers into her bonds, squeezing them until her knuckles turned white. "Have I not proved ever faithful to my duty to oversee the continuation of soaring Life on the broad-pathed Earth," she said in a strained voice on account of her efforts to crush the vines with her bare hands. "Have I not always found a way to live and thrive, first in the confines of my father's consciousness, then long after I left the House of Okeanos and Tethys at the ever-expanding boundaries of the known world? All these years, all these centuries, I have been ever a friend to Life and to the Earth, even if the darker impulses of my mortal charges compelled them to turn against me as mortals sour on their creators once they find their lives plagued with wretchedness and injustice. And even in my darkest hour, when the heroes born to bring glory to my name strove to destroy that which represents the Life that sustains us all, I have never turned against you. And yet you have, time and again, used me as a pawn, a bartered bride, since long before I became a Goddess-Queen in the land where Rhea bore me into Life!

"From the first, you have favoured the unworthy only because they proved powerful. From the first, you chose my father, the dastardly Kronos, as your husband's successor because he showed promise in defeating your King whose mind grew addled by the ceaseless pursuit of lust! And after my father rose to prominence, you stood by and did nothing as he and my mother turned on Okeanos and Tethys their Titan elders, and expelled them from starry Olympus to an eternity in exile at the farthest boundaries of the broad-pathed Earth. You bore witness to this injustice, yet you never came to the aid of your eldest Titan children, who by their very nature cared not for crowns and thrones, but instead set their minds to engender and nurse the Lakes and Springs and Rivers and Seas of the Earth, without which there can be no Life! And when my father, realizing how easily he could be supplanted, turned his fear against his own children, you plotted with my mother to save not the most worthy or virtuous, but the youngest among us who turned to be, in truth, his father's equal in depravity and greed! Though he never devoured his own children, Zeus ravished the daughters of others, and at least once his own, to satisfy his selfish, hedonistic desires without a thought for the consequences of his deeds. And to this favoured son, this despotic, self-indulgent, ill-chosen Saviour among us, who tortured my own child Prometheus for his kindly deed towards mortals, to this son all the primordial gods of Earth, Sea, and Sky plotted to see me wed long after I spread my reign across all the ancient lands of the inner Sea.

"Still, in all these years I have remained the staunchest advocate and friend to the Earth and the defender of the Life which you sustain! And now that I set my mind to the task of preserving Earthly Life by seeding it across the stars, so that our light can shine upon the Cosmos long after the Sun has swallowed the Earth, you insult me by threatening to turn the world to ice! You would destroy the last remnants of hope humanity has left to redeem and restore the Life that once was rife in your bosom, only to spite me for planning to leave with the noblest and most heroic mortals to worlds yet unknown!? You threaten to obliterate that which I love and protect, just as Zeus threatened to lay waste to the Nephele to bring me low, only to spite me?

"If that is your will, then so be it. Raise your hand against the learned enclaves where Prometheus' learned mortals dwell across the nations of the world, and I shall burn the rotting Tree of the golden apples in the

Nepheleid

Garden of the Hesperides! I will take its ashes and nourish the fertile soil in worlds yet to be found beyond the stars… Let its roots wither and the soil loosen and cave into the Sea. Then all three of my brothers will truly be the Masters of this world, while my sisters and I shall make the Earth anew elsewhere. Zeus and Poseidon can rule over a world of skeletons and ghosts, as Hades rules over the long and newly dead who shall be reborn and return to other Earths ruled by the Daughters of the Titans. Then perhaps I shall find solace and justice for having been borne by the womb of Rhea, when I should have been the Daughter of Okeanos and Tethys, the Father of Rivers and the Nurse of All, who by their daughter Asia and my son Prometheus are the true progenitors of humankind, the Father of gods and men be damned! Had the Fates been just, I would have been their child, and tasked with the glorious purpose of pushing the boundaries of the known Cosmos farther still by sailing the innumerable Rivers across the stars!"

Once Hera uttered these words, the Earth-Mother answered by calling forth a forceful gale across the once placid Garden of the Hesperides. As the wind tore at her long, ebony locks, Hera closed her eyes and willed the miasma of her rage to seep through the pores of her flawless skin to burn the vines holding her fast. Once she opened her eyes again, the goddess noticed that her bonds had grown translucent, as had her own flesh, now crisscrossed with small veins and capillaries filled with the dark venom. Once more Hera strove to expel the poison from deep within her being, but the bonds exerted their pressure and kept the rancour stagnant where it pooled under her skin in darkening bruises.

At a loss, Hera withdrew momentarily from her struggle to rest her back against the trunk.

"You cannot hold me bound this way forever," she said through gritted teeth. "I will not abandon my task before I see it to completion! I must seed Life elsewhere! Far from the Earth, far from *him*!"

As soon as she voiced these harried thoughts, Hera heard Kronos' voice echo in the recesses of her mind.

"Daughter," the Titan-King told her. "Do not struggle against your bonds; this is a fight you cannot win alone! Call to me, and I will see to it that your designs come to pass, and that your heir reaches the stars, as you so willed it at her birth. Do not struggle against your bonds, but instead stay the anger of the Mother to us all. She does not mean to spite you or to bring you low; she needs you now more than she ever has!

You are and have always been her most ardent defender. Call out to us, call out to your deathless children and kin, and we will all help you guide Prometheus' learned mortals to restore Life upon the broad-pathed Earth if you help us reinstate the Life-giving rhythms of Time and the Seasons. I swear to you, Daughter, you will prevail in bringing this task to completion, with or without allegiance to your King, if you call to us at once!"

Hera paused, pondering whether she had at last lost her mind. As exhaustion overpowered her consciousness, she heard Junia's voice calling out from across the farthest realms.

"Mom! MOM! We have the sickle!" the child said. "And we have Titans! Eris got the Titans free, and they have your back! Mom, we won! Where are you?"

"Junia," Hera whispered weakly.

She waited for the child to answer but heard only the wind threatening to unleash its fury should she resume her struggle. When she regained consciousness, Hera saw a black tear sundering the golden light of Sunset above her, casting the Garden of the Hesperides into the same cerulean twilight as that of the Elysian fields behind her brother Hades' palace.

Then she was alone, standing upon a starlit meadow illuminated by Rivers spanning an endless cascade of worlds far greater and stranger than she had ever known.

Nepheleid

Chapter Twenty-Six

Holding fast to the reins of his splendid chariot, loud-thundering Zeus rode ahead of the company of the blessed gods who dwell on starry Olympus, as well as Poseidon's Sea-Court, the Titans, and all other immortals who gathered by the shores of the Holy River Styx in search for their Queen. Determined to be the first to cross the opening in the gloomy firmament of the Underworld, Zeus sped towards the Garden of the Hesperides, hoping to reach Hera and cajole her into returning with him to the abode of the gods before Prometheus and his merry band of traitors could convince her otherwise. Once the swift chariot landed upon the nuptial garden where the King and Queen of Olympus sealed their marriage, Zeus' children and the rest of their kin quickly caught up to him, completely engulfing his conveyance.

The deathless mob halted all at once when they caught a glimpse of Hera, who sat by the upraised roots of the Tree of the golden apples at the centre of the orchard, looking as forlorn as what remained of the once lush and resplendent garden. To everyone's dismay, the spirited Queen neither greeted nor upbraided the uninvited crowd that suddenly invaded her haven. She appeared as though in a state of torpor, her usually impeccable hair uncharacteristically unkempt. The garments she wore on the Nephele to pass for a leader among mortals disintegrated around her arms and her waist, where she was bound by pale, diaphanous bonds which she held tightly in her right hand. Most alarmingly, dark bruises marred her usually milky flesh on her torso all the way to her throat, and on her arms where she seemingly struggled in vain to free herself from her bonds.

Almost as soon as the company finished crossing the breach from Hades' Kingdom, Eris grabbed hold of young Junia, took flight and carried the child to the foot of the Tree, with Prometheus, Kronos, and Kymene trailing in their wake.

"Mom!" the girl shouted, sickle in hand, once her feet landed upon the ground by the Tree.

Nepheleid

Hera's eyes opened, eliciting a loud gasp from all the immortals assembled. Turning her gaze towards Prometheus, the Queen took a slow, pained breath, and said, "Prometheus, take your sister. Klymene, see to it that our son and daughter remain unmolested as they journey to the city-ship Nephele. Take our children there, for Junia has chosen her fate. She is as one born from the clouds, not bound to any world, as I find myself in this garden of spite. Go, so that she may succeed where I have failed and be free..."

"Mom!" Junia cried out once more as Hera lost consciousness.

Junia raised the sickle and prepared to cut the bonds, however the blanket Apollo gave her earlier when she crash-landed on starry Olympus, which she draped around her shoulders like a shawl in the fashion of the mortal women native to Turtle Island, fell upon her arms, impeding her movements. Undeterred, Junia threw the garment upon the ground to better wield her blade, but before she could strike, Klymene shouted for her to stop. Demeter and Hades, who followed Eris and Junia closely in their flight, caught up to them and knelt by the Tree beside their sister.

The Cloud-gatherer leaped off his chariot and motioned towards his distressed bride, however Athena and Hermes appeared before him, flanked by Ares and stalwart Herakles, forming a wall. Zeus frowned at his children, wordlessly chiding them for their interference. To his surprise, the ground barely quaked as he furrowed his brows, shaking only a few dead leaves loose from the Tree of the golden apples. His children, however, remained steadfast in their efforts to thwart their King from reaching Hera.

"She draws breath!" Hades said calmly, looking immensely relieved as he removed the dead leaves that landed on Hera's head without waking her.

"Of course she draws breath!" Junia protested, her voice brimming with impatience. "She can't *die*!"

"No, young one," Demeter said. "She cannot die, but she would lie breathless for a year if she ever broke an Oath by the Holy River Styx."

"Well, she *didn't*!" Junia griped. "Now please move aside, I'll cut her free from whatever the hell that is –"

"No!" Klymene shouted again. "Kitten, look! These are no ordinary vines!"

"Look, child," Demeter said, pointing to the eerie bonds binding Hera to her derelict treasure. "It almost looks like an umbilical cord!"

Junia gasped. "What the fuck!?" she yelled out unceremoniously.

"The Earth-Mother and my daughter have become one in their struggle," Kronos answered, looking as though he had fully expected this sequence of events to come to pass. "Hera's ichor flows towards the Tree through these bonds. You cannot cut them, Moppet. Not until Hera becomes free, otherwise any injury to what binds her to the Tree will become as an injury to both."

Her demeanour betraying her utmost scepticism, Junia raised the sickle and with its tip cut a small mark in the bark of the trunk above Hera's head. At the same moment, a small, shallow cut appeared on Hera's chest, above the scar on her left breast where centuries ago Herakles stuck her with a three-barbed arrow laced with the Hydra's venom, when the demigod was still mortal and Hera's sworn enemy. Though Hera eventually prevailed and subsequently became immune to all the poisons of the Earth, it appeared that neither she nor Gaia possessed the same invulnerability against Kronos' mighty blade.

"Stop that!" Demeter scolded Junia. "And put that thing away – it has served its purpose!"

Instantly regretting her actions, Junia took a step back behind Prometheus, Eris, and Kronos, while Klymene took a seat at Hera's left and began to wipe the ichor from the cut with her shawl. Demeter gave the Oceanid a mildly panicked look, as the small cut had not yet healed with the preternatural speed of deathless gods born to the Titan-Kings of old.

Zeus looked upon the scene with growing despondency, trying not to stare at the frightful bonds holding his wife prisoner to the Earth-Mother. These accursed vines reminded him of the tentacular limbs of the Giants who used to lay waste to the Earth wherever they roamed. Most of all, they reminded him of the limbs of Porphyrion, the King of the Giants and successor to Eurymedon, who once tried to ravish Hera when the gods of starry Olympus waged their final battle against the sons of Gaia.

Nepheleid

"It looks as though Hera fell into a trap and tried to break free by tempering Gaia's fury with her own," august Themis pondered aloud from her place at Zeus' right. "Of course, only our Queen could match the Earth-Mother in her anger, and thus they find themselves in a stalemate without an end in sight."

Zeus closed his eyes for a moment and took a deep, steadying breath. *What course of action, dear one, would be wisest to undertake*, he supplicated Metis without uttering a word, lest the others think him weak and unworthy. As he waited for a reply from his oldest and most sagacious counsellor, he recalled the words of the strange and beautiful White Buffalo Calf Woman on the meadow in Turtle Island. Metis' silence towards Hera's predicament, the exquisite Tessa would say, constituted the very challenge meant to prove his worth, one he could scarce afford to fail if he hoped to win back his bride.

Fair Thetis, daughter of Nereus, tiptoed between grey-eyed Athena and swift Hermes to stand before Zeus. When the Father of gods and men noticed the sea-nymph's presence among his children, he spied Poseidon and their entire Sea-Court enclosing their emissary, as if poised for battle.

"It is as we feared," Thetis said, addressing Zeus as diplomatically as one could without drawing attention to the fact that the King of Olympus now found himself completely surrounded.

Zeus glanced at Thetis incredulously.

"If Hera were to choose to leave the Earth with Prometheus and his learned mortals," Thetis continued, "we feared that the Earth-Mother would abandon all hope and let the deltas and shores of the world turn to slime and rot where the Life-giving waters once flowed from the lands. We feared that she would allow the fields and woodlands and meadows turn to dust, and then cover her vast and withering form in a blanket of ice until all living things that feed off her bounty died off, only to awaken when Life in another, less threatening guise was ready to return."

"You knew this would happen?" Zeus asked august Themis, fair Thetis, the Earth-shaker and the Sea-Court all at once.

"We tried to warn you of this many times, Brother," Poseidon replied. "But you scarce listened, so we had to find another way –"

"We devised a contingency plan of sorts to compel Hera to stay," Thetis interrupted, "in case Aphrodite's scheme to coax Hera back into your loving arms failed, as we thought it would."

"Our sister has grown to despise you to a degree none of us would have thought possible even a century ago," Poseidon added. "And we knew that it was only a matter of time until you provoked the young Junia into casting her lot with Prometheus' learned mortals and choose her fate among them aboard the city-ship. And since we already knew that Hera would rather abandon the Earth than leave the fate of the Nephele and its crew to the random whims of the Cosmos, we arranged for the gods of Turtle Island to compel Hera to bid a final farewell to the Mother of us all in a place where she felt no one would find her."

"This is why Ptesanwin told you to find Hera where her trouble began," Demeter said, causing the Thunderer to almost jump back in surprise, as he failed to notice the goddess of the grain making her way from the Tree to the centre of the assembled Sea-Court.

"Then why were you all in the Underworld, pray tell?" Zeus asked crossly, hoping that at least one of his kin would provide a satisfactory answer.

"To make certain that Junia found her way to the Nephele without interference," bright Athena replied, her aegis raised in defiance. "Why were you there?"

"To find Hera –"

"Hera's trouble did not begin in Hades' Kingdom," Zeus heard his mother, the Titan-Queen Rhea, say as she approached the crowd from the edge of the Garden. "My heir fared rather well after losing her memory of that unfortunate day she spent in the Underworld, giving birth to Prometheus while you tried to persuade her to return with you to the surface. That is why I sent her to dwell the boundaries of the Earth with my elders. She would have ruled over the whole world, had she not faltered in her conviction to never fall in love with you. This place, this nuptial garden that bore witness to your bridal, this is where her trouble began, and if you do not make it right, this is where all our troubles will end, when the Earth swallows us whole under a blanket of ice and snow!"

"Then why do the lot of you insist on thwarting me from seeing my wife?" Zeus asked, almost at his wits' end. "I cannot help her if you continue to hold me here at a distance!"

Nepheleid

"You are the last one among us Hera wishes to see at the moment," august Themis answered. "If you say something to upset her, she might reconsider her stance of staying Gaia's hand, and in her vulnerable state also decide to end us all. I advise extreme caution until you determine a right and proper course of action."

"Hera would never doom all mortal Life, nor her own deathless kind, to oblivion!" Zeus replied sullenly. "She has always been of the mind that enough upright mortals remain, however scattered across the many diminished nations of the world, to spark hope for the resurgence of Life upon the broad-pathed Earth."

"That is why she is our Queen," Athena said.

"Then move aside, Daughter," the Cloud-gatherer told the Virgin Warrior. "Our Queen is in distress, and she needs her King."

Athena frowned at those words.

"Others have already begun attempting to free her from her bonds," Ares said, stepping aside to clear his father's view of the Tree of the golden apples.

Zeus saw Hephaestus standing before his mother, axe in hand, then dodging with surprising agility a rapidly-moving branch at it attacked the smith god before he could strike. The Father of gods and men then spied Aphrodite helping her husband to her feet, pulling him aside as the pair took great care to step over a half dozen hapless immortals who failed to elude the thrashing limbs of the Tree of the golden apples.

Prometheus and Eris held Junia where she stood, sickle in hand, while Apollo moved to the fore and wisely dropped his quiver and golden bow before kneeling before his bound and unconscious Queen. Without saying a word, the Archer placed his hands upon Hera's right hand holding fast to her bonds and whispered something in such a faint voice that even the immortals assembled in the Garden of the Hesperides could scarce hear his words. He closed his eyes and remained still as a statue, except for a few small shakes of his head as he appeared to delve into Hera's embattled mind.

Zeus bowed his head, saddened by the knowledge that his eldest son could speak with his wife with such ease in the fields of twilight where they once shared a dream, on the fateful night before Junia was conceived. When Apollo finally awoke, the Archer looked up at all the immortals assembled by the Tree, his gaze settling upon the young Junia.

"Zoe!!!" he uttered in a loud, clear voice, a daffy grin illuminating his flawless features, before losing consciousness.

For some reason, Hades shook his head and pinched the bridge of his nose.

Leto and Artemis emerged from the crowd and crouched as they approached the Tree to collect Apollo's inert form. As the Fates willed it, the Tree did not move to strike the two goddesses. Once Apollo, Artemis and Leto found themselves far from the reach of the Tree's belligerent limbs, Zeus gazed upon Junia, who now looked as horrified and surprised as one who had her most profound secret revealed before the whole world.

At that moment, Zeus made his way past Athena, Hermes, Ares, and Herakles, who predictably closed their formation around their father.

"I knew my wife would never give our child such a common name," the Cloud-gatherer told his gatekeepers, as well as all the immortals assembled in the Garden of the Hesperides. "Hera gave our daughter the name Zoe, a lovely name to honour me. That means some part of her still loves me as she did then all those years ago whether or not she cares to admit it."

Athena and Hermes stepped aside, with Ares and Herakles following their lead. As the Thunderer walked slowly towards the Tree of the golden apples, Junia bolted, breaking free from Prometheus and Eris' grip and put herself between Zeus and her mother. She raised her sickle hesitantly with both hands, as if she were genuinely afraid of her father for the very first time.

"Move aside, child," Zeus said benevolently, smiling at the girl while Ares took his youngest sister aside by her upraised elbow.

"I now know what must be done to free Hera from her bonds," the Father of gods and men added, picking Junia's discarded blanket off the ground.

Nepheleid

Chapter Twenty-Seven

Hera opened her eyes, blinking at the golden light of perpetual Sunset in the Garden of the Hesperides. Still bound at the waist to the ancient Tree of the golden apples, the voice of Gaia now silent in her mind, the goddess looked at the pale vines holding her fast against the trunk. The last thing she remembered before awaking was greeting the Lord of the golden bow in the fields of twilight where Gaia brought her consciousness once she realized that Hera would never yield the fate of mortals to the Earth-Mother's fury. Fighting off a wave of miasma swelling within her very core, Hera lifted her gaze and saw that she was not alone in the Garden of the Hesperides.

All the other blessed gods who dwell on Olympus were assembled before her, as were throngs of immortals from all realms. The ancient powers of Earth and Sky were there, as were her parents, wily Kronos and fair-haired Rhea, the boundary-dwelling Titans Okeanos and Tethys and their innumerable children as well as countless nymphs, naiads, dryads, and elemental spirits. Hephaestus was there with his Cyclops, Dionysus with his satyrs and Maenads, Artemis with her entourage of virgin huntresses, Poseidon with his Sea-Court. Even magnanimous Hades came though without his subterranean retinue. It took Hera a moment to notice that the long-imprisoned Titans who dwell in Tartarus were also there, though absent their chains. That all seemed so very strange, Hera thought, feeling suddenly very anxious and exposed, bound as she was before a gathering of immortals that looked very much like the one that came to bear witness at her wedding.

Hera closed her eyes, recalling instead the crowds of mortal revellers who came to her festivals each year, so many centuries ago, when her likeness was carried in a procession, then bathed in the river and bound to the sacred Tree until the mortals believed that their goddess had bestowed the fruitfulness of her sacred womb upon the land. Hera chuckled at the image conjured by her mind, considering her current predicament. Had these august beings congregating in the ruins of her garden come to witness such a preposterous spectacle, or had they come to watch the Queen of Olympus experience one of her fabled, powerful fits of prophecy? Hera opened her eyes again and looked at the gathering in the garden once more. The sight of her chthonic allies mingling cheerfully with the blessed gods who dwell on starry Olympus made it very clear that no one would be fighting for her release from Olympus, nor to grant her and Junia safe passage to the Nephele high above.

"Junia…"

"It will be all right, Sister," Demeter told her reassuringly, appearing somewhere to the left of her field of vision. "We all came to see Junia safely to the home she chose. Your will prevailed, your child will seed the stars with Life, as you so willed it from the days she was born!"

Hera closed her eyes and smiled. It was her oft-repeated adage that Junia ought to accompany her to the stars in order to spread Earthly Life across the Cosmos that prompted Apollo to guess her daughter's true name. Inspired by Eris' whimsical genius, Hera devised a challenge to her youngest daughter's suitors on the matter by presenting them with an anagram, in binary, of Junia's true name, which even for the most astute minds would prove impossible to solve through normal means. Apollo, however, accepted the challenge when he met his Queen in the fields of twilight beneath the starlit meadows illuminated by innumerable Sky-Rivers crisscrossing the Heavens, and guessed Junia's true name by surmising that it was Zoe, which meant "Life" in the ancient tongue by which mortals used to honour the blessed gods who dwell on high Olympus.

Though he remained the son of her most hated rival, Hera was glad that Apollo uncovered the stratagem and won the right to court Junia once she came of age, for he learned long ago the wisdom of listening to his Queen's words and taking them to heart. Furthermore, Apollo showed genuine gratitude once he understood that he won Hera's blessing if he chose to pursue Junia as his bride in no less than five years, once the girl achieved scholarly mastery of all the knowledge mortals needed in order to fulfil the Nephele's mission across the stars. When Hera opened her eyes again, she spied august Themis standing somewhere to the side of the Tree, looking after Apollo's motionless form as the Archer slept off his own encounter with his Queen in a realm not of the Earth. Hera's heart halted when she caught a glimpse of Junia standing defiantly before Zeus, armed with the mighty sickle that once belonged to her father, the Titan-King Kronos. As the Fates willed it, her son Ares mercifully pulled the young girl away while the Thunderer made his way towards the Tree and in turn beckoned gentle Demeter, who brings forth gifts, to stand aside.

"That will be all, Demeter" Zeus said. "I will unbind Hera, if she will let me."

Demeter threw Zeus a look of mild annoyance, though she smiled once more at Hera before joining the others gathered in the meadow bordered by the vast orchard in the Garden of the Hesperides. Hera willed herself to put aside her weariness and overwhelming disorientation as Zeus stood before her, looking amused and alarmed in equal measure at his wife's quandary, and holding a blanket he picked off the ground a few moments before. Hera tried again to pull at her bonds but remained bound tightly against the Tree. A feeling of mild dread swelled inside her chest as Zeus leaned over and began pulling at the vines around her waist with the same result.

"Are you not done lifting the veil, peeking through the fabric of the universe?" he asked her cheekily, gently brushing the loose strands of hair from her face and shoulders. This intimate, familiar gesture did little to comfort her.

Hera wrapped her arms protectively around her waist, grabbing hold of the vines with both hands.

"Where did you go, when you lost consciousness?" Zeus inquired, the concern in his voice unfeigned.

That is a truly inane question, Hera thought, staring at Zeus in disbelief. "I've been here all day and all night!" she replied. "I am bound to this Tree!"

Zeus could not help smiling. "Yes, you are, but that is not what I meant. You went away inside your mind for a long time, and you spoke as though with a voice that was not your own –"

Hera was aghast. "I spoke out loud?"

"You certainly did. The last time I saw you in this state, you secured our victory in the war against the Giants."

"Don't remind me..." Hera said faintly.

"Don't be like that," Zeus replied as he drew closer and cupped her face in his hands.

"Let me go," Hera muttered, knowing all too well that she remained in a vulnerable and unsteady state, her very form barely holding back the miasma she had conjured up in defiance to the Earth-Mother herself. It also did not help that Zeus' hands were cupping her face in such a way that her reply came out muffled and barely audible.

Zeus ignored her request. "Why are you still bound?"

Hera lifted her head suddenly. "What!?" she cried out, her apprehension and confusion quickly giving way to annoyance and anger. Hera gave Zeus a cold, hard stare. She would not be mocked, even if she let herself get caught in a cosmic snare by an ancient power whom she had sought to bid farewell before she became confronted with the full brunt of Gaia's grief at the state of the world. She tugged in desperation at the vines around her waist, but her bindings did not budge. As her anger grew, a sudden gale fiercely shook the remaining leaves of the Tree of the golden apple trees. This unexpected change made the countless immortals gathered in the Garden of the Hesperides turn their gaze toward the King and Queen at the Tree.

"It would appear that the only thing that the gods of Olympus and the other immortals who dwell at the boundaries of the Earth dislike more than having me as their King is the idea of losing you to the endless void between the stars," Zeus said as he bent closer to Hera and removed the few dead leaves that landed on her head. "This lot brought me here to tell you that, while you may engage me in a battle of wills until the heat death of the universe, you cannot fight the combined will of Gaia and the Sea-Court and Olympus alone." He drew closer, sliding his right arm with some difficulty between the tree trunk and the small of her back. The vines loosened at his effort, yet, Hera remained bound. Zeus then grabbed the bonds at Hera's waist with his left hand and pulled with all his might, trying to break them with brute force. The bonds loosened even further but did not break. Zeus then pulled the blanket he carried and slid it between Hera's tattered clothes and the bonds that held her fast against the Tree of the golden apples. Looking at the vines Hera now held tightly with both hands, her knuckles drained of colour from the force of her grip, Zeus slid completely behind Hera and the bottom of the Tree, once again, the bonds loosened but did not release their captive and increasingly distraught goddess.

"What is the meaning of this!?" Hera cried out, causing the gale in the Garden of the Hesperides to become increasingly violent. In response, Zeus pulled her closer to him with his arm at her back and cupped her face with his left hand. He held her for a moment, giving her time to calm her tempest. The gale subsided somewhat, though the leaves continued to rustle uneasily around them. Hera tried to will away the tears welling in her eyes. She would not show fear nor weakness, not now, not while she stood bound and helpless in this bizarre embrace, with all the immortals of all the realms watching them.

"Why is this happening?" she asked, trying to sound calm, yet unable to conceal her distress at her increasingly ridiculous and surreal predicament.

"We are not done negotiating a truce, my love," Zeus told her flatly.

"What!?" Hera looked away from Zeus, who placed his free hand under her chin and turned her head so that she could face him.

"Did you really believe I would let you leave before we had a long-overdue talk about our marriage?" Zeus asked earnestly. There was no longer any trace of mirth in his voice.

"What do you want from me!?" Hera said as she closed her eyes, as if this could prevent her from losing her mind completely.

Zeus waited until Hera finally opened her eyes, then told her, "I want you to come home. I want you to bathe in the waters of the Kanathos Spring, whether at Nauplia or in the pool on starry Olympus, so that we can properly renew our marriage. I want you to remain by my side and be the Queen that the Fates promised me as they sealed our bond when we wed. I want you to stop fleeing..." Zeus closed his eyes and took a deep breath. "I want you to stop fleeing to the ends of the Earth and in the places beyond the Heavens whenever you get angry with me. But I know you will not. You will not, because I constantly make you angry. And you become so cruel and vicious when you are angry. Cruelty was never in your nature, but you have had to act as though it were so that all would live in constant fear of your anger." Zeus lowered his head and rested his temple against Hera's. He waited a moment before he continued. "I know that I am to blame for all of your anger. I have wronged you, and in securing my supremacy among the gods I almost destroyed the one I love the most. But you are so strong. Nothing can ever break you, and this frightened me to no end. You are the only being in the Cosmos who can defy me and prevail. This is the reason why only you could be Queen. I was a fool for trying to undermine you, when we should have ruled Earth and Sky as one, as is the will of the Fates."

Stunned, Hera looked at Zeus, unsure whether his heartfelt confession was another one of his mind games. Zeus waited a moment before he found his voice again. "We have both made so many mistakes. but you cannot leave me, not even by sailing to the stars. You have tried so valiantly to leave me in the past, but there is a reason why you always came back, even if I had to trick you and use force at times. Do you not remember that it was Eros, the most powerful of all the beings of the Cosmos and presided over our union when the Fates sealed our bond? Neither one of us can be free from the another, no matter how hard we may try. Countless times you have crept out in the middle of the night after discovering another one of my indiscretions, yet you always returned without fail, and I always welcomed you back with open arms, because I would be lost without you."

Hera closed her eyes. This was a mind game, she told herself. It did not matter that she had once loved Zeus madly long ago, prompting Prometheus to question her motives for agreeing to return to Olympus a mere three years before. I cannot love my tormentor, she told herself. I will not allow him take hold over my heart, never again! I cannot give in to this madness!

As if reading her mind, Zeus drew her closer and whispered to her, "Was it not longing for our marriage bed that compelled you to agree so readily to return to me from your frozen fields? You must have known that I would never collect on your ghastly Oath, since I had not done so in more than three thousand years. Did you think that I forgot? I knew why you laid waste to Troy. It was not because of your hurt vanity at losing the beauty contest, and it was not because I dismissed Hebe as our cup-bearer and replaced her with the Trojan prince Ganymede, although that probably made sacking Troy easier for you. No, you did it out of spite after all my threats of replacing you with other wives. You did it because of the way I treated you when Herakles was mortal, even though you were in the wrong for trying to change the outcome of the War against the Giants. You did it because of the way that I tried to make you my slave after I ended my plans to marry Thetis."

Hera flinched and tried to look away from Zeus, but he still held her face in his hand. Forcing her gaze back toward him, he told her, "I treated you horribly back then. I tried to sour your triumph at remaining the Queen of Olympus by making you feel powerless and defeated. I was angry at your incessant wrath and murderous savagery during the destruction of Troy, but I came to the realization that you were unleashing your anger by destroying something that I cherished Oath so that I could hold it against you, but that was a mistake. I should not have used it to coerce you into returning to Olympus. I should have stayed with you in your hideaway and negotiated a peace until you returned to me willingly, because you do love me, underneath all the bravado and threats of separation."

"You are out of your mind!" Hera protested, perhaps a little too defensively.

Zeus chuckled softly, having caught the faltering conviction in Hera's voice. "Perhaps..." He kissed her on the forehead. "You sometimes forget that you love me, but Mnemosyne has a potion for that."

Hera scoffed. She released the vines in her left hand and attempted to hit Zeus in the ribs with her elbow, but he caught her arm easily and laughed softly as she tried to push him away and wriggle her left arm free of his hold. Zeus then grabbed Hera's hand into his own and held it against his heart. Surprised at this intimate gesture, Hera willed herself to look at Zeus, who was done with playfulness.

"If you doubt my sincerity," he told her solemnly, "then I will swear by the Holy River Styx, before all the gods assembled here in our nuptial garden, that you have no rivals when it comes to my affection. I may be a dreadful, faithless husband, but I have never loved anyone as passionately as I love you. Even when I thought that I could cast you aside and replace you with Thetis, I was reminded that you and I could never be apart, that the Fates would always avenge you in the end, and that I would have fully deserved being supplanted by my own son for treating you with such cruelty and hubris. Knowing you, you would have found your own triumph once again. I do not even doubt that you would have married the Crown Prince, if only to take your revenge on me. If you had, I would have told him that no one, not even myself, could ever be worthy of such a glorious Queen. I would have told him what the world once knew centuries ago, that your greatest glory came not from sleeping in my arms, but that my greatest glory came from sleeping in yours..."

Nepheleid

Zeus took Hera's hand off his heart and kissed her fingers. She gasped. He only kissed her like this when they were alone in their bedchamber, and now he did so in front of thousands. Zeus smiled when Hera began to blush. As she felt her resolve giving way, Hera stiffened and asked, "What of Junia? What about all my work with her and Prometheus?" There was a catch in her throat as she asked finally, "What have you done with Prometheus?"

Zeus leaned over and kissed Hera's eyelids tenderly. "Prometheus and Junia have already gone to the Nephele," he answered. "Prometheus will continue his work among his learned mortals, and Junia will remain with him on the city-ship until she comes of age. Although, defying one's father for ascendancy probably constitutes the truest measure of maturity among our kind. You would have been fiercely proud of her. She reminds me of you when you were a maiden." Zeus closed his eyes. "If you stay with us on starry Olympus, I have no doubt that Junia will be the one who seeds galaxies with Earthly Life in your place, and through her your descendants will be more numerous than the stars. We all agreed to this when Prometheus left with her a moment ago. He possesses incredible courage, and now, I understand that he inherited this from you as well."

Hera shifted uncomfortably in Zeus' embrace. It did not please her that Junia would leave without her. She tried to protest, but Zeus said to her, "Do not despair, you will see her often. She will dwell in the Garden of the Hesperides you planted at the base of the Nephele, until the city-ship is fully ready to sail towards the stars. And when the time comes, perhaps we will join them, once the Earth-Mother is again rendered whole. If that day ever comes, we will leave together, as husband and wife again, then said finally, "Now please, come home. Let us call a truce, and perhaps strive for a peace that we will both accept."

Hera bit back a sob. "I cannot! I am bound –"

"Hera, let go," Zeus said softly, looking at her waist. "There, with your other hand. Release the bonds."

When Hera looked at her right hand at her waist, she realized that she could no longer feel her fingers, so strong was her grip. She willed her fingers to release her bonds and, as she did so, the vines disintegrated into dust. Zeus pulled her away from the Tree of the golden apples, holding her tight so that she could stop trembling. Forgetting her usual reluctance at showing affection for her husband in front of others, Hera offered no resistance when Zeus embraced her in front of all the immortals gathered in the Garden of the Hesperides. She simply yielded, not hearing the loud cheering noise from the crowd as the garden began to bloom with flowers and new vegetation, and her treasured Tree of the golden apples sprouted buds upon its bare branches. When Zeus drew her closer for a kiss, Hera stiffened and clasped a hand over her mouth. The Father of gods and men released her, perhaps afraid that he had hurt her by pressing upon her bruised and poisoned flesh.

"The miasma has not left her!" August Themis told Zeus as she made her way to the Tree of the golden apples. "She needs to purify herself from the great venom she carries inside her."

Zeus threw a glance at Apollo's still-grinning, unconscious form. The lad was obviously in no condition to provide answers on the matter.

"What must be done to cure her?" Zeus asked Themis, his son's mentor in the oracular arts.

"Hera needs to bathe in a purifying stream, though far from the fragile waterways of the broad-pathed Earth," august Themis answered. "The miasma she carries must also be cured before falling back to Earth, otherwise the Mother of us all will be dealt the killing blow!"

"As the Fates willed it," Zeus said confidently, "I know of such a place, and it happens to be on starry Olympus." Looking at his bride, he asked her, "What if I take you there, my love, if only to relieve you of your sickness?"

Hera nodded faintly in assent, her hand still clasped over her mouth so as not to do befoul the ground beneath her feet. With a victorious smile, Zeus lifted Hera off the ground and carried her onto his swift chariot, while Hermes dispatched the other immortals gathered in the Garden of the Hesperides to their respective realms. Overcome with exhaustion, Hera let herself fall asleep for a spell in Zeus' arms as he drove his swift chariot away from this place. The last thing she saw was her brother Hades smiling back at her as he crossed back into his Kingdom through the closing breach in the Heavens above the orchard. Once the Host of Many had left, only the golden light of Sunset remained above Hera's newly resurgent nuptial garden.

Nepheleid

Chapter Twenty-Eight

When Hera regained consciousness, she found herself in Zeus' arms, though not upon the swift chariot that carried them back to the gilded halls of holy Olympus. They were now alone in the royal palace, sitting on a couch by the open door through which Hera spied the sumptuous bath she often shared with her King after performing the nuptial rite.

As she began to stir, Zeus leaned closer to Hera and whispered in her ear, "Welcome home, my love."

Hera looked up at Zeus, divining his intent before he set her down on the polished marble floor. He took her to the corner of the room beyond, where the smaller, refurbished baptismal pool near the far corner of the room had remained unchanged since the last time she angrily refused to renew her virginity upon her return to Olympus three years prior. The rejuvenating waters of the Kanathos Spring since froze into a solid block of ice, despite the warmth emanating from the countless lit candles strewn across the cavernous room. Had Hestia done this in their absence? That seemed rather presumptuous of her eldest sister, Hera thought, blushing slightly as Zeus caught her gaze and smiled at her.

"I hope you do not expect me to sit on a block of ice as I bathe," she told him wryly as she fought off a wave of sickness from the miasma rising to the fore.

"I have an idea," Zeus replied, pulling Hera closer and kissing her neck ever so gently so as not to press upon her bruised skin, his hands dexterously removing the blanket off her shoulders as well as what remained of her tattered clothing. As they stood in this embrace by the small pool, Hera felt wisps of steam rising from beneath them.

"Now look down," Zeus told her, looking very pleased with himself.

Hera looked at the pool in amazement. The ice had melted, releasing the clear, translucent waters. She drew closer to the edge of the water and dipped her hand in the pool. It was pleasantly warm.

Nepheleid

"That is very impressive, how did you know this would happen?" she asked him.

"I did not know, but I thought it was worth a try," Zeus said as he gently, carefully, caressed her naked back.

Hera suddenly froze at the thought of bathing in the virginity pool while Zeus watched. She sucked in a breath when her bridegroom leaned over and kissed her neck once more.

"These waters will cleanse you of the miasma you absorbed while matching Gaia's fury with unrelenting spite," Zeus told her softly. "You heard Themis' words, we cannot risk soiling the Earth-Mother with this venom, not after she capitulated and released you from your bonds. Look at your hand, the stain has already withdrawn. There simply is no other way, lest you bear this burden until we reach one of the cleansing tanks on the Polaris at the boundaries of the Earth."

Hera closed her eyes, fighting off another wave of sickness, her hands gripping the edge of the pool.

"Now, will you do me the honour of bathing in the waters of Kanathos, or must I beg it of you?" Zeus whispered in her ear, his voice almost a purr. He then wrapped his arms around Hera's waist and lifted her as if to help her into the pool. Hera stiffened.

"Wait!" She almost shouted. Zeus stopped moving, though he still held her.

"What is wrong?" He buried his face in her neck and kissed her again. Hera felt goose bumps cover her whole body. Grabbing hold of Zeus' arm, she pleaded wordlessly for him to pause, then turned to look at him.

"Is something the matter?" he asked gently, brushing back her hair so that her shoulders and chest were completely bare. "Are you having doubts?" Zeus suddenly looked very worried.

Hera shook her head. "As I've told you before," she said weakly, but determinedly, "I will bathe in the waters of the Kanathos Spring, after you go first."

Zeus raised an eyebrow. He stared at Hera for a moment, as if seriously considering her request.

"I've told you before," he said, shifting uncomfortably. "You would not like me as a virgin."

"You never know..." Hera replied, failing to suppress a grin.

"If I go into that pool and renew my virginity, I fear that the Cosmos might collapse onto itself. Do you really want me to have that on my conscience?"

Hera answered with a genuine, throaty laugh.

Zeus smiled as he gazed upon his wife, likely suspecting that a certain minion of Chaos planted this preposterous idea in her mind. Perhaps he regretted allowing Junia to remain under the care of Eris for all these years. He finally looked at the pool, then said, "I will do it."

"How do I know this is not a trick?" Hera replied, feigning shock that he would, at long last, seriously consider her request.

"You will have to trust me," Zeus answered with a look of utmost resignation.

Hera bit her lip, then took a seat at a low tripod by the pool.

"After you," she said faintly, as though the novelty of this dare kept her awake and alert despite the vast quantities of miasma sickening her very being.

Zeus suddenly affected the mien of a mortal who swallowed a swarm of live electric eels, which elicited more laughter from Hera.

"Do I need to hold you by the hand?" she asked facetiously. She sat up as Zeus climbed over the edge of the pool and placed a leg in the shallow water. The pool remained undisturbed.

"You have to go all the way in," Hera chided him, her face rapt with anticipation of witnessing a true miracle among the deathless gods of high Olympus.

Zeus heaved a weary sigh as he stood with his legs at either side of the narrow pool, then swung his other leg over the edge. The waters lapped his tall limbs above the knee, and the pool remained undisturbed.

Hera shook her head, then immediately regretting doing so. As she clasped her hand over her mouth, Zeus quickly leaned over, placing his hands in front of each foot, then motioned to submerge himself all the way to his neck while flexing his muscular arms and torso to impress his sole spectator. The moment his dangling manhood touched the sacred rejuvenating liquid, Hera heard a loud hiss coming from the pool, as all the water escaped upwards in a great column of steam. Hera stared in disbelief as the steam formed a cloudy whirlpool at the ceiling, churning furiously above the King and Queen. When she lowered her gaze to look at her husband, Hera saw that he had remained completely dry, except for his hair and beard which had curled to a frightful degree with the intense momentary humidity. As he climbed out of the now bone-dry pool, Zeus stared back at Hera with a completely neutral expression, or at least he appeared to do so since his features were now obscured behind the copious curls on his face and head.

Perhaps the sheer exhaustion of containing prodigious quantities of miasma within her deathless form had finally sapped her ability to maintain decorum, or perhaps millennia of pent-up frustration at having to undergo this obnoxious ritual each year to renew her marriage to the most faithless of husbands finally made her reach her wits' end. Nonetheless, Hera took a long look at her bridegroom, staggered towards the pool then doubled over the edge and fell into the empty vessel as she burst into laughter. Her bruises darkened and her legs gave out from under her, yet she laughed heartily for such a long time that soon the King and Queen heard timid knocks on the outer door facing the enclosed garden. Hera raised her head for a moment and saw her handmaiden Eirene, on of the three Horai, staring back at her incredulously through the open door.

"My lady, is everything all right? I thought I heard screams –" the Charite said.

Catching her breath, Hera tried to explain to her handmaiden what had happened, but all she could manage to say was, "Zeus... tried to bathe... in the waters of... Kanathos... and then his... his... BALLS!" Though she tried to clarify her words by pantomiming Zeus' misadventure, Hera could only point at the churning whirlpool below the ceiling before resuming her hysterical laughter. The confused handmaiden finally saw her father standing on the other side of the pool, his hair a nebulous, spherical force field of tightly wound curls around his face and head.

"Shall I fetch scissors, my King?" Eirene asked shyly.

"Not quite yet, child," came Zeus' muffled reply, barely audible over Hera's fits of laughter. "But stay close, your Queen will need you shortly."

As the handmaiden gazed upon her Queen's darkening flesh with fascination and alarm, Zeus told Eirene, "You might want to stay outside in the garden, Daughter, unless you wish to become a virgin once again."

As he uttered these words, Hera's laughter suddenly came to a halt. The Queen crouched into a ball at the bottom of the pool while the waters roiled furiously above her head. With a flick of his hand, the Cloud-gatherer caused to churning whirlpool to rain down on Hera, washing away the miasma under her skin with the healing waters of the Kanathos Spring. When Hera finally stood up and climbed out of the pool, her bruises were completely gone, though the waters in the vessel became as murky as a mire. Without being told, Eirene entered the room and immediately tended to her Queen, while Zeus sat patiently on the tripod, presumably entertaining himself with whatever witty remarks Metis could provide at the moment. Though cleansed from the poison born of spite, Hera did not yet know whether the waters had renewed her virginity, or whether the miasma shielded her from the waters' other wondrous properties. Still, she had no doubt that she would soon uncover the truth of the matter.

"What will we do with this?" Hera asked, pointing at the veritable bog within the pool as Eirene trimmed Zeus' hair and beard into a more presentable guise.

"We shall wait for the purifying waters to do their work, before we return what's left to the Earth," Zeus answered placidly.

"And how long will this take?" Hera asked, taking a seat upon a couch, as a wave of weariness began to take hold.

"As long as it must," Zeus replied.

"That's rather vague," Hera said.

Zeus shrugged, while Eirene asked him meekly to hold still.

"Does that mean we can no longer use the pool for its intended purposes?" Hera added cheekily.

Zeus sighed. "I supposed you will have to resume your journeys with a trip to Nauplia each Spring," he said with a hint of humour in his voice.

Hera answered with a cold, hard stare, though she gave in to another fit of laughter almost immediately thereafter on account of her sheer exhaustion. When Eirene finished her task and bid her King and Queen farewell, Zeus stood up and joined Hera at her couch. In her addled state, Hera noticed that Zeus looked rather stunning with his hair and beard cropped short. It reminded her of earlier times, before their marriage, when Zeus had occasionally completely shaved off his beard before coming to court her. She always thought that he was rather beautiful under all the hair, though he had worn a beard for so long that it was now difficult to imagine him without one.

Zeus did not fail to notice that Hera was staring at him lasciviously.

"I now need a bath of my own," he told her. "Would you care to join me?"

Chapter Twenty-Nine

Unsupervised and alone on the senior management deck of the Hesperides Autonomous Station, Junia stood with her back to the wide Earth-facing window, trying in vain to summon the courage to gaze upon the slumbering world beyond. She did not shy away from the wondrous sight of the quiet Earth at night because of a fear of heights, otherwise she would never have dived to high Olympus from the airlock of the Nephele's transport bay on the night of the meteor shower. Junia denied herself this breathtaking spectacle out of unrelenting guilt for the part she played in setting in motion a chain of events that sealed not only her fate, but also that of her mother. For all her boundless cleverness, Junia never once considered how unnecessarily harrowing it must have been for Hera to watch another one of her children fall to Earth from a great height, as Hephaestus did more than once centuries ago. She also never expected her Earth-dive to grant Zeus a splendid opportunity to bring back Hera to Olympus, which he exploited through manoeuvres so fiendishly shrewd that they remained, to this day, uncontested by even the Queen's most ardent allies.

Junia looked down upon the middle finger of her right hand, newly adorned with the fabulous ring Hephaestus made for her thirteenth birthday. This was, of course, a small consolation for her friends and classmates aboard the Nephele missing this landmark occasion. Junia inadvertently began her adolescence in the Underworld, where the passage of Time unfolds at a much slower pace than upon the broad-pathed Earth. When Junia leaped to Olympus on the night the stars fell to Earth, Winter had not yet come into full force; whereas Spring was already in full bloom in the Northern hemisphere when Zeus returned to the abode of the gods with Hera after their spell in the Garden of the Hesperides. Junia smiled at the trinket, admiring how adroitly the smith god concealed complex circuitry within the ornate vines and tree branches adorning this exquisite piece. This, she knew, was a tracking device, one their mother likely insisted that she wear at all times on the Nephele, lest she attempt to escape once more through the airlock and land somewhere else on Earth than outside the gilded ramparts of holy Olympus.

Somewhere beyond the observation deck, where Hera and Junia used to spend a great deal of time looking at the Earth after Junia finished her school lessons for the day and Hera her shift, the inner elevator rose swiftly towards the nearly deserted senior management deck. When the doors opened to Junia's left, she looked up and saw her brother Prometheus gazing amicably at her.

"You got me," Junia said with her hands raised as if caught in a compromising position.

"You were easy to find," Prometheus replied with a soft laugh. "At least you weren't microchipped like a house cat!" he added when Junia gave him an almost credible frown.

"Uh-huh."

"You are not the only one shackled to a ring, I'll have you know," Prometheus continued. "Here, you've seen my ring, have you not? Do you know the story of how I got stuck with this?"

Prometheus extended his right hand and showed him the ring on his middle finger, mounted with a small rock Junia could not easily identify.

"It's just part of the stone upon which I was chained for centuries," Prometheus said. "When Herakles released me, Zeus made me wear a piece of my rock wherever I roamed, for he had decreed long ago that I was to remain bound to my rock for all time, and that even though he allowed my release to increase the glory and prestige of his mortal son, his word was to remain law nonetheless."

"Is that why you wear your ring on your middle finger?" Junia asked innocently.

"Of course," the benefactor of humanity answered beatifically. "As do you, or so it seems."

"I was going to wear it on my ring finger, but it's still too big," Junia said.

"You will grow into it," Prometheus said, "provided you desist from leaping off space stations for the foreseeable future."

"I'm not going anywhere, and I'm not going back down *there*!"

"Not even to visit Ares and Eris?" Prometheus asked. "Not even to visit our mothers?"

"Klymene is back together with her husband, the Titan Iapetos," Junia said. "I don't think she will ever go back to Olympus either." Junia bit her lip. She did not quite know how she felt about Zeus releasing the Titans and their allies from Tartarus and declaring them the lords of the Elysian fields to thank them for the part they played in helping him find Hera in the Garden of the Hesperides.

"This was a kindness," Prometheus said.

"Get out of my head, Prometheus," Junia retorted.

"That is rather difficult to do when your thoughts are ceaselessly griping, little one."

"It's really messed up that the Titans got free, but Mom is still bound to Zeus and to Olympus after all that happened. What the hell, Prometheus? Did *you* see any of that coming when you have your episodes of prophecy? Because I can't even – "

"You will soon," Prometheus interrupted. "Your powers are growing exponentially as you blossom towards womanhood. You already proved at least as strong as Hera when you fell to Earth from the Nephele and walked off with only your clothes singed off. I have no doubt that you will gain the second sight before your first blood moon."

"Still," Junia pursued. "I find this unsatisfactory."

Prometheus said nothing for a moment, and simply gazed at Junia with a hint of a smile upon his lips.

"You know something I don't?" Junia asked.

"Prophecy is a funny thing," Prometheus answered. "Even the Fates, in their edicts on the course of events yet to come, have been thwarted by the random whims of chaos. You ought to know this well enough, for having spent the past few years with Eris as your shadow. Do not think this city-ship, and its laboratory sub-station, have seen the last of Hera yet. Always remember that the gods remain ever true to their nature."

Nepheleid

"What's *that* supposed to mean?"

Prometheus did not answer, though he gave Junia the sly look of a cat that ate a tasty little mouse and was rather proud of himself.

"Look, there in Mother's garden," he told her.

Forgetting her earlier reluctance, Junia turned to face the window and looked at the world below. There she saw Hera's slumbering form in her garden on high Olympus, under an ancient willow. Her handmaidens made a soft bed for her there, so that their Queen could gaze upon the stars and her children aboard the Nephele when she finally awoke.

"How long has it been since she fell asleep?" Junia asked.

"Ten days, perhaps a fortnight," Prometheus answered. "Sometimes she stirs awake, very briefly, before falling back asleep. She needs to rest, though. She did challenge a primordial power of the Cosmos when she confronted Gaia in the Garden of the Hesperides. Any other god or goddess would have slumbered for years thereafter, provided that they made it through the ordeal at all with their faculties mostly intact."

"And how is she?" Junia asked hesitantly. "You all told me that she would prevail! Didn't she lose her marbles when she agreed to let Zeus take her back to Olympus?"

"Not at all," Prometheus replied. "Right now Olympus is probably the safest place for her to recover. Even Zeus decreed that she ought to remain undisturbed during her convalescence, and he even tasked Hypnos and Morpheus to see to it that she sleeps until she is well enough to resume her duties as Queen. Now look, over there, someone is coming to visit her."

Junia leaned closer to the railing and focused her gaze on a graceful figure high on the hill making her way towards the willow. As if suspecting that others high above the Earth were watching her, the goddess looked up, revealing her lovely features to those who dwell at the boundaries of the Heavens and beyond.

"It's Aphrodite!" Junia said. "What is she doing? Why is she –"

"Wait for it…"

At long last, Junia saw Aphrodite place a small object in Hera's hand, then leave the garden in a hurry, lest she get caught defying Zeus' order to not disturb the Queen's restorative slumber.

"Was that – ?"

Prometheus said nothing, though his wide, impish grin gave Junia all the answers she sought.

"The gods remain ever true to their nature," Junia repeated Prometheus' words with a knowing smile.

"Now come," Prometheus said. "The entire crew is celebrating the vernal equinox with a game of laser tag around the centre of the gravity wheel. Young Derek requested that I recruit you for his team as you have the strongest stomach of all the pupils in school."

Junia giggled. "If they only knew," she said as she made her way to the inner elevator with the benefactor of humanity by her side and the blessed gods of starry Olympus beneath her feet.

Nepheleid

Epilogue

As the stars and wanderers brightened the cerulean hues of twilight, Eris kept watch over her mother's slumbering form, a task she volunteered to fulfill since Prometheus returned to the Nephele with Junia, leaving Eris otherwise bereft of her young charge and companion. Last night, when Eris foolishly asked Ares to watch over Hera for a spell, she caught golden Aphrodite sneaking out of the Queen's garden in a hurry and her twin asleep beside Hera at the willow in the quiet hours just before Sunrise. Ares swore that he possessed no recollection of his intermittent lover visiting their mother nor did he notice that the goddess of love left something in the palm of Hera's hand, something the Queen now clenched with all her might even while asleep. On this night, Eris would make certain that no one would disturb Hera's recovery, lest they find themselves in the throes of madness and chaos for their impiety towards the Queen of the gods.

Once the Horai retired to their own beds for the night, Eris sat beneath the limbs of the ancient willow, watching the stars appear then wink out one by one, as the bright lights of the Nephele eclipsed all other luminaries aloft in the Heavens except for the waxing Moon. After Hera made a full recovery, Eris might return to the Nephele and resume her duties as Network Security Consultant, a position she sometimes undertook when Prometheus' learned mortals had need of her special talents and whenever it was Ares' turn to look after Junia on and off the city-ship. Whether or not Hera decided to stay on Olympus indefinitely constituted another matter altogether. Regardless of how many times Hera fell into the honey pot of reconciliation with the Cloud-gatherer, Eris resolved that the option of returning to the city she helped build in the expanse beyond the Heavens ought to remain open to her mother, Aphrodite's scheming be damned.

Eris looked down at Hera's hand, which still clasped the offering the goddess of love brought the previous night shortly before Dawn. Without prying the object loose from her mother's white-knuckle grip, Eris already knew that it was an inscribed golden apple from the Garden of the Hesperides. Eris also knew that this was not the prize that Hera lost to Aphrodite following the judgment of Paris so many centuries ago, but rather a paltry replica of the device Eris cleverly deployed at Thetis' wedding to avenge her slighted pride for not being invited to the lavish celebration. The aftermath of Eris' elaborate prank also provided Hera the serendipitous opportunity to take revenge on Zeus for his hubris by destroying a city dear to his heart.

Aphrodite likely wanted Hera to believe that she willingly surrendered her prize as an incentive for the Queen to remain on starry Olympus with her King. If this were so, then perhaps Aphrodite's judgment of Hera's character and vanity had grown as ornery as that of generations of mortal bards and poets who relentlessly slandered the Queen of Olympus for wielding the kind of authority they would have deemed intolerable for a mortal woman. If Hera were even half as clever as Eris knew her mother to be, then she would quickly see through the cheap trick and demand satisfaction for the insult.

While Eris' thoughts lingered upon the means she would use to turn the odds in her mother's favour should a duel arise between Aphrodite and her Queen, Hera awoke, stirred by the light of the Nephele above her palace, and the cacophony inside her guardian's mind. It took Hera a moment to find her bearings, not because she did not know where she was, but rather because Eris' presence had that regrettable effect on even the sturdiest minds. Somewhere beyond the grounds of the royal palaces, the gods revelled loudly in the banquet hall on high Olympus. This was to be expected, Hera surely thought, for the blessed gods never missed an occasion to celebrate narrowly avoiding annihilation at the hands of an even higher power than themselves, even if their saviour remained sequestered in her garden, recovering from the burden of her glorious fate.

Hera turned her gaze towards Eris and smiled at her. Eris could tell that she dearly missed Klymene and Iris, her loyal companions now gone from Olympus to fulfill their own destinies, whether in the Elysian fields or with Prometheus and his learned mortals. Like Eris, Hera likely felt Junia's absence most keenly, even if she had spent most of her time sleeping for the last few weeks. As if conjured up from the Aether to specifically ruin this tranquil moment in Hera's beautiful starlit garden, someone emitted a loud moan of pleasure somewhere in Zeus' neighbouring palace. The voice to which the moan belonged was not that of the King of Olympus who eventually added his voice to the wordless chorus. Hera closed her eyes, knowing full well what transpired within her husband's dwelling in her absence, even if Zeus assured his Queen time and again that he never took lovers into their sacred marriage bed.

Hera looked down, then saw the small golden sphere in her hand as if for the first time. She examined it for a moment, then upon seeing the inscription in handwriting other than Eris' own, Hera took aim and threw the object far into the firmament with the incalculable force of her exasperation. When the apple's arc reached a terrific distance high above Olympus in the direction opposite to the Nephele, it exploded into a blinding blaze, then the bright collapsed in an infinitesimal pinpoint of light, until it disappeared completely. Hera stared at the Sky for a moment, mouth agape, not caring that Zeus and his bedmate had ceased their loud nocturnal activities.

When Hera finally looked down again, she gave Eris a knowing smile and said, "Gaia told me that I never knew what the golden apples were for. But now I think I do."

Eris gave her mother a sly grin. "The tree has begun bearing fruit again," she said.

"You mean devices," Hera replied. "Not fruit, devices. Was that not the word that came to your mind when you recalled what Aphrodite left in my hand the other night?"

"A device, like a holy hand gre–"

"No!" Hera interrupted. "Well, perhaps. I've got a theory!"

Eris raised an eyebrow. "Do tell, Mother."

"Gaia gifted me with the Tree of the golden apples not because of the sheen of its fruits, but because the seeds they bear are meant to take root in the soil of other worlds, which in turn are to become rife with Life like the Earth as it once was and shall be again. If a small, unripe seedling can open the way through the Heavens and point towards where to set a course, imagine what a ripened one can do!"

Eris gave Hera a look of awe, her grin widening into a dotty smile.

Nepheleid

"It is in my power to make the Earth bloom with Life; I will therefore seed new worlds and bestow my blessings and protection upon them," Hera said aloud, as if from memory. Turning her full attention back to Eris, she asked with an elated laugh, "shall we go apple-picking, Daughter? Perhaps later we can go visit your brother and little sister?"

Hera's joyful epiphany, and Zeus' horrified demeanour as he stood in silence from his neighbouring perch, were as mollifying to Eris' ears as the shrillest battle-cry of tyrannized rabbles about to unseat their oppressors.

Heartened by her brazen, hard-won victory against the forces of order and stagnation, eternal allies of entropy and impending doom against the ever-chaotic unfolding of Life and consciousness across all the realms, Eris looked at her mother and said as if to a long-estranged friend, "Let's."

Nepheleid